Seventh Wielder

Ken Decoteau

Quotes from *The Book of Five Rings* by Miyamoto Musashi, translated by Thomas Cleary, © 2003. Reprinted by arrangement with Shambhala Publications, Inc., www.shambhal

ISBN 978-0-578-00178-4

Chapter 1

The store

Walking around Los Angeles is a mixed experience. The moderate temperature would have made the place ideal, if not for the two issues of smog and rain. On a normal day before between summer and fall, the act of breathing deeply would leave you rather worried about the air quality. Today was a slight exception to the first issue, since it was raining hard. An afternoon shower does have the benefit of washing some of the smog out of the air. If you're not prepared for the rain though, it can really ruin your day.

I've done enough on-site consulting with clients to remember to pack an umbrella. More importantly, I've actually gone so far to make it an item I carry with me daily, even when the chance of rain is slim. What I haven't managed to do is break the awful college habit of not carrying cash. Thus I'm walking in the rain through the streets of Los Angeles, late for a meeting with a client. The three cabs I'd tried to hire so far all had broken credit card machines.

This little project in L. A. had turned fatiguing. It was one thing to design a system and sell it on the phone. It was another to hold the client's hand while they worked through the internal politics of making that system work with the smallest amount of crushed toes. Okay, so I'm a bit bitter. Apparently this was par for most Process Control Engineering firms. Dealing with this level of inconvenience is my penance for taking a job not quite in my field in the first place. There's at least enough mechanical engineering in the job to make sure I can be useful every once in a while.

Being late to the last afternoon of meetings was not a stellar way of ensuring that I'd live up to my alleged utility. Again. It was completely my own fault that I was still a good eight blocks from the client's offices. I looked down at my watch, telling myself not to let it get to me. After all, my job was essentially done two days ago when the new control systems went live.

Looking back up brought me face to down turned hat with a rather stocky man. I dodged to the side, swinging my umbrella up to keep it from hitting the man in the face. In the process, I accidentally struck the "close" button on the umbrella.

I stood there for a moment, dumbfounded. The man continued walking down the sidewalk as if nothing happened. Figures.

Two steps brought me out of the rain and under an awning in front of a bookstore. I shook off and went to work on getting the umbrella back open. It wasn't the first time I'd been sabotaged with this particular umbrella. It was a compact model, designed for car use. Stick it out, hit the button; it extends. Then when you get back to the car; step in, hit the button, and it retracts slightly so you can grab it and yank the wet mess inside. The same button. Why is it the same button?

It is rather funny. A mechanical engineer getting drenched by an over-designed mechanical release mechanism. I shook my head, snapped the umbrella back out and got hit in the back by the door opening behind me. The umbrella closed again on its own.

"Excuse me," said a woman, giving me a dirty look. "But you shouldn't have been standing in front of the door!"

"Sorry," I mumbled after her, moving aside to fiddle with the umbrella again. Pushed it closed, then pressed the button. It extended. I shook the handle, careful not to touch the button, and it collapsed again. Make that an over-designed release mechanism that isn't working properly.

I figured I could either try and hold the umbrella open or pop into a shop and wait out the rain. Since I had a company laptop with me, I was leaning towards the shopping idea. Add to it a lack of desire to go to the meeting and the decision was simple. I turned around, dumped the flaky umbrella next to the door, and went inside the bookstore.

The man behind the counter nodded to me as I entered. It looked like a good little shop. Mostly books with some antique items and memorabilia to add atmosphere. About one half was Science Fiction and Fantasy and the other Nonfiction. Everything was used. And some sections looked quite old. I started with the History section to the right with the intent of making my way towards the Science Fiction.

Just as I was about to slide over to the left side past the counter, someone in a dark raincoat quickly darted across the room past me and turned towards the door. It looked like they'd come from the Fantasy section. I honestly didn't remember seeing anyone over there at all in the ten minutes or so I'd been in the store.

The shop keeper saw my reaction. He smirked at me and shrugged. I got the feeling I was missing a joke. I moved over to the left side, and the old man followed me, the smirk still bending up the corners of his mouth.

"You by any chance have a later edition of Harlan Elison's *Approaching Oblivion*?" I asked, my attention still slightly drawn by the exit of the person I hadn't seen lurking anywhere in the shop.

"Good book. Short stories, right? Him in a pink bathrobe on the dust jacket?" he asked. I nodded. "Alas, no. I don't think I have one in. It's out of print I believe."

"Sadly yes. I have a copy, but I keep having to resist the urge to loan it out to people." He nodded to me and pointed to a table father along to my left, I turned to browse it.

"You may like what you find there then. Make sure and check the bottom shelf."

Early Scifi hard covers, mostly good condition. Some with intact dust jackets. I started looking for some that I knew I didn't have. A few caught me from the shelf below the table, and I picked them up. After a round about the lower shelf, I headed back over to the counter. The books didn't have prices on them. This should be interesting.

"Good eye," the man sighed. I set the three books down and he picked them up, one by one. After a brief examination, they were turned back around. "Eighty five."

I resisted the urge to whistle. Almost. Well, it was worth it after all. Small whistle past, I moved on to thinking about how much I wanted the three books added to my collection. The chances of me getting all the way back to this particular store in the near future were slim. And the chances of finding these particular books in a store in Jacksonville, Florida were slimmer. My eyes skimmed past the cash register front to make sure that those little logos for credit cards were there. Some of these shops were cash only. Of course the lack of cash cut my chances of talking the man down.

"Eighty okay?" I partially gave in. He nodded without too much of a pause. "I'll buy them."

The man smiled slightly and took the three books over to the register. I looked around a bit while he wrapped them in tissue paper and then slipped them in a plastic bag. The cash register itself was carefully located. One couldn't see it directly from the front door because of a narrow book display. A good idea. That way if you were counting down the till, it wasn't visible from outside. And a step to the right was all it took to get a look at someone after they came in the door. In case I wanted to come back at some time, I drew one of the business cards from the dispenser in front of the register.

"Charles?" I asked to be sure. The card was simple, with the name of the store taking up the top center; "Choice Tomes". A depiction of swords crossed behind two contrasting scrolls of parchment took up the center. His name was scrawled at the bottom in what looked like fountain pen ink.

"That would be me," Charles replied. I passed him my check card and went to looking at the items under the counter. Charles set the receipt on the counter.

I signed, passing back the top copy and pen. "Well, good day. I should be getting to the meeting I'm late for." I'd already killed almost a half an hour. It was still raining outside, but I'd decided to make a go at keeping the drenchomatic umbrella extended.

"Rain always does that here. Just blame it on a cab driver."

"At least I'll be done by tomorrow," I sighed, taking up the plastic bag and sliding it into the accessory pocket of my laptop bag. "What's in that box?"

Charles looked back up from stashing away the store copy in the till. "What box?"

"That one," I pointed to the long wooden one next to a flag under the counter. Charles gave me a probing look.

"Oh, just another bit of history."

I felt the guilt of being late setting in so I didn't press. Nodding and then offering a wave, I turned and left the store, picking up my umbrella on the way out. Strange too, as there was another one next to mine propped beside the door that hadn't been there before. I hadn't seen anyone else in the shop.

Taking a left and popping open the umbrella, I hurried off towards our client's offices which should have been about a twenty minute walk from here. That left me plenty of time to begin looking forward to reading my purchases. And plenty of time to think about the store. Something still bothered me about it.

It really bugged me. I felt like I'd left something there.

A quick check of pockets, belt and bag found everything in its rightful place. I always had a fear of loosing my cell phone. And after carrying around a Gerber for about eight years, I really didn't want to loose that tool. One becomes attached to things like that. Walking again didn't seem to help. Oh, well. Something to think about later.

I made the last turn and ducked into the entry way of the manufacturing firm's door. A few steps past the receptionist's desk and I popped open the door for the staircase up to the second floor. A quick check of the cell phone showed me only about forty minutes late, and two messages. In other words, I'd probably missed the status presentation, but was still in time for the question and answer session.

I saw most of the group milling about the coffee in the small break room across from the conference rooms. I just hoped they weren't waiting for me.

"Ah, Chris," said one of the senior plant engineers. "Good of you to join us."

The look on his face was not one I'd wished to see. It was the same look he had before the all nighter last week. At least I had something to read this time.

"Sorry about that Eric, missed a cab and had to walk."

"It happens. Well, we've discovered some new issues about the tuning coefficients. They were a part of the topic for the status presentation. Are you absolutely sure that using these PID's are really going to solve our consistency issues? Well, the results from the run last night show improvement, but nothing over what we have seen in the past using the old system."

"Yeah, but you're still missing some things," piped in Randy, a fresh engineer from Tennessee Tech.

I nodded. "What was the overall purity?"

"62%," said Randy.

"Then it was about what I expected," I said, repeating myself almost word for word from the first full test we had run two days ago. "And remember, that while you did get over 50% in the past, it only happened one batch per month."

Eric began going over the whole thing again from the start as the group migrated back to the smaller of the two conference rooms. It was looking like it would be a long day. At least I was leaving tomorrow afternoon.

But I still had one question that kept nagging me through the rest of the meeting. Leaving things unresolved is a rather difficult act for me. I just can't let things go until I figure them out. My thoughts were not on the meeting. What bugged me was back in the bookstore. I couldn't let it out of my mind.

What was in the box?

Chapter 2

Return

I woke the next morning to the bedside alarm and began packing. The nice thing about flying back from L. A. to Florida would be getting to go straight to bed. Since I didn't have a flight until almost one in the afternoon, I'd planned on taking the hotel shuttle to the airport, checking bags, and then a bus out to the Santa Monica Pier. I guess its one of those landmark attractions that everyone sees when they come here. I figured it would be a good way to waste the morning.

It took almost a half an hour for the shuttle to make its way to the airport bus terminal. One of the airport tram's completely cut off a black sedan to pull into a slot along the terminal. The Mercedes had to back up and cut around the bus. A little ways ahead of me, the sedan came to a abrupt stop, then made a double lane change and turned left. A brief walk across the street to the city bus stop reminded me again of why I'd refused to get a rental car. Los Angeles traffic was a bit crazy. I don't think I'll ever forget the audacity of some of the bus drivers around the airport.

Almost to the bus stop, and two more shocking near wrecks later, I thought I spotted the Mercedes again. It was around to the right on a side road parallel to the city bus terminal. The sedan pulled into a row of parking spots with a mild bark of rubber.

Moments later, the bus for Santa Monica rolled up. The small group of people waiting at the stop queued up, and I joined them. My eyes were still on the Mercedes. I'd not seen anyone exit the car. With a jerk, the bus moved out into traffic, cutting around to the left and away from the airport. I hunkered down in a seat on the left side of the bus, studying the map briefly. It had started raining slightly outside, the rain pattering on the metal skin of the bus.

Two stops later, the same black sedan slowly passed the bus. Now more than a little suspicious, I took another look at the map. We were now about three blocks from the bookstore. Through the front of the bus, I could see the sedan pull aside at the next stop. Someone got out of the back seat and calmly walked over to the bus stop. The sedan peeled off around the corner to the right.

The bus came to a complete stop. I let the guy from the sedan get to the hand rail before getting up. In two steps, I'd crossed to the exit stairs and hopped off the bus. I walked as quickly as I could across the street and kept moving. One more block, and I came to the street I'd walked down the day before. After making the turn, I paused at the corner. Sure enough, the tall guy had just rounded the other end and was heading at a jog down the side street.

I was being followed. Silly thoughts about my client having hired a car to escort me back to his precious proceeding plant flashed through my mind. Impossible; the guys in charge like their cell phones so much they would have melted my voice mail box before sending a physical message to me. A quick jog across the street, and two more stores and I was at the bookstore entrance. I pushed inside and ducked behind the book rack towards the front to catch my breath.

"Can I help ya?" said Charles, looking up hastily from reading a book behind the counter. "Oh. It's you. Back so soon?" I shook my head, and swallowed. "I, er, thought you wouldn't have made it through the books quite that fast."

"I didn't," I said sharply and glanced out the front windows. "I'm being chased. Or at least I think I am."

"Which is it?"

"I don't know!" I sighed. "It's too weird. A car started following the bus and well, look. Just let me use your phone to call the police." I finished, walking towards the counter. Charles picked up the handset, but paused before touching the keypad.

Suddenly I caught motion on my left. A shady looking character came out of a hallway to the left of the counter and moved quickly past me. He exchanged a nod with the old man and left the store.

Now, I'm not an unobservant fellow, but I really can't remember a better description than 'shady'. Worse, I didn't remember there being a hallway there. Looking back to the left, I got another shock. There wasn't a hallway anymore. The wall was five feet away and I couldn't make out the opening.

I knew I'd seen one, I said to myself. I looked for a few seconds, and then it appeared. Right there even with the end of the counter, where I'd seen it when the guy walked through. Weird. It was also in the same general direction that the person in the raincoat had came from the day before.

"Who exactly is it that's chasing you?" Charles asked evenly.

I nodded to the left without looking. I didn't want to have to run through the whole missing doorway thing again.

The man cocked his right eyebrow up and then looked at the alleged hallway. Then he shrugged.

"Where are you from mister? Not around here, eh?"

"What's that supposed to mean?" I asked in reply. "Hey look. Are you going to make the call or not."

"Well, I haven't seen you around here. I'm just wondering if this is where you're from."

"Nope," I said, reaching for the phone. Charles put it down on the base and leaned under the counter. He quickly slid aside the top of the box I'd asked about the day before. A drop of black fabric later and he slapped a sword on the counter. After closing the box, he moved to the end of the counter, flipped up a divider and grabbed my arm in one hand, the long sword in the other. We moved towards the, fortunately, still existing hallway. After a step in, he hit a light switch, turning on a small bank of fluorescent lights along the ceiling of the hall.

At the end, about fifteen feet in, there were three blades mounted on the wall at eye level with the tips pointing up. To the right was an opening to a room about half the size of the whole store. Although the lights were still off in this room, I could make out the shadows of full suits of armor, lots of racks of weapons, both mounted and in cases. Through a set of double doors, a workout room with sallies and mats.

I was still faced with two slight problems. One; the disappearing doorway that I'd just walked through. And perhapse more importantly, two; whoever was behind that black car.

"Again," said Charles. "Who is chasing you?"

"Black Mercedes. Tall guy with a dark sport coat ran out after me."

"And did you see this doorway?"

"What kind of question is that?" I almost yelled, yanking my arm free and taking a step back. I heard the front door of the shop bang open.

"Listen to me," he said softly. "Take this," he placed the hilt of the sword in my hands.

The sword was perfect. An absolute perfect blade. I almost felt a tingle when I accepted it from his hands. The balance seemed to adjust itself to me. The stone setting and hilt design was solid. Simple, functional, yet elegant at the same time. The stone in the end of the hilt was a brilliant ruby color. I couldn't do anything other than admire the work. I was frozen in place.

"Why don't you spend some time with her," he suggested while reaching over and hitting a few switches on the wall. The lights in the room to the right snapped on. He nodded to the room, then headed back to the front of the store. "My daughter makes daggers by the way. I'll be right back. Just going to check the front and make a phone call."

I've never touched a sword this good before. Crossing through the mini-armory to the workout room, I unslung my laptop case and set it down just inside the room on a bench. I had done some fencing a few years ago. Mostly recreation stuff with schalgers and epees. That had been a bit of a crash course, but I'd done well with the practice blades.

I set the blade down on the bench next to the laptop case and stepped back. Here I was, possibly being chased by someone I didn't know, and I'm now essentially trapped in a back room of a shop toying with a sword. And what does the fact that Charles' daughter makes daggers have to do with anything? At least there looked to be an exit through some double doors to the back alley.

I heard an odd noise from the store. I gathered my thoughts back to ground and picked up my laptop. Sword in hand and questions on my tongue, I headed to the hallway slowly. The noise turned into arguing, and then something breaking. And there was a big hairy hulk charging down the hall at me swinging what looked like a claymore at my head.

Chapter 3

Escape

There's not much I could have done. Since I realized this a little too late, my reactions had already taken over. I mean, there I was with a sword in my hand and someone was swinging a much larger sword at me. So I did what I was supposed to do. Planted, gripped correctly, leaned and countered. If I was religious, I may have prayed too, but it would have been a pretty fast prayer.

All I can say for myself is that I met the swing properly. Perhaps a little too perfectly. It was probably the strongest swing I've ever encountered. I mean the thing doing the swinging was at least six foot six inches and well over three hundred pounds. The blades met with a force which would have broken my arms if I hadn't been careful with my stance. I was sent back on my duff anyway.

Looking up, sword still in my hands and my arms stinging from the impact, I almost laughed. The claymore had split in half at the point of contact. The troll-like thing was staring at his shortened blade in surprise.

Then it was my turn to be surprised. I had a nice gash on my right forearm from the remaining half of the blade. I also felt a few warm spots on my face and chest. Probably from shards of the shattered claymore.

Taking advantage of the shock of Mr. Troll, I decided I had a perfect shot at cutting his legs out from under him. Leaning forward and swinging, I managed to catch his left leg right above the knee joint. I rolled back and up to my feet as he fell with a roar of agony. My laptop bag neirly tripping me in the process.

Yes, I'd now hacked into some big guy's leg with a sword that wasn't mine. But hey, he swung at me first. Since he still had about two feet of blade left to my three and was already halfwa back to his feet, I think it was time to leave the store.

My hopes of making a frontal exit were dashed by two more troll things heading to the hall. There was a guy in a suit coat behind them pointing the way. The sword he held at the shop keeper's neck looked even more useful at the moment.

Noting my presence, Charles yelled "Get it out of here, run!" and then collapsed as the man hit him with the flat of his blade. In light of the circumstances I was more than willing to count the "it" he mentioned as the sword in my hand. I really didn't want to part with my only defense at the moment either. Turing away from the hall, I ran to the workout room, grabbing my laptop bag and the sheath for the blade on the way. I skidded before the double doors and added a staff to my burdens.

After passing into the workout room, I used the staff to secure the door handles. It wouldn't hold for long, but it was a quick way of buying me a few seconds. The sword sheath was easy to attach to my belt one-handed using the double leather strap and buckle. I sheathed the sword, and thought for a second. The rain was starting to pickup up outside by the sound through the door. Shrugging, I grabbed a raincoat from a hook next to the door, throwing it on. Then I flew through the door with the sounds of battering wood behind me.

Head down, eyes up, I hung a left in the alley and walked briskly away. After about thirty feet, I hit a cross street and turned right into the crowd. Then I took a look around; this didn't look much like any L. A. I knew.

Actually, this didn't look much like earth.

The good thing was, I seemed to fit in. Except for the hand inside the coat on the sword pommel. Deciding upon a less conspicuous placement of the arm, I stuck both hands in the pockets of the coat. I'd deal with my bleeding right arm after I could be sure I'd lost the tail. Patching up a gash would basically ensure that I'd be noticed at the moment.

In the left pocket, I found a piece of paper. Pulling it out while making a pseudo random turn at an intersection past a stand that looked like it was selling the local version of hot dogs, I read the paper. It was an address, written in a female's handwriting. I made a guess that it was the shop keeper's jacket, considering that this coat smelled like his aftershave. Wherever the hell I was, the shop keeper got me into it. I could make my way back there (pseudo random turns; I knew where I was compared to the shop), but didn't want to encounter the troll entourage again if I could help it.

I stopped and held out the paper to the hot dog vendor, choosing to ignore the fact that some of the hot dogs still appeared to be moving. He looked at it for a few seconds and then nodded in the rough direction I was going.

"About eight blocks that way, hang a right on Grolsh Way, two more, maybe three and then a left. Should be on your right somewheres along there."

I nodded and headed off to find this woman's house. Now that I had a direction, I spent some attention on the people around me. All I can say is, this really wasn't like any part of L.A. I'd seen before or heard about. Almost everyone was armed with something resembling a blade. About one in ten people had tattoos completely covering their exposed skin. Several looked like they had way too much hair. No one met anyone else's eyes. So I followed suit after a few stares in my direction.

I arrived at the walk-up with no problems. It looked like a seven story apartment building. There was a 12 after the street address, so I looked at the names on the mail boxes. Looks like four apartments per floor. That puts this address up three. Judging from the floor size, these things were probably sardine cans. The stairs creaked something fierce on the way up.

After stepping over a mound of trash on the third landing and navigating past a dead refrigerator from the 60's, I found apartment 12. I put my hand inside the jacket on the sword, noticing that I was still bleeding, and knocked on the door with my left fist.

I knocked again.

After the fourth time, the door opened revealing a young women rubbing sleep from her eyes under her glasses. Her face was cute in an exotic sort of way. Even though she was wearing jeans and a hooded sweatshirt and half asleep, my breath was taken away for a few seconds. Maybe it was the long dark hair. I don't know. It doesn't matter.

"What is it?" she asked pointedly. Then yawned.

"You make daggers?" I asked.

"Yeah, sometimes, what..." then she paused and looked at the raincoat. Her father's coat. Then took in the fact that my right hand was obviously on the pommel of a sword because I'd forgot to remove it. Her eyes widened. I removed my hand slowly and spread my arms wide.

"It's a loaner. Sort of. Look, I–" she grabbed me by the collar of the coat and hauled me in the room, slamming the door somehow and shoving me up against it. I'm not a weakling, but I would have had no idea that this petite girl could throw someone my size around like that. I was shocked momentarily.

"Who the hell are you?"

"Look, I was buying some books in your dad's shop yesturday. Someone started following me today, so I went back there. Then some guys came in and started to rough up the place. He told me to run, so I did. Now I have no clue where the hell I am and he had your address in the pocket of the coat. I figured you might know what the heck I'm doing here, since this is NOT L.A."

"Actually it is, sort of." She sniffed, then got this hungry look on her face. "Oh, *hells!* You're bleeding."

With this she almost yanked herself out of my personal space and headed off towards what looked like the kitchen. "Bathroom's there," she said, pointing to her right while storming out of the room. "Your face too."

I almost thought of giving some snide reply, but fortunately stopped myself. I'd read enough books to know that a wounded male on a female's door step usually gets ministered to by the female. I mean, come on here, it's the wounded lost bird syndrome. Right? Guess not this chick. Oh well.

Disregarding the weirdness of the situation and heading to the bathroom, I gave a quick look around the cluttered living room. Glasses everywhere, plates, and some trash. Several books. A sword and dagger set strewn under a pile of papers next to the door. Clothes tossed around. I entered the bathroom.

After a quick inspection, I determined that the door would not be closing anytime soon. I did give a few thoughts to seeing this women in the dress hanging over the door under a pair of ratty jeans. The stockings drying next to the underwear in the shower also looked inviting. I continued looking around for some paper towels or something and finally gave up and pulled a fresh towel off of a shelf. I tossed the coat over the shower rack and dropped the laptop on the floor amidst the clutter and went to work on the arm.

Now that the adrenaline was wearing off, I actually started to realize my arm hurt like hell. My face was hurting too. I didn't see anything resembling a pain killer of any sort, so kept it in mind to ask when my hostess returned from her kitchen run. And screw her for leaving me in the lurch, I thought as I tore off a part of the towel for use as a makeshift bandage. Then I pulled a few of the shards out of my face. Only about three actually did any damage. The bleeding stopped quickly on its own, akin to a bad shave. No, I didn't fail to notice the definitively male razor next to the sink. Nor the remains of a recent shave of morning stubble stuck around the drain. And there were the evident two tooth brushes. I guess that explains the cold reception from my hostess.

Satisfied, I washed my face and neck and turned to find the girl standing in the doorway looking at the torn towel.

"What happened?"

"Yes, I'm okay," I replied, looking away from her and back to the mirror.

"I honestly don't care. What happened at the store?"

"I actually don't know. I said I was chased. Charles wouldn't call the cops. And then he passed me this sword, walked me through the side hallway and left me. Someone came in the front of the store. Next thing I know, I hear this really weird noise from the front. I head out to the main store and this huge troll-looking thing goes after me with a claymore.

"Then the old man sees me and yells for me to 'get it out of here.' Emphass on 'it'. He gets knocked up side the head by a dude in a suit, and I run."

"What sword were you looking at?" she asked calmly. Her hands on her hips.

I turned right and reached for the hilt at my hip. She rushed into the room, her hands out.

"For gods sakes don't pull it out," she almost screamed. Okay, now I'm getting a bit freaked out. "You wielded that?"

"Yes. Then, like I said, this troll took a swing at me, so I swung back. His sword cracked. I ended up on my ass with a slash in my arm. While he was trying to figure out what to do with his shorter spatula, I decided I didn't like him towering so much anymore and hamstrung him."

"Hmm," she murmured.

"What's you name?" I asked.

"Oh, Melina."

"Chris," I said. She didn't seem to hear me. "Look, Melina, I was just here on business. I stopped yesturday to get some books for my return flight. That's it. This has gotten crazy fast. I think if those trolls want this sword that I shouldn't be involved. I'll just pass this back to you and then if you could point me in the direction of downtown, I'll get out of your hair."

"I'm afraid it's not that simple," she said.

"I don't follow."

"No, you probably don't," she said. What the heck was that supposed to mean? "I can't take the sword from you. Actually, no one can. It's yours."

"But I don't even know how much your dad wants for it!"

"Like I said, it's not that simple. And he's not my father. I am his daughter, sort of. Anyway, the sword is yours. It chose you. Wait here, I have to make a call."

She turned and left through the doorway into the living room.

"What, here? As in right here in the bathroom?" In case you hadn't noticed, I was starting to lose patience with the situation.

"Oh, fine! Sit on the couch if you want, I don't care. At least try to be an adult."

So I gathered the coat and laptop bag and set them on the couch in the living room. I didn't sit. I heard her pick up a phone in the kitchen and I listened while pacing slightly. I missed most of her conversation. Words occasionally came through. I heard "sword" at least twice, "shop" and a few other scant terms.

Then she leaned in to the living room and asked, "what did you say you name was?"

"Chris Borden," I replied. She nodded and disappeared again.

Then a few seconds later I heard the phone drop and she came into the room.

"That's not a computer, is it?"

I nodded. She rolled her eyes and groaned.

"I need to ask you a few questions. But first can you pull the battery of that thing without turning it on."

"It's in a sleep mode, if I pull the battery it will crash."

"Let's put it this way," she said sweetly. Then turned to ice, "Take the damn battery out of that thing now and don't you dare even think about turning it on. If you have any cell phones or pagers, kill them too."

"No," I said. I'd had enough at this point.

"You don't have any choice," she replied, anger in her eyes. "You're not where you think you are. You don't know the rules here. No advanced technology. No exceptions."

She moved toward the laptop case. I considered for a minute and then remembered her man-handling me at the door. I cut her off and opened the case. With a flick, the battery dropped out and I just realized I may have fried last night's work. I similarly disembowled my cell phone, which had a dead battery anyway. She shook her head when I got to the watch.

"It's ten year old tech; it's okay."

"Can I get any answer about what's going on?"

"I should probably wait," she said. "Well, I guess I can tell you this much. Charles, the shop keeper, was holding onto the sword for some people until we could find its owner. That is apparently you. No one outside of the league knew where the sword was. Did you see the hallway before Charles led you to it?"

"Yes. Not at first though," I admitted. "Someone walked through it. Then it was kind of hard to see. Since I knew I'd seen it, I stared at the wall and then it kind of focused in. That didn't make any sense did it?"

"More than you know," she said. I mumbled "gee thanks" but she cut me off. "It's good that you saw it on you own. Remember how you did that. It may help you later. Basically, the sword is now yours for you to do with as you will. The problem is, once you wielded the sword outside a warded area, all those who were looking for it were alerted to it's location. It was kind of stupid of Charles to let you touch the sword outside of the practice room with it naked. But then again. They may have noticed you when you walked into the shop yesturday. Yes. That's probably it.

"And it's worse that Sir Neville was close when you did. He's one of the worst people to have after you. How much of a trail did you leave? Who did you talk to?"

"I took several random turns. I'm not stupid," she snorted. "I asked a hot dog vendor about the address. Well, really I just held up the piece of paper at him. He gave me directions, and I nodded thanks."

"You didn't speak?"

"No," I said. I'll guess for the record that it would have mattered. Melina wasn't exactly forthcoming.

"Good."

We heard a key in the lock. I tensed and put my hand on the sword. Melina covered my hand with hers and shook her head. The door opened, and she crossed to the guy who walked in the room. Figures, I thought, boyfriend. Great.

Melina kissed him on the cheek and they hugged. The guy didn't take his eyes off of me. Yes, he was clean shaven. He also had a bunch of pock marks on his neck. Looked like mosquito bites. He was also wearing a coat similar to my borrowed, and now blooded attire. He also had a sword on his left hip and a dagger on the other. I didn't like him. He didn't seem to like me either.

"This Mr. Spiffy?" he asked tartly. Melina scowled at him.

"Jameson, this is Chris Borden," she said, extracting herself from his arms. I extended my right hand. He looked at it and then slowly brought his hand up to grab mine in a crushing grip. I expected something similar and was fortunately prepared.

"Jameson," I said, with a nod and a smile. I hoped the strain didn't show on my face. It did on his, to my delight.

"Mr. Spiffy," he replied, his voice slightly strained. So I squeezed a little harder. He winced and tried to let go, so I let him. Melina giggled.

Jameson seemed to think this was because of him calling me Spiffy again. I was pretty sure it was because he got his hand crushed. This was affirmed when she giggled again when he shook out his hand after I turned around to retrieve the coat and bag from the couch. It was then that I noticed a rucksack and a sheet on the couch. Maybe Jameson wasn't that much of a live-in after all, I hoped to myself.

"So now what?" I asked. "Charles is sitting in his shop out cold from the flat of the guy's blade. I've got trolls after me and a nifty new sword for free. You hate the sight of blood and have no manners," I pointed to Melina, then turned to Jameson. "And you have no hand strength and need to do something about the bug biting you at night. And I'm in what appears to be some sort of refuge underworld for some rather unmentionable individuals."

The two looked at each other. I was satisfied that I got Melina to blush. And then I continued.

"And I'm late for a quick tour of Santa Monica and then a plane flight home, out of patience, thirsty, and probably not an all around good people person right now. So I'm planning on walking right back out that door and into the real world unless someone tells me what the hell I should be doing. And more importantly; why?"

"You didn't tell me he got injured," Jameson responded, looking at Melina with something bordering on anger.

"I said he got in a fight with one of the bears, James."

"Yeah, but," I decided to cut him off. "I happened to cut one down. The thing went after me; what was I supposed to do? Try singing?"

"Oh, great, you mean you actually wielded that thing? Crap!"

Melina sighed and rolled her eyes. I got the feeling that he hadn't been listening to her on the phone. I also got the feeling that he failed to listen a lot. I also decided not to answer him and made for the door instead.

"I'm going to go check on Charles and then get out of this crazy place," I said with finality and headed to the door, prepared to shoulder Jameson out of the way.

"No," Melina said softly. "Please."

"Why?" I asked. My hand paused over the door knob.

"Because we need you," she added.

"Oh, please," said Jameson with spite. "We're doing fine without a Wielder."

"No we're not. Look, Chris," she paused. "The last thing that you should do right now is head back to the store. Or the other side. You can't be warded well over there. Not yet anyway. We need to get you to the league elders and let them talk to you. I've probably already told you too much."

"Melina," said Jameson, his voice heavy with flint. "What did you tell him?"

"Nothing! Really. Just that the sword was now his."

"You had no right," he yelled. "That's-"

Melina slapped him. Good for her. He actually almost didn't keep his feet. This is one strong chick.

"I'm going. If you want to show me to one of your league elders, then lead the way. Otherwise, I'm off. I'm sorry for interrupting this little lover's quarrel."

"We're not, err," said Melina. "Fine. Jameson, stay here. Charles will probably come here after Neville gives up and leaves. Tell him where we went."

"Um, Melina," I interjected. "You're forgetting something? I've got his coat with your address."

"Oh, don't worry, that was from a few weeks ago when I moved in. He's been here since."

"A few weeks," I said, looking around at the mess. "I'm impressed."

She colored, "don't you start." So I stopped. It looked like Jameson was regaining his composure, aside from the red mark on his cheek. "James, you got it?" she asked sternly.

"What gives you the right to order me around," he replied venomously.

She glared at him.

"Fine, Mel. Go," he said, while rubbing his cheek. "But don't think I'm going to forget this."

Melina chewed her lip in thought for a few seconds and then shook her head.

"Lets go," she said, "it's getting late."

I was thinking it was only about 11 in the morning, but didn't say anything. Jameson plopped down on the couch and clicked on the ancient television. While Melina slipped the dagger from under the papers inside her sweatshirt, Jameson kicked some of the clutter off the coffee table and then propped both feet on it, dripping mud on the papers there.

I followed Melina out the door, which she locked behind me. I heard her sniff once in the dark hall on our way to the stairs.

"You okay, Melina?" I asked.

"No-Yes...I... It doesn't matter."

I put my hand on her arm and stopped her. "Yes it does."

We were in the light near the landing, I could see that she had tears in her eyes. "You don't know anything."

She tugged away from me, and put her hood up, her long hair tucked inside the front. We left the building into a pouring rain. It was nearly completely dark outside. Funny thing was, I couldn't muster up any surprise at this. I mean, it was at least five hours later than I thought it was, and I just didn't care anymore. Maybe Melina was right. It just doesn't matter.

Chapter 4

It does

It was a slogging trip through what was definitely NOT the city of angles. I stayed relatively dry, but I am sure Melina was getting soaked by now. I followed her steadily, resisting the temptation to offer her my coat. First off, I had my laptop to think about. Second, I didn't want to get this nice sword wet. Third, she was already well soaked by now. And fourth, I just plain didn't feel like it.

It's for times like this that I always wear waterproofed shoes. You never know when you're going to end up in the middle of a place you didn't even know existed. In the rain. Tailing a vamp of a girl with a trusty sword strapped to your waist. In the rain. Who wasn't talking to you at the moment.

Did I mention it was raining? Good. Because it was.

Although I tried hard to convince myself that I was still in Los Angeles, nothing along our walk did much to convince me. Or I guess a more acurate destinction would be I didn't see much to convince myself that I was in L.A. NOW, in 2004, rather than the late 1980's. After what felt like a good thirty minutes of fast walking, we made it to a warehouse. It didn't look like anyone was home. Melina opened the door with a key from her pocket and went inside. I followed, sloughing water off the coat and dropping the hood. She dropped the hood to the sweatshirt and I was surprised that her hair wasn't soaked. It looked wet at the front, but dry on top. She unzipped the apparently soaked garment and hung it on a hook. She had on a black soft looking shirt under it which was just as unbecoming as the hoodie, yet I still thought it somehow attractive on her. And it was dry.

Apparently the hoodie had some sort of lining. Her jeans I noted, were soaked. She kicked off her shoes and motioned for my coat. I hung it next to her sweatshirt and waited while she wiped her lenses off.

"You'll catch cold in those things," I said for lack of a better opener.

"No I wont," she replied flatly. "This way."

I followed her through another locked door and then around to a stairway that lead down. We took the set at a fast walk. She didn't seem to mind taking the steps in her bare feet. The lower level opened out into the main area of the warehouse. Apparently there was some sort of meeting in progress. I counted sixteen people, all sitting on chairs in a circle. A few brooms along the rear wall, and some random dust piles indicated the floor had been recently swept for the meeting. One person was talking and gesturing and the others were listening. Several others surrounded the warehouse, and looked like a guard contingent. These outnumbered the people in the circle about two to one. All looked attentive and sure of themselves.

A rather pale looking fellow with blond hair broke off from the group and headed our way. He also looked at least partially damp. And was tall, at least six foot eight. Skinny as a railroad track.

"Melina," he said, inclining his head.

"Sir Finely," she said in response, inclining her head just a little bit more.

"And this is?" he asked. Then his eyes dropped to the sword at my hip. They widened. He stepped back, his hand going to his own sword. I backed up away from Melina as well, miming his movements and giving myself room to draw if needed. I head Finley mutter something under his breath.

"Melina," I said. "What the hell is this?"

She said nothing. Behind Sir Finley, the rest of the group stood almost as one and turned in our direction. I sensed more than felt someone behind me and moved to one side, still ready to draw, but not wanting to force anyone else to do the same. I didn't have any misconceptions about my skill level. A stupid troll was one thing, an intelligent and skilled swordsman was another.

Sure enough, there were two of the guard types at the foot of the stairs behind me. Hands on their hilts.

"Melina," I said very slowly. "You're friends don't seem to like me much."

Sir Finley continued to advance towards me, but the guards held their ground. I noticed that all the other potential exits were similarly blocked. I dropped the laptop bag to the ground and hoped it wouldn't get stepped on. I moved a bit away from the wall, putting Melina between me and Sir Tall. This was not looking fun.

Melina put her hands in her wet pockets and turned to Sir Finley.

"The wards are in place as usual, I guess?" she asked.

"Yes, Melina. Thank you," said the pasty guy. He glanced at the group standing in a circle and one of them nodded. I didn't like that one bit. Sure enough, Sir Tall looked back at me, drew and charged.

I don't even remember much of the next few minutes. All that I can say is that I don't think I ever came close to getting an attack in until the end. It was all I could do to make an effort at defending myself. And he was going easy too. I knew enough to see that. He kept opening up my feeble defense like a tin can encountering an axe.

Rather than just running me through, he continued to play with me. It wasn't that he didn't touch me at all, he did. I still have scars from that fight. But he was just drawing blood, not trying to do anything permanent. I was both grateful and enraged. I thought a few times about just giving up, but something told me that he would have really ran me through if I did something that stupid.

He managed to open up the cut from the troll on my right arm and kept trying to get me on that side. I knew I was nearly exhausted at this point. My knees were starting to shake and I was bleeding from eight or nine cuts. But he kept hammering my right guard. I frankly decided I'd had it and from somewhere managed to draw a reserve I didn't know I had.

He wanted my right so I damn well gave him my right. I shifted my sword to my left hand, dropped beneath his swing, then delivered the best roundhouse I could straight to his jaw. He staggered back in a daze, his left hand dropping down from the sword to try and catch his balance. Pressing the advantage with the last of the strength I could find, I chopped at his right hand, shifting all my weight into it, catching his sword right at the guard. He screamed and dropped the blade and fell back cradling his hand.

"Stop," said someone softly from the circle of watchers. I was still seeing red and puffing for breath, but moderately satisfied. Melina had a slight smile on her face. I looked at Sir Tall. He definitely wasn't smiling. Not at all. He had been annoyingly calm throughout the fight. And now was anything but. He spit some blood out in my direction. Yeah, mister pasty face. You had your fun, but I'm still standing with my sword in my hands, thank you very much!

"Enough play for now," said the same voice. I cautiously looked away from the fallen and enraged Sir Finley and saw that the speaker was the same woman who had given him the nod.

Sir Finley hadn't gotten up yet. I sheathed my sword and offered him a hand. As much as I wanted to in this case, I am not the type of person who can gloat. He made a mistake, I took advantage of it brutally. And it felt good. But I still felt guilty. He could have killed me in the first ten seconds if he wanted to.

"You gave me my hat more times than I can count. I got a cheap shot in. I'm sorry," I managed, with a bit more sincerity than I thought I could get out. He gave me a solid glare, but grudgingly extended his left hand. I hauled him to his feet as best as I could.

He stared at me for several seconds. "I guess I deserved that too," he said finally. "I'm sorry for getting carried away." I nodded. He let go of my hand, and I almost fell over, the energy gone. His arm quickly went out to my shoulder to steady me.

Melina came over, as well as the speaker from the circle, an older women in a flowing red dress. Her hair was black and long like Melina's, but she wore it in a braid.

"Your name, Wielder?" she asked.

"Chris Borden," said Melina, now at my elbow. I heard her take a deep breath, and then back away a little from me. I was still trying to catch my breath so was grateful for not needing to talk. I nodded instead.

"I am Samantha," said the woman. She turned to Sir Finley, who was massaging his jaw with his left hand. A guard came up and passed him his sword. He took it in his left, examined the guard and then threw it down in disgust. I guess I'd done it in with that hit.

"Your opinion?" she asked of the disgusted Finley.

"He has a lot of good basic training, but little more than rudimentary study. His guard is actually rather strong for his level, and his reflexes are faster than most. He thinks faster than I do actually, as we just saw much to the demise of my family's sword."

He winced as he said that, and I almost said something smart. But I was beginning to realize I was getting a little bit light headed. Actually, more like very dizzy. Fast. I decided to speak my piece.

"He's also standing here bleeding and about to collapse," I said. Then realized I didn't have much of a choice anymore. They both turned in my direction. "Actually, I am going to collapse, I think."

With that, my knees lost their battle and I began to slip to the floor. Melina reached forward and grabbed me, slowing my decent to a relative sitting position. She sunk down with me. I noticed she was acting kind of strange. She seemed to be excited, and I couldn't figure out exactly why. She also kept really close to me, with most of her attention in my direction.

"Melina," said Samantha. "Leave him be for now. Someone get some bandages and some water. Better make it wine too. And an ice pack for Sir Finley's wounded pride."

Sensing an order, Melina pulled herself away from me almost reluctantly. I was actually beginning to like the few seconds of contact. I heard a few people leave the main warehouse area, probably in search of the ordered items.

"Well, it seems we have a practicable Wielder once more. Where are you from, Mr. Borden?"

"I work for an engineering firm in Jacksonville, Florida," I replied. "I'm here on a contract."

"Interesting," she said. "Here, as in L.A.?"

"He was looking at books in Charles's shop," interjected Melina, who seemed to have calmed down a little. "Sir Neville was there as well." I chose not to mention that there were two visits, rather than one.

"So we heard, actually. Good job with the bear, Mr. Borden. Thank you for bringing Mr. Borden to us, Melina. We'll have to actually ask you to take charge of him now too. There's no one else who can break free for this."

"But-"

"No buts! That's actually what we were discussing before you entered."

Melina looked stricken for a few seconds, then straightened and nodded.

"Good. He's your responsibility until we get things in order. This is Charles's fault. And you are his responsibility, so the task goes to you."

Melina's face darkened for a second, then she nodded her acceptance.

A short woman and a tall black man who I'd first seen on one of the catwalks appeared. The man sat next to me and started to bandage up my right arm. The woman passed me a glass, then moved off to give another to Sir Finley.

"Drink up, Wielder," said the man. I sniffed at the wine and took a sip, hoping it wouldn't go to my head. "My name's Chris too son. We ain't had a Wielder since I was a kid."

I tossed down a healthy swig of wine and set it down. "Thanks," I said gratefully, flexing my right arm. I then waved him away, grabbing a long bandage and putting it around the stab wound on my left thigh. I would be a wreck in the morning one way or another at this point. The pants were bloody and ruined. My polo shirt had several tears in it and wouldn't last a wash.

"Now, you," said Samantha, looking once more in my direction. She must have said some words to Sir Finley, but I didn't hear them.

"I'll try to meet with you tomorrow to answer your questions. But I will tell you this tonight. You must stay with Melina. Do not try anything brash. You are, as you suspected, not in Kansas any longer. This is quite unlike your land. Rest assured, Sir Neville, and others more ruthless than him, are watching every gate right now with careful eyes. You need to rest, Wielder."

"I'll take your advise, ma'am. I don't think I could be good for anything else tonight anyway," I finished with a weak smile.

"Good night then," she finished and turned away to the circle. Sir Finley walked over to stand above me.

"I did not realize you had already been in an altercation today and had wounds before we began. For that, and my arrogance, I apologize."

"Apology accepted. It's okay, Sir Finley. How bad is the sword?"

"It is destroyed. Split to the core. I'll have another made."

He turned and left.

Melina, put her hand under my right arm and hauled me to my feet.

"We need to go soon. They still have a lot to talk about," she said.

I ignored the heady wine on the floor, nodded my thanks at Chris, who was still standing a few feet away, and then let Melina lead me to the stairs. She passed me my laptop bag, and I slipped it painfully over my shoulder. I felt like I had a bruised rib or two.

In the area near the door we retrieved our outer garments. I left the hood down, but she put hers up. Habit I guess. It had stopped raining. We began the walk back at a slower pace, with me favoring my leg.

"It is 427 years old. But it will never fight in a battle again," said Melina a few blocks away from the warehouse.

"What," I asked.

"The sword. The Finley Sword. You ruined it. It was kind of fun watching that arrogant prick get his, how did you say it, 'hat' handed to him."

"I didn't expect that to happen, but I had to end that, I didn't have anything left."

"Chris," she replied with emotion. "You have no idea what you did, do you?"

"Give me a break, dammit," I replied a little stronger than I'd intended. "You could have warned me I was going to get attacked!"

"Actually, I couldn't. Not really. I am already probably in trouble for telling you the blade is yours. That hasn't been confirmed yet. Well, actually it is now just a formality, since you passed the testing. Finley's family have been testers for centuries. He was to get you to use the blade. It took a while, but you finally did."

"What do you mean, use the blade? I was using the blade for like fifteen minutes like mad."

"No, you weren't," she replied critically. I decided to give up. To make it worse, she added. "Actually, it was more like a bit under ten." Then she grinned. "But you did hold you own better then you might think. You are very fast on your feet and with your mind. I have to struggle against Finley, and he wasn't holding back that much. His reach is phenomenal."

"But his left side is weak and he tends to dip his rights a bit when he pivots his elbows to change angles. And his footwork is leading his own mind. I don't think he was consciously doing it, but you could always tell which side he would go based on how he was moving his feet before he'd do anything. I couldn't take advantage of it, but it was there, infuriating the heck out of me."

"See," she said bluntly, guiding us left at an intersection. "I've gone against Finley in formal bouts and never seen the feet thing. I'll watch for it next time."

"You're welcome," I said. I had a strong feeling she was just trying to be nice to me. "This isn't the way we came."

"You're right."

"Well?" I asked. We were heading into what looked like worse territory than before. I noticed her arm reaching for the dagger behind her back a few times. More street lighs were out; more windows cracked slightly. The feeling of being somewhere we shouldn't permiated the air.

"I never take the same route. Amd since it's only a few miles, a couple streets one way or another don't matter. This one's just not as good as some of the others I could take. Don't worry, we're almost out of this section."

"Good."

"Can you limp a little less?" she asked.

I snorted in reply. She took it as a no and quickened her pace. After a few more minutes, things got noticeably better and I relaxed.

"Drat, you need to eat, don't you?" she asked.

"And you don't?" I asked back. "Unless you bolted down a lightening fast meal in the kitchen, I didn't see you have anything. I was thinking about lunch before I even ran into your dad's shop. Sorry, Charles's shop. He's not your dad, but you're his daughter."

"Right."

"Yeah," I replied. "I don't know what passes for food around, here, but I refuse to eat anything that's not dead yet."

Melina laughed rather loudly. I smiled back. It was nice getting a good laugh out of her.

"Don't worry, most of it's dead. I'll take you by Sparky's and you can grab something to take with you. You have money?"

"Cash, as in US dollars, yeah. That work?"

"No. It takes at least $100 to get it exchanged. You have that much?"

"I usually don't carry more than a $20. If any at all. Just habit from my college days. That's actually why I went by your, ah, Charles's shop in the first place. I didn't have cab fare."

"Funny," said Melina with a frown. I guess it wasn't funny after all. "You're on a tight budget then. I haven't gotten much work this month."

"So what do you do?" I asked. "Other than make daggers, sometimes."

"I look after Charles's shop occasionally, but that doesn't pay. When I can afford the materials, I make some blades and try to sell them. Charles buys some and sells them through the shop. The rest I usually hawk. I get special requests every once and a while. That's more of a hobby. I get paid to run errands, mostly. At least now."

"Do you try hawking those blades at any of the festivals on the 'outside'?"

"Usually. But I haven't been able to get reliable passes recently."

"You have to get a pass to go to the other side? I don't even know what to call the two. Realities? Realms?"

"Let's just say it's difficult for some of us. The penalties are pretty stiff if you violate things. Don't worry. You wont have a problem. You don't need a passport," Melina sighed. "Main-side and other-side. Or under-side. We're in what amounts to a small pocket of protected reality, attached to L.A. for the safety of those with strange ways. "

"What-"

"Just leave it, okay," she snapped. Cutting me off. Okay, fine.

"Sorry, I'll leave it."

"Good, here's Sparky's."

I looked up. It was a dump. But things smelled good. She opened the door and I limped in like I knew where I was. I waited for Melina to enter and followed her to the counter.

"I'll have whatever you're having," I said softly.

"I'm not having anything," she replied just as softly. "Grab whatever you'd like. But it's got to be under about 6 even."

"Well, what would you suggest?"

"Trust me, you wouldn't like anything I'd consider ordering."

I let this slide without comment.

"Okay. Order me what Charles would have."

She sighed and shook her head, defeated. Apparently she had been trying to get me to play a guessing game. I wasn't playing. Melina went to the counter and nodded to the tattooed kid behind the counter. She held up four fingers, two on each hand. "To go."

"Three fifty," said the kid while tapping a few keys on an old fashioned cash register. She passed a few yellow bills to him and he passed her back a few coins. I looked around the place. Did I say it was a dump?

Well, the kitchen area actually looked clean. The eating area most definitely wasn't. I almost asked if they had a bunch of toddlers in there for a food fight. I decided not to comment.

The kid set a bag on the counter after a few minutes and then nodded at us. Melina turned to walk out. I picked up the bag and limped after, nodding to the kid.

After I caught up with Melina we walked side by side for a few minutes.

"You were trying to have a little bit of fun back there, weren't you," I asked.

"What makes you say that?" she replied playfully. "And what makes you think I didn't?"

"Oh, I think you didn't have half as much fun as you could have. You did honestly order me what Charles would have gotten?"

"Yep," she said with satisfaction. "And you have no idea what that is."

"No."

"No what, Chris," she said, looking at me. She took a left turn at a corner. I could tell from the style of walk-ups that we were near her apartment.

"This is a cheeseburger with fries and an apple cake."

Melina mumbled something under her breath.

"Charles has take out from that place almost every day for lunch doesn't he? There were wrappers in the trash bucket behind the counter and I saw a half eaten sandwich sitting on top of one of these bags."

Melina shrugged, and then laughed again. "Okay, fine, you win."

"Aren't we on the wrong block?" I asked. "You're apartment's one over that way." I pointed left.

She shrugged and turned at the end of the block. About halfway along the side street, she turned left again into a little, almost hidden alley between the buildings. I followed single file. My left hand was on the sword hilt to keep it from hitting the stones. After several feet, we got to a door. Melina opened it and I followed her in and then up the stairs to her apartment. The smell of the food was getting to me.

Melina opened the door and pushed me through. She closed it and locked it behind me and tossed her dagger back on top of the pile of junk next to the door. I don't know how it stayed. Jameson almost flew out of the bathroom at the sound of our entrance. He had his shirt half buttoned and was obviously getting ready to go out. It looked like he had up-ended his rucksack on the couch. I set the food down on one of the side tables where it looked reasonably safe and then headed to the kitchen.

"Is the tap water okay?" I asked. Not that I'd care much.

"Yeah," said Melina. "There's a few clean glasses in the cupboard on the left of the sink." Jameson snorted. "Maybe," she added.

I grinned, checked and didn't find any, so proceeded to wash a few for myself that looked most salvageable from the sink. After I finished, I filled one, downed it, refilled it and then headed back into the other room. To find Jameson half way through MY cheeseburger. He noted my entrance and nodded.

To add insult to thievery, he lopped off a huge bite from the apple cake, and followed it up with a handful of the fries. "Thanks," he mumbled through the mush. Then Jameson tried to lean in to kiss Melina, who moved away from him. Seeing it as a lost cause, he opened the door, coat in hand.

Having gotten most of his mouth emptied, he managed to communicate, "I wont be back till tomorrow late. Careful Spif; she gets hungry in the mornings, man. Wicked."

With that warning, he left. Melina looked like she was going to kill him. I went over to see what I could recover from my supposed meal. Passing on the slobbered burger leavings, I attacked the fries and the remaining half of apple cake. Melina went to the kitchen and returned with some crackers which looked good and some cheese. She also had used one of the fresh glasses for water. She sipped a little and sat down on the chair across from the couch. A few seconds of silence later, she shut off the television.

"I guess that means that you can take the couch if you want," she said.

I swallowed. Then looked at the couch. Took a sip of water. "I'd actually prefer the floor. All I need is a towel for a pillow and a sheet and I'll be fine."

"I'm really sorry about that," she said. I could tell she was. Actually, I could tell I really wouldn't want to be Jameson right now.

I ate a few more fries and the last of the unviolated apple cake. After I swallowed, I replied, "it wasn't your fault, Melina. If he wants to be a jerk, he will be a jerk."

She nodded. I chased some fries with a solid hunk of cheese on a cracker. It was far stronger than I'd expected. Like the type of cheese you walk by in the supermarket because it's twice as much as the steak you were planning on grilling. I wondered where she'd got it.

"You're probably pretty sore already. Sleeping on the floor wont help that much," I made my thoughts shut themselves off real quick at this line of reasoning. "I'll take the couch. You take the bed. Seriously, it doesn't matter to me. And the sheets are clean."

I swear, I could hear an unsaid "almost" there, but didn't care at this point.

"I normally would be in a position to argue that, but I'm afraid I can't muster the energy right now. Sir Tall longed me out."

Melina had been drinking from her glass of water and almost choked on her laughter. Then she smiled. "I'll have to remember that one. 'Sir Tall.' He does have the ability to long one to the point of exhaustion. Beanstalk limbs and all. Probably would have been a good basketball player if we were allowed to play organized sports main-side."

I finished the partly meal and tossed the remains of the defilement and my leavings into the bag and got up to head to the kitchen. Along the way, I compulsively grabbed a few wrappers and other bits of trash and tossed them in as well. In lieu of the non existent trash bucket, I set the bag on the counter next to some similar items. Knowing I needed it, I downed the rest of the glass and then refilled it. Then I went back in the living room to head to the bathroom. I wanted to check the ribs before I fell asleep.

Melina was still sitting in the chair when I got back out, apparently deep in thought. My decision was that I had one bruised for sure, but not badly. I almost didn't want to interrupt Melina's reverie, but couldn't fail to give her a second chance.

"You sure about the arrangements?" I asked. She shook herself and then looked up at me.

"Yes, you dolt. Go! It's through the kitchen. The light doesn't work. Move anything that you need to."

"Okay," I said. And then. "Thanks for this, Melina. Good night."

"Good night, Chris," she replied, almost wistfully. I nodded and followed her instructions.

The bedroom was quite small, about twice the size of the bathroom actually. Pretty much just a bed, dresser and a small walkway between them. The closet looked like it could hold about eight to ten items if they were really skinny. But overall the room looked relatively uncluttered in comparison. And the sheets were clean.

"Almost," I said softly with a grin. I set the water down on the edge of the dresser and then sat myself down on the edge of the small bed. Of course, it's rather difficult to sit on a bed with a sword on you hip, so I almost got flipped off the side as it caught.

I managed to get it and myself straightened out and took off my shoes and the remains of my polo shirt. I don't remember laying back at all. I just passed out.

Chapter 5

Morning

Waking was actually a bit better than I'd feared the night before. Not much, but a little. My arm and leg felt like shit, and my chest hurt every time I breathed. I could also feel an ache in my right hand when I opened and closed it. Courtesy of the impact with Sir Tall's jaw bone.

Deciding life was worth living, injuries aside, I opened my eyes and began a slow process which would end with me sitting. Then I stopped. The spot to the right of me on bed was warm. Like someone had been there recently. Adding up the options in my mind, I decided to ignore the obvious conclusion. Maybe she got lonely or something. Maybe the couch sucked. I don't know, and as much as I find Melina attractive, there's apparently something going on between her and Jameson and I'm not going to get myself involved.

My resolution to ignore the evidence aside, I sat up and reached for my boots. After finishing the ties, I realized I heard the shower running in the background. I looked at my watch. 7 am. great. A little early for Melina, from what I could tell of her habits. What was that warning that Jameson gave me; 'She'll be hungry in the morning'?

Oh well, whatever. I reached up and grabbed the glass of water I'd set down on the dresser the night before. The second drawer had been opened and not shut all the way. Another clue that Melina had been in the room, but it's her room and her apartment and her clothes.

Yeah, and you're in her bed you moron. And her boyfriend probably suspects it. I slurped down about a quarter of the glass. My stomach growled in response. I set the glass back down, and noticed a roll of gauze bandage set on the dresser which wasn't there last night. I still heard the shower, so there wasn't much chance of getting a mirror soon. Who knows how long this chick takes, could be an hour in there.

Setting the roll aside for now, as I'd rather a shower first, I poked at my chest a bit to survey the damage. The rib was definitely broken, and looked horrible from the side. About midway through my assessment, I heard the front door open. Jameson, I thought.

And then immediately followed that through with a series of curses. I quickly finished my healh check. For some odd reason, I also noticed my neck itched on the right side. There were a few tender spots. The skin wasn't broken, but I couldn't figure out what had caused it.

I looked up to find Jameson in the doorway with a smirk on his face. He looked jittery. Like he was hopped up on something. It figured. And this was not what I needed right now. I stood and reached to buckle the sword on my belt. His was in his hand and he moved it to my throat. I stopped and straightened up to face him, bare chested. I regarded him levelly.

"I guess this would be you caught in the act," he said. I didn't answer, instead, I grabbed the glass without looking and took another swallow, setting it back down in the same place. He glanced at my neck. And then looked at me in confusion.

"What act do you think you've caught me in that you can actually determine through the haze of the stuff you're on?" I asked. I know, not my best, but I was actually hoping to confuse him.

"Want some?" he asked. I was amazed that it was that easy to get him off track. Then again, he still had a sword on my throat. Who was I kidding?

"I think I'll pass," I raised my hand to the flat of his blade and shoved it aside. He almost toppled over, but managed to catch himself on the doorway. He made an attempt to get the blade back up, but I was already through door with the glass in hand once more. He followed me into the room and set the edge against my neck while I filled the glass. He pushed and drew blood. Now I was ticked. I moved away and set the glass down. The shower cut off.

"If you do that again," I said rather loudly, "you'll regret it."

He moved the blade back up to my neck. I heard the bathroom door slam open and the pat of wet feet on the tiles in the living room. Then Melina was behind me, though I didn't turn to look.

"Jameson," she said. "What the hell are you doing?"

"Protecting my interests," he said levelly and moved to prick my neck again. I wasn't there this time. He staggered around to his right to track me.

"Good morning, Melina," I said, still not looking in her direction. I could tell in my peripheral vision that she was at least wearing a towel. I felt blood running down my neck, and resisted the urge to dab at it.

"Aren't you hungry, Mel?" Jameson asked, his attention slightly drawn to her dripping wet form. I wasn't letting mine get drawn anywhere with this hopped up jerk in the room. He moved over in her direction and began to reach for her towel.

I decided I'd had enough of this guy. Damn the consequences. I moved with all my speed. My right fist chopped at his wrists. The blade dropped to the floor easily. My left grabbed his left ear and used it to yank his head around while I kicked at the back of his legs with my right leg. He spun around like a top and went crashing to the floor face first. I resisted the urge to kick him in the side and instead slid the sword away under the table to the opposite wall.

Jameson tried to rise, then cried out and collapsed again. My right arm was in agony and the rib was screaming, but I'd had enough. I looked at Melina in apology and shrugged. She seemed like she was shaky. I guess she had a right to be. She was also very attractive and her hair was wet. And there wasn't much towel there. I made myself look away. Jameson made it about half way to his feet at this point, gathered himself together and then staggered to a standing, almost level, position. I think he lost a tooth on the floor.

"You bastard," he said. I nodded in reply. And then he reached in his right back pocket with his left hand, almost tipping himself over in the process, to pull out a piece of paper. He tore it in half and let the pieces drop into the sink. Melina choked, and then sniffed. I had no clue what was going on so I just stood there.

Jameson mumbled something like he'd be back for his stuff and then stumbled toward the door. Melina moved into the kitchen to let him by, then looked up at me, almost pleadingly. She was definitely shaking. The door slammed. I walked a little closer to her and she leaned in to put her head on my chest almost sobbing. I did what anyone would under the circumstances, I put my arms around her.

"I'm sorry Melina, I should have handled that differently," I said softly. "I've just had it with people taking swords to me these days." She snuggled a little closer, but had seamed to stop shaking. A good sign I guess. I started to say something else, when I noticed that I felt something very much like a tongue on my chest. Right under where that jerk had pricked me. Then I felt it again, longer and a little higher up. The wheels began turning and then managed to get to some sort of conclusion just as I felt Melina suck right on the cut, her teeth scraping slightly against my neck, longingly. I was almost lost in the moment as it was one of the most seductive things I've ever experienced, and I felt myself reacting to it.

But my mind took over as I felt the teeth pressing harder against my skin. My mind went back to the marks on Jameson's neck. To Melina's strength, to her not eating. And a few other comments. The only possible conclusion. She was a vampire. The hell was I supposed to do now! All I could think about is that people become a vampire by being bitten by a vampire. And I wasn't sure that's how I wanted to spend the rest of my time. I did the only thing my spinning mind could do, I shoved Melina, hard. And she went sailing into the cabinet and sunk down to her knees.

I looked down at her and she returned my look and then began to cry and shake again. I crossed next to her near the sink and looked at the piece of paper Jameson had torn up. The two halves read "Vampire Stabilization Permit". It was made out in Jameson's name with Melina as the signed vampire. I skimmed the rest, dropped it, and sat down cross legged next to Melina on the floor. There were parts of the agreement detailing consumption limits and expectations and requirements for both the stabilzer and the vampire. Melina had her head in her hands. I tentatively touched her shoulder. She looked up at me, a small amount of blood on her lip. She was clearly shaking and her eyes didn't look so good.

"So you're a vampire?" I said softly, as neutral as I could. "I've never met a vampire before. I didn't know they existed until about twenty seconds ago. So I'm sorry for my reaction. I apologize for shoving you, Melina."

She nodded. Tears were still streaming from her eyes. "I don't know what you were going to do Melina, and I was afraid of what you might have done. That is why I did what I did. Do you understand that?"

Melina sniffed and nodded. "Is it safe to assume from that permit up there that humans can be bitten without being turned into a vampire?"

She nodded. I reached up and pulled a mostly clean napkin from the counter top and handed it to her.

"Now, I'll ask this question, and please answer truthfully. You're hungry aren't you?"

"Yes," she said softly.

"Was that what you got from the kitchen yesterday, when I showed up, with blood all over me."

"Yes," she said again, a little more evenly.

"But you didn't have any left?"

She shook her head, no. I sighed. Jameson probably hadn't been keeping up his part of the deal very reliably.

"He was on drugs most of the time too, wasn't he," I asked. I'd guess that that would taste pretty bad to a vampire. She nodded.

"You could have bitten me any time this morning, couldn't you. I know you were next to me."

She nodded again and looked down.

"But you didn't," I touched her chin and pushed upwards until she looked at me. "Can you promise me you won't turn me into a vampire?"

"I promise," she said, almost pleadingly.

I'd never been bitten by a vampire before, but with evidence, physical and written, that one could be bitten and live as a human, I decided what the hell. I grabbed both of Melina's wrists and pulled her into my lap. She didn't resist. My left hand circled around behind her and my right slipped around her neck under her hair. I pulled her mouth to my neck and felt her quiver as she gently sunk her teeth into my neck. It hurt a little bit, but was actually kind of nice in the long run. Getting to hold onto a rather nice body during the experience and then having her rest in my arms after was also interesting.

I'm not sure how long we sat entwined together, but it must have been at least a half an hour. I finally decided I needed to move my legs and gently roused Melina from her nap. She sleepily yawned and managed to realize that the towel had slipped away in the midst of the process. She blushed scarlet and gathered it back up, extracting herself and standing up slowly. She did seem a lot better than before. I stood up much more slowly due to loss of circulation in my legs. The left leg was killing me, and it was looking like it was bleeding again.

After I made it to my feet, Melina leaned into me and put her head on my chest.

"Thank you," she said. "I...I don't expect anything from you again. And I shouldn't have then. It's just that Jameson..."

"He kept himself hopped up didn't he?"

"Yes, it tasted horrible, and he knows it. It usually makes me sick. And half the time he doesn't let me have that much. I...I that was the first time I've tasted anything clean in several months. You actually taste very good." She finished and I could feel her cheeks heating up.

"You don't need that much, do you?" I asked.

"To keep me alive, very little. What I took from you was more than enough to keep me pretty well off. If I get it regularly..."

"And let me guess, it's either illegal or prohibitively expensive to buy it on your own, isn't it?"

"Expensive."

"Figures," I sighed. "Well, I don't regret it Melina."

There was a knock at the door. Melina pushed away.

"I'm going to get dressed, you get it, okay," she asked. I followed her out of the room. "It's probably a package from Samantha."

"Package?"

"Yeah. Clothes."

There was another knock. Melina went into the bathroom. I heard the towel drop the the floor, and noticed that the door was not quite shut. I didn't let myself think about that, and went to the door.

Well, I'd just met a vampire, so now it was my turn to meet an elf. The elf passed me a heavy paper bag, gave a small bow and then left. I looked around the hall, I guess for candid camera minions or something, then closed the door. I looked in the bag. There was a note:

> Pick one. Melina should be able to help if you need it. Expect to do a lot of walking and talking, and listening. But don't worry; you will not face another swordsman today! I hope the fit is well.
>
> Samantha.

I went into Melina's bedroom and pulled out the contents for inspection. It looked like three shirts and three different styles of pants. All seamed formal, similar to the clothing worn at that meeting in the warehouse last night. So, did Samantha not count Jameson as a man, or was she clairvoyant in the use of the word, "another?"

The hose were immediately passed on, simply on a matter of principle. Of the two other pairs of pants, I chose the more loose, which also appeared more durable. All three of the shirts were white with high necks. And there were a few different vests which looked like pared down jerkins. All were dark blue with a crest on them. I picked the least flamboyant, which also once more looked the most durable and simple in cut. I sensed a theme in their design.

Then I got to the bottom of the bag. The underwear was about what would be expected from ten years ago. But the shoes most definitely were not. I refused to wear pointy shoes; I'd stick with my leather boots. I heard foot steps again and reached to gather up my chosen attire. Then stopped.

Apparently I wasn't the only one required to wear something formal today. Melina walked right at me, holding the top of a very flattering strap-less black dress to her chest. She turned slightly and motioned for me to zip up the back. So I did, almost with regret. I didn't miss the fact that the dress seemed extremely functional too. The sword and dagger from the paper pile out front were strapped around her waist in elegant matching sheaths.

"I guess I should say something nice about that but I can't form rational thoughts at the moment," I said honestly.

"You're not going to wear the hose?" Melina asked, almost innocently.

I snorted.

"Why not?"

"Are you kidding me? I wouldn't be caught dead in those things."

I re-acquired my bundle and went to the bathroom.

About twenty minutes later, almost feeling human again, I emerged from the bathroom. Melina was pacing across the livingroom, deep in thought once more. Wrapping my chest had been more difficult than I'd thought, but I'd managed okay.

"You're a troubled little vamp, aren't you?"

"There are probably some other things I should tell you," she said, biting her lip. Uh, oh. She walked over and passed me my sword. I strapped it on over the jerkin-vest thing.

"Good or bad," I asked, fearing the latter.

"Well, it depends on the point of view, I guess."

"And..."

"Okay," she said. "You know about the permit system for us now that you've read over that bit of paper. Basically, unless we are really wealthy, we have to find someone to willingly give blood to us. We get in lots of trouble for biting without permission. I'm actually up for destruction if I get caught for anything again.

"Things may have been different a few centuries ago, when vampires hunted, but not now. Not anymore. Since 1862 we've been under the current rules. The side effect of only taking one person's blood is rather, *sensitive,* for some vampires."

She moved to the door and opened it. I moved to follow.

"Well, basically we tend to be a bit, ah..."

"Sensitive," I offered.

"Yeah," she took a deep breath. "Sensitive to those whose blood we take. It almost makes us predisposed to... Oh, hell, basically, Chris, if you tell me to do something right now, regardless of my own choices, there's a very good chance that I'll obey."

"That could be bad for vampires, at times, no?"

"Yeah..."

"And Jameson?"

"Pushed things a little bit. His blood was weak, so his control was weak. But I believe you see the point. And the dangers. A lot of powerful people have pet vampires. I've struggled not to be one of them."

"And will I be meeting some of those today," I asked.

"You already have. Samantha has one that's her lover. Sir Finley has several in his staff. Charles's wife is one, which is my dam, actually. She turned me to save my life though. There are a lot of others."

"Anyway, that's just in our league. Sir Neville has at least thirty in his house. And he is a lot less scrupulous about using them. Our league is responsible for what little rights vampires have left. Four of the elders at the meeting you saw last night were vampires, but they're fairly powerful, and rich."

Melina looked over her shoulder at the wall clock. She tossed me my borrowed coat, and then spun one of her own over her bare shoulders. I finally gave up on using my wrist watch, it didn't seem to track well with whatever schedule this place was on. She pushed me out the door and closed it behind us. I began down the stairs, with her in tow.

I turned back to Melina at the bottom and waited for her to walk down beside me.

"It's almost a form of slavery, isn't it?" I asked, referring to the vampire stabilization practices. I could see her frown.

"It can be, but there are logical reasons behind it," she said. "The up side is, we're not hunting humans in the night anymore. We have the possibility of being productive individuals. But you saw how I was yesterday. Every time I scented blood I went ape. And I've been subsistence living for almost a year now. Since, well, never-mind."

We exited the building and turned left. The sun was pretty bright, and I laughed, nearly choking in the process. I turned to look at Melina expecting her to react in some way. She just kind of stared back.

"I guess there's nothing to the myth about vampires and sun."

"Nope. We don't hate silver either. Several vampires I know are actually catholic and wear crosses and carry bibles. But we do live for several hundred years."

"Wood through the heart?" I might as well get through the usual checklist.

"Dust," she said softly. "But only after we've been bled and dried. It takes about a week in the sun." Melina crossed her arms over her stomach and looked down, but continued walking. I didn't miss the slight shiver.

"Sorry," I said.

"Sokay," she replied. Then she gave herself a shake. "I've been dried last time. It's not something I ever want to go through again."

"Ouch," I said for lack of a better response. "So how old are you, Melina?"

"I was turned at 16, which was about 7 years ago. So I'm probably a little younger than you. Our appearance ages about 1 year for 10, depending on how healthy we are. I'll look this young for quite a while."

"Are we heading back to the warehouse?" I asked, though I thought not.

"Nope, this will actually be a public meeting. We're going to the league hall for the first time in a while. Did you think Samantha sent you hose for your health? It's a formal event of sorts."

Then I just realized, I'd been asking questions for about ten minutes and getting answers. Something seemed strange about this all of a sudden. Comparing it to the day before, this was a veritable flood of information.

"Melina," I asked, beginning to get worried. She looked over at me. "You're allowed to tell me what you just did, right?"

"Parts of it are public knowledge, others are common league knowledge. So those, yes. Who turned me. No, I shouldn't have told you that, but it was my choice. I'd just like it if you didn't talk about it with anyone else."

I nodded. It didn't seem that bad.

"Can you do me a favor? If I ask anything that you shouldn't answer, let me know. I don't want to get you in trouble."

"I'll try," she said. "So, what project were you working on in L.A.?"

Glad of the change of topic, I launched. "I'm not supposed to tell you."

Melina giggled and covered her mouth with her left hand.

"I had that coming, didn't I," she said, smiling.

"My firm was contracted to renovate a control system on an extruding process here. Pretty basic stuff for us. The process itself wasn't working quite the way they thought it was, so our systems didn't work as predicted. I got sent out to figure out what went wrong and make some changes.

"One of their old pneumatic controllers wasn't working because of a broken line, and that had apparently been throwing their whole process off for years. My part of things was essentially done two days ago. But they will probably be tuning things for a while."

Melina gave me a blank look. I sighed. The story of my job. No one has any clue what I'm talking about half the time.

"How does this," I asked, tapping the hilt of the sword, "change things?"

"I..I probably shouldn't answer that," she smiled. "But, I'll mention this, which may help. Samantha is a prosperous lawyer on the other side, and she's also the leader of our league at the moment. For you it may be easier since the Wielder mansion for our league has its own gate."

"Mansion?"

"Uh," Melina frowned. "That I shouldn't have said. Not that it matters. There's an estate house for each of the seven league Wielders. The swords are the keys to the houses."

"Do I have time for one more stupid question?" I asked. For it looked like we were approaching a large cathedral of sorts.

"Fire away," said Melina.

"What the heck does a Wielder do?"

"No, I shouldn't answer this, but I will anyway. No one can face a trained Wielder in combat and live except another Wielder. If two leagues disagree, the Wielders must settle the dispute. That is why our league is so weak right now. We can't challenge any of the other leagues. It was tried once, but that person failed."

I stopped and stared at her back, as she kept walking up the steps to the entrance of the cathedral. She paused and turned in my direction.

"You seem to be the type of person who wants to make a difference, Chris. Well, consider this one more way of doing that for a lot of people."

I took a deep breath and climbed the stairs to stand next to Melina. With more gumption than I felt, I offered my right arm. Melina put her hand on my forearm.

"Let's be about it then," I said. I proceeded up the steps and into the Cathedral of the Seventh League. I couldn't shake the feeling that I was walking down the isle to my doom.

Chapter 6

Training

We entered the cathedral anteroom and were greeted by the sounds of raised voices. Melina yanked me back from the door and was probably going to push me back out the way we came, but I thought I recognized the voice from the bookstore.

"No, Melina," I said, and she stopped, and moved next to me.

"Remember the hallway," she whispered in my ear. "Remember how it felt to see it. Remember."

I took a deep breath, put my bluffing hat on and stormed through the door while drawing my sword.

"Do you want to die today, Sir Neville," I yelled at the top of my lungs. The argument between him and Samantha on the dais stopped. His eyes widened at my entrance, but he didn't seem too impressed. Melina was right behind me, with both blades drawn. Already giving evil eyes at one of Sir Neville's non troll tag-a-longs. From the looks of the room, there were about even numbers of both parties. But it was the Seventh League's hall, and it didn't seem like this other group was invited.

Sir Neville looked like he was about to laugh. Then he did. I just stared fire at him and waited for him to speak. "You even know how to use that thing, Wielder?" His voice was calm.

"Why don't you ask Sir Tall there, or his family's sword? Or rather what's left of it." I replied in the same even tone, waving the sword carelessly in the direction of Sir Finley. He paled slightly (if such a thing was possible) and lifted his right arm from its sling in answer of my reference. His scabbard was empty.

"Bah," replied Neville. "How could you possibly?"

"I did."

Neville looked down his nose at me, and then focused his attention to Melina to my right. "Do you think that pathetic thing will help you? She shouldn't even be here!"

"She's here at my request," I said, taking my left hand off the blade, I pulled down my left collar and moved my head to the right to show the marks. Several people in the room inhaled in response.

I decided my bluff shouldn't include patience.

"I'll ask again," I seethed. "Do you want to die today?"

He started to make a reply, but noticed members of his party were starting to exchange glances. I took the opportunity to begin a slow approach to the dais. Neville glanced in their direction, then at Sir Finley, his exterior cracking. I saw doubt cross his face. He slowly raised his hand off his sword hilt and spread his arms wide.

"We leave you to your advisers, Wielder. Till the next congress," he bowed slightly. I inclined my head to the same degree and moved my sword to a rest position. As they left, I continued to keep my gaze focused on Sir Neville.

After the doors shut, there was a palatable silence. I sighed with relief and sheathed the sword as quietly as I could. It echoed in the chamber much louder than I had hoped. Melina, still at my side, did the same. I walked the last few steps to stand in front of Samantha, who was still in the center of the dais.

"Well," she said. "That was the stupidest thing I've ever seen in my life young man."

"Have you read your Miyamoto Musashi, Lady Samantha?" I asked. My voice calm once more.

She stared at me blankly.

"'Flustering is the essence of battle; it should be studied very carefully.'"

She laughed. The tensions in the room began to slack off.

I turned to Sir Finley. "I apologize for my remarks Sir. I meant what I said last night. I regret the loss of your family's blade that you have suffered through my actions then, and I regret the comments I just made against your honor."

"Your apology is not necessary, Wielder. You realize that you've only delayed a conflict with Sir Neville? And that only because he couldn't afford to have the mages come. He was probably hoping to get in a clean kill and be done with you."

"I'd be surprised if it was anything more than a delay," I said. "I figure; he came here to kill me, and he left with me still alive. That would have to count for something."

"That is does," said Samantha. Then she looked around the room at the other fifteen league elders. "Is there anyone in this room who does not concur that Chris Borden has been tested, and passed?"

No one spoke.

"Are there any who deny that Chris Borden has the right to be the Wielder of the Seventh Sword?"

Again silence.

"Does the chosen Wielder accept the blade?"

"I accept," I said. What else was I supposed to do?

"Then as leader of the Seventh League, I acknowledge the decision of the Sword in its Wielder. Chris Borden is now affirmed as the eleventh wielder of the Seventh League."

"You will now sit in on meetings as your schedule allows. You will attend all congress of the leagues as our representative. You will answer any challenges as they arise to our league. You will issue any challenges that you must for the league."

I nodded. Samantha stepped off the dais and walked over to me. The others in the cathedral began to get up and leave, taking members of their guard with them. I noticed the other Chris from last night and waved to him, he smiled back.

"Melina," Samantha said. "He needs to learn to ward fast. Take him to see Trevor with my regards. After that, we need a schedule setup with Sir Finley. Starting this afternoon. And take him by the library. As I said last night, he is your responsibility for now. You are the best suited to train him. And I see you have taken care of one of the issues..."

Samantha pulled my left collar down to examine the bite mark. I imagine she probably had a pair or three of her own.

"Chris," she continued. "You could do a lot worse than Melina. I chose to ignore your 'announcement' of sorts, as I'm sure others may. I'm not going to formally acknowledge it. However, I must ask to make sure. Did you allow her to bite you?"

"Yes I did. I asked her to."

Samantha smiled slightly. "That was probably very kind of you," she said. "And was that before or after that druggy voided his agreement."

"After," I said. "And after he pricked my neck with his sword too."

"Well, looks like I haven't gotten any promises right today, did I?" Samantha gave Melina a smirk. "Just don't forget to file a form as soon as possible for both the void and the bite this morning. Rest assured, Sir Neville will try and cry foul if he can. And we know what that would mean, Melina."

Melina nodded, and bowed her head slightly.

"Do you have enough charges left," Samantha asked. Melina looked up, and then thought for a second.

"Should be. Just though, I had to use several already last night and this morning."

"Very well," Samantha motioned for Chris. The other Chris. The one I was pretty sure was her vampire lover that Melina mentioned. "Give Melina a few hundred for Trevor, Christopher dear. Melina, go ahead and get Trevor to recast the spell. You will probably need it before this situation has equilibrated. Although, as we saw today, it may not take that long after all."

"You know you were glowing, Chris," said Melina, while accepting some bills from Christopher. I looked at her dumbfounded.

"The sword, you were using the sword," she elaborated, a fire in her eyes.

"All right, you should go soon, before word gets out of Sir Neville's pseudo defeat and people come to see if this place is in ruin."

She reached out and offered me her hand, I shook it firmly.

"Till tomorrow night. Stay safe. And don't forget those forms!"

Samantha, Christopher and several others took off through one of the side entrances, Melina walked in the direction of another.

After we went though the doors, she stopped and turned around and kissed me about as passionately as I've ever thought a kiss could be. After several seconds, she let the kiss break and slipped away from me towards the door.

"Um, Melina," I said rather huskily, after I finally found most of my voice.

"Yeah," she replied, dreamily.

"Not that I'm complaining, but what was that for?"

"That is the first time anyone has ever gotten that man to back down in quite a while."

"That's not all is it?" I asked. "He knew you."

"He should," she paused. "Please, Chris. Ask me later, but not right now."

"Okay," I replied. "Who's Trevor? No wait. I'm going to stop asking questions. Now. I withdraw the question."

Melina laughed, "You're silly. I'm not going to just pour my guts out every time you ask a question."

I chose to stay quiet.

"You should like Trevor. He's an old friend of mine, yeah, he was *that* kind of friend for a little while, but his girlfriend didn't like it much. They're married now. He was giving me his blood, so I was pretty much fawning after him. She didn't like the thought of competition."

"I take it that he is a mage of some sort," I asked. Melina pushed me into a left hand turn. She didn't take her hand off my arm after making the redirection.

"He's intelligent, and skilled, but not very powerful. He usually contracts with us for wards and such since we can afford his rates. He doesn't have all that much business. My dagger has been enchanted with a warding and hiding spell. It ensures that we can't be tracked or watched by anyone who would do us harm. I'm actually not supposed to have it by law, but there's a loop hole since I made the blade."

"And did he also waterproof your hoodie," I asked with a grin. Her face darkened.

"That was actually his wife," she said flatly. "She kind of, um, got ticked at me. I had gotten into a habit of walking to their place in the rain. She kind of wanted to make sure that it wouldn't happen again."

"Right," I said. I think I understood the issue. "I guess it would be too much to ask to stop for breakfast on the way?"

"You darn mortals and your eating habits. At least I have some cash now," said Melina. "We can try and bum some stuff off of Trevor, if you want to chance it."

"Whatever you think is best, Melina. I'm still feeling it from not having much to eat yesterday. I've also been pulling near all nighters for a good part of the last two weeks."

I laughed and then said, "I'm not sure which is funnier; a vampire admonishing a mere mortal for his need to eat, or the fact that that same mortal provided said vampire with her breakfast."

Melina gave me a look. I don't think I can write it down. Then her face changed and she looked like she was about to cry.

"Ouch," I said. And then I had little choice but to stop walking and try and hug her. "I'm sorry," I mumbled while pulling her into an embrace. I'd apparently stepped on that same central vampire in trouble nerve.

After several tense seconds, with one hand around her waist, and the other on the back of her head, Melina began to relax. Slowly, she pulled away, her face dark, but more under control.

I think she was about to apologize, but I cut her off. "Stop, I shouldn't have brought it up. I know your life is probably more in danger right now than mine. At least until I meet Sir Neville again. Tell you what; where do you need to file the paper work for what happened this morning?"

"Local control office," she said softly. Her arms were still on my sides, and I still had a firm grip on her waist. "About six blocks away."

"Is there a temporary form of some sort for that 'stabilization permit'?"

Her face softened and she seemed to melt a little. "You can't mean you're willing to–"

"Melina, it looks like I'm going to be here for a few days more, one way or another. I'm not sure what will happen after that, but at least for now, I'm here. Furthermore, you've pretty much been told to keep my nose clean for now.

"I cost you your source of blood this morning. And since you'll probably be walking me around this town in your spare time for a while, I don't see where you will have the time to go 'hunting' for a new source. It seems I've been giving a lot of blood away recently to guys with swords. Well, honestly, if I'm going to be losing blood anyway around here, I'd much rather give it to a cute little vampire like you."

Melina looked like she was going to fall apart. I glanced around, and it was starting to look like people were paying attention to us, so I took the lead and turned Melina aside. I kept a hand on her arm and got us walking again. She sniffed.

"You sure?" she asked. "You don't have to do anything for me. I'm just a vampire."

"From what I can tell, you're a good person who just happens to be in a society which treats her kind as little better than slaves. I hate seeing it and the last thing I want to do is try and make you dependent on me either. But I seem to have a choice, and I think it's obvious which one I should make. It's pretty much become apparent that I need someone to show me the ropes. Or at least to not hang myself on them at first. And that person, for various reasons, is you, Melina."

"There are week permits," she said, a little more composed. "And you'll need to sign as a witness to Jameson voiding and then sign for the bite this morning. But I can't accept your offer without a promise."

She had recovered enough to navigate into a left hand turn.

"And that is?" I asked. Yes, I may be getting a little ahead of myself with this whole other world thing at the moment, but I wasn't going to just promise my life away.

"I'm probably going to need you to be very understanding at the end of that week. Let's put it this way," she sighed. "I've had nothing but muddy blood for more than a year now. Just promise me that you'll try to understand. I'm probably going to be pretty well hooked after a week."

"How bad a problem are we talking about here?" I asked with a grimace. I had a mental image of claws flying. "Enraged cat in a cage bad?"

She giggled. "You can make light out of anything, can't you?" After a few seconds, I saw the sign a few buildings ahead that said *Special Controls Office*. "Probably, crashed and depressed bad. But I may not be very personable for a while. I may not be very personable for several weeks, depending on what I find for options. I just wanted you to be aware."

"I promise to be understanding, when the time comes." I almost added if, but then again, I didn't want to get this girl's hopes up. I didn't miss the fact that she separated herself from me when we got nearer to the front doors. She opened the left one and I walked around her and inside. She followed, brushed past me and then got to the back of the line.

There were about six people ahead of us in line and one more at each of the three teller windows. One of the groups in front looked like a couple. The young woman directly in front of Melina looked terrified. She had a fresh mark on her small neck. She gave me a shocked look and then glanced at Melina's neck. Not noticing any bite marks, her eyes widened and she tried to back further away from us. She ended up resigning to defeat since there was another vampire right in front of her position. The woman lowered her head and clutched her hand bag. Her knuckles were white.

All is not well in the land, I thought to myself. Melina ignored the woman in front of her and began tapping her left toe. I crossed my arms over my chest and looked around the room. My gaze stopped cold on the bulletin board. It was absolutely plastered with adds offering blood sources. Everything from unmentionable supplys, black market close outs, dime a dram's. Then the other offers. One caught my eye: "Got Blood? We do. For You. If you have Skills... Call Today!" The rest were the same.

I could see where a desperate Vampire could go wrong. It would be so easy to believe the ad hook and get drawn in. I looked back to Melina, now biting her lip and wringing her hands. A cute and intelligent young woman, probably with lots of the "skills" required, barely able to survive. The woman in front of us; probably picked up some handsome guy at a club last night. Had a bit of a wild time of it and ended up with two holes in her throat and a quart low. Tough to blame her for being stupid. Tough to blame her would-be beau for being desperate. The line moved up.

I left the line to get a drink of water from the fountain. When I leaned down to sip from the stream, I noticed the building right across the street was a blood bank. Figures. A steady line of people leaving with pricks in their arms. And a cache of ready blood there for the tempted, desperate vampire to take. They probably transported blood in armored cars here, I thought. I wondered how many vampires there were.

Then again, I wondered why I was getting so strung out about the rights of vampires. I crossed back to the line. Melina looked up at me and gave a weak smile. I resisted the urge to squeeze her shoulder. Couldn't hurt to ask I guessed.

"About how many vampires are there?" I asked quietly. Melina frowned for a second.

"Probably several hundred thousand," she said after some thought. "At least half a million now world wide? Only about fifteen thousand here. Overall about twenty percent of the population of the underside."

"That's a lot of people." I said. The woman in front of us snorted, then sobbed. I wondered if she knew that being bitten didn't turn you. Then for a second I realized I didn't know for sure myself; I only had the word of a very hungry, sexy vampire. I shook the thought from my head, and rested my left hand on the hilt of the sword. The line moved up two more people. It was now the couple, the woman and us.

My thoughts then went to the sword. I realized it felt a bit warm. Which was strange for a blade. I'd once worn one for a fortnight retreat a few summers ago. That hunk of borrowed metal never did what this one was doing now. It was always cold as hell when you first touched it. This one wasn't. What was it that Melina said, "remember the hallway." Something like that.

So I thought about the hallway, and the sword. The couple moved up to the center window, and began arguing with the teller. I began to see a difference in the room. Kind of like a glow on things. The people I thought were vampires showed up slightly differently than the humans. The woman in front of us showed up like Melina, almost. Similar but, well, fresher. The woman moved to the teller on the left. Another vampire came in the door and took to the line behind us, looking at the bulletin board from the end of the line. I turned to Melina.

"She was turned, wasn't she?" I asked very softly, indicating the woman.

"Yes, she was, how did you," then she looked at me, and reached over and slapped my hand gently away from the sword.

"Stop that, you're glowing, damn it!" she hissed. "The ward's not that strong!"

"Sorry," I replied sheepishly. The right teller cleared out just as two more vampires came into the room. We moved to the window.

"Yes?" asked the dumpy male behind the counter. He seemed bored.

"I need to confirm a void of a stabilization permit, as of this morning. I have three complaints against the human on file already for this permit," she passed the two halves of the permit across to the teller. "He tore it up this morning."

The teller stared at it blankly and then looked at her.

"Yes, I have a witness," she said flatly. Then pointed over her shoulder at me. I nodded.

"You saw mister..." the teller looked at the scraps. "Jameson, tear up this permit and void the agreement?"

"Yes, I did."

"Are you a vampire, a werewolf, elf, or ink?"

"No, I am none of the above." Ink? What was an ink?

"I need to see some ID," he said, finally pulling a form from a stack and beginning to fill it out with information from the voided permit.

I pulled out my wallet and showed him my Florida drivers license.

He looked up at it in surprise, and then up at me.

"I'm just visiting for a few weeks," I said

"Yeah," he replied. "Right." He didn't seem to think humans had any business visiting vampires.

He scratched down the number and my name. He spun the document around. Melina reached forward and signed it. I read it over and then did the same.

"You have three days to make other arrangements or you will be brought in and assessed. Do you have any questions?"

"No," said Melina. So three days, huh. Not much time.

"Anything else," he said. If he could have gotten any more ennui into that, he'd have put down roots. Then again, I couldn't see under the counter. Maybe he already had.

"Yeah," she said. "Consensual Feeding Report." She said and then looked over at me. I waved her on. "A...And a Temporary Stabilization Permit."

"You too?" asked the teller looking at me. I nodded. He shrugged and pulled a form off a stack, filling it in with information off the other form. He frowned and then pushed back in his chair to look behind him. "Hey, Shelly! Get out here. We need a truth test."

The girl that came out from a back room and walked at us past the filing cabinets couldn't have been more than eight or nine. Her eyes were sunken and she looked underfed. She walked over behind the tellers chair, her head hanging.

"Go pull vamp V-1972-0320-006749," he told Shelly. She turned around and lumbered back to the cabinets. After a few seconds she had a file folder and brought it to the teller. He pilfered through it and wrote down a few things on the form.

"Ah, so this would have been your third strike, I see."

Melina remained blank.

"You should have gotten the void processed before the bite," he admonished her. Then to me, "show me the bite."

I did. He looked at it closely.

"Why's it look funny?" he asked suspiciously.

"I cut myself while shaving," I improvised.

"With what, a dagger?" he retorted. No, a long-sword you prick. Let her sign the damn form!

"As long as the bite happened after the permit was voided, it's okay," he said, and turned to Shelly. She looked up at me. I looked down into her green eyes.

"Is your name Chris Borden?" asked the teller.

"Yes," I replied.

"Did you witness the voiding of the stabilization permit between Mister Jameson and Vampire 1972-0320-006749, also named Melina Long?"

"Yes."

"Do you also affirm that this event occurred before you were bitten by Vampire 006749."

"Yes."

The teller looked at Shelly. She looked at him. She nodded, and then turned and trudged back to the rear of the building. The teller wrote down several things. Then passed Melina two forms to sign. She did. Then I got them and read them over. I signed both of them and passed them back.

Mister teller tore off the top of the Temporary permit and passed it to me. The bottom copy went to Melina. He kept the middle and stapled it to the inside of the folder. All of them went into a "processing" in-box already stuffed with forms.

"Anything else?" he said. Forget a tree, this guy had the energy level of bedrock.

"Actually, I do need to setup a quarterly while I'm here," she said.

I turned away from the counter, and looked around. The line was filling up, it was about twice as long as when we came in. The new vampire was crying with her head down on the counter on the other side. For a second, I seriously wondered what I was doing here. I mean, seriously. Who does this kind of stuff? Apparently I did.

Melina signed another form and then turned away from the counter. I looked outside again. What was I doing here?

More importantly, what the heck was that guy doing outside staring at me.

Chapter 7

Run

Well, I shouldn't say at me. More like staring through me. I wasn't convinced he knew I was there, but based on his interest, he apparently knew something was here that he was having trouble seeing.

I turned to Melina in alarm. She looked up at me, her face clouded. I put my back to the window, and thumbed over my shoulder.

"There's a dude from the cathedral outside, and I'm pretty sure he was with Neville's troupe," I said. "I think he was the same guy that followed me around L.A." Melina frowned, and glanced over my shoulder. Then looked to either side along the street.

"Do you think you can find the warehouse?" she asked, then looked me in the eyes. Another person had moved to our spot at the teller.

I thought for a few seconds. I had a good idea where I was, but no idea where that was in relation to the warehouse. I shook my head. "Your dad's store, your apartment, the cathedral, and probably Sparky's, yes. The warehouse, no. Sorry."

"Okay, the store's out due to its gate. But go north past it two streets and over six to the east. Take the sixth south. About thirty yards from the corner on the right there's a small faded shop sign. It'll smell like frankincense. It's a small step up."

"Got it, 2 north, 6 east, 30 yards, 2 up. Use the nose," I recited. "What are you going to do?"

"They can't see you, which means they haven't broken the ward. But I think they know we're here. Which means one of us has probably been tracked. My guess is it's me."

We moved farther away from the line towards the bulletin board. I pretended to read some of the crud.

"How so?" I asked.

"Like begets like," she intoned.

"Sympathetic magic?"

"Blood magic," Melina replied. "I didn't think Neville would wait until the congress, but I didn't expect him to already make a try for you. He probably has Jameson. I still have enough of his blood in me to scry for it."

"So I head to the shop," I asked. "Trevor's?"

Melina nodded.

"And you meet me there after losing them?"

"Sort of..."

"Melina! What do you have in mind?"

"Don't worry," Melina smiled. "Nothing permanent. It's not illegal to attack a vampire anyway. And I'll be giving you the dagger. It has a wooden core."

She unstripped it from her belt and began to pass it in my direction.

"You must think strongly about a cloud hovering over you. It doesn't have to be constant, but at least once a minute or so. The more you do it, the stronger it will be, but the more quickly it can be shattered. When I leave, go with me, but keep walking. Stop when you are almost out of sight and make sure they get distracted. Then head to the shop. Do not draw your sword unless you absolutely have to."

"Got it," I replied, taking the dagger and strapping it to my belt behind the sword. I'd probably cut myself if I put it on the right side. "Good luck."

"Thank you, Chris," she said and leaned forward and kissed me softly on the cheek. "I'll see you in about an hour and a half. Maybe a bit more. Ask Trevor to show you how to ward with the sword. He'll recognize my dagger, and your blade too, so you shouldn't have a problem getting him to help you."

I touched my cheek with my left hand, and then turned to follow Melina out of the office. I thought about a cloud and then began walking steadily away in a roughly easterly direction. Melina shouted to the vampire who had been trying to see in the office. He shouted back. Swords were drawn. I kept walking. A troll came out of the bushes right in front of me and began heading towards the clash. I side stepped him and kept going. The sounds of blades striking got louder. I counted to ten, thought of a cloud, and then turned behind some trash buckets to examine the situation.

I almost cried out. Melina had faced off the vampire I saw through the window, and apparently three others who had been waiting. Also a total of six trolls. Cute little Melina, coat and skirts flying, was a whirl wind on tall grass. Two of the trolls were on the ground, and one of the vampires was trying to pull his own sword out of his chest. Another troll was staring down at his missing hand. A woman vampire and the the peeper from before were struggling together against Melina's sword work.

I've seen some virtuoso performances of blade work at festivals, but nothing compared to what I was seeing from my vantage point. It made my bout with Sir Finley look like a bad boy scout skit. The third vampire had extracted himself from the heap of trash cans across the alley and was trying to get the remaining trolls to go after Melina. They refused, so he recovered his sword and a nasty looking dagger from the dirt and went in to help out his fellows. I thought about a cloud.

Seeing the approaching vampire, Melina disarmed both male and female vampire in three moves. The pair went sailing back and skidding across the street. Then, she kicked up one of the fallen blades and flew at the remaining vampire. Just as the two would have made contact, Melina stopped. The vampire fell off balance by the sudden reversal and stumbled forward, right in time to meet the up swing through the center of his guard of both Melina's swords. He flipped backwards, and didn't stir.

Melina dropped the borrowed blade and surveyed her handiwork. The trolls had shrunk away from the street. The remaining vampire with a sword stuck in his chest gave one last try at pulling the blade out and toppled over when he lost his balance. Melina looked in my direction, winked, and then was off at a slow jog the other way, skirts and hair flying.

I thought of a cloud and began my search for the shop, thoughts on the one sided battle I just witnessed. A few streets down, I took a left, since I had to jog a little more north. Then I remembered the number, V-1972-0320. Sounded like a date to me. But that would put Melina a bit older than she mentioned. It's 2004, and she quoted 16 + 7 which would put her at 23. Not the 32 since 1972. I'd have to ask her. Then again, she probably shouldn't tell me.

I grinned to myself and then thought of a cloud again. Seeing a familiar looking cross street, I hung a right. It should be about 10 minutes walk from here, I thought. I resisted the urge to put shapes in my cloud. I figured, if someone's looking for me, they're not going to appreciate shapes in the cloud anyway. It's best to keep things simple.

Then again, how can I tell myself to keep things simple when I just signed up for a week as food for a vampire. It just seemed like the right thing to do. But what the heck happens when the week is over? From what I just saw, I'd hate to see Melina mad. Well, I think I can deal with having her mad at, say, Sir Neville. But he's a Wielder, so they probably shouldn't get in a fight.

I thought of a cloud, without shapes, just a simple cloud, thank you very much. And then I remembered something. Mansion. Melina said that all the Wielders had mansions. I'd have to remember to ask her about that next. Okay, fine. I'll ask her about whether or not I should ask her about it. Is that better? Good. I took a right.

Several minutes, and a bit under twenty clouds later, I turned left on the sixth street and crossed to the left side. Okay, twenty four clouds later. I had to double back a little bit. At least this meant I came at it from a different direction. Whatever that's worth.

I stepped up the two small steps to the shop, opened the door, and almost coughed at the smell of frankincense rolling out at me. My breathing under control, I approached the counter. There was a short, but handsome black man behind the counter with glasses. He looked up from a huge tome and squinted in my direction. I met his gaze and crossed to the counter.

"Are you Chris?" I asked. No, I'm not feeling okay, but I did know what I was doing.

"No, I'm Trevor," he said with a frown. "I own the place. Can I help you with anything?"

"Actually," I said. "I'm Chris."

He laughed. I set Melina's dagger on the counter. His eyes widened in alarm.

"My clouds are starting to get funny car shapes and maybe some wings. Should I keep thinking about them, or are there wards on the place?" I asked.

"Where's Melina?" he asked sternly.

"She's on her way," I was tempted to flash my neck at him, like I'd seemed to have to do to everyone else this morning, but I resisted the urge. "I'm almost at 30 seconds."

"Don't bother. This is a magic shop. It has to be warded. Save the charge."

"Okay," I said, and relaxed. I was going to have clouds on the brain for the next week. No wonder Melina was a bit nebulous recently.

"I believe you can probably help me, Trevor," I said as I pushed my cloak back a bit to reveal the pommel of the sword. He recognized it immediately. If his jaw dropped any more, the glass on the counter would have gotten wet.

After several seconds of his jaw collecting itself, he took a deep breath.

"Well, this does change things," he said. "You're definitely the Wielder?"

"As far as I can tell. I've used it, and the league affirmed me this morning."

"Did Samantha send you to me for warding and other basics?" Trevor asked. I nodded.

"That, and she gave Melina some money to recharge her dagger. She has it with her. The money, not the dagger."

"I don't have any appointments," he said, looking around the shop after checking his watch. Yeah, there wasn't anyone there, confirimg Melina's comment about his business being slow. "So I guess I'd better get you started."

"Uh, two things," I said. He motioned for me to continue. "First, Melina said she'd meet me here, but that was before I watched her mow down like ten trolls and five vampires. Is there anything we should do to make sure she's okay?"

"She is pretty amazing, isn't she," said Trevor, almost wistfully. "Melina should be all right. Was she being tracked some how? I don't think my ward was broken."

"She thinks it may have been something to do with blood from her former, ah, I'd don't know the term for it. 'Victim' just doesn't seem appropriate."

Trevor grimaced. "The guy that is giving her drugged blood?" He asked coldly.

"Yeah, was."

His left eyebrow jumped up about six inches on his forehead. He looked worried.

"Is this where I'm supposed to show you my neck?" I asked in exasperation. His expression dropped several notches of concern to severe worry.

I guess I was going to have to tell him the whole story. Then again. Maybe he needs some excitement in his life. I could wait for Melina to tell him. Actually that's a good idea.

"But that means," he started. I motioned for him to continue. He regarded me coldly, then softened a little. "You didn't know, did you? Until she bit you?"

I didn't answer.

"She was probably pretty bad off. I saw her a few weeks ago at the last congress. You could tell she wasn't healthy. And then that *bastard* drove her to bite you. But this would be her third..."

He looked like he was going to cry, so I gave in and decided to go easy on him.

"Whoa there Trevor," I said, holding my hands up. "Slow down. You're digging your own coffin, and her's while you're at it. Jameson voided their agreement before she bit me. She had plenty of opportunity to have stolen a bite before that and didn't. Including at least two times when I was bleeding from sword cuts. And I made her bite me after I found out what was going on."

Trevor deflated like a popped balloon. He wiped his brow with the back of his left hand and then shook his head. Man, this guy was either a really good friend, or had a thing for her. I felt a hint of jealously fire up inside, but swatted it away.

"I'm sorry I went on like that," said Trevor. "I just, well I helped bring her back after last time and would hate to see her go through it again. And the way the laws are written now, its three and your staked. She's up for three."

"Brought her back?" I asked.

"Yeah," he replied. "She got bled and dried in, oh, probably early 97, late 96. It was her second time, so it went for six years. She got up about a year ago. I was one of the people who helped bring her back up. It used to be, you do three years for each infraction. Now you add three each time. And after three times, you're out. And the regs were less strict. Blood was also cheaper. That was back when the Seventh League still had a wielder. A long time gone now."

"So she was, what, asleep, for six years?"

"They drain all the blood out of them, hang them up in the sun for a week or two to make sure they're dry, and then put them in a box. They don't even need to lock it. Without the blood, they can't move. But their minds still work. They feel constant pain the entire time, but are still able to think about anything they want. It's horrible."

I didn't say anything. I was getting a little ticked at this system. And not just because I was getting soft on Melina.

"So did she bite someone for that?" I asked. Why not? This guy was answering questions! Wow.

"No, actually, that was part of the controversy," said Trevor. "Sir Neville, Wielder of the Fourth League, got a complaint passed through congress. They wouldn't let him challenge her, for obvious reasons. So he petitioned to have her actions count as an infraction and have her put to sleep."

"That's odd," I said in thought. "That would explain this morning."

"Huh?" he asked.

"Oh, I guess that was the same Sir Neville that showed up this morning at the League Hall for my head."

Trevor blanched.

"I bluffed him and he left."

The relief in Trevor's face was instantaneous. I was starting to feel sorry for this guy. He seemed to not be dealing well with this conversation.

"Oh, the second thing, since we've pretty much decided that Melina can take care of herself. I hate to ask this, but I've only had about half a meal in the last twenty four hours. I talked Melina into going to file some paper work instead of going for breakfast, and then we kind of got interrupted."

"I've got some sandwich fixings in the back. You go ahead downstairs and I'll scare up a plate and meet you there." I nodded my thanks. Then he reached out his left hand. I looked at it.

"This will save a few minutes later. I can 'show' people things. It's usually how I teach most of the basics stuff. If you allow, I can pass most of what you need to do on to you. You'll still have to go through it step by step later, but it speeds up the learning process."

I was a little dubious about this sort of thing.

"So, you like flash my brain, and then I go meditate on it while you get some stuff together?" I asked.

"Essentially." Great. I extended my left hand and he grabbed it. A few seconds later I felt an itching sensation behind my eyes. After a moment, it was over and I suddenly felt enlightened. He released my hand.

"You got it?" he asked. Yeah. I got it all right. I just didn't know what the heck to do with it.

"Go slow," Trevor added, stepping away from the counter. He then returned and lifted Melina's dagger and put it under the register. "Don't try anything until you've 'looked' through the whole package."

I nodded and went to the stairs at the back of the store. As I walked down the rickety stairs, I began looking through what I had been given. It was kind of neat. The package started out with some basics about warding. That it is used first as a way of protecting oneself against mistakes. The way a ground in an electrical outlet protects against surges. A secondary effect of warding is to block the warded object from being seen or located. By establishing the "ground" a warded object is easy to blend into the background noise.

I learned that warding is only a little more complex than what I'd been doing with Melina's Dagger. The main difference is that the dagger had been imbued with the ability to form a ground. I would have to do it manually through the sword each time I needed to ward. I could feel how it was done, and couldn't wait to try it. Man, that was easy, I thought. I sure wish I could have taken that Environmental Chemodynamics course using this method. It would have been a breeze.

Continuing on with the package, things got a little more interesting. I won't bore you with the details. But I was pretty confidant I had the basics of how to use the sword to defend myself in some non standard ways. I did note that there were no offensive tricks in the package. Trevor probably didn't want his store leveled this afternoon.

Speaking of, my reverie was interrupted by him walking down the stairs with a plate of sandwiches, cheese and crackers. In his other hand he held two glasses. He was carrying a bottle of water and one of red wine under his left arm. Trevor set the plate down on a small table after pushing aside stacks of papers and small books. He sat down on one of the two chairs next to it. I got up from one of the benches and walked over and sat in the other while he poured both glasses half full with wine. After he topped it off with water, and I'd half devoured the first sandwich, I took a healthy swig. Pretty good stuff, even watered down.

Trevor picked up the second sandwich and took a bite, then lowered his hand and sipped the mulled wine.

"Do you have any questions so far," he asked. I had a feeling he had some.

"Not really," I answered between mouthfuls.

"That's funny," he said. "I use almost the same package for starting mages. Of course the one I gave you was tailored to the sword a lot. Most people I show that to immediately ask why I didn't give them the 'good stuff'. And then they complain about it and go elsewhere."

"I thought that was the good stuff," I said. "I mean I almost can't wait to see what happens when you try and link someone else's shield into ground."

"What?" asked Trevor, his mouth full. "That wasn't in there. Anyway, it doesn't work. You can't bring down a shield, or a ward, since that's what the shields are based on from the outside. It's impossible. All you can do is overload it."

I looked at him. It seemed perfectly possible from an electrical engineering point of view.

"Um, it's just basic circuits. There's one ground. You have the wards set up as antenna, sort of, and the 'transceivers' are who ever is making a link between ground and the 'antenna'."

"I see the parallel, I think," he said, then thought for a few seconds. I began on the second sandwich. "But it would never work; everyone's ground is different."

"Is the potential the same, every time you touch ground?"

"Yes, essentially," he mumbled out, then washed down with some wine. "But you're missing the whole point. Each person grounds differently, it's just one connection. You can't just link someone's shield to your ground. Even if you could, it'd be meaningless because it would still be different than their ground. The shield would absorb it. Most good ones wouldn't even flicker."

I almost asked for some paper to start drawing him the circuit. Instead, I decided a live demonstration would be in order.

"Can you make that chair disappear with a ward?" I asked, pointing to a chair like those we were using which was about halfway across the basement. "I guess I need to try this out."

"Are you kidding me," Trevor said. "I'm not that strong. You may be able to do that, eventually, but making something simply vanish is very hard. Since you know where the chair is, anyway."

"What can you do to it?"

"I can shield it from harm. Say, about a half reduction in damage, or so. If I had time, I could refine that, but about half is all I would expect," he finished looking at me dubiously.

"Humor me," I asked, then polished off the second sandwich.

Trevor sat still for several seconds and then gave a deep sigh. I could almost see the chair change. Thinking through the lesson, I shifted perspectives slightly, like I had when I saw the hallway back in Charles's store. The shield became apparent. I could see its structure and links. I also could feel the wards in the building, stronger wards around this room, and the shields around Trevor.

I regarded the chair. Just like I thought, tracing the ground Trevor established from the "center" of the chair lead right into the same potential as his shields and the wards. I grounded myself and erected my own shield. Then pulled myself out of the ground so that I was out of the circuit. "Reaching" out, I did the same thing I'd done to make my ground connection, but between the shield on the chair and ground.

The result wasn't quite what I'd expected. Although I am quite pleased.

I'm not sure of the order, but three things pretty much happened at once. The chair exploded. Or perhaps that isn't expressive enough. The chair instantly turned to an expanding dust cloud as violently as you can imagine. Trevor screamed and fell out of his chair. And the wards on the building dropped out.

"*Lord!*"

"Cool," I exclaimed. Yep, definite possibilities. Trevor glared at me from the floor.

"It's one ground, dude," I said. Trevor sneezed. They needed a bandpass filter. I didn't quite hear what Trevor said in response, but it wasn't pretty.

"You ever put a wrench across the terminals of a car battery," I asked.

We heard the door open upstairs in the shop. Trevor tried to get up and then fell back on his butt. A few seconds later Melina came walking down the stairs. She quickly crossed over and gave me a peck on the cheek. I could get used to this. She had apparently gone by her apartment, since she was back in jeans and a hoodie. She set down a rather tall and thin bag which looked suspiciously like her sword in disguise on the bench.

"Hey Trev," she said, plopping down in my chair. She drank down some of my wine and then stuffed some cheese in her mouth. "The hell happened here?"

"Your friend here almost managed to kill me, that's what," Trevor almost yelled. Melina looked up at me, her mouth still full.

"I was just demonstrating the practical application of shorting out a power source," I replied in my defense. For lack of a better thing to do, I reached down and popped the cork off the wine bottle. Melina nodded thanks as I topped the glass off. I guess the fact that we were watching a vampire chow down wasn't as strange as I thought, as Trevor didn't seem to find it out of the ordinary. Then again, he was still sitting on his ass and practicing his Medusa impression.

"He freaking vaporized a chair," he said. "And managed to fry me, and all my wards in the process. I can't even... Crap. All my spells are... Oh hell!"

Trevor stumbled to his feet and flew up the stairs, tripping twice on the way up.

I plopped down into the remaining chair. Melina pulled her feet up onto the edge of her chair and sipped some more wine.

"It happen about a minute or two ago?" She asked, then went to work on the remains of Trevor's sandwich.

"About that."

Melina swallowed. "Looks like lots of people felt it," she sipped some more wine and then continued. "Kind of a weird surge, was what people were saying on the street. I heard some vendors talking about it around the corner."

"Sorry for pissing off your friend," I said. "Melina, are you okay?"

She stopped eating and looked up at me. Then swallowed.

"Didn't have much choice," she said. "Had to stop the trail."

Melina held up her left wrist at me. I could see a partially healed set of cuts along the forearm, which would have done quite a lot towards opening up the main veins in the arm. The other arm looked similarly abused. Her color did seem a little paler than it had been this morning.

I was essentially horrified. The concept of just dumping all of one's blood to evade detection just seemed rather extreme to me. I set myself a notch lower because it was essentially my fault that she did it.

"It's okay, Chris," she said. "I'll actually feel better in the long run."

"Isn't that painful, though?" I asked, putting my hand over her left, which she set back on the table. It felt rather cold.

"Yeah, a little," said Melina. She took a long drink from the glass. Then frowned. "Actually a lot, but it's like a headache. You kind of ignore it."

My hand tightened on hers. Thinking back to the recent conversation, I had a good inkling of what that feeling was like for her. And that she'd spent a lot of time with this feeling.

"Is there anything I can do," I asked tentatively. For a second the pain was completely obvious on her face.

Melina looked away from me and said very softly, "No." She also pulled her hand away, almost reluctantly.

This was a bit of a tough moment for me. Looking at the details; this girl had basically threw her life on hold to help me out the other day, which cost her her life support system, of sorts. Yes, I'm being a little inaccurate about Jameson's relative worth. Then she shows what I'd view as admirable inhuman restraint in not biting me through the night. Then she goes against like ten trolls and five vampires so that I can get away. To make the escape complete, so that she can keep helping me out, she probably bled herself dry.

And I can pretty much guess that her need for blood right now is about as high as it can get. And she probably won't ask for it. Damn her!

Trevor picked that time to storm back down the stairs. He had Melina's dagger and a few other small objects in his hands. I could see steam coming off his bald head. No, the last part was a joke. Almost.

He poured the assortment on the table and stood glaring at me. I took a close look at a few of the items. Yes, that kind of look. To me, it felt like they had broken wires on the ground loops. It seemed like the ground connections had "melted" like a fuseable link. I didn't see what the problem was, just replace the link. I said as much.

"What do you mean, 'replace the link', Chris, they're gone!", he seethed. "That's like six months worth of work right there!"

I picked up one of the amulets laying on the table. After a few seconds of concentration, I'd fixed the link. A few more, and I added in a sort of diode on the ground line and bandpass filter on the shield part. It was actually kind of fun. You don't get to play like this in industry. I passed it back to him.

"Okay, done."

He took it from my hand and looked at it.

"What, how'd you...," then he saw the filter setup. "The heck is all this stuff?"

"It's a filter. You wanted this to be some sort of personal shield, right. The spell works to pull energy that would have gone into the wearer to ground. But it was limited to the strength of the spell. But you designed the spell for a DC circuit, but in reality, you have AC. Sort of. The diode on the ground side makes sure you don't get a spike back into the system. Like what burnt out the ground link today, and like what vaporized the object formerly known as a chair.

"The filter section looks like this," I continued, pulling a scrap of paper from the pile. It took me a few seconds to locate a pen, and then I went to work. I drew up a quick RC bandpass filter and wrote out the equations on the side.

"The RC filter probably isn't the best, but should pretty much half the effective gain. You may find an RLC is easier to tune, but I didn't want to try and think about how to make an inductor. Capacitors and resistors are easy. Capacitors discharge current in the opposite direction when their charging voltage is removed. Inductors keep current flowing in the same direction when the charge is removed. Since it's AC, they're constantly charging and discharging. The other bit is a diode, which just limits 'current' flow to one direction."

I looked up. Trevor was dumbfounded. Melina drank some more wine.

"Look, get yourself a copy of Rizzioni," I paused and thought for a second. "Ten year limit, right?"

Melina nodded, Trevor didn't seem like he got the point.

"Okay, make it Giancoli, *Physics for Scientists and Engineers.* It's a little weaker on the application but possibly better in the theory section. And that's what you'll need more. You really have to think about these things as AC circuits, Trevor. They're really very rudimentary. Its straight out of college physics or basic elecritcal engineering."

"You sure this stuff is more than ten years old?" Trevor asked, finally catching his thoughts.

"Oh, easily. Most of it's probably twenty plus. I think the Giancoli second edition is 1989 or 90." I wrote it on the paper, and added "chapter 25 or 26" under the title.

"What did you say you did for a living?" he asked, while examining the amulet.

"I'm a process control engineer," I said. "But about half of what I do involves designing or troubleshooting electronics. The other half is fluids, but I try and leave that to the chemical people if I can help it. They get twitchy whem someone with a mechanical degree pokes their fingers in to their work."

"I think I'll definitely take a look at this," he said. "I don't know what this is, but I can see what it does, and it's nothing like anything I've ever seen before."

I looked back to Melina, she seemed to be fading a little bit, but was still sipping wine occasionally.

"Trevor, I hate to set aside the conversation temporarily, but Melina just got back from bleeding herself out and tried to tell me she didn't need anything more substantial than that wine. Should I believer her, or should I think she's too selfless for her own good?"

Trevor looked like he needed to sit down. And of course the third chair was still settling. He did a controlled crash on the bench, nearly landing on Melina's sword.

I looked expectantly in his direction. It didn't look like Melina had heard me.

"I'd say she's probably being her usual self," he said finally. "But I can't..."

Having heard enough, I took matters into my own hands, which stopped Trevor's train of thoughts. Using Melina's dagger, I held my right wrist over her half full wine glass and gave myself a good prick. I inhaled sharply and held the wrist there for several seconds, squeezing with my left hand. Then I looked around and spotted the towel Trevor had brought down with the wine. After I decided I'd added a fair amount to the glass, I pressed the towel to my wrist, and managed to hold it in place against my chest while tying it off. It would do for now.

I stood and picked up the wine glass. When I kneeled down next to Melina, she stirred a little but didn't meet my eyes. I didn't like what I saw. No, she wasn't doing well at all.

My right hand on the back of the chair, I swirled the glass under her nose. This perked her up quite a bit. She stirred and reached up to the glass with both hands, but they seemed shaky. I helped her bring the glass to her lips and had to keep her from drinking it too fast. She still managed to polish it off in one go.

With a long sigh, she sat back in the chair with her eyes closed. I extracted the glass from her hands and set it on the table.

"Thank you for doing that," said Trevor. "I hate to see her in that condition again. I'm surprised that she'd be slipping this quickly after bleeding though. I mean, it usually takes several days to get where she is."

"Probably has something to do with the fact that she'd barely been getting any blood for months now," I said coldly. "And from a druggy."

Trevor looked sadly at Melina. We heard the door slam upstairs and heavy footsteps across the floor. A female voice made something akin to a curse coupled with a scream. "Trevor!"

Chapter 8

Yes dear...

The woman's voice was loud and high pitched. But it was upstairs. Trevor jumped like it came from two inches behind him. Wife.

The footsteps stopped, then started down the stairs after checking the back room. I stood up.

"Trevor," she bellowed. "You were supposed to drop off that amulet hours ago! And where the hell are the wards! What kind of shop are you running here!"

She said the last sentence as she hit the basement floor. One hand on the railing, and one foot on the bottom step, she regarded the basement's occupants. Melina turned around in her chair to look at the newcomer.

"Oh," she said emotively. "That kind of shop, eh? You and your..."

"Excuse me ma'am," I said, cutting her off. "But an emergency came up which required Mister Trevor's skilled services for the Seventh League. Please accept my apologies for interrupting the normal running of this establishment."

She glared at me. I seemed to be getting that a lot today. I felt her *looking* at me, and decided I'd give her a show. My "shield" probably wasn't that impressive as it sat. So I decided to try a bandpass filter and a ward and see if I could disappear. I threw myself at the problem as quick as I could.

It worked. Later Trevor said I just vanished from the room. It's actually not that hard even for him now. It's just a matter of tuning the filter to only block visible light. Just trying to "vanish" the old way involved trying to block all frequencies of energy, and there's a lot of spectrum out there to deal with. Just a minor conceptual difference, but a major practical advantage.

After allowing for the shock to set in, I reappeared.

"Now if you'll excuse us," I said kindly. "We are almost through with our business here. If you'll give us about five minutes..."

I tried to make it sound like a dismissal, but she didn't seem to want to be dismissed.

So I did the unthinkable, I waved at her to go upstairs. She harrumphed, gave each of us an individualized look designed to strip paint, and stormed up the stairs. I understood why they were rickety.

"Melina, are you feeling any better?" I asked softly. She looked up at me and nodded, then looked down. I touched her chin, lifting her head back up. "You have ah... just there."

I pointed out a small dribble of red liquid along the left side of her mouth. She blushed and wiped it with her sleeve.

"I, ah.." started Trevor. "I should really get up to Lucy."

"I understand," I said. "However, I want you to promise me something. Two things really."

"And they are," he asked back, already getting to his feet. Thinking slightly ahead, and noting the fact that the footstep of Lucy ended just at the top of the stairs, I erected a quick sound barrier and pushed it around us.

"First, don't build anything like what we talked about without understanding oscillation concepts first. And work them out on paper. Even extremely simple systems using those elements can get wildly unstable, or do unpredictable things. You can do it all with variables. No numbers, since I don't know exactly what the units are and such. But from the variables you can get ratios which will make the systems work. It should be enough to keep things safe."

"Sounds fair."

"And second," I continued. "Don't tell her. Actually, it's your field, so your judgement is the best indicator for telling anyone else. Just please don't tell her. I'm not sure why. I know she's your wife, but I really don't like the idea."

Melina giggled, but it didn't sound like it had much energy behind it.

Trevor shrugged. "Okay, I won't tell her. It'll probably drive her nuts. But I kind of agree with you. On one condition."

"Go ahead?" I said.

"We spend a good day on this after I've had a chance to do some reading in your Giancoli book. You'll need to come by and pick up some other 'packages' too. But at least give me a chance to have you here when I do some experiments. I mean, seriously Chris, I'm the best at this sort of thing, small clean imbuements and passive work. And even though I'm almost pitifully weak as a mage, I know I'm damn good at it. But that amulet is better than anything else I can make that's that size."

"It's a deal," I concluded.

I picked up Melina's dagger from the table. I knew how to recharge it quite well now though setting up one of my own would have been beyond me. Melina could probably use the money anyway. On second thought, so could Trevor. And he did just help me out a whole lot.

I passed the dagger to Trevor. He took it.

"How much for a recharge?" I asked. "For the League's service."

"Generally 100," he replied quickly.

Melina got to her feet slowly. From her pants pocket, she withdrew some bills and pealed most of them off. Trevor accepted them from her. He looked like he wanted to say something else, but looked over his shoulder up the stairs, and then nodded at us and quickly climbed them two at a time.

Since I was in a giving mood, I sent my attention at the wards around the building. Being very cautious, I reset their ground connection and added in a very carefully hidden diode in each line. The diode method probably wasn't the best. But fortunately, the reverse bias 'voltage' looked like it would be what I wanted. I didn't know how many surges like the one I'd created with the chair the diode could stand. I guessed not that many people would be shorting out shields like I had either. That done, I turned to Melina. She did look a lot better. I crossed over to the table and popped the top off the water bottle, downing several ounces. Melina followed me over to the table.

"Are you well enough to get out of here?" I asked. "I think we've pretty much ruined Trevor's day."

Melina moved a little closer. I felt a strong temptation to put my arm around her shoulders.

"I'm better now," she replied softly. She moved the last step to place her right next to me and gently grabbed my right hand. I set the water bottle down on the table and moved my left hand to her elbow. Melina then turned and walked over to the long bag with her sword. From the bottom zipper pouch, she withdrew a roll of gauze and a small bottle of antiseptic.

She returned and removed my hastily tied towel. The antiseptic stung a little. The wound did start to bleed a bit after the pressure was removed. Very carefully, she wrapped my wrist with the gauze roll, tearing the strip off and tucking the end expertly into the wrap. After she finished, Melina returned the items to her bag and slung it over her shoulder. I walked towards the stairs.

"So, where to now?" I asked, stopping intentionally closer to Melina than was strictly necessary. She moved closer. Figures.

"Well," she said softly. "I should take you by the archives. And then the Finley estate. But Sir Finley won't be free until much later today. He will setup some practice sessions. You'll probably have them scheduled regularly. I'll probably be your primary practice dummy, for obvious reasons. But I don't think I'll be good for much today. "

"You've got to be kidding me," I said. "Melina, I saw you take on those vampires. You're phenomenal! That stalling move at the end was perfect."

Melina turned slightly red.

"I had some good training when I was young, and, well. I also had a lot of time to think things through," she said. "The mountain and sea changing is just habit."

"So, I'm not the only one who reads Miyamoto?"

"Sorry Chris," Melina said with a small smile. "I had the Thomas Cleary translation memorized when I was six. It was a rather simple application in this case though. He was stronger than I was, as I found out the first time we closed. And his defense was tough. Mountain and the sea, 'doing something completely different.'"

Melina frowned and then continued, "I guess we could take you to the congress library. The only thing that's set is the meeting with Finley. He also has to walk you through some things that he is keeping in trust. Until then, probably the archives are your best bet. It's a walk though."

I set my hands on her shoulders, she looked down.

"You look like you're not up for a long walk," I said.

"I'll be fine," she replied flatly.

I sighed. I didn't think so.

"That may be," I said. I was still reeling a little bit from the concept of draining oneself. "Let me ask it this way, Melina. I'm not sure I'm up for a walk either. I'd actually like the chance to go somewhere and practice a few things. I don't think Trevor's up for that at the moment. And it really looks like you could use a nap."

Melina nodded. "You can't go back to my apartment though," she said. "And I don't think I should either. It's being watched. Actually there's a vampire sitting on the couch with the phone open. He's probably recovered by now."

I was about to continue, but Melina interrupted. "Oh, Chris," she continued. "I'm sorry about your laptop. Jameson must have messed it up when he came back to get his stuff. Or they did. I'm not sure. It was in pieces."

"I've got backups," I said, but still winced. "So that leaves...Didn't you say there was some sort of estate house with this job."

She nodded. "Yeah," she said. Her face darkened a little. "And it has a large practice room."

"But it's probably watched too?"

"Of course," she said. "But there's an entrance that they don't know about. Well, probably don't know about. They didn't catch me when I used it once."

"Okay, so lets head over there. You take a nap while I play with some of this sword stuff, and..." I paused. "Wait, you said you used it before. But I thought you said the key was the sword?"

"I did," said Melina, swallowing. "Both actually, I said that and it is. Ask me later, I'll have more energy to tell it. It's a long story, Chris."

"You weren't the last wielder were you?"

"No, silly," she admonished. "Later. And I really do thank you for..."

"I should be thanking you, Melina. Just let it go."

"And if I can't?" she said, leaning against me. "That's twice in one day. If I didn't know any better I think you were trying to spoil me."

I was starting to get an overwhelming urge to spoil her. I pushed it aside.

"I seems you've been due for some kindness," I said. "Oh, well. If you think the archives are too far. Lets head to the estate, and let you take a nap."

"I'll make it fine," she countered. "Congress Archives it is. It wont be the first time I've slept in the Library. Then you can practice at the estate later. It's not as far as the warehouse was."

It took some effort, but I pulled away from Melina gently and pushed her in the direction of the stairs. She went ahead of me, but seemed a little tipsy. On the first step, Melina stumbled a little and then giggled.

"I guess I'm a little drunk," she said lightly. I put my left hand on her arm to steady her, her right grabbed the rail. She began moving again.

"You did polish off most of a bottle," I replied. Great, a drunk, sexy, vampire. Just what I needed. "You're going to be okay, right? No wacko tendencies when you're drunk?"

"I don't know," she said. "I've never been drunk before."

Great.

"Just wait until Mrs. Lucy sees you now," I added as we neared the top of the stairs, and entered in to the still ongoing domestic dispute. Melina moved to my side and clamped down on my left arm with both hands. I made a steady path for the door. The conversation stopped.

Lucy stared at Melina, who returned a blank expression. I smiled my business smile and waved as we walked past them and left the store.

"She doesn't seem to like you much," I said after Melina turned us right and we made it about half way to the next block. "Kind of all bound up inside, isn't she."

Melina giggled, and then hiccupped, then held her left hand to her forehead. I slowed.

"You okay," I asked.

"Yeah," she replied. "Head hurts...Lucy still thinks something happened between me and Trevor."

I picked the pace back up. Melina put her left hand back on my arm. I didn't ask the obvious question. It was between them, I had no business asking. And it was at least a year ago. Or was it. And why did I want to ask anyway? Anyway to my credit, I didn't ask. Yet.

"Aren't you going to ask?" Drat.

"What?" I replied. If the girl wants to tell me; let her.

"If there was something between us," she elaborated. As if I didn't know what she was talking about.

"It's really none of my business."

"Well, there wasn't," she said with finality. I almost heard a "much" in there somewhere, but I may have been imagining things. A part of me was slightly relieved.

Melina stopped us abruptly, almost losing her balance. She closed her eyes for a second then opened then in terror. "Please tell me you're warding us, Chris. Please.. I'm so sorry I forgot earlier.. I..."

Using two fingers from my right hand, I put them across her lips.

"Shh... don't worry, Melina. I've been warding since before you showed up at Trevor's. I have a feeling I'm going to have to get good at it."

Melina relaxed, and turned back to the sidewalk.

"I still should have made sure," she pouted.

"Why are you so hard on yourself?" I asked. We took a lazy left hand turn with the road past a small market area. I tried not to look at what they were selling. The chilled blood in little hand held coolers set my teeth on edge. The sign said 300/bag. And the little bags looked like a days supply. This was probably diluted down stuff too. And still expensive as hell. Yep, these vampires had a slight problem.

Melina didn't answer. I also noticed that she ignored the market area as well.

Several blocks later, the scenery started to change. We were getting back into a more commercial section. After another minute or so, a guy went by on a motorcycle. He looked familiar. Probably one of the vamps from the Special Controlls office. Anyway, he didn't see us.

"I see he got himself back together," said Melina, almost spitefully. "He had a little split personality earlier."

Melina was grinning at her own joke.

"Was he the one with a sword and dagger?"

"And an absolutely splitting headache," Melina laughed maniacly.

"Isn't he caught up in the whole system, too?"

Melina frowned. "Yeah, some of Sir Neville's troupe is. But not this one. Jules has a great deal of money. And power. He goes along with Sir Neville by choice, not for blood like the others."

A few minutes later, we were in front of a large block building, and the oldest thing I'd seen so far. It had an unmistakable facade that clearly showed its origins as a church. Although at some point it looked like the spire had been lopped off and then bricked up. Melina nodded at the steps. I began walking up them towards the trio of double doors. The center set was open. We walked through into a foyer, and then through another set of doors into the main library.

An elf waved a greeting at us from behind the counter. He was clearly sitting on a stool which brought him up to our eye level.

"He needs a card," Melina said, pointing at me with her thumb. The elf raised his eyebrow and shook his head. I lessened the ward a bit and he refocused.

"Wielder," he sniffed. "Hmm. Must be number seven?"

"I'd say I'm definitely running in last place," I offered. He laughed while pulling a form out of a drawer and sliding that and a pen across the counter. I filled it out, and passed it back to him. The elf knocked a plastic card out of a sheet of them and wrote some numbers down on the form.

"Sign the back please," he ordered. I accepted the card, read the warning and was about to sign. Just to make sure no one was pulling my leg, I read the agreement on the back and then looked around. Maybe trying to find cameras or something.

"Is this a joke?"

"What about literature protection do you find funny, Sir Borden?"

I stared at the elf for a few seconds. He was staring right back, highly amused. I gave up and signed the card.

The elf gave Melina a look over the top of his glasses. Which reminded me that Melina was wearing hers again.

"Watch this one, Melina," the elf said.

"I will, Nadav," she half smiled back at him, then gave me a push. We started off toward some of the stacks to the right wing.

"Are they serious?"

"What, Chris? About cutting fingers off? Yes. I don't know if they've had to poke anyone's eyes out in a while. But yeah. They're serious."

I swallowed.

"Well, look at it this way," she yawned and shook her head. Which caused her to clamp down on my arm. "Crap, I can't even walk straight."

She caught me giving her a raised eyebrow.

"Most of the books in here that really matter are small production texts. Or only copies. They don't have that good a cataloging system. So they have to be rather heavy handed in their care. Here's the section you should start in."

I got pushed down into one of four chairs at an old wooden table. There were a few books on the end. Two tables away, a teenager and two young children were talking about a book. I noticed they were all covered in tattoos. Melina dropped a thick text in front of me and then turned to walk away, looking a few rows down for a book. I popped open the cover. It was a history of the leagues.

"This one's specifics about this enclave," said Melina, dropping another small book. "There's more than one underside. All created in different places and for different reasons. Some are linked. Some talk, others don't. About every five years most of them that do meet. And these books are about the original council and then the other enclaves around the world. And this one's about the technology ban. Mostly current information. Probably should read some of it, since you've already violated parts."

"Am I supposed to read all of this stuff?"

"Nah," she said. "Just do some skimming or something. The technology piece is only about twenty pages, so I think you can manage all of that."

Gee, thanks. Ah well. I flipped to the table of contents of the league history. Seven, four, and then the rest, I decided. Melina sat down across from me and cracked open a very old looking book. The bindings were completely black, thick leather. I didn't see a title.

"What's that?"

"Volume 17."

I smiled. "Helpful. Thanks."

She ignored me and dropped her nose into the book. So I started reading some interesting history. Most of what is in the texts you don't need to know. Some you'll find out in the course of this story. I found myself rather intrigued by the founding of the enclaves; these constructed pockets of alternate reality. And as with any good exercise in learning, I ended up with more questions as I got more answers. Melina ended up with her head on the book and the book on the table. A careful move extracted her glasses from her hair and set them next to her arm.

The penalty for misshelving books was a fingernail per text, so I left the books on the table. Heading to the section Melina got them from, I began hunting for something that answered one of my questions. I didn't find much at all about the making of the swords in her selections. And as I now apparently had one to myself, I was more than a little curious about its origin. I found a likely title, "Sword and Artifact: the founding era." I pulled it from the shelf and flipped to the contents page.

Just as I was about to take it back to the table, I noticed a little girl was standing right in front of me. And almost dropped the book. Since it would have fallen on her, I'm glad I didn't. I thought I remembered seeing her with the family a moment ago. She passed me a small book.

"Hello," I started. "Sorry, I didn't see you there."

"Read this one too," she said with half a smile. I heard someone hiss, and looked up to meet the eyes of her mother. The girl waved at me and then went back to the other table. Her mom yanked her arm and spoke quickly in her ear. Strange.

I sat back down with the two books and set the small one over my selection to get a better look at it. It was an overview of the special creatures of the enclave. Most of the text was related to vampires and elves. Another third comprised a brief history of the Weynrely, the tattooed people; clooquieally refered to as "inks". And there was a small section on other creatures. Werewolves and bears appeared under those subchapter headings. I assumed the girl wanted me to see a bit about her history, so I flipped to that section.

The pages were blank. Not torn out, not destroyed. Just blank. I frowned and shut the book, moving on to the artifact history. Those pages weren't blank. They might as well have been, for all the information they offered. With a sigh, I closed the cover, stood and crossed to Melina. I gently touched her shoulders.

The vampire stirred, and sat up. Melina looked over her shoulder at me, squinted, and then clawed for glasses. After they were in place, she looked at the clock on the wall.

"You okay?"

Her response was interrupted by a yawn and half a stretch. I went back over to the other side of the table and retook my seat. It looked like she needed a few minutes before moving. She brought her feet up into the chair and stared at the table top. I had the book she was reading halfway across the table before she shook herself out and then snatched it back. It was instantly added, closed, to the stack I'd started off to the side.

"Well?"

"Well what," I smiled back. "The thought behind the enclave was nice. It looks like its provided a good place for a lot of people. Not much about the swords though. And I don't have any answers."

"I didn't pass you anything about them," she mused, then caught the title of the book I'd found. "That wouldn't have anything detailed anyway. Probably nothing will, since it is not known. Why did you get this?" she fingered the small book with the blank pages.

"I didn't," I explained. "A little girl gave it to me."

Melina shook her head, "I guess I'm missing something."

"Probably sleep?"

She yawned at the thought, then gave me a weak smile. "Yeah, sorry."

I sighed and looked up at the clock.

"I think we could go to the wielder's house, Chris. Shouldn't be that dangerous. As long as I take you in the back way."

"It would give me some time to practice?"

"That would be the plan."

"And you'd get your nap?"

She darkened slightly and stood up, then sat back down again with a half uncontrolled crash in the chair. Her hands went to her head.

"You sure you're okay?"

"I'm fine."

I snorted. No, she wasn't fine.

"Try it more slowly next time, Melina."

So she did, and made it to her feet without any acrobatics. I followed her towards the exit. The family had left some time before. Curiosity almost made me stop and look through the books they left behind. But concern for the weakened vampire brought my thoughts back to order.

It was a silent fifteen minutes walk after that. At least it was a rather slow walk. My thoughts were mostly on those blank pages. Which of course mattered a lot. Why were the written works of a people so fond of written art mysteriously missing form two books? Fortunately, I had several months to deal with that. And also, as per my tendencies, I completely forgot about them until it was almost too late. Well, what do you expect. I kind of had other things to worry about at the moment.

Chapter 9

Encounter

"Here's the alley," Melina said, pushing us to the left across the street. We crossed two more streets along the same narrow alley. It was relatively clean compared to most I'd seen. Other evidence that we were in a different area of the town. One more street, and half way between the buildings and backyards we came to a small opening between the backs of two well built apartment buildings.

Most of the buildings on our left were walk ups, or town houses. On the right were individual houses and some nicer town houses, but very few complexes. The alley definitely represented a division. We squeezed through the split and Melina kneeled down to go to work on a small grate. Since it was so narrow, I couldn't get by to help. After several attempts, Melina swore and then stood up and turned sideways to look back at me.

"I'm just too weak," she said, I squeezed past her to give it a shot. I bent down and heaved. Nothing. Man. I stripped off the coat and passed it to Melina, then leaned down and examined the grate closely. I think it weighed about as much as Melina, and it looked rusted in place. She may have been able to pop it like a bottle top in her heyday; I could give myself a hernia on the thing. I wasn't about to let her try again.

Looking around for a pry bar, or something, my thoughts immediately flicked to the sword at my waist. No, I was NOT considering using it as a crowbar! But I could use it to make things happen. Thinking through what I knew about the blade, I quickly saw something that may work. Just gently apply opposing "charges" to the grate and the sill and I should be able to get this thing open.

I gathered my thoughts, put my hand on the sword hilt, and stared at the grate. Here goes.

POP! ...CLANG!!

Oops.

Melina squeaked. I would have jumped, but I knew something was coming. No, I didn't vaporize the grate. I did succeed in blowing it out of the sill and up about ten meters in the air. That part was about as loud as a gun shot. When it came back down a meter from the opening and hit the concrete, it was almost as loud.

I stood there staring at it for a little while. Melina gave me a few moments. Or maybe she didn't and my hearing was going or something.

"Chris," she said. "That was a little loud."

"Yeah. I noticed."

"So did half the neighborhood."

"Probably."

"Um... Can we..."

"Yeah," I said, taking her point and looking down into the hole. It was only about two meters to the bottom. I hopped past and then motioned for Melina to go down. I'd move the grate back after us. Or at least try.

Melina ignored my hands and just jumped down the hole. Figures. I heard a slight splash at the bottom. It hadn't looked like there was more than an inch or so of water. Ideal for finding rats.

I pushed the heavy grate over to the edge and then clambered down and lowered myself into the sewer. It was tough, but I managed to get the grate back over the hole and dropped down in the sill and still keep all ten fingers. A few didn't like me anymore, but they'll deal with it. I hoped no one would notice that the grate was slightly deformed. Not to mention the unmistakable chunk out of the concrete surrounded by a smattering of loose rust flakes.

Melina had trudged a few paces north of the grate, toward the house district. I followed.

"You really don't do things by halves, do you," Melina asked playfully after a few paces.

"So I didn't quite gauge the amount of force necessary. I was trying to be careful this time. Oh, well. I keep thinking of this stuff like electrical energy because that's what I know. It's close, but doesn't seem to behave quite as my intuition for electricity has developed."

"Yeah," she said. "But you're first attempt didn't just turn a chair into match sticks, it vaporized it. That's pretty bad, I mean, like-no chair, gone poof! bad. Then you manage to launch a hundred pound grate like fifty feet in the air–"

"–thirty," I interrupted. Mentally switching back to English units. Hey, I was an engineer. I thought in SI half the time.

"Thirty," she allowed. "while being 'careful'? All you needed was two inches or so."

"Well, looking at it from an engineering perspective, I have gotten a lot closer in just two tries. For a PID controller, my gain is still a little too high, but the derivative and integral constants are actually doing good. I mean, I went from a completely unacceptable 'gone poof' situation to only being off by a factor of about 200. I'd say that is a marked improvement."

Melina stopped and turned around. I ran into her.

"Chris," she said, awfully close all of a sudden in the near dark. "I'm sorry, I shouldn't have gone off like that, I-"

Well, I couldn't use my fingers this time to shut her up, since they were covered in rust, so I used my mouth instead. It seemed to work. Melina stopped admonishing herself.

After several seconds, I let the kiss break and realized that Melina was pressed against me. She sighed and leaned into me more. I started to put my arms around her, but she pulled away.

"Please," she said in almost a whisper. "Not right now. I can't deal with this."

"And I can't deal with you beating yourself up."

Melina didn't respond, but turned around slowly, took another deep breath, and continued down the tunnel. I followed. Maybe I couldn't deal with it just now either. I was starting to get a little hung up on Melina.

I guess it was bound to happen. I mean, cute girl, who you were immediately attracted to. Through the evening, kept giving you really hungry, turned on looks. Ended up sleeping next to you most of last night, scratching at your neck. Then you got to send her boyfriend out on his duff, come to her rescue. Then she had you for breakfast.

Yeah, I think I was a little hung up. But so was she. I'll watch myself. If I have the choice.

We came to a ladder, just like the last thirty or so that we saw before. Melina stopped next to it, sniffed a few times, and then went left. Another two intersections, and we went right. Three more and another left. I was almost worried about getting lost. Most of these paths looked the same.

Fortunately, we came to another ladder, this one much less substantial than some others we'd seen. And it had a slightly damp looking vampire who was staring in our general direction. I recognized her as the female vamp from the office. She saw us, the ward broken most likely by the splashing of water. Darn.

Well, then again, it wasn't like there was any chance of us getting up the ladder without getting her off of it first. Melina stopped forward motion and let me come up right behind her.

"I'll have to take this," I said. I set my left hand reassuringly on her shoulder. My right went to the sword hilt. "Won't I?"

"You need the practice," Melina replied, sounding a little forced. Yeah, I'd have to take this. Did I want the practice? Hell no. But I wasn't about to let Melina get ran through as my personal shield. I let her slide behind me, and regarded the lady vampire. My thoughts were flying through how to approach this situation.

"I can smell your fear," said the vamp, untangling her long legs from the ladder and settling down to the bottm of the tunnel with an unmistakable grace. She had a naked blade in her hand. And it looked like she was just a little bit ticked from getting stomped earlier.

"I'm just afraid of hurting you too much," I said calmly. She sniffed. What's with all these vampires sniffing recently. Do I smell bad? I took a shower this morning.

Melina giggled behind me. It kind of ruined my poor attempt at a bluff.

I think I knew what I was going to do. I stopped, about ten paces in front of Melina. The vamp closed to about three in front of me and held her sword at the ready. I matched her angle. I thought tentatively about trying to talk her out of this. To appeal to her "ensnared vampire" side or something like that. I actually wish I had, now.

I don't like focusing on any one thing while facing an opponent. Some teach to watch the feet, some the hips or the shoulders. Others stress the hands, the sword. A larger group stresses watching the eyes. I always liked the theory of looking at all of them. Not getting lost in one detail, and getting drawn in. Fixation was bad. Especially in poor light conditions like this one, where the only light was what came down the tunnel from grates in dark places.

So I stood there, calmly waiting for the lady vamp to close. She did. Fast. But not fast enough that I didn't see it coming and have time to react.

Well, this wasn't a "man" coming at me with a sword, so I guess Samantha's promise still held. Discounting Jameson once more of course. But this lady was coming at me fast, sword already descending in an arch, her arm muscles bulging. This was going to hurt.

I leapt forward to meet her the instant she moved. I hoped this was going to work.

It did. But I almost wish it hadn't. I didn't get it perfect, but it was at least within a factor of ten this time. There was a reason why I waited. I wanted to be sure to have her sword above me, and her momentum in my direction. It wasn't that loud this time either, I'm glad to admit. Although I seriously do regret the outcome.

The vampire's blade met mine just above my left shoulder and at arms length, my blade held almost horizontal and straight out. I tried a modified grate launching thing between the two metals. It worked. Her sword shattered at the touch, and the vamp kept moving forward. Right into my blade.

I took a bit of a chance with the horizontal, extended defense. If I'd been any sooner in deploying it, or if she had been any faster in reacting, it would have been trivial to dip under it and have her way with me. She may have been overconfident in her skill and strength and chose to swat my weak defense down anyway. I'll call it lack of reaction time and be done with it. But part of my issue is; I was done with her too. Well, she was done anyway.

I didn't know that the league swords killed vampires. I really wished I'd been warned. I didn't want to kill this lady, even though she worked for a man I was getting pretty angry at.

My sword went right through her heart, to the hilt. Her hands first closed around my neck, with murder in her eyes, and almost an exuberation at having me at her mercy. I felt those vise grips clamping down. Then realization hit her, and me. Something was wrong. Her face lost all evidence of success and turned to sheer horror. Her grip slackened, and she instead tried to push me away, to get at the sword. But it was too late. She died in my arms, a plea on her lips and tears in her eyes. As she started to fall, she turned to dust. I almost dropped the sword, as I staggered to catch my balance.

I was shocked. I'd never killed anyone before. I don't remember Melina moving, but she was suddenly at my side. And I was kneeling down, my left hand touching the pile of dust which was all that remained of the vampire. It was already blowing away. Some of it had landed in the water, and the clumps were dissolving into the stream and being carried off.

Melina regarded the pile for a few seconds and then went up the ladder. The grate here popped easily up, and she disappeared. I automatically followed her, but it wasn't a conscience effort.

Unlike the entrance, this grate opened into the basement, or at least a lower storage room of some building. There were stacks of old crates around the grate. Some barrels of what looked like water, and rack of wine bottles, several of which were broken. I got the impression from the placement of the crates that a defense of some sort had been established at the foot of the stairs leading up to a stout door.

Melina was standing on the other side of the crates on the bottom step. She looked back at me. I guess it was my turn again. I had the key anyway. With the sword still out, I stepped through the crate line and took the stairs two at a time. The door was covered with soot, as if someone had tried to burn it down, or blow it up. There are huge scratches in it and the surrounding walls. But it appeared to have survived the onslaught rather well.

I reached for the handle, felt a resistance, and then it relaxed and I was able to grasp the knob in my left hand. The door opened with a creak. I pushed it and walked through into a large kitchen area. Melina followed to find me plopped down on a bench, which was probably for the serving staff to rest. It was next to the large pantry and the near antique refrigerator.

Like I said, I had never killed anyone before. I dropped the sword on the tile floor. It clattered, echoing loudly in the empty kitchen. My head in my hands, I began to cry. I just wasn't ready to take a life. It didn't matter that it was her or me. It didn't matter that she was "just" a vampire. I had just made a living, intelligent, sentient, human being cease to exist. Gone-poof!

Some time later, I realized Melina had sat next to me. Her right arm was laying across my shoulders and her left was around my waist, her head against my left shoulder. I don't know how long we sat like that, but it was apparently long enough for her to have fallen asleep. Or at least pass out, which was probably more likely.

I shifted a little, and almost succeeded in dumping Melina on the floor. I managed to get my arm around her, and held her up, with her head lolling at a bad angle. As gently as I could, I shifted around, my left arm around her back, and my right under her thighs. She weighed even less than I'd expected. I stood up and left the kitchen in search of somewhere to let her sleep. The ground floor looked like mostly empty ball rooms and sitting rooms.

There were two large dining areas.

I went for the double staircase. Kind of like the one in the house in *The Sound of Music*. You know, kind of sweeps up to both sides. Except only the small front room was open on both floors. Small as in, the size of a small house. Up the stairs with my sleeping vampire I went, and kicked open the first door on the left side of the second floor. What I saw wasn't reassuring. It was a bedroom, and no, there wasn't anyone there. But the bed had been slept in. Rather badly. It looked like the sheets had been soaked with blood. There were rags next to the bed, similarly inundated with dried fluid. And a white dress, torn almost to shreds was in a heap next to one of the night stands.

Someone had died on that bed, of some pretty nasty wounds. Or at least come very close. And that someone was probably a female, judging from the dress and its condition. I had no idea how blood aged, but it felt like this room hadn't been touched in several years. I pulled the door partially closed with my right toe and went to the second room. Also a bedroom.

I went in and set Melina down on the bed, pushing the covers aside. Then I pulled her shoes off, dropping them on the floor. After I realized her sword was downstairs, probably on the floor next to the bench, I also noticed that mine was similarly absent. I remembered dropping it. I hoped it would forgive me.

Seeing nothing else to do, I pulled the covers over Melina and tucked them in. I pushed a lock of her hair out of her face. She seemed to be breathing regularly, so I guessed there was nothing else I could do but let her sleep.

I was exhausted. Not just physically. I couldn't even think straight. I had just faced too much in too little a time. Going over to the other side of the bed, I crashed into it head long and passed out.

Chapter 10

Evening

I awoke with my nose being tickled by someone's hair. And it wasn't mine. Some how, I'd ended up under the covers. And Melina had ended up snuggling up to me. Her face was buried against my chest. My neck felt fine, thank you very much; no new bites.

Melina must have felt me stir. She woke slowly and yawned while turning over and wrapped my right arm around her waist. I didn't see anything really wrong with this, so I let her.

It was almost dark outside, judging from the small amount of light entering the room. We probably had been out for at least four hours.

"Good morning Melina, " I said gently. Melina groaned. And pulled my arm a little tighter to her stomach.

"Feeling any better?" I asked.

"Quite," she said softly. "Are you?"

"I haven't given it much thought yet, actually. I guess so."

"You don't do things by halves, do you Chris?"

"I really didn't know, Melina. I had no idea that would kill her."

"I guess I should have mentioned that," Melina said. "I've seen a lot of vampires destroyed. I've done several in myself, but that takes the record for the quickest dusting I've seen. Not many vampires have been cried over either. Not like that, anyway, not by the person who destroyed them."

I remained silent. I wasn't sure I could talk about it yet.

"Which room are we in?" Melina asked after a few seconds.

"Second one, left side of the house. The first one was a little, um, used."

I felt a shudder go through Melina. She twined her fingers into my right hand.

"I guess it would be that," she said. I was starting to have a sinking suspicion of what exactly went on in that room.

"Should I ask?" I asked.

"You already have, actually," said Melina. "Yes, that was me. I died in that room. Well, almost died in that room. The league was trying to get me away to safety after a fight. They made it here. The sword let them in, and they were barricaded inside by Sir Neville's people. I was dying from my wounds. Ginny turned me, and I lived. We escaped because they thought I was dead."

"A few days later, a group of mages came for me at Charles's place, where I was learning how to become a vampire. Neville got the congress to put me to sleep for three years as punishment for my actions against him."

"That's got to be kind of creepy. I wouldn't suggest going in there," I said. I don't know how well I'd react to a room with my blood all over it. "How did you-"

"Get the wounds? It's most of that story I've been avoiding telling you."

I waited calmly. She'd tell me or she wouldn't. I wasn't going to push her.

"I had been trained to fight all my life. I think I remember getting my first sword when other girls were asking for dolls. By the time I was twelve, I could best Sir Finley about half the time. I showed all the signs of a wielder. Everyone managed to convince themselves that one day, I'd take up the blade for our league, and bring some balance back to the congress.

"Things started to worsen in the mid '80's. By 86, Sir Neville had almost a choke hold on the congress. He was using his vampires to intimidate the other league members into backing his policies. Their league grew. At the expense of ours, which had nothing more than a voice. Without a wielder, we couldn't do more than argue with the other leagues. If they proposed a change, we could not challenge. Anyway, this got worse.

"Early in '88, things ran to a head of sorts. We were running a grass roots campaign to educate people about what Sir Neville was doing with his entourage. It was starting to work. Some of his vamps were defecting away from his blood-for-service slavery. Word was starting to get out about what he was doing from the vampires that left his house. And we were starting to get people to listen.

"His response was about what you'd expect. He pushed the incidents off as rampant vampires. Things got worse. And we were looking at much stricter vampire laws. Which is where I came into the picture. Several vampires who we'd got to leave Sir Neville were taken in and sentenced for destruction. I couldn't let it happen. So I did the only thing I could think of."

"You were the one that challenged a wielder?" I asked.

"Yeah," she said sadly. "For all the good that it did. But I'd been trained my whole life to essentially be one. I just didn't have the sword to use. On a level field, I probably was more than a match for Neville. I borrowed the sword, with the league's blessing, and came here to use the gate. When the congress began, I entered through the terminus for the Seventh Wielder and issued the challenge to Sir Neville. He had no choice but to answer.

"The fight was actually a long one. For both of us. I arrived with the sword strapped across my back and my own in my hand. I could not use the sword of course, but I had it with me as a symbol that I had the blessing to hold it. He thought he was going to face a naked blade with naught but a fiery girl and a prayer behind it.

"He faced a little more. And he got hurt severely in the battle. But it was not enough. I was not strong enough, nor did I have power to match what the sword could do. After minutes of wearing away at me, he ended it by running me through. I knew I'd failed. But the challenge was not over until one had died or been knocked from the circle. I was still alive, and in the circle.

"I rose and charged Neville, the broken hilt of my sword before me. With my life running out of my chest, and with no breath, I grappled with him. My half-blade found a home in his side and I lifted him off the ground, using the hilt as a handle. Two steps, and I collapsed, and he fell outside the circle. But I fell with him, caught again by his blade as well. The challenge was over.

"Charles and Willie grabbed me and ran through the gate back here with Ginny trying to hold me together. I remember Ginny asking if she could turn me. She said it was the only way I'd live. Willie held my hand. Charles was crying. I nodded and passed out. When I awoke, I was a vampire."

I wrapped my left hand around her shoulders to hold her tighter. I could almost see tears streaming from her eyes.

"And Neville," I asked. "He obviously lived. But didn't you essentially win?"

"Not really. There was an uproar for several days while things straightened themselves out. His league was out for my blood. They didn't know I had none left of my own. Neville was in recovery and enraged because his minions had let us go from the mansion. It was because they thought I was dead, but all of a sudden there I was, obviously walking around while Sir Neville was in hospital with a rather nasty gash in his side. Rumors abounded.

"Then he got his act together. Ginny's filing for the consensual turning vanished. It came to public that I was a vampire, and had been one for quite some time. It came out that I'd used magic, for the league; a very serious offense. He produced witnesses. The congress overturned the ruling. They sent mages to come and get me for "punishment befitting such a vile creature" or some such drivel. I was bled, dried and put in a coffin for three years."

"I guess that explains a little bit," I said. A lot actually. "And that brings us here."

"Well mostly," said Melina, while extracting herself from my arms and sitting up. "There are two other parts to the story, but those will have to come later. After I get some water."

I began to sit up, preparing to ask if there was something else she needed more. She pushed me back down gently but firmly.

"Oh no you don't! You silly, compassionate creature. You are trying to spoil me!"

Melina picked up the pillow from the other side of the bed and threw it at me. She then rolled off the bed and leaned down to put her shoes on.

Wait a minute, I thought. This house has been essentially abandoned for a while. I didn't see any lights on, but hadn't tried to check the electricity. Were the utilities connected?

Melina left the room and I heard foot steps move away from the door to the right. She seemed to know where she was going. I kicked off the covers and sat up on the bed, to find my belt and empty sword sheath on the floor. I'd have to do something about that. Can't be hanging around in bed with vampires without my trusty sword.

Oh, god. The sword that I killed a vampire with. My mood sunk again, and I almost broke down.

Thinking to Miyamoto's Fire Scroll once more, I picked the words I needed from its pages. "Becoming New." In like, I tossed the mood aside that was tearing at me. I would go and apologize to the sword for dropping it so harshly. And I would deal with my actions, and not let them rule me. I left the room while buckling the belt back in place and went down the stairs.

When I got to the kitchen, I reached down and retrieved the fallen blade. So this blade and I had a job to do, it seems. And I was already beginning to think of a few things that needed to be done along the way. I sheathed the blade and went over to one of the spacious sinks, and tapped both faucets on. It took a few seconds, but the water started to run. While I waited for the water to clear the sediment out of the pipes, I looked around for a glass. In the third cabinet I tried, I found a few hundred. Taking two, I went back to the sink and filled them up.

While the second one was filling, I drank down most of the first. I refilled this most of the way and then left the kitchen to go find Melina. She was leaning over the sink in a bathroom upstairs with the light on. Since the door was left mostly open, I didn't see anything wrong with entering. She had just been reaching down to drink from the tap. I clucked my tongue.

"We civilized people," I said, employing my best Monty Python accent, "drink from glaah-sses."

Melina giggled as I passed her the clean glass and she shut off the tap.

"Thank you," she said.

"Now, I guess it's my turn. I'm hungry. Feed me."

This got a little more of a laugh.

"I suddenly have an insatiable urge for Chinese take out. What are my chances of taking you out on a date."

Melina made a face.

"What, you don't like Chinese food?"

She shook her head, while drinking from the glass.

"We should get to Sir Finley's. It's very late."

I looked down, it was like 2 in the afternoon. Then I remembered I was supposed to be ignoring my watch. Okay, so it was late. No food for me. I frowned.

"And the chance of food at Sir Finley's is?"

"That depends on how pissed he is at you for breaking his wrist. And then humiliating him in front of Sir Neville and our league."

"But," I sputtered.

"Oh, don't worry Chris. I'm sure there will be supper involved. Sir Finley doesn't eat until he gets back here from the other side. This will probably be nothing more than an organizational meeting anyway."

"And will this involve another hour of walking?" I asked. And dodging Neville's goons and facing more non "guys" with swords. I really had to take that promise up with Samantha next time I saw her.

Melina shook her head and pushed past me out of the bathroom. I drank some water and followed.

"So do we get to use the 'gate'?"

"It's two blocks down. I think we can walk," she replied.

"Drat, I wanted to use the gate," I said, feigning disappointment. Like hell I wanted to use something else that I didn't understand at the moment. "Um, aren't we forgetting something rather substantial. Like the probable presence of vampires and trolls right out side."

"Oh, they're probably gone."

I didn't think that deserved a reply. Why the heck would they leave? They seemed to want me out of the way before I got the chance to learn the ropes and become a political pawn. Oh, yeah. That's later.

Melina looked at me, as if she expected a question. I decided I wasn't asking one. She gave up.

"Chris, you pretty much guaranteed that Sir Neville's minions are up in arms at the moment. With him. They were probably under the impression that you were some loser low life who ambled in off the street in the other side and picked up the sword and started waving it about for kicks. They were a lot more cautious after your flustering show in the league hall. But now you've spontaneously destroyed a vampire, which isn't usually that easy even for a Wielder. And you dusted an experienced vamp, who I might add was over a hundred years old."

We'd made it down the stairs to the front door between the two staircases. I suddenly had an idea.

"'Arresting Shadows'," I quoted.

I got a look. Okay, miss smarty pants. You know the text. Figure it out.

"Last time you guys had a big quarrel with this guy Neville, you actually may have won, but it got defaulted six ways from Sunday in the public opinion, right?"

"What I told you wasn't the last time," said Melina with a frown. I had an inkling that the other time was also something to do with her. "But yeah, essentially. The second time it was a little more removed from the league. But the net effect was pretty bad."

Yeah, removed from the league and put right on her pretty shoulders, no doubt.

"It seems like we need to do more than just fight the fight, so to speak," I said. "It's one thing to follow the course and face this guy in a challenge. But I don't think that is the best way to approach this. First, we can perceive his intentions. He'll try to use his connections to spin this situation so that the congress wants to do me in. Maybe even escalate it to him doing them a favor by ensuring my demise. And thus hurting the league. Second, he's done this once before-"

"Twice." I didn't miss the fact that Melina winced when I mentioned the part about the "favor". It was essentially what they did to her.

"Okay, twice before. You'll have to tell me later. But this looks to be a classical case of the need for 'Arresting Shadows'. We need to do something to arrest his probable course of action. And this means now, when he's in the process of deciding what that action is."

I was about to launch into a whole speel, but Melina stopped me with a hand.

"Okay," she said. "But I'm not the one you need to convince. Actually I'm the last one. By a long shot. You're right. Let me get my sword and lets go to Finley's. I'll tell you part two of the situation and you can use them both to get Sir Tall off his short."

I laughed. She made a funny.

I watched her leave the foyer for the kitchen. The Fire Scroll sure seemed to be getting a lot of action tonight. She returned momentarily and passed me my coat, which must have made its way into the kitchen somehow. I realized I hadn't had a hand on it since I passed it to Melina before the grate launching incident.

We both turned to the front door. I downed the last of the water and set the glass down on a side table. I held out my left hand, and Melina took it in her right. We left the mansion. It was time to get the ball rolling.

Chapter 11

Willie

The walk out to the edge of the small estate was rather pleasant. The moon was out. The garden was overgrown, but still quite a contrast from anything we'd walked through so far. We opened the main gate, and headed off to the right down the lit street. There was no sign of a watcher.

"So, you were involved in the second time too?" I asked to get things started. We only had two blocks after all.

"Yeah," she said. Then after a short pause. "It was Willie. Er, sort of."

"Willie?" I asked. She mentioned that name earlier indicating someone helping Charles get her away from the challenge.

"He meant a lot to the league. He had kind of been an uncle to everyone. He was a mentor to me for most of my life. Anyway, Sir Neville was trying to get a change passed through congress which would have made things very difficult for vampires. It was essentially custom tailored to give him a tool to call for Willie's destruction.

"He was really pushing things this time. I'm not sure how many vampires he'd gotten, but it wasn't just them. Sir Neville had started using bears, didn't you call them trolls?"

I nodded. I'd just read a bit about them in a book.

"Well, they call themselves bears. Not sure why, they are very troll like," Melina paused and bit her lip. "Anyway, Willie was there, up on the scaffold, bled and most of the way towards being dry, and..."

She stopped. I gave her hand a reassuring squeeze.

"And I had had it. I was strong then. A lot stronger than I am now. I had a good source of blood. So I did what I was trained to do. I went after the tools Sir Neville was using to get the congress to cooperate. I hunted. I'm not proud of it, but I did what I felt I had to do. And it did manage to make things a little better in the long run.

"I went after every vampire and bear and non human he had in his service and gave them two choices. They either ran and disappeared, or I destroyed them."

I looked at Melina from the side. So this cute chick went on a rampage. Interesting.

"I managed to get through a good portion of his personal army before he realized what was really going on. Fortunately, most of the minions I approached took the offer of running. Those that didn't, I took care of. Word got through the ranks, and things got a little easier.

"Before too long, Sir Neville was really hurting in the congress. All the plans he had to put pressure on the members from the other leagues were falling apart. His guard structure for illegal activities was gutted. It looked like his days were numbered.

"Then it all changed. He spun it, as you guessed, with just the right angle. All of a sudden, I went from being this avenging angel of sorts to the nemesis of humanity. It was a mess. But it worked for him. Almost overnight, I was turned into the very justification for the changes I was struggling to prevent."

"And they went through?" I asked. Melina had stopped us at a rather dingy gate.

"They went through," she said sadly. "Willie was dusted that night. I had been brought in by mages to watch. Sir Neville wanted to be sure I realized that it was my fault for him being destroyed. He tried to get me destroyed too. In the end, it would have compromised the chance of getting the change instated.

"Sir Neville had a vampire tear half this little boy's throat out. Then he scared the mother into making a confession that I'd done it. It was my second mark. Six years."

"Thank you Melina," I said.

She snorted. "For what? Telling you what a screw up I've been?" I hugged her. She tried to push away, but not very hard.

I noticed a pair of eyes looking through the gate at us. I resisted the feeling of embarrassment and squeezed Melina a little tighter. She seemed to know we were being watched, so she broke out of the embrace. But I did catch a rather reassuring glance from her which at least gave me the impression that it had helped.

The gate was pulled open from within by a young woman, probably in her early twentys. Clearly a relation of Sir Finley. I guessed daughter. After the creaking gate stopped, she walked around the it and waved us in. It looked like she had been going for a run. I mean, it was a little cold, and she was wearing a sports bra and lycra pants. And a dagger in a sheath in the small of her back.

"Welcome Wielder," she said formally. "I'm Tracey Finley. Please follow me to the house. Dinner should be ready shortly. My father just arrived."

I swore that the young miss Finley ignored Melina completely. Maybe it was just my imagination. I thought that was strange, because my original impression of Tracey Finley was that she was a vampire. As we began walking down the drive a few paces behind Tracey, I made a motion with my hands which was intended to mime a vampire biting and then pointed at Tracey.

Melina shook her head sharply. She thought for a second and then made a hand motion distinctly communicated as a stick figure with something up its rear. I got the point and had to cough to cover over my laugh. Tracey turned and looked over her shoulder at us. I coughed again, into my hand, hoping that she'd keep going.

She did, and I behaved after that. The grounds to Sir Finley's estate were a lot more expansive than those of the Wielder's estate. And they were definitely maintained with more care. We arrived at a slightly larger house, and Tracey bounded up the stairs. I caught Melina glancing in my direction to check if I was looking at Tracey. To my credit, my attention was ignoring Tracey and examining the house.

We climbed the stairs behind our hostess and she opened the front doors before us and went through. We followed. I decided I didn't like the insides any more than the facade; it was too showy and too modern. And hard to maintain. I'll stick to simple, functional and stout designs, thank you.

Tracey unhooked her dagger with controlled practice and set on a side table. I thought I would probably keep my sword for a little while if she tried for it. She did move in my direction, motioning for my coat. I agreed, it was rather hot inside the house. I took it off, and passed it to her, not failing notice that she had gotten a little closer than necessary to me to take the cloak.

Almost as an after thought, Tracey turned to Melina and accepted her unzipped hoodie. Tracey made a face. Melina didn't. My breath caught. Melina may have been wearing a little more than the elegant and taller blond, Tracey, but not by much. Whereas the shirt Melina had on last night was a tribute to 80's dumpy styles, this was clearly 90's. It was white, thin, two straps, and ended about five centimeters below the belly button. I immediately gave a mental nod in Trevor's direction. It was torture dry. Poor guy.

Tracey's face turned into a deeper frown as she took the sweatshirt and hung up the two garments on a rack next to the side table which had received her dagger. Melina set down her bag next to the rack with a clank. Tracey sniffed.

"I'm going to take a shower," she said pointedly. Good for you. "The drawing room is that way, past the library. Feel free to pour yourself a drink."

Tracey walked briskly to the back of the foyer and bounced up the stairs. Rather than watching her go up the stairs, I looked toward Melina.

"Should I have mentioned that I prefer the library?" I asked softly.

"There's a pool table in the drawing room," replied Melina. I looked down at her shirt. And quickly decided against the drawing room. The library door was locked, so I was resigned to my fate. Melina crossed to the pool table and selected a pool cue. I crossed to the wet bar and selected a bottle of cognac. I felt my stomach growling at me and changed my mind, setting the bottle back down. I looked up at Melina, but she shook her head.

After a moment I realized my attention was focused on her breaking. What the heck, I said. This may be fun. The rack broke and a solid went in. It looked like three more were setup. While Melina worked on those, I picked a light cue from the rack on the wall and checked the tip. Melina knocked another in, making it two total, and missed the third shot.

"I really suck at pool," I said putting chalk on the tip. Melina smiled, and sat on one of the stools next to the bar. Let the girl win, I told myself. I settled myself down for an easy shot on a strip across the table, took my time, and missed. The cue went right towards a pair of solids ready to go in the corner at the other side of the table.

"The third part of the story, you mentioned it involved Willie. But if he died in the second, how?"

I sat on the stool, watching Melina line up for the easy shots. She smoothly knocked the first one in, and set herself up for the second.

"The short story is Willie recovered the sword from Germany during World War II after the last Wielder was killed." She knocked in the second easy shot and the cue ball flew across the table to the other side, almost knocking a third ball in. "He was captured on the way out, and the blade was lost for a while." Melina looked up at me as she talked, though she was still bent over the cue stick in preparation for the next shot. I made it a point of staring at her face. "In '84 he began looking for it."

She knocked in the ball and then nailed another, but scratched. Good, since she was on the 8 ball and I hadn't gotten any in yet.

"But found it by the time you faced off Neville," I noticed, dropping the honorary intentionally this time. I stood to try and redeem myself.

"Yes, he found it about a year into his search. Charles took it in trust, since he can hide it well in his shop. Or at least was able to until you walked in."

I lined up and took an easy shot, but didn't concentrate on the cue position, so had to struggle for the second shot. It missed, wobbling between the bumpers. Melina grinned and hopped off the stool to finish me.

Tracey took that opportunity to enter into the room, skirt swirling. I actually have to be reasonably impressed. That was one of the fastest showers I'd ever seen from a college age female. It couldn't have been more than ten minutes, and here she was in gauzy white dress. Her short blond hair was still wet, but she'd taken the time to put on some makeup.

"Can I play the," she paused, Melina knocked in the 8 ball, "loser?"

Figures. Melina shrugged. I went to rack.

"You break," said Tracey. She poured herself what looked like a brandy and took a large swallow. I thought she may have been under age for that kind of thing. She didn't seem to think so.

I set the rack and prepared to break. Melina had acquired one of the two stools farthest from the brandy glass now set on the bar. Tracey moved to the end of the table. I broke, sinking both a stripe and a solid, then looked up to the two women. Melina looked unhappy, Tracey looked like she was trying to ignore Melina. I decided to not let this girl win, and plunked in a solid, confirming my set. Tracey would have a harder time with the stripes.

Going to work, I smoothly knocked in another but missed the third. I left Tracey with no leave. She was tucked close to a corner pocket behind the eight ball and two of mine. Melina flashed me a smile as I walked toward the stool while Tracey was walking to select a cue and try to salvage the horrible position.

She should have taken a safety, I thought as I returned to the table. I cleared all but two and left her behind the eight ball again, on the wrong side of the table from the only easy shots. Tracey wasn't too happy, as she lined up for a near impossible shot around a solid, she inhaled.

"So, Chris, what do you do for a living?" she asked.

"I'm a process control engineer," I said. "Well, I work as one. My background is mechanical."

"Mechanical, interesting," she said. It sounded a little forced. She missed the shot. "I'm a student at UCLA."

Good for you. I knocked in a pesky 3 ball and then swung around the other side of the table to go for the 7. "What are you studying?"

"Art history," she said. Melina choked on a laugh. It was one of those empty sort of degrees that people joke about. Most art history majors end up doing nothing with either art or history. Daddy's money; probably. It's a shame, since there is a lot that can be learned by studying art. But there just wasn't much of a market for that type of degree. Kind of like music. It doesn't matter what you think you're getting into, you'll probably be either a band director or only playing on weekends. And there weren't that many band director jobs.

The 7 was easy. I glanced at my leave for the 8 and decided I'd end this now. I heard voices in the hall. Perhaps dinner was close. I glanced at Melina, who was waiting patiently for me to finish the game off. Tracey looked like she would have rather had things go a little differently. I lined up and sunk the ball with finality. Tracey gave a weak smile and raised her glass in salute, then downed it.

A butler came through the door. "Dinner is served," he said formally. And then left.

"Shall we?" asked Tracey. Melina slid off the stool and stood next to her, motioning her ahead. Tracey refused to budge, so Melina left. I set my cue down and stalled, hoping Tracey would go ahead and leave. She didn't. So I headed for the door. As expected, Tracey tucked in beside me, a bit closer than I'd like. I could smell an annoying perfume.

The dining hall was opposite the drawing room, and about the size of that room and the library combined. It had fireplaces on either end, which were both going full bore. Although the room was warm, it wasn't stifling. The table was set on one end for five. Sir Finley was standing near the head with his double, minus about twenty five years right next to him. His son, I assumed. About 6 inches shorter than his father, but otherwise identical. He couldn't have been more than about eighteen. Probably a wet behind the ears freshmen in college. His eyes got locked onto Melina as soon as she entered the room.

Just before I crossed the threshold, I evaded a try for my elbow from one of Tracey's hands. I think I'd have to watch this girl. She seemed to have ideas. We all crossed the mostly empty room to stand near the father and son.

"Chris Borden," said Sir Finley. "I'd like you to meet my son, Martin. He's a freshman at Georgia Tech this year."

The poor kid drug his attention off of Melina and reached out to shake my hand. His grip was firm and sure. I liked this kid. Well, he did have good taste after all.

"That's a tough school," I said. "Good engineering program there."

He shook his head. "I'm in physics. Wanted to do computer science, but the 10 year rule..."

As he trailed off, Sir Finley motioned me to the seat on the right of the head. And then he nodded to Melina to head to the one opposite on the left side. Figures. And who would be sitting next to me, I wondered?

We took the offered seats. Sure enough, Tracey sat to my right and her brother across from her next to Melina.

"I'm sure you're as famished as I am," said Finley. "We're not a family locked in formalities, so dig in. I'm afraid it's not more than what you see, plus some dessert, but should be filling."

I uncovered the plate. Noting that the cover was definitely silver. Solid. Roast and potatoes. Nice. With some stewed carrots and fresh broccoli. I think I'd make due.

"Melina," said Sir Finley. "We weren't sure how much you'd be wanting. Word got around about what happened earlier. Let us know if you need anything else."

"Thank you, Sir Finley," Melina said. Tracey frowned. "I'm sure this will be fine. I've already, ah, started to take care of it."

Melina gave a shy glance in my direction. Martin grinned, his mouth full of roast. Tracey inhaled sharply. I guess she didn't like vamps much. It was a shame she was on my right. Otherwise I'd make a point of scratching at my neck. Oh well.

I cut into the roast. It was tender, and just about juicy enough. The taste was average, but I was more than satisfied. Several bites later, I felt fortified enough to begin talking. Sir Finley had been asking Martin about his studies. I decided to interject. I also needed a distraction from how much of Tracey's legs she was showing me under the table.

"Martin," I said. "It sounds like you're just getting started."

He almost looked put down.

"No, I'm not saying anything bad about your progress, just that there are other options besides physics."

"How so?" he asked almost pleadingly. "I mean, other than *humanities*," Tracey stuck her tongue out at him, "there's really not much else that meets the ten year tech limit."

"Have you thought about engineering?"

"Yeah, right," he took a swallow of wine. I had noticed we all had a glass. "I wish."

"Well, if ten years is the limit, I'd say you could argue quite strongly for chemical engineering. It's more than just a running joke with Chem E's that their entire field hasn't changed since the 60's."

"Really, but with computers and all?"

"Not any more than physics has. Less maybe, since there have been a whole lot of advancements in certain areas of physics in the last decade. But the premise of most of the chemical engineering discipline is rooted in transport equations which were known back in the 20's and 30's. A lot of refinements took place in the 60's. But since then, all that's really been done is work to get better approximations from the same laws. You might look into it."

"Thanks," said Martin, through a half eaten potato. "I will."

"I still think you should have just gone with something safe," Tracey fired. "I mean, look what happened to mom!"

I looked expectantly at Sir Finley. He signed and set his fork down.

"Casey is a surgeon. She thought she could keep behind the decade limit, but it wasn't working out. They tried to revoke her permit, so she elected to stay over there, and continue with her career."

After Sir Finley's explanation, the table was silent for a while. I noticed between vegetables that the wine glass in front of Melina was a little darker than the others. She also hadn't appeared to have touched it the entire meal. I actually felt myself anger for a second, then brushed it aside. I didn't know what proper etiquette was for being hospitable to a vampire, so I'd keep my mouth shut and ask Melina later.

The meal was wrapping up a bit. Thus, it was time to start talking business. I gathered my thoughts.

"Sir Finley," I said. "I'm not quite sure what the purpose of this evening is to be. Not that I'm in any way questioning the happening. But I'd like to strongly request a slightly different agenda."

"You do seem to be full of surprises, Wielder," replied Sir Finley. Such as the one which was causing Sir Finley to eat with his left hand. I'd noticed his roast had been cut for him.

"I've been fully surprised, so it seems fitting to reply in like."

Both Melina and Martin laughed.

"Ah," he replied. "I'd imagine so. What do you propose?"

"Well, Melina's told me the basic details behind the league's last two major conflicts with Sir Neville. And I-"

"Did she?" asked Sir Finley, a little more sharply than I was expecting. "She had no right to do that."

"First, since they primarily involve her as a central player, whom I might add suffered greatly in the course of the events, I would say she had a right. Second, I asked her."

Sir Finley stared at me.

"Which brings me to my point," I continued. "Sir Neville is off balance right now. What do you people intend to do about it? And what have you done already since this morning?"

"You may be this league's wielder, Chris Borden, but you are just beginning. You as yet do not have a clearly defined role in this political organization; other than the position you hold. And determining that role is the purpose of this meeting, and others to come. The process will take some time. I must ask you to be patient with us."

"Perhaps we should discuss this more in private," I snapped. It seems the wheels would need some greasing. Melina looked slightly amused. Martin just looked shocked. I still refused to look at Tracey. Perhaps I was being mean. But she really wasn't my type.

"You don't seem to understand how this league works," Sir Finley replied. His feathers were slightly ruffled, but he sounded like he was admonishing a child. It looked like I had to convince him of more than I thought. I'm not a child and I don't play games.

"If you choose to ignore my request, I will go back home right now."

"What makes you think you have the right?" he all but yelled back.

"Now, now," said Melina. "This isn't getting anywhere. But he does have the right, Sir Finley."

"That is open for interpretation!"

"No." Melina replied to Sir Finley's objection. She continued just as calmly, "It is not open for interpretation. Nor can a league elder deny the request for counsel of the wielder. You know that Sir Finley!"

He was getting quite red at this point. I felt another tact was necessary.

"Melina," said Sir Finley with force. "You have overstepped yourself! Dictating to an elder in his own house!"

"If it is necessary to remind an elder of his or her responsibilities; I will do it. I no longer care what happens, as long as the job gets done," she replied.

"And that's been a problem for us in the past which shall not come up again!" I knew very well he was referring to Melina's stint as a pinch wielder, among other things. At this point I decided I was done with this conversation and needed to move on to other things.

I set my knife and fork down gently on my plate, wiped my mouth with my napkin and dropped on it top of the silverware. Tracey tried to grab my arm as I stood, but I pushed her hand away gently.

As respectfully as I could, I bowed in Sir Finley's direction.

"Thank you for the meal and the hospitality, but I fear I have much to do tonight and must get started."

As I walked towards the doorway, Sir Finley threw his fork down in disgust. Good for him. His chair scraped as he launched himself to his feet and started after me.

"This is preposterous!" He yelled and began after me. I kept walking.

He caught up with me as I was pulling my coat down off the rack. Borrowed still. I'd have to do something about that. I was almost tempted to throw his hand off my arm, but decided to give him another chance.

"Yes?" I asked calmly, my eyes on his offending left hand, with my right arm through the cloak and in the middle of reaching for the left arm.

"Mister Borden," he began. I cut him off.

"Chris," I offered. He looked taken a back for a moment.

"Chris," he continued, a bit more composed. "Perhaps I, we, have not been as understanding as we should of your situation. But you must know that procedures have to be followed. This is an established organization with set practices which must be followed. And there's the addition that we have not had the opportunity to bring in a wielder in several decades now."

"I understand that Sir Finley," I said. "And that is precisely why I desired a conference with you on this issue."

"But, I'm sure Melina can answer your questions on most of the basic issues at hand," Sir Finley replied smoothly. *Yeah, and you were just ready to string her up a moment ago for telling me some of those answers.*

"You don't understand, sir," I replied. Sir Finley took his arm off mine, I finished putting my coat on. "I don't have any more questions, really."

"Then what the hell is this all about?" he asked, his color rising again.

"I see that you still don't get the point," I said. "I'll put it this way. You must act now. Tonight. As quickly and as surely as possible, or else I don't think there's anything I can do to help you. Actually, I don't think I will live through the week if you do not act. It may already be too late."

"What are you getting at, Chris?" At least he'd calmed down a little and seemed to be listening. I'd apparently got his attention.

"Melina told me enough to be able to predict what Sir Neville will do. And that even if you get me to challenge Sir Neville at the next congress, or whatever, it will not matter. Even if I am still alive by then, which I doubt. Even if I win, which I can actually say wont matter either. It would probably be better for you to strike me down right now in your hall and hang my body on your front gate.

"Just take one cold hard look at what he's done to your league! Hell, ignore what he's done to poor Melina in the process if you want, but don't be stupid. He will spin this to his like. He did it twice before, if you open up your eyes and look. Twice before things turned for the worse for him. Your league was heading towards success, he was knocked off guard. And you did nothing!

"Well guess what! He's off his guard right now. And all I'm asking is what the hell you're doing about it. Because if the answers 'following practices' then you have already lost. I might as well head on back to Florida, grab a six pack of Sam Adams and watch some Star Trek reruns."

Sir Finley looked like he was going to go ballistic. I held up my left hand.

"But I will tell you this," I said. "If you do act. If you do arrest Neville's intentions now, before he can get things in place, what happened to you has the possibility of being avoided. I don't know for sure, since as you pointed out, I obviously do not know everything there is to know about the situation. All I can say is that if you take care of the political situation by keeping what happened to Melina and me in the past two days from getting spun out of control, I promise you that I will take care of Neville when the time comes."

During the conversation, the rest of the dinner party had followed us into the hall. Tracey barked a laugh at this promise of mine. I turned in their direction. Melina was leaning against a doorway with her arms crossed over her chest. She gave Tracey a dirty look at the laugh. Tracey and her brother were a few paces behind us.

"You intend to kill Sir Neville?" Sir Finley asked. I shook my head.

"No sir," I said. "I have no desire to, nor intention of, killing Neville. I don't believe it will be necessary."

"Then what exactly are you 'promising' which will take care of him?"

"Neville seems to have been intent on refusing to allow your league a wielder. I'm going to deny their wielder the sword of his office. I'm going to break his. "

"Bosh," he said. "That's preposterous! The swords can not be broken!"

"My professional opinion as an engineer says otherwise," I replied. "It can happen. And I know how to do it. You put me in that circle cleanly against him, and I will destroy Neville's blade."

Chapter 12

Footwork

According to Miyamoto Musashi, footwork should be simple. It should be dictated by the terrain you are on. And it should not be a distraction. Above all, it should be logical. That was what we needed; a lot of logical footwork.

I'm not sure what made Sir Finley believe me, but something clicked at the end. I'd challenged him in his own house, at his own table. And he responded to that challenge with cunning beyond any that I could have thought up on my own. This man knew his business. Now that he'd been awakened from his little nap of righteousness, that is.

With near surgical precision, he set us out on our tasks. Melina was to go to her apartment with Martin and two of Sir Finley's vamps to retrieve all of my "technocrap" and dispose of it permanently. I winced at the loss of my noble laptop, but couldn't justify hanging onto the stuff. They were going to then head to the Special Controls Office where they would be met by a friend of Sir Finley's to make sure certain paperwork went through. I suggested the addition of getting Melina's permit cleared to allow her to cross to the other side.

After they left, we repaired to his study. I was assigned the task of going to a few of the elders individually and giving them suggestions, and asking for advice. Tracey was to go with me, since, as the heir to the Finley estate, she could proxy his authority. I will add though that her father shut the door on her. He wrote down a list of things for each of the elders to do. More often than not providing detailed hints to get them done quicker. For a few of the notes, he asked me to be sure that the understanding was clear. All went into little envelopes which he sealed with a wax stamp and passed to me.

Sir Finley sat back in his chair after I'd stowed the notes in my coat pocket. He laughed and then threw back most of the scotch his butler delivered to him almost a half hour before.

"It really is a shame Samantha's out on the other side at the moment," he said. "She would have gotten a kick out of our discussion a little while ago. I feel she would have been in agreement with you from the start."

I let him munch on his own hat for a while.

"Go on Chris," he finally said. "Get out of here. And don't forget you have my permission to smack Sir Naber around. But watch it with Lady Weiss. She's a handful. Actually, it's best if you just let Tracey do the talking with her. Well, maybe not. No, on second thought; don't. The lady doesn't much like Tracey."

"Thank you," I said. "I'll do what I can."

"No, Chris," said Sir Finley. "Thank you. For getting my head out of my ass."

I smiled weakly and turned to leave. Finley's butler came in the second I opened the door with some ice packs for Sir Finley's hand. I made way for him, and then collected Tracey. I headed towards the front door, letting her follow. She had kept the flimsy dress for some reason, but yanked an 80's jean jacket off the rack and threw it over her shoulders. Her dagger went inside in an internal holster.

We collected two vampires who had been waiting just outside the front door. I recognized the woman who passed the ice to Sir Finley last night, but couldn't remember her name. The other was a rather short man, possibly half Chinese, half American. He definitely looked like he could handle the sword at his side. I nodded at them.

"I'm Sara," said the ice bringer, extending her hand.

"Chris," I said, shaking it firmly and giving her a smile. I turned to the other.

"Johny Danger," he said, we shook.

"I once knew a rock band by that name," I said, while smiling. "They were pretty good."

He laughed. "Just as long as they weren't country. I hate country. My cousin's always listening to that crap. No freaking key changes, all the same tempos."

I nodded. "Nice to meet you Johny, Sara." Tracey gave me a look. She didn't seem to think much of my exchanging pleasantries with vampires. Well, guess what. They were here to keep me alive, and I happened to be grateful for it.

"Well Miss Finley," I said to the heir, while motioning her down the path. "Shall we?"

She shook her head and descended the stairs. The three of us turned after, and I moved up intending to walk almost next to Tracey. For a second a thought fluttered through my head. This may actually be nice, walking behind her for the next while. She did have rather nice legs.

Then I couldn't throw the thought away fast enough. I heard that unmistakable sound of a cigarette lighting up. I ducked under the cloud and held pace next to Tracey.

"Doesn't the whole coffin nail thing kind of cancel out your run earlier?" I asked. Johny walked ahead of us and opened the gate. We walked through and took a right, then crossed the street. I heard Sara close the gate and skip a few paces to join us.

Tracey took a puff. "What's it to you?" she said while exhaling. I didn't fake it, I just sneezed. It was perfect.

Tracey groaned and flicked the cigarette away. I looked at her, and sneezed again.

"Great," I said almost hurt sounding. "Now you're going to make me feel guilty for making you litter."

Johny laughed from his position a few steps ahead of us.

"There just isn't a way to win with you; is there, Chris," she said in exasperation.

"Of course there is," I replied quickly. "There's always a way to win with everyone. I just happen to feel treating people in a manner befitting who they are is more appropriate than treating them based on what they are."

Tracey winced, and I could see Johny give a quick look back in my direction.

"I guess I had that coming," she said, sounding apologetic. Hey, I wasn't the one she should be apologizing to. There's two of them well within hearing distance.

We walked past a few more gates, then Johny hit a buzzer on one.

"Lady Weiss's house," said Tracey. "Kind of drab. Watch out for the dogs. She's got a pair of them and they're always dirty."

Said beasts came running up at the gate. Two nice labs, both jet black, were hopping up and down on the other side of the gate barking at us. I kneeled down at the gate and offered them my hand through the iron. After sniffing me, they decided I was okay, so I patted them in turn through the gate.

Aw... they were sweeties. The larger one let me spin her over on her back and start rubbing her belly. They both jumped up as a figure came walking through the trees. The dogs went bounding in excitement back to the figure, barking and having a good time. The swish of skirts identified the person as a woman. And a few more steps brought her and her canine escort into the light enough to see it was the lady of the house herself who came to the gate.

She opened the gate for us and pushed it wide. I entered, with Tracey close behind me. Although I'd intended on crossing to greet the woman, the large lab had other ideas, jumping at me. I gave her a solid head rub and scratch behind the ears, and then she tried to get me to finish the belly rub, I saw no choice but to give in. Johny had drawn the attention of the other lab. He was trying to be nice, while keeping the dog down at the same time. I smiled and glanced up at our still quiet host. Oops. She was glaring at Tracey.

"Sorry to disturb you so late, Ma'am," I said, giving the sweet lab a final, at least in my mind, pat on the belly and standing up. "We only ask a few minutes of your time."

"You're the new wielder," she said flatly.

"That's my understanding. My name is Chris Borden" I replied evenly, my hand getting licked by a lab. I used the other to keep her slobber away from my clothes.

"Raven likes you," she said, just as lacking in emotion.

"I like her too," I replied.

"I know your name," she replied. This was getting to be a little strange. I see what Sir Finley meant about the potentially difficult part.

"Who's the other one?" I asked, nodding to the other lab, who had circled away from Tracey to sniff at Sara.

"That's Canarie," she replied. Just a touch warmer. Then she went all cold again. "What do you want?"

"Actually, I have a letter from Sir Finley. And I have a few questions to ask."

"Which couldn't wait," said Lady Weiss. I shook my head.

"I'm afraid I was rather insistent with Sir Finley," I admitted. Honesty had to be the best policy with this lady.

"And are you to be rather insistent with me, Mister Borden?"

"That is not my intention, but I will be if necessary, my Lady."

"How's Melina?" she asked. Tracey snorted.

"Excuse me?" I asked, taken off guard by the question. And I think I was also getting a little bit tired.

"Is she well?"

"That is Melina's business," I said. "I do assure you that she is being taken care of. So, yes. Or rather she will be."

"Good," she said, then turned and motioned me to follow. I did. We began walking up the small path from the gate to the old house. This may have been a grand estate once, but the grounds were literally untouched. What little I could see of the house looked unkept. There was only a single light on in one of the front rooms on the ground floor.

"Some people in this league find it convenient to forget what Melina has sacrificed for us," said Lady Weiss.

"That was part of the reason for my insistence earlier, my Lady," I replied. "I feel certain events have transpired which may put her in danger of another, ah, problem. And since those actions were almost directly related to saving my life, I do feel a personal duty to avoid any problems those actions may precipitate."

"So, you're cutting into this old woman's sleep for Melina," she said. "If so, I'd suggest you leave now."

"I said that was only part of my reason, Lady Weiss. Not the whole of it."

"You've read too many fantasy books, Chris Borden."

Johny laughed at this I grinned slightly too.

"There is a great deal to be learned from the musings of writers," I replied in my defense. The lady snorted.

We had reached the stair. I stopped at the bottom. Raven sat next to me, looking up at Lady Weiss.

"I'll leave if you want me to, but I will not forget it."

"No doubt," the lady spit back. She opened the front doors. "You're really going to be that wishy-washy? Just leave if I tell you to with only that for a threat?"

"I was advised to use restraint in dealing with you, my Lady. I'll be very firm with the others, I assure you. I've actually been instructed to spank Sir Naber if necessary."

She leaned her head back and laughed quite loudly. Raven cocked her ears at her mistress. It was not a sound that I'd imagine had been heard much from this woman.

"All right, come in, Mister Borden," she said, and entered. The dogs followed with me on their heels. Tracey and the vamps came, a few steps behind me.

The house was a mess. I wasn't sure what was up with this lady, but she didn't seem to have a staff of any sort. With a house this size, that essentially meant that a house went to pot. This one was about there.

Lady Weiss motioned Tracey and the others into a small sitting room to the left of the main door. It was clearly one of the used rooms, and relatively clean. Well, the shelves had been dusted in the past year, and most of the books were organized. A few sat open in various places. There was a small reading desk near a window covered in notes, and a really small wet bar in one corner. Tracey flicked the light on and sniffed.

"Brandy, I believe, Miss Finley?" asked Lady Weiss. "Help yourself."

Then to the vampires, "I'm afraid I can only offer you my couch. I apologize for my limitations, and beg your forgiveness, friends."

Johny bowed toward her and Sara shrugged, plopping down on one of the couches and picking up a book. Johny went to look out the window. Tracey was in the middle of pouring herself a tall brandy when we left the room. The dogs and I followed Lady Weiss across the hall to the room which had the light on. It was a lavish study. The walls were lined with bookshelves almost completely full. There were hundreds of manuscripts piled against a closet door. On the inside wall, there was a sofa, coffee table, and a pair of lamps. The small low table was covered with more books and notes.

I noticed two stacks of dead typewriters in one corner, totaling nine typewriters. This woman wrote. A lot. The desk in the center of the room was as neat as any working desk could be. A typewriter was setup on the side table, stopped in the middle of a blank page.

Lady Weiss sat down at the desk chair, and I took the chair in front of the desk which didn't have any papers in it. I went to move my right hand to extract the envelope for the Lady from my cloak, but found Raven's snoot on top of it. I patted the old girl in apology for not being able to give her more attention and located the envelope. Upsetting Raven, I leaned forward and passed the envelope across the desk to Lady Weiss.

Saying nothing, she opened it, read the contents, and then lit it on fire from a lighter she had extracted from her desk drawer. I was momentarily shocked by the sign of flames in a room with this much loose leaf, but the fire soon extinguished itself.

She looked up at me, so I looked up from Raven. She sighed.

"Damn you," she said. I nodded. Then she laughed again. I smiled slightly. "Tell me," she ordered. "Tell me everything."

I did.

I finished about almost twenty minutes later. It wasn't easy; she asked a heck of a lot of questions. But she was satisfied, and I was worn out.

"So you'll do it?" I asked. I didn't actually have a clue what was in the letter. But I was supposed to get answers.

"Tell that overgrown bean stalk I said yes. But it'll be 200 barrels. No less."

A new form of blood money? Interesting. Wait a minute, was this Lady a vampire? Either way, that was a lot of blood. I nodded again.

"Now get out of my sight and take your little band of bullies with you!"

I think she tried to put some spice into that, but she hadn't gotten the smile off her face yet. I stood up.

"And give my regards to Melina. Oh, also, watch that brat out there. She smells funny."

"She smokes," I said.

"Yes, I know that," she snapped. "That's not it. She just smells funny. Close the door behind you and put out the light."

"Yes, ma'am." I said, leaning over to give Raven a pat on the side. She went over and laid down on a carpet near the windows next to Canarie. "Is it okay if I wash my hands on the way out?"

"Bathroom is under the stair," she said. "Good night."

"Thanks again," I said. "Good night."

I collected my party of "bullies" from the sitting room, made sure the lights were off and all doors closed, and shooed everyone out the front gate. We had several other places to hit and people to annoy.

"So?" asked Tracey as we crossed the street and took a turn down a side road.

"So, where to next?" I replied.

"Sir Naber's," said Johny helpfully. Tracey glared at him. Just keep it up girl, I thought, you'll end up with some teeth in your neck one of these days.

"So what did the old hag have to say?" Tracey offered in elaboration.

"You're doing it again," I said.

In anger, Tracey pulled out another cigarette and lit it.

"What did the Lady Weiss have to say about the situation?"

"Much better," I replied. "See, Tracey, was that so hard?"

Tracey made a reply, but I missed it. I'd felt something. Something bad and strong echoed in my head.

"Hey, Johny," I said. "Pull back a second."

He slowed his pace, instantly a little more alert. I waited until he was next to me.

"I just felt something," I said softly. "It pushed at my wards. Hard. Like really hard, twice, then was gone. Anything to be worried about?"

"Probably," he replied. "I actually didn't know you was warding, so I'd not be too worried about it. Some people who live around here have really wonky defenses around their houses. Ya know. And sometimes the things drift off a little bit. Gotta be cautious about where you ward sometimes where things can be setup permanent like. I don't actually know who's house that was we just walked by. Could have been them."

"Thanks Johny," I replied, barely understanding what he'd said. "So should I tell you if I feel it again, or anything else?"

"Right-o, boss," he replied. The only thing that was missing was the wad of gum in his mouth. I smiled at him.

"Thanks man," I said.

He gave me a thumbs up and stepped up to take point again.

Tracey looked at me, she had been biting her lip between puffs. The cigarette was about half gone.

"Do we have to go through all this again?" she asked.

"She nearly told me off. I instead received a message for your father," I replied.

"And it was..."

"A message," I replied. "For your father."

I couldn't resist. This was actually getting fun.

"I think I see why Melina likes you," she said, apparently deciding to give up this time.

"Hmm?" I dithered. That's not the type of statement I can usually reply to. The fact that I happened to like Melina too made my possible response more difficult.

"You're absolutely unwavering."

"See, most of that is a farce," I admitted. "I like to always be on the ball, so to speak. Part of the best way to do that is to appear to always be on top of things. When all that I really do is make every effort to keep myself in check and rational. It works, usually."

"I heard about this morning," said Tracey. "Sir Neville is not one with a history of backing down. Are you?"

What kind of question is that?

"If I need to reverse directions, I do. It's as simple as that for me, Tracey. I pick a position and justify it as best as I can with the evidence at hand. If I am given new evidence to support another path, I take that one. It's a kind of 'Zen of Engineering Applications'. Engineers spend most of their time, money and effort making sure that they aren't fooling themselves. Because as Richard Feynmen said; 'you're the easiest person to fool'."

"That's kind of pragmatic," Tracey replied. "I.."

I kind of lost her. I felt something again. Maybe we were fooling ourselves.

"Hey, Danger-son!"

"Yo," came the reply, he dropped back with his hand on his sword. "Sup? Again?"

"Yeah."

"Um," mumbled Tracey, looking around. Sara had turned around slightly to look behind us. It came again. This time it pounded. I went to my knees, desperately throwing up a filtering system to block it the hell out of my way.

"Johny," I said. "Again, bad."

His sword was out, back to us, looking around. Sara pulled hers the same instant, guarding the rear.

My right hand closed on the hilt of the sword, and my left reached for the ground to hold myself up. The blows picked up their intensity. I was getting nailed.

Chapter 13

Rounds

It hit about ten more times before I got my filter network in place the way I wanted it. I almost lost the whole thing with the second blow, but the third was dampened a lot more. The tenth and after went right to ground.

I found myself looking at a very short skirt and very long legs. So I looked, up, and accepted the hand in getting to my feet. I was a little unsteady, but reasonably whole. The waves of whatever the heck was battering at us were washing safely away to null land.

I looked down at Tracey's left hand on my lapel, still holding the smoking cigarette. I guess my expression was a little indicative of my feelings toward the object.

"Sorry," she said, quickly holding it away. I nodded thanks, and then looked around. I had no clue where this was coming from, but it wasn't very nice of them. Since I couldn't figure out what this was coming from, I tried figuring out where it was going to, what it was aimed at.

It didn't seem horribly directional. It seemed to be localized to within about this general area. Then it stopped. A few seconds later it started again. Then I knew where it was. I shrunk the size of the ward rapidly to only enclose me and stepped towards Johny.

A cell phone rang. Sara and Johny looked around at Tracey quickly. I laughed, in sheer relief. Tracey frowned and reached in her jacket pockets to find the phone.

"Hello," she said into the small phone. It looked similar to the main-side models, but I had a feeling it was made here and worked on a much different system. And that system didn't like wards much.

"No, I'm busy," she said after listening to the other side of the conversation. "I'll call you back later... Yes."

Then she hung up the phone and put it back in her pocket. She took a drag from the coffin nail and then motioned for us to get going.

I refused.

"What's the problem?" asked Tracey.

"That's the problem," I replied with just as much snap. "Please turn the hellphone off."

"Sheesh! Fine," she said, extracted the phone and flicked a switch on the side. "There! Now can we get going?" Sara was shaking her head with a grin on her face. I waited until Tracey walked past me to return Sara's smile.

Weapons resheathed and thoughts regathered we proceeded as before. I asked Tracey a bit about her classes at UCLA, and she told me. At least she actually had to take a real math class or two, but it was about what you'd expect for art history.

We arrived at another non-descript gate. Considering the state of some of the other gates we passed, I definitely got the impression that this particular league was a little down in the dumps in comparison. Johny hit the buzzer. We waited.

Tracey finished her cigarette and twirled the butt away into the bushes, still smoldering.

"Do know how long it takes a cigarette but to dissolve in the wild?" I asked.

"Like 4 years," said Johny. He buzzed the gate again. I didn't know, but it sounded right. "Just imagine all the mommy and daddy birds picking them up for use in their nests. And the squirrels..."

Tracey sighed and made a face at Johny. This gate actually had an intercom. The channel opened.

"What do you want?" said the sex-less gruff voice from through the old speaker. "It's late."

"It's Tracey Finley, on business from her father, Sir Finley to see Sir Naber," said Tracey, before I could get anything out.

"With the wielder," I added. Tonight was not my night to be ignored.

"Just a minute," came the reply. After about ten seconds, the gate lock snicked open. We walked through towards the house. This one was definitely in better repair than Lady Weiss's, although it was of a more simple design.

Tracey took to the steps, and I followed, almost at her elbow. We stopped at the top landing and waited. The woman who opened the door could have been any age between 40 and 60. You just couldn't tell. She was wearing a robe over a dressing gown.

"Come in," she said. "Sir Naber will be down in a moment."

We were ushered into the main hall. The woman leaned against the railing of the stairs and crossed her arms. Just as her eyes started to waver closed involuntarily, a man trounced down the stairs from the second floor wearing a purple robe over pajamas. Him I could place more in the late 50's. And he didn't look happy.

When he got to the bottom of the stair, he regarded Tracey and myself with an expression designed to convey extreme annoyance. I was annoyed too. Maybe that was the point.

"I apologize for disturbing you so late, Sir Naber," I said. "But the situation, I'm afraid, does not permit waiting."

"I seriously doubt I need to be woken to hold your hand. What could possibly be important enough that it can't wait until a reasonable hour?"

"I have a letter from Sir Finley which I'm sure will answer your question fully," I replied. Tracey didn't seem likely to intervene, so I was on my own.

"Well," he said, reaching the bottom stair. "Give me the damn let–"

I passed it to him in midspeech, anticipating his request. I was not going to let this guy get the upper hand.

Sir Naber remained up on the staircase, as if to maintain his stature. Since he was also the shortest in the room by a good three inches, it may have actually been intentional. With stubby fingers, he broke the seal, dropped the envelope to the floor and read the letter.

"The answer is no," he said without a thought. The letter went into the pocket of his robe. "Absolutely not! Out of the question. Now get out of my house!"

"No." I said. Tracey glanced at me. "Sir Finley said you would say no. He said to remind you of Thomas McQueen and allow you a second chance."

"Thomas McQueen," he sputtered, flushing scarlet. "What did he tell you about that? Wait, 'allow' me a second chance?"

"Yes, Thomas McQueen and the fate of, oh, what did he say, Johny, was it 70 barrels, or 700."

"Probably the latter, Sir," said Johny, playing along nicely.

"He wouldn't dare!"

"Actually, he would. But he would prefer not to....If you get my drift."

"The answer is still no, Wielder," said Sir Naber. "Tell him he can bloody well blab if he wants to. It'll hurt him as much as it will me."

That was interesting, I'd have to ask Sir Finley about this later. All he said was mention a large quantity of barrels and the name.

"Very well," I said. "But I'm not finished yet."

Sir Naber began to gather himself for a verbal onslaught. I was gathering myself for something a little more, ah, physical. I beat him to the punch by a small bit.

The small side table right under the railing, and Sir Naber's hand, turned to match sticks with a loud crackle. I'd gotten the gain right this time. Tracey squeaked, Johny and Sara both jumped slightly. The woman just glanced at the pile of toothpicks and backed away. Sir Naber deflated and looked down at the mess.

"You have a lot of really nice furniture in the sitting room, Sir Naber. Is there any piece you're particularly fond of?" I asked.

"What the hell do you think you're doing?" Sir Naber glared at me. I was getting my job done. That's what I thought I was doing. A small corner chair cracked to bits in the room beside us. I didn't take my eyes off of Sir Naber's face.

"Stop it," he yelled at me.

I cracked another piece. I think it was a writing desk. I wasn't really looking. Papers went flying in the air as the table blew.

"Would you rather I switched to the paintings?"

I think I blew up a lamp. Anyway, the lights in the hall flickered. I felt a little back lash and resisted a wince. Okay, Chris, don't mix the two. Not yet. Stick to kindling. No electrical appliances or devices thank you.

At my suggestion Sir Naber lurched to the wall next to him. There were at least twenty paintings mounted up the stair case and along the second floor balcony. I started to point to the first one.

"Oh, heavens! NO!"

I lowered my hand.

"No? Still? Are you sure the answer is still no," I asked. My finger was pointing at the ceiling like a gun. I mimed taking aim at the painting.

"NO! Oh, wait! No, yes!" he sputtered. I brought my arm down at his "no" and brought it back up when he said "yes."

"Which is it?" I asked for clarification.

"Yes, I'll do it," he was almost panting. "Just stop this madness! Please!"

"Okay, Sir," I said, holstering my hand in my coat pocket. "I'll tell Sir Finley that you've been most cooperative."

Sir Naber nodded.

I was tempted to push things, but I didn't need this man any more ticked at me right now. He was still hugging the painting on the end.

"Good night, Sir Naber," I said, then to the woman, still unintroduced, "Ma'am."

I don't think he heard me. The woman nodded and then I turned around and motioned for us to depart. She closed the door behind us.

I noticed on the way to the gate that my companions were silent. Tracey had this horrified expression on her face. Johny looked grim. And Sara seemed to be avoiding looking at anyone else. What was this about?

"Um, what?" I asked. Tracey looked at me.

"What do you mean, 'what'?" she snapped. "You just like started blowing stuff up!"

"Yeah, man, like cool," said Johny.

"Well, it was that or start slapping Sir Naber like your father suggested," I replied in my defense. "At least this way I'm just making kindling. It's kind of preferable to assault in my book."

"What Miss Finley is trying to get at, sir," said Sara, "is that you're little display in there would have brought most mages to their knees. And that's if they were prepared for it."

I sniffed. For some reason, I decided against telling them that what they saw was me toning down the effect quite a lot. It took some energy to make the shields. But shorting them out was relatively easy. Compared to just blowing them up I guess. Instead of commenting, I shrugged. I did feel drained, and I don't think it was just the day of activities either.

"Oh, and Sara? It's Chris. I'm only 26."

"Okay, Chris," she replied.

Tracey was reaching for another cigarette. Disgusting. I walked around her and joined Johny as he opened the gate.

"So which one next?" I asked, stepping around the gate. We walked on down, the two women came through and closed the gate behind us.

"I'd say we could do either the Hausmann's or the Lady Whitacre. They're about a block away from each other."

"Which do you suggest, Johny?" I asked. "I'd say get the harder one out of the way first, but then again, it's getting late and I'd prefer not to get to the easy one past their bed time."

"It probably wont matter, man. They're both about as uppity as Sir Finley. But I don't think they'll just plain out laugh in your face like Sir Naber."

"I could just give the letters to her smokiness back there," I said, pointing back to the puffing Tracey.

"You may wanta watch her a bit, Sir Chris. She had a few back at the Lady Weiss's."

I frowned. A brandy before dinner. Two glasses of wine and...

"About how many we talking here?"

"Least two tall right as she got there. She sipped the last one for a while. I'm not sure how much was in it. Sorry."

Crap. I'd be drunk after that, or at least buzzed to fuzziness. I looked back at her. She didn't seem too plastered. Maybe she was a little more stout than me when it came to the witches brew. Last thing I need is to bring Sir Finley's young daughter back schnozled after a night out on the town.

"Thanks, Johny," I said. I'll keep an eye on her. We crossed a side street and made it a little ways past a corner mansion.

"That the Hausmann's?" I asked, pointing a head to the right.

"Yep," he said, slowing to a stop.

"And can you think of a conceivable reason for their gate to be wide open and all their lights off?"

"I can conjour up a few bad ones for ya," he said, drawing his sword. I did the same.

"What is it?" asked Tracey, flicking her cigarette into someone's yard. I pointed at it with my left hand and atomized it. Yes, quietly. I warded the hell out of the air around it. She blinked at me in shock.

"The Hausmann's gate is wide open and it looks like nobody's home," said Johny.

"They're usually up rather late," said Tracey, looking concerned. Her dagger had manifested itself in her left hand with a quick practiced motion. At least she knew how to handle the thing. She was probably better than I was.

We heard voices. And a muffled scream. I nodded to Johny and we began a fast walk, toward the gate.

"So, you can like, just blast people apart, like poof?" asked Johny. I cringed.

"I don't think I have the stomach to try that on someone," I said. "Let's just say, I can probably disarm someone who isn't otherwise wanting to be disarmed and leave it at that. Well, until I run out of energy."

We got to the gate just as a group of six people were leaving. Two had blood on their hands and shirts. One of those also had some on his mouth. He was in the process of wiping it away. It was mister split face.

Both groups skidded to a halt. Split face frowned. One of the men behind him cursed.

They began to advance on us, and swords came out. The one that cursed had a rather nasty axe in his hands.

"How's the headache?" This was directed at the friend from this morning, Jules, Melina had called him. He spat at my feet. There was still a definite mark up the center of his chin and forehead where Melina had caught him. Come on Chris, think... Six to four. Two vamps verses at least two in the other party, possibly up to six. And only three swords on this side. They may have just murdered an elder and family. Or at least had a snack.

I had seconds to make a decision. Attack, run, or... or what? An idea formed. This wouldn't be pretty, but it may just work.

Just as they rushed forward, I dropped a extension of my shield over them like a net, with lead weights attached. All six were pushed to the ground. I grabbed Johny's arm for support, as he stared at the sight. It was too much for me to hold them on the ground, so I let the shield off, and let it shape itself into a hemisphere. It seemed to settle into that shape on its own.

Split face bounded up to his feet and rushed us, but bounced off the shield after a pace in my direction. He struck out at it with his sword. The blade sparked, but rebounded. Then he really struck. I felt my feet slide back. I'd stupidly anchored it to myself. Glancing around, I found the good sturdy footing of the wall corner and anchored the shield to that instead.

The enraged vampire went nuts against the shield. The others got to their feet in disbelief. One had a bloody nose, and had edged away from the others, holding a handkerchief to his nose. I guess they weren't all vampires.

"Johny," I said, still gripping his arm for dear life. This was tough. I kept the strain off my face as best as I could. Each of that vamps wild blows was battering on my reserves.

"Yeah, boss," he said.

Then very softly I said, "I can't hold this for long."

"Sara," he said, "go run up to the house and call the mage police. We'll keep these goon dolls company."

The axe bearer swore again and said something to split face. Another full force blow landed on the inverted shield, then the next was less. He stopped, and glared at me.

"Wielder," Jules said. His voice was very scratchy. Probably due to Melina's handiwork. "You better let us go, Wielder. If you know what's good for you."

"You better hope those people are alive," I replied evenly. My voice sounded too strained for my liking. "Or I'll show you personally what happens to a vampire when a wielder's blade finds their heart."

I almost fell when Johny suddenly stepped away from my side. Blades clashed. I turned, my guard up. Tracey hadn't been doing a good job of watching our backs. Four more armed individuals were on top of us. Johny already had one on her back after a strong shove. Another was crossing swords with him in rapid blows. Each brought sparks out of the night. A third had engaged Tracey, but she was doing well, having already put a deep mark on his right forearm. I saw him switch to his left hand.

That left another female, who I rushed with as much speed as I could come up with. I hoped I could hold the shield and this woman long enough to get a hand. I didn't have much left.

The momentum of my rush helped a little bit. At least with the first exchange. It was the first time I'd struck swords with a vampire without any trickery. I felt that blow to my toenails. My right arm screamed in agony where I'd been cut the other day. And I was instantly reminded of the broken rib. The next few blows were not much better, but she was relying on strength, and I had a speed and reach advantage. For now.

She seemed bent on going for my arms. It wasn't a traditional assault, but I didn't let myself get caught off guard by it. The vampire came in with a low swing up towards my head. I dropped under her blade, but noticed she was drawing me in instead. Almost too late, I dcked further under her lunge downward, managing to cut her across her left side on the way. Back on my feet, I met a series of quick chops at my shoulders while losing ground. I could feel my left leg protesting where it had been cut the night before. And she didn't seem to mind the gash on her stomach much.

I thought of trying to do the blade shattering trick again, but quickly abandoned the idea, as the shield instantly began to fall apart. I stumbled back from the vampire to put myself back together. Time to change things. Planting my feet, I calmed myself and gave the woman a respectful bow, my sword was almost dangerously low. She didn't seem to like it much and charged me, swinging at shoulder height like one would with a baseball bat. It's a sword. Not a bat.

I lunged under the blade, right foot first. My left arm knocked her sword up as she tried to correct. Since the edge was horizontal, I struck only the flat. Mostly. My leg tied up with hers and she began to topple towards me, and my blade. Already hoping I was going to miss, I followed through. I didn't miss. She was now on top of me with her sword at my neck. My left hand was fighting to keep the blade from cutting my head off. And my sword was already halfway to the hilt. She turned to dust. Now twice today, a vampire died at my hands.

I laid there for several seconds with my eyes closed. Concentrating on keeping the shield up and hoping nothing was standing over me ready to get frisky. I heard the sound of approaching vehicles with sirens. The engineer in me immediately thought about the height of the gas prices to make vehicle travel so scarce. I'd have to ask about that. With my left hand, I set the deceased vampire's blade aside. I opened my eyes and sat up. That was as far as I got.

The two vampires Johny had been sparring with were dragging the one Tracey had launched into the bushes next to the wall to his feet. He looked pretty dazed and had lots of cuts on his arms. She's pretty good with that dagger.

Johny came over and kneeled next to me. He sniffed.

"You okay, boss?"

I nodded weakly. He passed me a handkerchief. I laid my sword across my lap and took a look at the left arm of the raincoat. The tough material had probably stopped most of the blow. But after the blade made it through, there was a nasty slice off the arm. It wasn't deep, but it was stinging pretty bad and bleeding. I doubled up the handkerchief and pressed it to the wound.

"Thanks," I said. I think I may have been zoning out a little.

"Hey," he said, putting his hand on my shoulder and squeezing. "You okay?"

"No, I'm not" I said angrily. I'd just killed again. No I wasn't okay, damn it! "Sorry, Johny, I guess so. I just need a minute."

"Sure thing, man," he said. Tracey looked up to watch the two old 80's minivans that turned the corner with flashing lights. Horrible front wheel drive things which seemed to be smoking a little. Oil past the rings no doubt.

"They going to play straight with us?" I asked, nodding to the oncoming vans. They had slowed, and were pulling onto the curb before the gate area. I noticed Sara standing with a sick look on her face nearby, staring at the ground.

"Yeah," he said. "Mister Hausmann's got his throat ripped out and Lady Hausmann's been turned. I'd say they're going to be playing very straight with us. Considering you've caught them."

"Good," I said, reaching out with my left hand to Johny for some help. The cloth had essentially stuck to the wound on the arm. It would have to do for now. At least I wasn't actively leaking. I had police to greet. Joy. Johny pulled me to my feet, my sword rolling smoothly off my lap and into my right hand. I sheathed it. "Cause I really don't want to have to kill anyone else today. I don't think I could. I'd probably fall on my own sword first."

Three men and one woman in robes stepped out of the vans and headed our way. Johny glanced at me.

"You serious, dude?"

"Yes, I just killed a woman who probably hasn't had a sword for more than a week. I'm not finished dealing with the lady I killed earlier today, and she was like a hundred years old or something. So yes, Johny. I'm serious."

He shook his head. The woman mage came up to us, and I stepped forward.

"We have a complaint of a ravage killing and a forced turning," said the woman with authority.

"Yes, ma'am," I said. "They're the Hausmann's. Husband murdered and wife turned. We were here to talk with them, and ran into these six coming out the gate. Those two had blood all over them. That one still has blood on his face."

When I indicated split face, he bowed away and tried to wipe at his mouth. Gotcha sucker!

"Did a mage put up that shield?" she asked, staring at the corner of the wall, and my anchor. Two of the guys headed toward the house at a jog.

"No, ma'am, I did," I said. And I can't keep it up for much longer.

"And you are?" said the man to her left.

"Chris Borden; Seventh League Wielder, as of this morning."

"Interesting. And the wounds, they occur from these guys?" he asked. It looked like he was taking over.

"No, sir," I said, shifting my attention. "There were four others outside. After we confronted and detained these six," I almost pointed at Sara, but had a second thought, "we checked the house and then were set upon by the other four. I killed one, and three more got away."

The guy's eyes widened.

"You killed someone?" he asked dangerously, looking around for a body. Yeah. Twice. And I hate it!

"Yeah," I said forlornly, I pointed at the pile of ash and taped some more of it off my cloak. "She was a vampire, but I don't think she had been one long."

"Oh," he said relieved. "I thought you'd killed someone." Then he walked towards the anchor.

The woman took over with me. "Just make sure you file a Destruction form in the office in the next day or so. If you're worried about it. Just collect a small sample to confirm identification of the destroyed creature if you can. Unless charges are filed, you wont have to pay any fines."

Was that it? A day or so? Fines?

"Um," said the guy from the corner of the wall with a frown. He motioned at the caged goons. "I, ah, can't bring it down."

"Sorry," I said. The shield dropped. My head swam. The mage had a glowing dagger out and was motioning to the six guys to head towards the vans.

"Wait here," said the woman. She went over to help. Tracey and Sara both came over to stand near us. Sara picked up the sword of the fallen vampire and offered it to me. I shook my head. She shrugged and slid the bare blade through her belt. It was then that I realized. Not only did the vampire turn to ash, so did the clothes. Her belt and sheath were gone. But the sword was left. I'd had my hand around it.

I felt like I was going to throw up. Johny put a hand out and touched my right arm, I yelped, which caused my chest to hurt anew. Overloaded, I began to collapse, got tripped up by my sword, and crashed down in a heap on the ground. It was better down here anyway.

"I think he needs a minute," said Johny to the others.

My right hand went to my cloak pocket. I still had three letters left, not counting the undeliverable one to the Hausmann's. Somewhere I found the energy to look up at those around me. That energy blossomed into a resolve which drove me to my feet. After a minute.

Chapter 14

Midnight

I crossed quickly past my startled companions to the vans. The two leading mages were finishing loading the last few guys into the back of the second van.

"I've got three more stops to make tonight," I said. "And it's already later than I'd like. Do you need us for anything else that can't wait until the morning?"

The woman looked at the man and he shook his head. She pulled a card out of her robe and passed it to me.

"Where can we find you?" she asked.

"Either the wielder's mansion, or Sir Finley's. Is that okay?"

"Sure. We'll contact you if we need anything."

"Thank you," I said, and went past the vans. When I got to the corner, Johny was at my elbow, he motioned right, and I followed his lead. Tracey and Sara were slightly behind us. Tracey yawned.

"Like the man said," piped Johny. "He's serious like. Two up on the left."

I vectored in that direction.

"Lady Whitacre?" I asked.

"Right-o, boss," said Johny. I laughed.

"You're really caught in the 80's aren't you. I mean, your skate or die lingo, her jacket, Melina's hoodie."

Johny looked slightly hurt, but then grinned at the reaction from Tracey.

Her mouth dropped open. And almost by reflex, her hand found a cigarette to lift there. I stopped and stared at her. She almost ran into me, already inhaled and primed to flick the switch on her lighter. Slowly and cautiously, she put the cigarette and lighter away. I turned and continued to the gate, hitting the buzzer myself.

A young female voice answered.

"It's the league wielder and Tracey Finley, we have a message from Sir Finley for the Lady Whitacre. And very little time. Tell her that Neville just offed Hausmann's husband

and turned her into a vampire."

I heard a gasp from the background. The channel closed and the gate clicked.

It was a short walk from gate to the house. We were met halfway by the owner of the young voice from the speaker. I was wrong, it was actually a young boy, probably about six or seven. Guess I should have watched my language. He showed us to the door and offered to take our coats. I extracted the letters from the cloak and passed it to him. His eyes went wide at the sight of the hole in the arm and the blood on both.

A tall and elegant black woman, appearing to be in her late 30's approached us. She had on a business pants-suit, which was a dark navy. I recognized her from this morning and the warehouse the other night. She gave the kid the unmistakable "bed now" thumb over the shoulder. He was gone. She extended her hand, but I arrested mine in mid reach.

"I'm sorry, my Lady," but I've just been in a rather nasty situation and killed a vampire, you probably don't want to touch me; I've got her ashes all over my clothes. "I fear my hands are a bit dirty."

"I understand, Chris, I'm Janice" she said warmly, and noted my left arm. She also surveyed the others for injuries. "Kitchen. Now, and you can tell me all about it."

I moved to follow the order, but paused. Lady Whitacre waved my companions down a side hall.

"Sitting rooms just past the ball room opposite the... well. Just follow Tracey. Make yourselves comfortable."

I followed the Lady to the kitchen. She made me push my shirt sleeve, or what was left of it, past my elbow. I clenched my teeth as she pulled the handkerchief off the wound under the faucet. Or rather out of the wound. It looked a heck of a lot worse in the light. I went to work on it gently with the indicated soap while she located a first aid kit from near the doorway.

"And it's Janice," she said. "My house. My rules." Okay, so I don't get to blow up the furniture? Darn. I was looking forward to more fun.

I gave her the story while she patched up the arm. Then passed her the note after I sat down on one of the stools near the center counter. She read it. Frowned. Figures. Here it comes. I sipped the glass of water I'd received in the middle of my tale. The door opened from the back of the house, a man stepped through.

"Honey," he said loudly, then he saw us. "Oh, sorry, Janice. I didn't know you had a guest."

"Several, actually. Could you give us about five minutes, Tom? T.J's upstairs and he should be to bed by now." Tom nodded at me and walked past, giving Janice a kiss on the cheek on his way by. She smiled at him.

"Where were we?" she asked.

"Right at you saying no, Janice, and kicking me out on my bum," I said, attempting humor. It fell a bit flat.

"Actually, I am going to say 'no'. But you didn't know what this was asking, did you?" I shook my head.

"The Office of Technology. My office. Will not be a problem. Sir Neville smuggled firearms in in the past due to oversights. They have been corrected since I took over. And I have already made sure the bits about your technology breach have been delt with properly. Finally proceccing happened before I left today; so you're in the clear for that too."

Ah, that explains why I haven't been shot at yet. Cool.

"That's a relief either way," I said, then downed the last of the water.

She pocketed the letter.

"Thank you, Janice," I shook her hand. "Now, I must away."

Janice nodded, and I followed her out the other side of the kitchen across the back of the house to the sitting room.

Tracey had apparently had a few more. She was now almost obviously a wee bit tipsy. Johny shrugged his shoulders at me and held up three fingers and mimed drinking. I snapped, pointed at the glass, and vaporized the contents just as she was preparing to throw it back. Tracey looked at the glass in shock and set it down, then I walked to the door. Janice covered a laugh with her hand.

"We leaving? Right?" Tracey asked. I was amazed, almost no slurring. Without waiting for an answer, she headed toward the door. Johny went through behind her to make sure she was going to be able to navigate. Sara and I followed. Janice walked us to the font door. Tracey had already gone through it. I retrieved my coat from the rack near the door.

"Take care, Chris," said Janice, then shut the door behind us.

We met up with the others at the gate. Tracey looked like she wanted a smoke, but was too scared of what I'd do. Good. I realized I was over-reacting. I didn't really care.

"Next?" I asked. "Two left. What, an hour walk, right?"

"They're not home," said Tracey, she brightened up a little bit.

"Yeah, it would be," Johny said. "But she's right. They're not home. At least it's not likely. They're at the club. About twenty minutes walk back in towards town."

I nodded, we headed out.

"I never asked what the gas prices are here," I said. "So they up a factor of ten or something?"

"I saw 24.95 this morning," said Sara. "I had an errand near the station on this side. Pretty low actually." So that about a factor of 14.

"We don't mind though," said Tracey a little whimsically. "It keeps us fit."

Her "f" had some problems, but it looked like she was still walking all right. For now. I was hoping this "club" didn't have a bar.

"Do you always have to sample the hospitality at everyone's house?" Perhaps I was getting tired, I didn't manage to get my disgust out of it like I should have.

"Do you always have to knock a girl off her high horse?" she replied, then frowned, biting her lip. I decided to let her off the hook. It wasn't my place anyway. She can have what's left of that horse. It didn't look like the tack was going to make it to the morning with all its straps and buckles, though.

"So both these elders usually hang out at the club," I asked. "Together?"

"Yep," said Johny.

"They're the youngest two members of the league, and like to live life a little," said Sara. Seems to describe our other companion as well. "That pretty much means the club. Pool, gambling, cards. Sometimes organized dances. Drinking..."

The last she said softly, but I already thought our little tipsy miss knew all about the possibilities of the club. I hoped it wouldn't be a problem.

We talked a bit more about automobile availability and I found Sara to know quite a lot. Turns out her dad had been an auto mechanic in the 40's. She grew up passing him wrenches and spanners with grease in her nails. I smiled. Then I asked Johny about his past.

"My family back in China paid to have my brothers and sisters and I sent to the States on a ship," he said. "When the hold opened, a bunch of vampires came in and killed all but a few, the youngest. Those they turned. I got to see the rest of the kids slaughtered. I think there were about fifty of us in with the crates."

Before I could finish processing this, he added.

"Actually, I need ta thank you," he said. "That lady you killed earlier in the sewers; she was one of the vampires who dined that night."

I couldn't find words for a little while. Sara, patted my arm reassuringly.

"Here's the club, ahead on the left," said Johny. We headed on over to the other side of the street. Slightly more elegant than a store front. It actually reminded me of a bookstore for some reason. No, not the book store that started off this whole mess.

The bouncer was standing next to a small podium. I saw a binder with papers in it. Probably a door list. He nodded at us as we approached and crossed his arms over his chest. The guy looked a lot like those bear-troll things, but with a shave and a hair cut. More careful examination verified; he didn't have any hair. I had no idea what that meant.

"We're here to see Sirs Dallas and Cleary," said Johny. The troll didn't seem impressed.

"And you are?" he asked, looking at me. Okay, a smart troll. Great.

"Chris Borden, Seventh League Wielder." Johny replied for me. Thanks. The troll looked down at the open binder, flipped a page, then another and frowned.

"Sorry, you not on list."

"Maybe you need a new list," I said with just a touch of flint.

The troll shook his head. "Nah, list is good. You not on it."

I was going in the door. He didn't seem to realize it yet. I smiled, pointed at the binder and vaporized it. The binder went with a loud bang. The paper gave off a crackle of small flashes. Each sounded about as loud as a rim shot on a snare drum.

"Yeah," I said. "I'd say you definitely need a new list."

The troll stared at me as we went by and through the door. I wondered whether I should have waited for him to open it, but decided he didn't need the time to reconsider his need for a new list. We entered.

Gambling is obviously legal, judging from the piles of chips at the various tables in one quarter of the room. There were a few craps tables, some slot machines and a roulette wheel. The room was about the size of a basketball court, with a few hundred people. Mostly men, with a few woman hanging on peoples arms. One of the craps tables looked like a young woman in a red dress was running the table. On the outside wall, street side, was a bar. There were some tables in front of it, mostly packed. Only a few stools weren't occupied at the bar itself. The opposite wall had a few hallways leading back to what private rooms.

Johny vectored us over to a trio of gentleman in tuxes standing near a partition talking. Tracey immediately broke ahead of us and almost sloshed into the man on the far left. Actually, it looked a little more professional than that. In the blink of an eye, she had encircled his arm with both of hers and reached up on her toes to kiss him on the cheek. I wondered where the heck her jacket was. She must have hung it up on the way in.

"Oh, Daniel," she said, bubbling out the charm. "It's so good to see you. It's been a dreadful night."

Daniel gave me a questioning look. I shrugged, and extended my hand. Since his right was occupied, he shook it half way backwards with his left.

"Daniel Cleary," he said. "Nice to meet you in person." I did the rounds, extending my hand to the next person.

"Chris Borden," I said. "'Wielder' makes me feel like I forgot the acetylene torch at home. " The next guy laughed and shook my hand with a weak grip. Extra 'i' aside, I felt confident in my little bit of punishment.

"Michael Beacham," he said. "I'm somewhere down a long line of ascension for an elders spot in the second league. I'm actually glad that the seventh league finally got a wielder."

I nodded, the third guy, one of the league elders, had a small sandwich in one hand and a beer in the other. He gave a slight bow. "Thomas J. Dallas," he said, his mouth half full. He threw back a swig of beer to wash it down.

Tracey was on her toes again, whispering really close to Cleary's ear. He seemed to be paying a lot of attention to her. Cleary waved towards a waiter, who came over with a tray of champaign glasses.

"Nice to meet you Beacham, Dallas," I said. I'd better get this done quick, or else Tracey would probably end up making a scene. "I'm afraid, though that I can't properly develop our acquaintance. I'm actually here on league business." I moved forward a step, and glanced at first Cleary and then Dallas. "Is there some place we can speak? It's urgent."

Dallas looked over to Cleary, who wasn't paying much attention. He was in the process of passing Tracey a glass from the waiter's tray. I sighed and rolled my eyes. With insistent caution, I set my hand on Tracey's elbow and pulled. She pealed off Cleary and her eyes aimed daggers in my direction. But they seemed to be missing their points. Cleary glanced at me in surprise, his hand still holding the champaign glass and face slightly flushed.

"Tracey," I suggested. "Would you mind entertaining Mister Beacham for a few minutes while I talk to Sir Dallas and Clearly?"

Tracey seemed to deflate a little bit, she dropped the daggers and instead turned on the puppy dogs. Which were probably a little stabbing too. I almost felt guilty for being mad at her. I mean, here she was, a college girl, getting drug off to escort a lame like me around town. When she could have been out with a boyfriend, or doing homework, or something.

Cleary seemed to be paying attention. Helped I think by an insistent comment from Dallas, which I missed. Dallas motioned towards the back and dropped his beer and sandwich on the waiter's tray. I released Tracey, who didn't seem to want to be released, and followed. The look in her eyes reminded me of something, but I had other things to think about at the moment. Sara hung back by Tracey and Johny tracked with us.

We were almost to one of the hallways at the back when I noticed a familiar face. One that I'd seen only a little while earilier in the evening get tossed into the bushes by my escort. The bearer of the face crouched down near one of the tables in the back right corner to talk in someone's ear. I met the gaze of that someone. He didn't look happy. Good for him.

"Neville," I growled to myself. Dallas heard me.

"What?"

"Nothing," I said. Hey, it was a public place. I threw away the thought of drawing my sword and taking out his little card game. It wouldn't have accomplished much.

Dallas opened a room with a card table and no occupants. We entered and sat down. I strengthened my wards to the best of my abilities, pushing them out to surround us. No sense letting anyone listen in, with Sir Neville in the very building. Then I passed them each a letter. Johny shut the door from outside.

"This is from Sir Finley. I don't know what they say, but I may be able to answer questions. Also, you need to know that there's now an extra vampire in the elders. Hausmann's been turned, just after they killed her husband."

Dallas blanched. Cleary tore open the letter while cursing. Then he read it and cursed again. Having read his also, Dallas seemed to agree. I made three.

"So?" I asked, expectantly.

"You have no idea what this says," inquired Dallas. Cleary looked like he was readying another curse.

"None whatsoever. But I do know that these letters were written after I convinced Sir

Finley to do something. And I already have answers from other elders. All toe in line with their letters, I might add. Except for the Hausmann's of course. Although we did catch their assailants."

Dallas raised an eyebrow. Cleary lost his train of thought and looked up at me.

"Caught," he asked.

"Yep, all six of them. With blood on their faces, on the way out of the yard."

Dallas whistled. Cleary's eyes opened a bit wider. Yeah, that's right. Just the four of us.

"So, gentleman. What are your replies?"

They both spoke at once. I heard "insane", "nuts", and a few other terms in there.

"Okay, now that we have that out of the way. I'd suggest that you reconsider." They looked at each other. Dallas swallowed. "And no, I'm not kidding."

"Kidding or not," said Cleary. "I will not do as this letter suggests. It's a violation of my professional integrity."

"Would you be happier with a violation of your personal integrity. As in your body, as Mister Hausmann experienced less than an hour ago?" He sputtered for a response. I didn't let him get it out."Or, how about the Lady Hausmann?" I continued, struggling to keep my voice down. "She's now going through a slight diet change. Is that what you'd prefer, Sir Cleary?"

"Calm down, Sir Borden," said Dallas. So I guess I was entitled to the honorary. Oh well. "I fear I have to object for the same reason. I don't know how Sir Finley found out I know this person. But I can't, in good conscience, ask for what he suggests.

"Why not?"

"It's absolutely none of your business why not," spouted Cleary.

"Okay," I said, feigning satisfaction. "Thanks."

Cleary almost visibly stumbled at my apparent acquiescence. Dallas recovered more quickly, his relief at me backing down quickly turning to suspicion.

"Thanks. I just wanted to know why so that next time I have to kill a vampire, I can first tell them that the reason why I'm killing them is none of my business."

"What," exclaimed Cleary. "You killed a vampire?"

"Two, actually." No, I didn't gloat. At least I hope not.

"Really," said Dallas, almost to himself. "You're serious?"

"Absolutely!"

"Okay, I'll do it."

"Thank you, Sir Dallas," I said formally.

Cleary glanced at his companion, and then reached for the note in Dallas' hand. Dallas held it away. I couldn't resist.

"Now that," I said smoothly. "Sir Cleary, is none of your business."

Cleary sighed.

"I still can not do what Finley asks," he said. "I am sorry, Sir Borden. It is unethical. I can't do it."

I nodded.

"That I can give in," I said. "I was given no instructions to push the issue with you, Sir Cleary. So I will respect your professional judgment. I will however ask if there's something else that you may be possible of doing which may push things along in the direction of the suggestion?"

He thought for a moment. Then slowly nodded. "I may be able to align a few things in this general way. So I guess, tell Sir Finley, no, but I'll work on it."

"I appreciate it," I said, still slightly unsure of what exactly I was appreciating. Oh well. "With that, gentleman, I need to find a place to collapse. It's been a long day."

I shook both their hands, and then went for the door. Johny gave me a worried look when it opened.

"We might want ta," he started.

"Yeah," I know. Hurry. "Lets pick up the chicks and split."

"Uh, boss," Johny asked, then pointed to his ears. I relaxed the wards.

"That better?"

"Yep. But we don't have a check; we didn't order anything."

"Never mind," I replied. "Let's just get out of here.

Neville was gone from his game, and others had broken up a bit around him. Perhaps a mass exodus? Hopefully nothing would be waiting when we got out there. We located Sara and Tracey sitting down at a table. There was a glass of water in front of both of them. I'd have to thank Sara later.

"You girls ready?"

"Sir Neville and company left about a minute after you guys went to the back. I almost got slapped, but she'll be happier with me in the morning for not having as bad a hang over."

"Witch," said Tracey in response. She stood up, almost losing the chair behind her. I reached to steady her elbow, but then changed my mind. I saw that look in her eyes again, and backed away, nodding to the door.

Sara led the way this time, and Johny took up the rear. I walked back a little. Tracey crossed her arms and walked with her head down. As we made it across the street, Johny stepped ahead of me and passed Tracey her jacket. She took it, put it on and recrossed her arms.

I think Johny asked me a few questions at some point, but I can't remember answering them. I didn't care. I was done for the night.

Eventually, we got to the door of Sir Finley's house. Finley greeted us in a robe and slippers. I gave a terse report of the answers, the Hausmann's fate and the capture. I passed him the remaining letter, ignored his questions and staggered into the sitting room. There was a couch with my name on it. In a few seconds, there was a couch with my face on it. I passed out.

Chapter 15

Suspicion

I awoke with hair in my face again. The sun wasn't quite all the way up yet. I didn't know why I was. And I also knew that my hair isn't that long. I was still on the couch, but had turned over on my back. My sword was on the floor next to the couch on top of my raincoat. Yes. It's still borrowed. Get over it. I also couldn't help but notice that my arms were wrapped around something soft. Melina.

This was a relief for two reasons. First, because it meant that she was okay after her sojourn last night. I felt a stab of guilt for not asking about her when I got back. Second, because I was very glad there wasn't any other soft object in my arms. I was thinking of one blond in particular who happened to be acting very strange last night.

I squirmed a little, beginning the process of sitting up while trying not to wake the sleeping vampire in my arms. She felt the shift and woke anyway.

"Hi," she said softly. Then she moaned and stretched a little, turning slightly and sliding up to a sitting position. I propped my arm under me, and pulled myself up to lean against the side of the couch.

"Good morning," I said. My previous line of thoughts were short circuited slightly as Melina scooted over and kissed me. After the kiss broke. Her arms were around my neck.

"How's your arm?" she asked after setting her head against my chest.

"Fine," I replied. "How's the headache?"

"I've had worse," Melina said softly. She looked up at me. I can say that that particular look is one of the hardest to deal with for me. There's just something about a girl asking for your blood. I know, it's a little twisted. But it pretty much tops out my list.

I nodded and leaned forward slightly and kissed her on the forehead. My left hand reached behind her head, and pulled her gently toward my neck. She leaned in to me, and I felt her teeth nip at my neck. I shuddered. Then almost painlessly, Melina bit me.

When she finished, Melina kissed my neck a few times. I hugged her a bit more tightly and felt her relax into my arms. "Hmm," she mumbled. "You're spoiling me. You didn't even make me ask." Then she looked up, alarm in her eyes. "You did want me to do that, Chris, right?"

"Yes, Melina," I said, then laughed softly. Melina grinned, relieved.

"Okay," she said. "Then thank you."

"You're welcome," I replied. Melina set her head back down. Then I asked, "so, how was last night?"

"Successful," said Melina. Then she brightened up and lifted her head to look at me. "I got my permit back!"

"Good for you," I replied, returning her smile.

"It wasn't quite as eventful as yours, from what I hear, Chris. The Hausmann's was already all over the news when I got in last night. The papers this morning will probably read 'Novice Wielder Captures 6 vampires and Destroys four more in response to a turn-kill of a League Elder.'"

"Just as long as Neville's name gets smeared all over it, I'll be happy," I said. Then added, "well, I'd be a lot happier if the Hausmann's hadn't been ravaged in the process. And there were only 5 vampires and one human that they captured. I killed a vampire, but the other three got away."

Oh. Yeah. I killed another one. I felt myself falling back into that mood again, fast. I was rescued by Melina kissing me soundly. The kiss broke, and Melina turned away from me, leaning back against my chest. She drew my arms around her and lifted her feet up onto the couch. My thoughts were still whirring through last night, but I had an anchor. This nice little vampire in my arms was keeping me in place.

There was something that bugged me last night, other than the vampire killing part and the murder. It seemed to be an undercurrent of the evening. And it was slightly familiar. And it had something to do with Tracey. Why hadn't she called out to us when the four vamps were sneaking up? She should have been watching our backs. Then later, at the club. The way she was looking toward Cleary, and then toward me. It reminded me of something.

Almost like. Almost like someone else recently.

Almost like, oh.

"Crap," I said out loud.

"Huh?"

"Oh, no," my heart sunk. It was the only possible explanation. "I think we may have a problem. You remember yesterday morning, just after Jameson left?"

"Yeah," Melina said, a hint of worry in her voice.

"Before the bite, when you stood real close," I continued. "The way you acted. Well, that was almost the exact same way Tracey felt last night."

Melina stiffened, and pushed at my arms. She managed to hit both wounds, while breaking out of the embrace and whirling to face me. I'd forgotten about them. The reminder was fairly painful.

"What do you mean, 'felt'!" If the situation had been less potentially grave, I would have laughed.

"Not physically," I replied quickly in my defense. "The actions and manner. She acted, well, hungry, just like you were yesterday morning. She'd been drinking a lot all night, and kept going for cigarettes. I swear, she latched on to Cleary just like you latched on to me yesterday morning. And the look in her eyes was right on."

Melina relaxed slightly, then frowned.

"But she's not a vampire, Chris. She may have just had a few too many. Anyway, vampires don't really get drunk. Unless we're really pushing things as far as blood intake is concerned."

"Melina," I asked. "How did you know the girl in front of us in line yesterday at the office was a vampire?"

She thought for a second, then turned around and leaned against me again. "She smelled neutral. Not like any human. Not like any animal. Just neutral. Since the bite on her neck was fresh, I knew she'd been turned recently. Probably hadn't figured things out, and hadn't yet taken blood."

"And if I said I could 'see' the difference between her, you and the other humans in there," I said. "And that you looked much more like her than the other humans?"

"I'd say that you were probably able to. I do remember that you went all glowy once. If you saw Tracey like that, then I think we should be checking on her as soon as possible."

"Crap!" I was a moron. I didn't even think of it.

"Let me guess, you didn't check, did you Chris?"

"No, I didn't," I said sheepishly. "So all I have is a suspicion. But I tell you Melina, she acted just like a hungry vampire."

"If all you're comparing her to is me from the other morning," said Melina, frowning. "Then you also have to factor that some part of that was a girl attracted to a guy. Not just being hungry."

I didn't know how to respond to that, so I wrapped my arms a little tighter around her waist.

"It probably didn't help that it was mutual," I finally managed to get out. It sounded a bit lame.

"Assuming Tracey is a vamp," said Melina after a long silence. "She could be getting blood from here through the estate sources, or some other source. And that could be either here, or back on the other side. I don't think she's hunting for it. That usually is only a last resort. And this is a well trained, resourceful and intelligent woman we're talking about here."

"Whoa, there," I replied. "We haven't even confirmed she's a vampire yet. I was stupid, and didn't even think about checking. My little "glowing" sessions were before I had a clue what I was doing."

"And you do now?" asked Melina playfully. I pinched her side and she jumped a little, which hit my left arm again. I winced and cried out slightly. "Sorry! What's wrong?"

"I seem to be working on symmetrical injuries," I replied flatly. Melina had captured my left arm in her hands and was pushing the remainants of the sleeve back to look at the bandage from Janice. She turned my arm over and clucked her teeth. It had bled through the bandage a bit.

"We'll have to change this," she said. "Edge parallel to the arm, sideways stoke, downward slope? What the hell were you doing?"

"Yes, Ma'am."

"Oh, be serious, Chris. These are a lot worse than plain stabs or slashes. Grazes like this love to get infected. Were you on your knees or something?"

"I'd really rather not talk about it."

"Another?"

"Fine," I sighed. "Yes, another. I'm now at a whopping two. This one couldn't have been more than a little while turned. She was still figuring out how to use a sword. Strong, but not skilled. I dove under one of her baseball bat style swings. And..."

I choked up. Melina turned around in my arms and kissed me. Finally, I relented and let go of my despair, and let myself enjoy the kiss. Melina broke away. Her breath fast, I could feel her heart beating quicker than before.

"I think we should probably get moving," she said softly. I nodded. Yeah, it was probably a pretty good idea. Melina slowly pulled her arms from behind my neck and stood up from the couch. She then bent over and picked up the coat and my sword and set them in a chair. I just noticed her hoodie was on the back of another chair with a backpack, her sword purse and her dagger. I guess she'd retrieved it from Trevor.

"Sir Finley said something about a lunch meeting with Samantha," said Melina, "Tracey should be starting back to classes today at UCLA. And since Samantha's in L. A. on a case, we can probably try and get by Tracey's. Do you think you can do your "glow" thing and tell? I'd hate to just like, ask her. That would be bad if we were wrong."

There was that "we" again, I thought. Twice in a few minutes. I think I was beginning to like it a little.

"It's not Monday, is it?" I asked, fearing the worst. I was supposed to have been back in Florida and at work by Monday. Wait a minute. I went into the store on Friday, spent the night at Melina's. Then all day Saturday, which was yesterday, tramping around town. Now this morning. Should be Sunday. Right?

"Of course it's Monday," she said. I looked up at her, wondering if she was feeling okay. I looked down at my watch. The one that had been off bad in the past few days. It read 7:13 am California time. Monday. The heck?

"Um, I hate to sound like a stupid little kid. But what the heck happened with the extra day. I mean, two here and three there. It doesn't seem to add up."

Melina smiled. "You just answered your own question. It's about a 2/3 ratio between the two sides. If it hadn't been for all the extra physical activities you'd been engaged in Chris, you probably would have noticed it more. Days are longer here. It takes some getting used to. We have a different calendar."

I shrugged. What the heck. Everything else was wacko, why not the day cycle too. I looked at Melina, then shifted to that "other" perspective that I remembered from the office. Melina looked about as I remembered. Now I just needed someone for comparison. And some water. And the restroom wouldn't hurt much either.

"I'm pretty sure I can get the "glow" view to work. You look like I remember, but I'll need a human as a control just to make sure."

Melina nodded.

"Think we can scare up breakfast? And what are the chances of me bumming a set of Sir Finley's clothes? On second thought, I think they'd be a little long."

"Martin's about your size," Melina offered.

"Oh, you noticed, did you?" I asked playfully. Melina blushed slightly. Then she held her hands out to me. I reached for them and was pulled to my feet. I think she was getting her strength back. He right hand never released my left, as she pulled us towards the door.

"It's not my fault he's had a crush on me since he was about ten. In his defense, he was the perfect gentleman last night."

"While, I'm afraid I was a little lacking with patience where miss Finley was concerned. At one point I vaporized a bunch of brandy just as she was trying to sip it."

Melina laughed. "I guess you have gotten past your little control issue?"

"More or less. I learned not to blow up anything electrical. But I had a lot of fun turning Sir Naber's furniture to twigs. He saw reason when I began to go after the paintings."

"You serious?" she asked. "You were blowing up things?"

"Sure, like I did the chair."

Melina was silent with thought. Great. So does that mean I shouldn't have been causally demolishing wooden objects? Maybe I should have been killing more vampires instead. Yeah. Right.

"Is that another one of those, 'how they heck did you do that' things?"

She nodded, her hand on the door knob. Okay, so I guess I'll just forget to tell her about the drop net shield thing that I used on the goons. Or the cigarette skeet shoot.

"Breakfast, Tracey's apartment, then launch with Samantha," she said after a few seconds of thought. "That sound okay? We'll have a little time between the two to kill."

"Fine with me, but I have two questions," I replied. "One, what do we tell Tracey? I'm assuming you have her address," Melina nodded. "Okay, then two, can I call my boss during the dead time. I was supposed to be back in Jacksonville this morning. About, oh three hours and twenty minutes ago actually." I hoped calling it "dead time" wasn't some sign.

"Should work," said Melina. "But please don't mention anything about, ah, what we discussed until we..."

Melina had changed gears, and then stopped all together. I head steps in the hall, and nodded my agreement just as there came a knock from outside. She opened the double doors and the butler peaked in from the hall.

"Breakfast?" he asked. The guy didn't seem phased by how fast the door opened. I didn't remember catching his name the night before. Drat.

"Perfect timing," I said and then put my hand on the small of Melina's back , ushering her through the door. I had a thought of returning for my sword, but felt it may be a bit rude. "Is there a chance I can appropriate a change of clothes from Martin?"

The butler frowned and began walking toward the dining room. "If Sir wishes, but the young master's clothes are, well..."

"That's quite okay," I replied with a wave of my left hand. My right had stayed on Melina's waist on its own accord. "I'm only a few years out of college myself. I'm sure just a pair of jeans and a plain shirt will do."

"In that case, Sir, I believe we can manage. Will Sir be requiring a bath be drawn?"

I was almost grating my teeth. This was too much.

"Please! Just call me Chris," I pleaded. "And no, but I'll probably just need to be pointed at a shower. Or I could head back to the Wielder house."

The butler looked shocked. Actually, shocked wasn't the word. Mortified. Melina giggled. I wasn't sure whether it was asking him to use my first name, or the suggestion that I'd find what I needed at another house. It was rather funny.

Just as we neared the doorway to the dining room, Melina pulled off to the side a little. I slowed and glanced at her.

"I think I'll go up and take one of those myself," she said. I saw her eyes glance at the doorway for a second. Strange. I nodded, and let my hand slide off her waist as she turned and headed back to the sitting room. I walked through the door. Some part of me seriously wished I'd grabbed my sword. Then again, maybe it was best that I hadn't.

Sir Naber was sitting at the table with Sir Finley working himself up to a frenzy. It sounded like he was making a connection between my rash behavior and that of a certain other character. A character who, I might add, had just managed to weasel her way out of the confrontation which was about to begin. Trust me. It was better that I didn't have my sword.

"Good morning, Sir Finley," I said loudly from just behind Sir Naber. He jumped and bumped his arm on the bottom of the table. Silverware hopped in response and all the glasses on the table showed little waves. I put a working smile on my face and went around to the other side of the table, opposite the sputtering elder. Just to be courteous, I nodded in his direction before sitting. The butler looked at me expectantly. I looked at him expectantly. He didn't look like he was going to relent.

I looked at Sir Finley's plate, and then pointed to it.

"I'll have what he's having. And coffee, black. And a tall glass of water," I said. No sense in making them work too hard, I thought. Just order what's already out. Makes things simple. The butler nodded and went out through a side door in the direction of the kitchen.

"Oh, don't let me interrupt," I said, breaking the silence. Sir Finley looked like he was amused. "Please, Sir Naber, do continue."

"I think David would rather not," said Sir Finley. "Did you really turn his Victorian roll top desk into this." Finley indicated a few splinters of wood on the edge of the table cloth.

"That looks more like the end table that was next to the Victorian roll top desk," I replied. Naber rolled his eyes. "But I guess it would be pretty hard to tell."

"'Was' being the operative word," inquired Sir Finley. "I assume?"

"Exactly," I replied. A tray came through the door followed by a woman probably in her early twenties. She seemed rather shaky with the tray. The reason was immediately obvious as the butler steamed out on her heals, his full attention focused on her back. She set the tray down in front of me with precision. I thanked her. She curtsied and left, ignoring the butler. He examined the tray, shook his head, and left. Yeah. It was like a picometer to the left and just an femtoparsec too far from the front edge of the table. Shame shame.

The coffee was really good. And so were the eggs and bacon. The pancakes weren't quite my thing, but I put enough syrup over them to make it work for me. I realized I wasn't paying attention when my name got called. I looked up.

"Hmm," I said, mouth full of bacon and some pancake.

"I was just telling Sir Naber of the Hausmann's."

"Oh," I replied, then swallowed. "How's she doing?"

"Resting, and mad as hell. But she should be recovered in a few days. Violent turnings like that can be rather rough on people. Added with George's death, and, well, it's a lot. On the up side, she expressed her gratitude for the capture of her assailants. Good thing you guys got them before the shift change in the mage police. Everything got processed just in time. It's all over the news."

"Yeah. Sir Neville didn't look too happy about it," I said.

"You saw Sir Neville last night?" asked Naber. Yeah dude, I went over his house and we like bonded, man. Just kicked back and got to know one an other.

"Club," I murmured through a mouth of egg. I think it sounded enough like the word to let it ride.

"Oh."

"Well, I'm already running late myself, David. And I'm sure Chris will want to get going soon as well. So if you'll please..."

I looked up at Naber. He looked at me. Yeah, you. Not me. That sounded like you just got dismissed. Naber didn't seem to get the point.

"Sir Naber," said Sir Finley with a little more strength. "Sir Borden and I have some things to discuss and I am already running behind for the day. If you would be so kind as to..."

Ah, the sun rose. Naber stood and gave a slight bow. "Good day gentleman," he said. After giving me one last dirty look, he turned and left the room. I drank down some coffee, then looked over at Sir Finley. He was holding his napkin to his mouth and laughing into it. I grinned slightly.

He finally got a hold of himself and set down the napkin with a sigh.

"Well, Chris," said Finley. "I'm sorry you had to walk in on David's venting session. He's broken up, ah, probably not the best word; lets try peeved, about his furniture. But he did say he didn't hold it against you. Actually the first words out of his mouth when he got here were 'what the hell are we going to do with such a competent wielder on our side.' Of course, that quickly took a side seat to an all out rant."

"I am sorry about the furniture," I said. "Anything I should know for the lunch meeting with Samantha?"

"Yeah, ward the hell out of place and the heaven too. Other than that? Keep Melina close. She hasn't been out in a while. I assume she's going with you?"

"That's the plan."

"Good," he said. "Oh, and some people in this league aren't quite as appreciative of her as others. David for example. Just ignore them."

"I figured as much," I replied. "And where are you, Sir Finley?"

"I'm definitely on her side," he said. "I think we should dispense with the pleasantries too. Just call be Bob."

"Gotcha," I said. "So is that why you offered Melina the wine last night?"

"You caught that," he asked. Of course I caught it. And I also noticed she didn't drink any. I nodded. "It's supposed to be common courtesy. A teaspoon full in a glass of wine. I'll always offer it to Melina, but she'll probably never take any. Not from me, at least not anymore."

I looked up from my coffee in askance.

"You'll have to ask Melina," said Finley. "Basically, I made a big mistake where Melina was concerned once. She called me on it, and I lost her service. I'm still trying to find a way to get her forgiveness. It's turned into a bit of a ritual."

Interesting. Melina walked through the door with a fresh pair of jeans and a baby doll t-shirt. I had trouble looking back to Finley.

"Well, Bob," I said. "I'm sure you need to get going. And we should too. What's your butler's name? I need to track him down about some borrowed clothes from Martin."

Finley stood, and looked over at Melina as she plopped down into the chair next to me.

"Morning, Melina. His name's Mister Graves." Finley moved to leave.

"Fitting. He have a first name?"

"Not that I know of," Finley frowned. "Actually, I have no bloody idea. It never came up."

I laughed, Finley smiled in response and left. I looked over at Melina, who had snatched a piece of bacon from my plate and was nibbling at it. I pushed the remainder of my breakfast toward her; one egg, three more pieces of bacon, a piece of toast and a pancake.

"Well, I'm going to go take a shower," I said. "Do you have any idea what Mister Graves' first name is?"

"No clue Chris," she said shaking her head. The side door opened and the maid came through.

"See if you can get it out of her," I pointed. The maid stopped in horror for a few seconds, then came forward and set a tray with a glass of red wine and another with water in front of Melina. I left to track down that shower.

Fifteen minutes later I emerged showered, shaved and rebandaged. I felt a world better. I was starting to get concerned about the blood loss I'd undergone in the past few days, both consensual and forced. But I seemed to be working okay at the moment. I'd really have to try and cut down on the forced blood letting though.

I found Melina talking with the maid in the dining room. She was laughing at a joke, but stopped abruptly when I entered. Oh, well. The maid took the two trays from the table and left.

"Hey, you," I said. "You look nice." Melina blushed. "So, did you get his first name?"

"He doesn't seem to have one," she replied, standing up and walking towards me. She checked both forearms and seemed satisfied with the new bandages. "We ready?"

"Just need to require my weapon," I said, taking her left hand. We headed to the sitting room. I realized as I strapped the belt back around and picked up the coat that I had no idea how we were getting to the other side.

"Um, I know this is probably another stupid novice main-sider question. But how are we getting over?"

Melina laughed. I was starting to like hearing that. "Silly, we obviously can't use any of the gates here since they're all tuned to their people. We need to use yours."

"Obviously," I said. "I have a gate? Oh, yeah. Comes with the house."

She nodded and lead the way to the front door. We let ourselves out and walked hand in hand back to the wielder house. I let my thoughts go, enjoying the slow walk, and thinking through the previous day. Melina seemed happy to leave me to my revere. After a few minutes, we entered the gate to the house and walked through the garden up to the door.

"I guess I'll have to find someone to tend to this place," I said almost to myself.

"Just wait a few days," Melina replied, a half smile on her face. I wondered whether I should be worried. I let it go. I opened the door, and went inside. Yep, still unlived in. But

I actually had the mental capacity to notice that it wasn't dusty. Probably a spell.

Melina walked us towards the rear of the house. And then into a room which was the mirror image of the front foyer. I shifted and looked at the door. It was strange. I guessed it was the gate. Melina put her hand on the knob.

"Oh, you'll probably want to shut down your wards. I hear they can be pretty nasty when mixed with gates."

I swallowed. My thoughts returned to that hellphone call the night before. Yeah, Chris, don't go mixing there. I dropped all of them. She opened the door and we went through.

.

Chapter 16

Los Angeles

I gasped. The view was breathtaking. Then I noticed I didn't have much yard space. I spotted a building on the left which was probably a garage. The house apparently had a presence on both sides, like Charles's store. This half was in the hills overlooking LA. The view was probably only good this time of the year, when the rain washed away all the smog. There were still pockets of it, but much of the valley appreaed clear due to the recent rains.

The weird part was, the house faced the view. The driveway went around the front of the house from the garage and must have met a road somewhere. I wasn't sure how much land this was on, but it may have been a lot. All I saw around the house was trees.

We walked towards a nondescript sedan parked on at the foot of the stairs. Obviously a rental. The doors were open and keys in the ignition. I glanced at Melina.

"You driving, Melina?"

"Can't," she replied. "Never learned."

She hopped in the passenger side and fastened her seatbelt. I went around and opened the drivers door. The seat was way forward. I slid it back, then popped the hood. Melina gave me a look. I went and checked the brake fluid, oil, coolant and power steering fluid. Then, I took off the sword and raincoat and set them in the back seat. I then hopped in and started it up.

"I think that's the first time I ever saw anyone check under a hood unless something went wrong, Chris. That was weird."

"Just checking for bombs," I said flatly. She looked over at me in shock. "Just kidding! I just don't like driving a car without knowing if there's any brake fluid in the reservoir. Chalk it up to a silly engineer's habit."

Melina shook her head as I put the automatic in gear and pulled around the side of the house along the drive. She withdrew a manila envelope from the glove box and showed it to me. It had my name on it.

"What's inside?" I asked. She opened the flap and extracted a few pieces of paper, a check book, and a small envelope with what looked like a few hundred dollars. Real money. This side money.

"It's from Samantha," said Melina, setting the envelope on her knees and examining the documents. "She says she's sorry for not getting a permanent vehicle, and that this was a rental. The letter," she held up one of the other papers, " is a bank note certifying that there's enough money in the account to buy a new one if you want. She suggested doing it today, and returning the rental as soon as possible."

"Cool," I said. "How much." Probably like 3 grand or something.

"Only a hundred and seventy five thousand."

I almost forgot to put on the brakes that I'd gone through so much trouble to make sure had hydraulic fluid before exiting the drive. A dump truck heading to the right beeped at me. The car skidded a little and halted inches from the road.

"That's quite a lot of dough," I said. On an starting engineer's salary, that's still like 3 years worth of work. I pulled out, taking a right. It looked like I had a better chance of acquiring a major road following the truck. It was empty, so was probably returning from dumping somewhere. "You know where we're going?"

"I haven't been out in a while," Melina replied grimly. "But get us near campus, and I can find her apartment."

"So what's between you and Sir Finley?" I had to ask. I mean, maybe I was looking out for her. Maybe I was just curious.

"What do you mean?" she asked slowly. You know what I mean. Probably.

"He mentioned something about him making a mistake where you were concerned sometime ago..."

"Oh," she said. At first I thought she was relieved. "Yeah. That. He did."

Okay, to be relieved seemed a bit too presumptuous at the moment. I let it go. I took a right into town on a promising two laner. After a little ways I found a freeway ramp and took it as well, speeding things up a bit.

"What did it take to get the permit?" I asked, trying to get some sort of conversation going. At least without getting into dangerous waters. It didn't look like it was going to work.

"Blood test," Melina replied, her expression blank. She was fiddling with the latch on the glove box. I saw a sign for the college. 8 miles.

If it wasn't for the crazy drivers, I'd have tried to grab her hand or something. I seemed to have a slightly troubled vampire on my hands again. I preferred the laughing, giggling, bright one. Finally, I couldn't take it anymore.

"What's wrong, Melina?" I asked, risking a quick look in her direction. She was still focused on the glove box latch. Of course, not one, but two drivers saw my moment of weakness and both tried to take the gap in my lane. I snapped my attention back, checked my six and hunkered down. Fortuitously, the two lane changers sorted themselves out and I didn't have to do anything to disturb the woman in the car behind me. Who was doing her makeup. With her bumper six inches away from mine. At seventy five miles an hour.

I noticed Melina hadn't replied. I risked another glance. She didn't look too good. Then it dawned on me.

"You don't get car sick, do you?" Could be. I mean, this chick probably hadn't been in a car in a while. May not be used to it. "You do, don't you?"

Melina nodded slightly. Figures.

"I'd highly suggest looking up, then," I said. "Look at the horizon in front of us, and not out at the sides. It'll help."

I saw her look up in my peripheral vision.

"You're not going to laugh, are you?" she asked softly.

"No," I replied. "If you're not used to it, you're not used to it. There's nothing to laugh at."

I noted the exit sign. It took some slice driving skills, but I cut into the right lane, and caught the ramp with a few feet of run to spare. Several horns went off as the traffic went past the ramp. Melina's left hand was locked into the seat edge. Her right was making rents in the arm rest.

"Easy, Mel," I said. "It's a rental."

She looked down at the arm rest she was in the process of mutilating and then relaxed slightly. I took a left toward campus. A motorcycle whipped past my mirror doing about 30 over. Melina yelped. I guess I should have mentioned it was coming. The whole lane splitting concept was still foreign to me, being from Florida.

Melina mumbled something.

"Say again?"

"Right turn," she said a little louder. I took it. After a little ways, Melina looked around and frowned. "Sorry Chris, last road, left."

"Sokay," I replied, hanging into a turn lane to pull a u-turn. There was a 'No U-turn' sign up. The two cars in front of me both pulled U-turns. I came up to the line, thought hard, and pulled into the parking lot of a strip mall. Just as I was swinging around a row of cars to get back around and complete the "turn" a cop came out of a gas station parking lot and pulled over the car that had been behind me in the turn lane. I turned right and went past them, taking the road Melina indicated.

"I think it's about eight or nine blocks on the right. Look for something like 'Periwinkle' or 'Penington' in the name."

That was helpful. I slowed, someone beeped at me, so I flashed my brake lights. The huge suv took a run at my rear bumper, and then went around me when I didn't flinch. "Piccadilly?"

"Yes! That's it!"

I threw the directional on, yanked on the wheel and screeched into the parking lot, a pickup truck inches from my tail. I slowed the rental and hit a speed bump a little too fast with the front tires. The rear transition was more sedate.

"Which apartment is hers?"

"P17A," she said.

I swung the car over a few more speed bumps around the back side, located P building and saw from the numbers that 1 meant first floor up. I found a spot and pulled the sedan into it, yanking on the parking break and putting it in park. I turned the key and popped the door, releasing my seat belt. Melina rushed out of the car and rested her hands on the hood, with her head hanging. I got out, and went around to her side.

"You okay?" I asked, setting my hand on her elbow.

"Just give me a minute," Melina replied. I squeezed her arm reassuringly and then went to the driver side to pull my coat and sword form the back seat. Using the coat as a wrapper, I wound it around the sword and tucked the long bundle under my left arm. Melina looked up at me.

"You could just ward it, you know," she said. I guess I could. I went past her to the passenger side, tried rolling the sword out of the coat and managed to drop it in the process. It clattered in its sheath on the ground. Melina winced. With the coat back in the back seat, and the sword strapped to my belt and warded, I returned to Melina.

"That bad?" I asked. Melina turned to glare at me.

"There's no possible reason for so many people to be going so fast with complete disregard for people's lives! That is absolutely insane! How can you possible stand it!"

I weathered the onslaught. Then smiled slightly. "Feel better now, Melina?"

She cracked a smile. "Yeah, I guess. I forgot how much cars scared the shit out of me. It will probably take me a little while to come to grips with the fact that we got here in one piece. Oh well, let's go."

I extended my hand, and she took it. We headed for the stairway to the 1st floor balcony of P building. Room 17A was to the left of the stairway about three doors down. Melina stopped a little before the door way.

"Any thoughts on how to handle this?" she asked quietly. "If she's home?"

"It's your plan," Melina gave me a look. "Okay, so I had a major part in it too. Well, just say I'm apologizing for treating her like a little spoiled brat last night. I'm here 'calling', without calling first, I might add, to make amends."

I got another look.

"What?"

"That's pretty bad," she said. "You've been reading too many books."

"Someone else said that to me recently," I paused. "Lady Weiss. Nice lady. She said to give you her regards."

"She did?"

"Yes. Also wanted to make sure you were well."

"Really," said Melina. Okay, fine. Don't be happy that the lady was thinking about you. I gave up and walked the remaining steps to the door, giving it three knocks. Nothing. I rung the door bell. Nothing. Waited for a little while. Knocked again. Nothing.

"So now what?"

"You're asking me?" Melina replied sweetly. "It's you're plan, remember? I could always open the door if you wanted."

"You mean..."

"The jam's not that strong. If you ward out the sound, I can be in in a second."

"Melina, I'm ashamed that you'd even think such a thing. I mean really," I was having a little bit of fun. I was also concentrating on the lock. Hard. "I mean, how could you even suggest breaking into this girls apartment forcibly. Especially when there are other ways."

Melina raised an eyebrow at me. I reached forward and tried the handle. It wasn't locked but there was a dead bolt. The door wouldn't budge. I used six little shields in the air under the tumblers to push them into the right place, then another pair with opposite polarities to cause the whole core to spin, pulling back the bolt. The lock snicked open, I turned the handle and pushed. Melina giggled. We stepped into the apartment, shutting the door behind us.

I actually expected the place to be neat; clean. It wasn't. Well, I shouldn't say that. I felt that it most likely had been at one point. But that point had passed into near oblivion. It seemed that the miss Finley had undergone a change in lifestyle. Or at least in what aspects of her life she cared about.

The open living room and kitchen area had been painstakingly decorated at one point. The coffee table had stacks of magazines and howto's relating to popular fashions. On a little table in a corner, there were neat little dividers in several inboxes. All of which had neatly stacked bills and papers folded out and arranged chronologically. On the same table, on the kitchen counter, the sofa, and the floor were more recent bills and papers. They were not quite filed as their like documents on the table. I checked the last date on the neat stack of phone bills. Almost eight months ago.

Melina had gone into the kitchen and opened the frige. She sniffed and clucked her teeth.

"Let me guess," I said. "Blood?"

"You better look for your self."

I swallowed and crossed the living room to the kitchen. Melina moved aside to let me look in the refrigerator. I looked. I closed the door. "We have a vampire here?" I asked, tentatively.

"Probably. It may not be Tracey though. She may also have one hanging out with her." I sniffed. "A lot," she added. I went to the check the bathroom. No, I'm not going to tell you what was in the frige. Use your imagination. I don't want to think about it.

What was it with girls and hanging sexy underwear up in the bathroom. It was just plain wrong. Why not just hang it out the window or something; like a flag. Well, then it wouldn't be quite as much of a tease. I did not see any signs of another inhabitant in the bathroom. I followed Melina to the bedroom.

"If there's someone living here besides her, he or she either has blond hair, or is extremely meticulous with their body's leavings. I didn't find anything other than Tracey Blond in the bathroom."

The bed was a mess of sheets and bed clothes. It looked like someone had thrown a slight temper tantrum in the room. Most of the furniture had war wounds of some sort. The desk was missing a drawer. Which was in pieces on the other side of the room where it had encountered a lamp and the wall forcefully. A second lamp had been used to hack at the surface of a night table. Or at least that's what I thought could have caused the slashes in the wood surface. One side of the bed had several marks that looked distinctly like fingers had pierced through the covering and torn at the insides. There were also holes in the walls. Lots of holes in the walls. And some in the floor. The ceiling fan was missing a blade.

"I'm thinking she either really doesn't like her neighbors, or she's absolutely ticked at someone."

"Or herself," Melina said biting her lip. I had a strange feeling that was coming from personal experience for Melina. I had a strong urge to hug her. Instead, I took another look around the room, trying to ignore the damages. Other than the fact that Tracey wore predominantly thong underwear, not many bras, and hadn't been swimming in the past 8 months, I didn't know what else to look at. The swimming goggles and several speedos were folded neatly on the corner of a desk under a shirt which was missing a few buttons.

Melina held up an undershirt, then sniffed at it carefully. I glanced at it. She waved it back and forth in front of me.

"That doesn't fit."

"Not one bit, Chris," said Melina, dropping the shirt back where she found it. I'd missed it entirely. Probably the overload from all the other clothes hanging around which were a little more interesting. Some detective I was.

"That was blood on the collar, wasn't it, Melina?"

"Yes, it was.," she said. "And I can't imagine Tracey wearing that shirt. It smells male. And with the blood, would indicate... Well, it still could be something else."

"Sure. That, coupled with this mess, plus the refrigerator," I shuddered. "Seems to point towards a vampire who is suffering."

Melina looked at me with wonder. "How do you do that, Chris?"

"What? Point out the obvious. But you're right. It's still all circumstantial based on an illegal and highly improbable keyless entry. I think we should probably leave."

"There's a class schedule on the refrigerator door," Melina offered helpfully. "We could track her down on campus, let you have a look at her, and then know for sure."

"You look. I don't want to step within five feet of that fridge again. I don't..." I paused. There was a sound at the door. Then loud banging.

"Miss Finley," a gruff male voice yelled loudly. "I know I heard someone in there! You owe two months rent! And I know you're good for it! Open up." Then more banging. I went, unlocked the door and opened it. The guy on the other side wasn't very tall, but he had the forearms of a lifetime worker. And the gut of a lifetime beer drinker.

"Can I help you?" I asked. Acting like I hadn't heard his bellows through the door.

"Where's Tracey," he replied. As if I knew exactly where she was. "You her boyfriend? Oh." He saw Melina behind me. "Brother than?"

"How much does she owe?"

"1300. Should be 1500 because its late. And another 750 in a week!"

"Can you get my check book dear?" I asked Melina. She nodded and walked past us through the doorway. I passed her the keys on her way. The guy tried to use the opportunity to come inside. I didn't move from the doorway. This is our business, buddy. Keep out.

"I assume that full payment, including next month's rent will be sufficient. Since you'd be getting it all at once?"

"How do I know the check'll clear?"

"How do I know you're her landlord," I replied. "Who do I make it out to?"

"George Williamson."

He frowned, then tried to look past me again. I stepped forward. Melina returned with the check book and a pen from the car and passed it to me. The landlord backed away to give me room to write the check. Of course, I made it out for only $2,050. He didn't need the late fees, since he was getting next month early. I tore the check off and passed it to him. He examined it, then smiled slightly.

"Is there anything else?" I asked, prodding him along.

"No," he replied. "But she better have the next few in early. And I still have to deal with her changing the lock. She hasn't given me a key yet."

"Thank you," I said as dismissively as I could. He took the point and left.

Melina put her hands in her jeans pockets and stepped inside past me. I went over the to the refrigerator door, Melina took a look through the papers on the table in the living room. I checked my watch.

"What time are we meeting Samantha?" I also just noticed we may be a little under dressed for the occasion. I'd have to find out where we were meeting her first.

"Two hours," she said, glancing at the wall clock. "It's at a small Italian place near her office." I nodded, then examined the schedule on the door from as far away as I could remain. Looks like our vamp would be at economics for the next half an hour.

"Someday, Chris," said Melina almost whimsically. "You're going to tell how you take in what you just saw and come to the conclusion of 'suffering vampire'. Then you pay her rent. I mean, she could be enjoying herself. And don't go and give me that, what is it, 'Occum's razor' thing either. Because you haven't eliminated anything major yet, and it just so happens that the simplest solution is for Tracey to be living her life as vampires naturally tend towards."

I glanced up at her. "Ah," I started. So that's what she meant earlier. I'd have to ask her about the physics reference later. I also couldn't tell whether Melina was mad at me, or amused, or what. I picked exasperated and went on. I also decided not to answer. She did say 'someday' after all.

"Tracey has Microeconomics for the next half an hour," I said. "I think we can catch her at that, I do my glowy vampire detection thingy, we tell her about the rent, and then leave. We can make it to the meeting in plenty of time."

"Two things," replied Melina, while looking at a bill. I think it was a phone bill, but couldn't tell for sure from across the room. "First, you don't know if she's at class. And second, you were going to call your boss back in the sunshine state. Also, you just ignored me."

She was smiling, so I stuck my tongue out at her. "I think Tracey's more important right now. The last thing we need is a vampire, hunting out on her own, and the daughter of one of the league elders. Curtis can wait a while. He probably hasn't shown up to work yet either. He tends to take a long time getting in on Mondays."

"Any chance we can walk?" Melina had crossed to the refrigerator to write the class location on a post it note recovered from the table. "It's only a little ways."

"Nah," I said. "We take the car. And I'll promise to try and be good." Melina pocketed the post-it, dropped the pen on the counter and grabbed my arm, pulling me towards the door.

"You're getting me back for all the walking, aren't you?" she asked as we walked through the door. I nodded.

"Of course," I agreed, turning to the door lock. A quick thought set the tumblers and another turned it over, setting the bolt.

"I think Trevor would hate you if you did that in front of him," Melina said, pulling me towards the stair.

"Wait until I get to practicing," I replied. "Then I'll show him my super-man impression." Melina gave me a reproachful glance. "I'm just kidding," I added hastily. "Honest."

"Sure."

Back in the car, I pulled out of the parking lot onto the busy street towards campus. Melina pointed toward a side road, and I took it.

"I threw myself off a building," she said without expression as we stopped with a row of cars going through a 3 way stop sign.

"Huh," I didn't make the connection.

"Sir Finley ordered me to do something he shouldn't have. I threw myself off a building. He apologized."

"Oh," that wasn't cool. "Ouch."

"He's now a little more careful," said Melina. She cracked a slight smile. "Actually, a lot more careful. I happened to have landed in a rather public place. I believe it was a bit tough for him to cover up on this side."

We were now second in line for the intersection. "I'm sorry, Melina," I said. "But wasn't that a little drastic?"

"Perhaps," she said, then rubbed her side, almost as if remembering something. "The point was to stop myself from doing what he told me to do. It worked."

"I'll bet," I reached out and set my hand on her leg. She covered it with hers. We came to a stop. I started to bring the car forward after the guy opposite me in a pickup truck entered the intersection going straight. Well, I thought he was going straight. It wasn't as if he had his directional on, or anything. He turned left in front of me. I slammed on the brakes and the wheels slid a bit on the dirt over the road. The truck honked at me and continued his turn.

I continued through the intersection.

"Sorry about the super-man comment," I said, after a few seconds.

"It's okay, Chris. That was a few years ago. I'm not going to ever take wine from Sir Finley again, but I'm also over it. He was in a bad situation, and made a poor decision. I don't hold it against him."

"Okay," I said, hoping it was. "So where to?"

"Keep going for a while. Then we'll have to find a parking space. I never got to drive on this campus. And anyway it's changed a lot since I went here."

I looked over at Melina in askance, then back quickly. A bike hopped a curb in front of me and cut across the street. She was going fast enough that I didn't have to slow. My kind of transportation.

"Yes, I went here for a few terms," said Melina, answering my unasked question. "I had to drop out when...Well, that was about the time of the whole Willie thing. I never got to come back. My GPA sucked anyway."

"Not a morning person?" I asked. I could see her blush slightly. "What'd you major in?"

"That's the building right there," she pointed. I nodded and began looking for a parking space. Fat chance. "I was in criminology for a while. Then switched to biology, which is what I had wanted to do originally. I was about two years into the major, with some general stuff out of the way."

"I don't think I'm going to be able to park. Well, not legally anyway. I don't have a decal." I pulled a U turn, and then went into a full lot next to the building. Passing a few cars idling in wait for people to leave the lot, I hopped a curb with the two passenger side wheels and nestled the car in as far out of the way as I could. "This should do," I said.

I shut the car off, unclipped my seat belt and opened the door. Melina hadn't moved yet. Then finally unfastened the belt and opened the door.

"Hey," I said. "It should be fine. It looks like it's going to rain. Parking services people hate to give out tickets unless it's sunny and warm outside."

Melina shook her head and began walking across the grass toward a sidewalk that lead to the building. "You don't know this campus, Chris; it will have a ticket when we get back."

"We'll see."

Melina laughed. "You warded it, didn't you? Well, I hope no one hits it."

I looked back over my shoulder at the car, suddenly a bit worried. Yeah, crap. She was right. I dropped the wards. It still looked like it was going to rain. Hopefully it wouldn't get a ticket.

"You have no idea how much I always wanted to just hide my car on a campus. Thanks for bursting my balloon. It was kind of stupid."

Melina laughed again. I followed her closely into the building and up the stairs to the second floor. She stopped at the doors of a large lecture hall on the second floor.

"This the room?"

"Yep," she said, standing on her tip toes and looking through the small square window in the left door. The right door didn't have one, so I waited. Melina frowned and looked over at me. "I don't see her."

I considered for a moment, and then looked through the window at the board. They were going through marginal cost and average total cost stuff for a monopoly market system. I knew that stuff. It was horrid. The professor, an average height, gray haired white male, advanced the slide and began comparing two graphs. It looked like one was for a monopoly system and the other for a competitive market system. They had about 40 minutes left of class. And this guy looked like he was good for another hour. Most of the students looked like they'd glazed over some time ago.

"Shall we end class early, Melina?" I asked with a hint of a smile on my face. "Or just wait."

Melina stepped closer to me, her eyes alight a bit, sharing my mischief. "What do you have in mind?"

I laughed maniacally. She grinned. I glanced through the window at the projector screen behind the professor. With a thought, I opened up a new web browser window on the computer screen, and closed the presentation he was using. From memory, I brought up a web-site which deals primarily with hackers, www.2600.com. I browsed around a little on that, while the professor kept talking about how the two market styles maximize profit.

A few people were now actually paying attention to the screen. Deciding I needed a little more of a distraction, I opened up the volume control dialogue and turned it way down. Then I switched over to a new browser window and brought up a college radio station from one of the Florida Universities that had an online stream. As usual, this particular station had some pretty wacko, but good, music. It loaded up. I slowly increased the volume.

The professor tried talking over it at first, then gave up and looked around at the class, trying to find our where it was coming from. Some girl in the front row pointed behind him to the screen. He glanced back over his shoulder and frowned in surprise. He then looked over at the computer screen in perplextion. I chuckled, then switched back to the hackers site. I continued reading through some of the front page articles. The professor walked over to the PC quickly and grabbed the mouse. He started to close the window, but before he could get the mouse to the button, I'd opened another three on the same page. Deciding he wasn't savvy enough to just close the program, I kept popping them open. Within a few seconds, I'd generated a memory error on the machine. I wasn't quite finished yet.

Conversation was starting to ramp up in the lecture hall from the students. The professor's face was bright red, and he was closing windows like mad with the mouse. A few students saw things as they were and began packing up. Then I couldn't resist. I closed all the open windows, and opened a text editor. After increasing the font size to 42 point, I typed rhythmically;

"All your base are belong to us."

I think that did it. The professor turned away from the computer and looked out at the class.

"I think someone it playing a cruel joke on us," he said, almost calmly.

The same girl who pointed earlier piped up, "It may be a virus."

"Well," he continued, ignoring the comment. "It seems we have been the victim of a hacker. I believe that concludes this lecture. Remember to read chapter 15 for next time. And look over the sample problems on the web-site."

Most of his comments were lost as 80 students all began moving around at once. Melina and I moved back from the door and stood together in a small alcove near the water fountains where we could watch the doors.

"You looked like you were having fun," said Melina, she was standing a bit close. I was looking over her shoulder towards the doors.

"Oh, yeah," I said. "That was just getting an economics professor back for making me sit through an hour and a half lecture on time rates of change without ever mentioning the term "derivative". I was ready to shout it out at the end of it. He was a nice guy, though. I think I got an A in that class."

I shifted into glow mode. "Let me know if I'm being too obvious."

"Um, you are," she said immediately. I toned it down, she nodded, and turned around a bit to glance back at the door. Tracey came out a few moments later, definitely not quite as well put together as she seemed the night before. Miss Finley was wearing a short skirt, a loose shirt draped off one shoulder and tennis shoes, and had her short hair up in a messy bun and bags under her eyes. She was checking her watch and opening her cell phone at the same time. Bringing the phone to her ear, she took a deep breath in expectation, taking a left at the junction and heading toward one of the building's exits.

Melina tapped me with her elbow and looked over her shoulder, her eyebrow raised. I sighed.

"Vampire?" she asked.

"Yes, Melina. And she didn't feel too healthy either."

Chapter 17

Chase

We headed after her, Melina holding my hand and pulling us through the crowded hall after the uncovered vampire. We went down the stairs and through the doors, picking up the pace in the clear. A few steps behind Tracey, Melina dropped my hand. Tracey slapped the cell phone shut and looked like she was going to throw it.

"Tracey," I said firmly. She stopped in her tracks and whirled around. Yeah, she wasn't too happy.

"What the hell are you doing here?" she asked, glancing back and forth between me and Melina.

"Are you a vampire, Tracey?" What the heck. I knew she was, but might as well give her a chance to come clean.

"How dare you?!"

"We've been to your apartment," said Melina. Yeah, thanks Mel, that was breaking and entering. I'd have preferred not to mention it. Then again, maybe it wouldn't have mattered.

"It's been, what, seven or eight months, Tracey," I asked. This was getting a little more confrontational than I'd have liked.

"I..." she paused and glanced over her shoulder. When she turned back at us, she had an expression of relief on her face. A black Mercedes sedan had pulled into the loading area where Tracey had been heading to. The driver's door opened a crack.

Then she swung at me. I didn't react in time and caught her fist on the left side of my chest. Of course, it was the same side with the bruised rib. I saw her fist coming in again at my chin, but hadn't recovered from the blow to the chest yet. Fortunately, Melina was faster. She struck Tracey with both arms and sent her sailing back off the sidewalk about four feet away onto her butt in the grass. She must have gotten up and ran off. I couldn't tell for sure, because I was found myself on the ground, struggling for breath.

It was all I could do to make my lungs draw as slowly as possible. I felt Melina's hands on my shoulders, she was asking if I was okay. No, dammit! I wasn't. My left side was on fire. I was sure I'd just learned what it was like to have a rib go into your lung.

I don't know how long it took, but the pain began to ebb slightly. At least enough for me to take slightly bigger breaths. I touched my side gently and probed the area. Maybe I'd just gotten lucky again. I took an extremely slow deep breath and didn't feel much. Letting the breath out, I slowly rose to my feet, opening my eyes. Melina had a hand on my right elbow, steadying my assent.

I tentatively lifted my left arm. After about 15 degrees, changed my mind, deciding that was about as far as I'd feel like going for a few minutes. The pain was slacking off more with each breath. Okay, so it wasn't that bad. Whew.

"Chris?" asked Melina, facing me. A steady stream of people were walking around is. Someone bumped into my left arm from behind, and I winced. Melina insistently moved us off the sidewalk.

"I'm okay," I said. "I think. Sir Finley probably cracked one of my ribs the other night."

Melina nodded. "And his daughter just tried to put it through your lung."

"Pretty much," I was breathing a bit more regularly now. "I'm sorry for dropping out... I assume Miss Finley took off in that slick black Mercedes?"

"Yes," she said.

"Did you get a look at the plate or the driver? I think I may have been tailed by it before too."

"I was a little more concerned about making sure you were going to live, Chris. But I recognized the car. I think."

"Do you recognize that," I asked, indicating a black van that just pulled into the loading area where the black sedan had been. The driver was looking around and locked his attention on us. I didn't like this much.

Melina turned and froze when she saw the van. And the six burly guys getting out of it. I take it that was a yes. My vampire friend swore in a language I'd have to ask for lessons in, grabbed my right hand and took us back towards the building fast. We went through and out the other side, heading towards the car.

"Are you okay to drive, Chris," she asked, pulling harder to move us along.

"Yeah," I panted, making sure to keep my breaths short. I was holding my left arm still across my stomach to minimize the movements on that side. "I'll manage." One way or another.

I had the keys out and unlocked the doors as quickly as I could. The sword got tossed next to me between the drivers seat and the door after it was shut. Melina hopped in the passenger side. I cranked the car over, and threw it into gear, launching it off the curb. A parking ticket was flapping on the windshield. Melina barked a laugh when she spotted it. "Sorry," she apologized. Figures.

I cut off some clueless freshman trying to get into a spot with a full-sized pickup truck.

Then screeched the tires, flying out of the parking lot into traffic. In my mirrors, I saw the black van stop and pickup the goons which had gone after us through the building.

"Who's after us here? Those don't look like Neville's men."

"They're not. The Mercedes was." Helpful. Very helpful. I sniffed. I cut through a yellow light just as it turned, out onto a fast three lane road. The van cut the red light behind us, nearly causing a wreck. I sniffed. The van was gaining on us quickly. It didn't look like they had any care about laws. So I decided I didn't care about them either. I floored it and then braked hard, almost skidding through a right hand turn. As soon as I had the car straight, I gunned the engine again, red-lining it before letting the transmission shift. I hated automatics.

As fast as I could get the car to go, I hit another right and then an immediate left on a side road. Three more full tilt random turns walking towards the right, the temperature gauge was starting to move up a bit. I slowed and got into another major road, heading towards the general area of downtown. There was no sign of the van in my mirrors.

"Take a left after you pass Wal Mart," said Melina. She sounded slightly shaky. There were new hand marks on the handle above the passenger door. I grinned. I tried not to, but I couldn't stop it. Melina tapped my leg with her left hand. "You enjoyed that, didn't you!"

"Only from a purely academic point of view, I assure you Melina. Actually, I'm still wondering who the heck that was."

"Oh," she said. Yeah. Talk. "I should probably let Samantha tell you."

"Melina! That's mean."

She sighed. "I really shouldn't. But of course, I'm going to anyway."

I began to protest, fearing I was getting her to say something she shouldn't again, but she cut me off. "This is general knowledge, Chris... No sensitivity factoring in here. Just listen."

I shut up.

"Not all the vampires, mages and otherwise inclined came over to the other side when they had the option. Some elements stayed here."

"Some of the more violent elements?" I offered.

"Yes," Melina agreed. "And that also means that some of them do not hold to the separation of league and magic, as is the case in the other side. Also, there's no technological restriction."

Guns, I immediately thought. They had guns, magic and vampires. I didn't like the thought. I said as much. Melina shrugged, but remained silent. A few minutes later, both of us deep in thought, I spotted a Wal Mart, and turned left at the next stop light.

"Strip mall, just before the next light on the right," said Melina. "The Italian place."

I pulled into the parking lot, and saw one of the stores didn't have a name, but there was a leaning tower depicted on the door. Looked promising. I found the best spot I could which hid the car from the road. It was between a hedge at the end of an isle and had an

SUV in front and to the left of it.

I shut off the car, and moved to get out, but Melina put her hand on my right arm. Then she leaned over and kissed me on the lips. She broke the contact and then opened her door. I sat dazed for a second, and then followed suite, strapping the sword back on my belt and warding it as before. I acquired Melina's right hand in my left, and we headed toward the door for the Italian place. I could smell some good stuff going on inside.

I opened the door for Melina, and she walked through, still holding my hand. The Maitre'd looked up at us, almost frowning. Probably placed us for a pair of college students. Well, not too far from the truth; and we were dressed for the part.

"Reservations," said Melina. "Samantha's the name it would be under."

The Maitre'd nodded, but didn't seem convinced. He looked down at his folder and began scanning the names. I began scanning the restaurant. Nice place. Good solid decor. Very quite, even though there was at least fifty people in the place, all having conversations. About two thirds full. The tables and furniture were all solid and well worn. The table clothes were spotless. We were a bit under dressed. But not by much. We were also ten minutes early.

The Maitre'd finally found the name, and sniffed. He grabbed three menus from a rack behind the podium and without seeing if we were following, took off toward a corner table towards the back. It was also the least occupied side of the room. He set the three menus down and I took one of the chairs with a view of the front. Melina sat across from me. The guy snapped his fingers twice. Loud. Melina took off her hoodie and hung it on the chair. I didn't see where she packed her dagger, probably in the hoodie. Her sword was in the car.

The snaps brought over a waitress wearing black pants and a tux shirt. She was probably a college student working between classes. From the apron, she withdrew a note pad, then shoved it away again after a reproachful glare from the Maitre'd.

"Good afternoon," she said, forcing a smile. She looked tired. "I'm Jennifer. What would you guys like to drink?" I motioned to Melina.

"A Pinot Nior," Melina said. "Nothing expensive, just rich and red."

"And you sir?" She asked, turning to me.

"Do you have a good Sauvignon Blanc? I guess that goes well enough with pasta?" Jennifer nodded.

"That and a water," I added. The waitress turned to Melina.

"I just need to see some ID?"

Melina sighed, and fished in a pocket for a small wallet. She flipped it open and then showed something to the woman. Jennifer's eyes went slightly wide, but she seemed satisfied and left. I was curious, of course.

"Well," I said playfully. "You do age rather well for a 32 year old, Melina."

She made a face. I was tempted to try and see the picture on her ID card, but Samantha walked in, brushed right past the Maitre'd, and vectored over to us. She sat down with a huff and plopped a shoulder bag onto the floor. The league leader was wearing a rather conservative pant-suit, her hair in a neat arrangement that kept out of her way, but still seemed free. The white shirt under the jacket had a high collar, I noted with a smile. She kicked off her shoes and pushed back in the chair.

The Maitre'd had apparently recovered from her entrance and materialized at her elbow, just as she was about to speak. She looked up at him, and smiled.

"Brandy," she said. "And then I'll have anything white and fresh that's open with the meal."

The guy nodded, and walked toward the kitchen. Interesting change of etiquette.

"Hi guys," said Samantha, tuning back to us. "Did everything work out with the car this morning?"

Melina and I looked at each other. "Ah, the rental's fine," I replied, aside from a few claw marks in the door. "We didn't, ah, get a chance to get a replacement for it."

Samantha raised an eyebrow.

"We had to check on someone," said Melina. "It took a little while, Samantha. And I think you probably need to know about it."

I gave Melina a look of thanks. I wasn't sure how to broach the subject.

"Yeah," I said then softly. "We got to find out that Tracey Finley's just like Melina and Christopher."

Samantha's eyes widened in surprise. "Really," she said, looking at Melina for confirmation. "Is that so?"

"Afraid so, ma'am. Chris suspected it yesterday, but I'd told him she wasn't. Then this morning, he had second thoughts about it. Turns out, he knows how to spot them somehow, when he tries. We tracked her down after one of her classes after checking at her apartment."

"And you're sure, Chris," asked Samantha. "This is serious."

"Yes, Samantha," I said. "I'm serious."

"Okay, if you can tell. How many vampires are there in this room?"

I looked around. Two including Melina. Then Jennifer walked back in with a tray of drinks. Make that three. She set them down in front of us in turn. Samantha got hers first, then Melina, then me with the wine and water. I tasted the wine. It was a step up from what I was expecting. Melina sipped hers. Samantha downed a fair amount of brandy. It looked like she needed it.

"Three," I said, then I took another swallow. "The beautiful Melina here, our waitress, and the fat man behind the plant in the other corner who looked up at you when you came in."

"How long," she replied. "Or can you tell?"

"Our waitress is relatively new. Say less than a year. Maybe a little more. The guy in the corner feels very old. Melina has been around for a little while. She feels about maybe a tenth as old as the man in the corner?"

"That's about right," said Samantha. "Jennifer's actually my daughter. She's Christopher's. We turned her a few weeks before she would have died of cancer. The man in the corner is a crotchety old bat, I think he's Lady Weiss's. And Tracey?"

"Less time than Jennifer," I said immediately. "Probably 8 months or so."

"That's about right," said Samantha, tossing back the last of the brandy.

"What," exclaimed Melina, almost choking on her wine. "You knew?"

"Of course, dear," replied Samantha. "Well, it was a strong suspicion for some of us. I fear the recommendation was to use her. We're guessed that she was turned forcibly. But we're still not sure who she's taking from. And that has been worrying us a little."

I'd set my glass down. I was actually getting a little mad at this point.

"What exactly were you planning on using her for," I asked as calmly as I could manage. Samantha didn't seem to notice my raising ire, but Melina found my hand under the table and gave it a squeeze.

"We presumed she had been turned by either Sir Neville, or worse, one of the main-side leagues. We're still not sure, since there seems to be a bit of a congruence between the two of late. And with this trial going on, we didn't want to force their plan by indicating that we knew she was turned."

"So you let her life fall apart," I said. My voice slowly rising. "You left her hanging out as bait for what? Well, I believe you have another problem, because she knows that Melina and myself know she's been turned."

Samantha motioned for me to be quieter, and I nodded, forcing myself to calm down.

"First, Chris," said Samantha. "Your concern for Miss Finley, while touching, is unfounded. Unlike others, Melina for example, Tracey does not deserve the concern you're wearing on your arm. I assure you, Chris, she is a worthy recipient of what ever misery she is going through just now."

I held back my remark, for Jennifer had arrived. I realized I'd not quite decided what to order, so looked down quickly, picking something almost at random.

"What will you have, Ma'am?" she asked Samantha. Kind of formal for a daughter not-mother relationship.

"Chicken Parmesan. And only 2 bread sticks this time. I'm filling out a bit, dear."

Jennifer nodded.

"Miss," she asked of Melina.

"Uh, I'll just have a salad, with oil and vinegar."

"And?"

"And that's it, just the salad. And another glass."

"And you sir," she asked, glancing at me.

"How sweet is the chicken marsalla?"

"Not very," she replied.

"Not very, as in not at all?" I asked. Like chicken marsalla was supposed to be. No sugar, save what was in the wine itself.

"Oh, it's a sweet sauce, but it cooks down a bit."

"No thanks," I said. "I'll take the "Mother's Lasagna" instead. With broccoli on the side. And extra mushrooms."

Jennifer looked like she wanted to pull out her pad and write it down, but felt the eyes of the Maitre'd on her back. He was watching from across the room. Nodded and glanced at my wine glass, which was barely touched. "And another with the meal?"

"Yes, probably," I said. "Thanks."

The waitress turned and left.

"Well, Samantha," I said. "I think you can perhaps conclude that Tracey's being influenced by someone other than Neville."

"How so?"

"We saw Tracey get picked up in a black Mercedes just after we confronted her outside of her class. Soon after, a van showed up with some main-world league stiffs and they chased us. Until Chris lost them through an experiment in the balance between gravity, centerifical force and friction coefficients."

I laughed. She made a geek joke, and it was funny. Samantha didn't seem to think much of it.

"Are you certain?"

"Yes, Ma'am. They weren't Neville's men. They had main league written all over them."

"And what exactly went on between the time you confronted Tracey and the time the van came up?"

I sipped my wine. "I was trying to decide whether one of my ribs had made a whistle hole in my lung." Samantha looked concerned. Melina winced. I shrugged. "I'm not sure, I had my eyes closed for a while."

"What happened, Chris? Are you okay?"

"I guess so," I replied. "Sir Finley probably cracked one of my ribs the other night in our little sparing session. If it can even be called that. Then his daughter spooked, saw the black sedan waiting for her, and swung at me."

"I knocked her down and then she ran to the car. I wasn't going to leave Chris," added Melina. "He'd pretty much collapsed. It was about two minutes later before the van showed up and we left."

"Hmm...Two minutes. Interesting."

"I'm sorry I'm still having trouble with this, Samantha," I said. "But have you seen her apartment?"

"No, why?"

"Who ever's playing her isn't doing a good job of keeping her stabilized," said Melina.

"So, is it your intent to let Sir Finley's daughter run around, crazed and starved, looking for a fix. There was a male shirt in her apartment with blood on it too. Not to mention, well. I can't mention what we found in the frige. But the short of it is, she was fairly hungry last night, and deep in her cups. There was no blood in her apartment this morning, and it didn't look like she had had any when she went off with the Mercedes."

Samantha thought for a moment. "I didn't know they were keeping her like that. It does change things a bit. We assumed they wanted her strong. It almost sounds like they were trying to get her to look elsewhere. Perhaps, to look to you, Chris?"

"It wouldn't take much," said Melina. "If she was half as hungry as where I was the other day, she'd have been into you pretty fast." Then she turned slightly red.

I chalked the color up to the wine, and went on. "But it takes days to get a vampire to this point, right?"

Melina nodded.

"Weeks, more like, Melina. Be honest." Samantha gave a small smirk at her. Melina turned a little darker and stared at her glass.

"Well, in that case, it definitely wasn't me they were setting her towards. It was someone else. I wasn't on the scene when they would have started this. So that leaves, what?"

"Who," Samantha corrected automatically. I frowned at her. She didn't get the point.

"Others with strong blood. Wielders, mages," said Melina. "Usually anyone with a strong personality has strong blood. It's just a predictable phenomena."

"Oh, no," I said, then sat back in the chair. I had a thought. But was still chasing it around. My thoughts went back to the store. To what was parked outside the store front. And who came in that vehicle.

"What, Chris?" Asked Samantha.

"Who," I corrected, Melina giggled. Jennifer and a server were coming toward our table with three trays The kid set down the two trays where Jennifer pointed; one in front of me and the other had the salad for Melina. Then Jennifer set the third tray in front of Samantha. With only two bread sticks. Jennifer looked over the table and then winced. The Maitre'd noticed the hesitation from across the room and shook his head.

"I'll be right back with refills," she said, and left, shooing the server in front of her. The Maitre'd broke off his conversation with another waiter and took off after our waitress. I had a feeling she was about to be dressed down. Jeeze.

"What kind of car does Neville drive?" I asked slowly, while setting my napkin across my lap and surveying the lasagna. It looked absolutely perfect.

"A black..." Samantha started. Then dropped her fork. It splattered spaghetti sauce onto her pants.

"Yep," I said. "I saw the same model black Mercedes that chased me right into this mess."

"You're reaching a bit, Chris," said Melina, then she took a fork-full of lettuce.

"It's reaching, yeah," I said. "But, how far's the question. You okay Samantha?"

She hadn't recovered from the fork drop yet, and was still staring into space. At the mention of her name, she shook her head to clear it and looked over at me. Our waitress arrived with refills of the wine all around. After she left, Samantha took a long swallow of her wine and then patted at the sauce stain with her napkin.

"Chris has a point," she said finally. "A nasty point. But one which is actually related very closely to the reason for this meeting."

I took a bite of the lasagna. This should be good.

"First, I guess I should thank you both for last night," she said, then took a bite of the chicken with the recovered fork. I nodded, my mouth full as well. She sipped the wine and swallowed. "I'm still hearing bits and pieces of it falling into place. But overall, I don't know what would have happened if things hadn't gone as they did. Two disasters were, if not completely avoided, at least diverted. Other things are well along.

"However, the reason for my unavailability last night goes almost beyond the events which transpired. Simply put; the status of the underside is in question. It's looking like we have a choice in front of us. The choice will involve either abandoning the other side entirely, and returning to the main-side, or changing internal regulations and adjusting the way we do things."

Samantha took a few bites of pasta and then continued while chewing, "therein lies the problem. The path we take is up for discussion and ruling at the next congress, which is tomorrow night. As you would expect, the leagues were split on the issue. A deciding vote was expected to come from the third league, and their wielder is currently in a rather nasty position; being in jail at the moment. I'm defending him in a murder trial, here, which may be wrapping up in the next day or so."

"Which explains part of Sir Neville's antics the other morning," I replied.

"And the moved up congress date. Just so," said Samantha. "We now have a vote ourselves, which puts us back ahead. The unfortunate part, Chris, is that the third wielder was the only one who was willing to defend the vote of maintaining the other side. That pretty much means..."

I swallowed. "That pretty much means I may get to hold up the oath I spoke the other morning, doesn't it?"

Samantha nodded. "I'm afraid that things have came to a head far quicker than we had hoped."

"So, how does this challenge system work. I thought it was like standard voting, but with the option of one league to challenge the vote of another. But this seems more complicated, Samantha?"

"It is, as you say. Sir Neville and two other leagues had setup a vote position with him as the champion. It's considered three votes, but they're consolidated vote, with one possibility for challenge. The challenge can be either from an individual league, or another consolidated position vote. We had one set with the other leagues with wielders, and ourselves, though we didn't have a wielder to offer in the challenge. That consolidated vote was stricken when Seamus got himself in trouble. One of the witnesses disappeared, and another was later killed in a mugging just before testifying. I don't think we shall win the case"

"I take it there was an issue in the past with multiple challenges?" I asked.

"You have no idea," Samantha began. "It was quite nasty. The consolidated system was an attempt to avoid such events." I could see how that could keep the number of challenges down.

"And Seamus was also the only one willing to face Neville?"

"Yes, Chris," answered Samantha. "I'm afraid I have to ask you to consider issuing the challenge," she held up her hand to stop me from replying. "Seriously consider it. But I must state that we do not expect you to take it up. Though you have shown a great deal of cunning, intelligence and initiative in the last 48 hours, our official position is that we will be able to survive after the vote regardless. We do not feel we have the right to order you to do it, given your relative inexperience, lack of training, etc. Sir Neville is not to be trifled with lightly!"

"I understand, Samantha" I said. "However, I meant what I said. I will take the challenge and face Neville regarding this vote, if it is what the League needs done."

"Are you certain? There is no guarantee that a challenge will leave both wielders alive."

"I understand, Samantha. I will challenge Sir Neville."

"Okay," said Samantha. "The league formally acknowledges your decision to challenge Sir Neville on this matter."

I nodded and downed the last of my wine. I then switched to water.

"So, about Tracey," said Melina, cutting through the moment. "I think we were at the point of discussing the possibility of Sir Neville picking up Tracey from campus."

"And a van full of nasties right behind the wielder," I added.

"Pretty much," said Samantha. She sighed and motioned to Jennifer for another wine glass. I declined, and Melina accepted. The waitress went to the kitchen, taking Melina's empty salad plate with her.

"Would it be safe to assume that there is a connection between Tracey's turning, and treatment and Sir Neville? And that it may also be related to the current vote?"

Melina took the words right out of my mouth. Since my mouth was full, this wasn't such a bad thing.

Samantha cleared hers, then set down her fork. "All I can add is that we were at the point of taking bets on which main-side league or leagues were interfering with our issues. That was about it. Nothing more than suspicions, thoughts, and shadows."

"Then should we consider continuing "arresting shadows" on this side?" I asked, then frowned. "It seemed to have helped last night. I seriously wish we could have arrived at the Hausmann's sooner, though."

"As I," said Samantha. "I don't think we can do anything at this moment over here though. I've already pissed off all our friends and prodded all of our enemies trying to track down the witness. And to no avail. No, we wait and watch over here. For the day, at least."

She checked her watch. Jennifer arrived with refills for her and Melina and topped off my water. I nodded thanks.

"Tonight," Melina mentioned. Sipping the fresh wine.

"Ah, yes," replied Samantha, pushing her plate back after picking a few more bites off of it. "Tonight. Yes, a much better turn of events. Did you two pick up a car yet?"

"Nope," I said. I thought we'd already told her about that.

"Hmm... Go ahead and take care of it. Seriously, grab anything. You'll need it tomorrow, and that rental has to go. Then get back to the other side for the evenings festivities. Melina knows where to go. Just make sure you're there before 6:00 at the storage house, so you can escort the stuff. It'll be good to have a wielder there."

I was now more than a little curious. Melina seemed to brighten a lot at this. I just wanted to know what the heck they were talking about.

"Should we tell him?" asked Melina, almost grinning.

"Nah," Samantha replied. "Let him suffer. He'll enjoy it a lot more."

Great. Women.

"Do you think your sister would take a walk in?" asked Melina, pointing at me. Samantha nodded.

"Yeah, good idea. She should, since all she does on Mondays is read journals. The brat. I'll write down her new address."

Samantha fished around in her bag and found an address book. While she wrote a number out of it onto a napkin with a pen, I knocked a few more bites off the awesome lasagna and chased down some more water. I was done. That was quite a meal. Two, actually. I was still chewing on the thought of facing Neville in a day and a half.

Melina accepted the napkin from Samantha, and I pulled out my wallet, getting ready to track down Jennifer to get the check. Samantha gave me a dirty look.

"What?" I asked.

"Put that away," she said. "I own the place."

Oh. Yeah. I guess that explains a little bit.

"Well, then I have to say that was the best lasagna I've had in quite a while. If ever."

Melina laughed. Samantha looked over at her, slightly pleased at the sound, then looked back at me. I had a slight grin on my face. She then nodded and stood up, managing to get her bag to her shoulder in the same movement. I rose and shook her offered hand. She hugged Melina and whispered something in her ear, which I pointedly ignored. Jennifer was standing close to us, waiting to clear the table.

"Thanks for a good lunch, Jennifer," I said. "Nice meeting you."

She nodded and moved to the table past us. Samantha stopped her and gave get a quick hug, which caused the waitress to turn scarlet. The kiss on the forehead probably didn't help.

"Stay clean, kiddo," she said, then released her and shoed us towards the door. I wondered how much I should try and get Melina to tell me about the evening.

It was raining. Samantha cursed softly and the Maitre'd was instantly next to her with an umbrella in hand. I didn't even see him coming. Melina and I ran towards the rental, her hoodie held over her head. I unlocked the doors and we dove in. Seat belts on, I started the car and put it in gear, waiting for a car that was backing out of a spot behind me to clear out.

"So, what did Samantha whisper to you about?" I asked.

Melina let out a girlish giggle which turned into a full laugh. She covered her mouth with her hand and took a deep breath, shaking her head.

"Maybe later?" I asked.

"Maybe." She tried to look serious, but her eyes were still sparkling.

"Fine," I sniffed. "Which way am I heading?"

"Right, then," she checked the slightly damp napkin. "Take a left at the third light. Go about 10 minutes, and look for the hospital. Turn left before it and then there's some side streets."

"Okay," I replied, checking the lot and backing out. I turned the wipers on, then realized Melina was looking at me. "What?"

She colored a little and turned away, shaking her head.

"Nothing."

Great. I pulled out into the L.A. traffic in the rain. My spirits were most definitely not a reflection of the weather. That would come later.

Chapter 18

Sister

Samantha's sister turned out to be Sir Finley's estranged wife. Melina and I showed up at her office both huddled in front of the door under the borrowed cloak. It took her several minutes to answer. She was a nice looking, but severe woman. She told us to go away. Then she recognized Melina and stiffened.

"If you think you're going to get a handout here, vampire, you're mistaken. Go elsewhere!"

"Oh, please, Dr. Finley," said Melina. "I'm not here for blood! Get a grip. He's got a broken rib. Samantha asked me to bring him by."

"Really," she replied. The suspicion flashed across her face. "What happened?"

"I ran into the flat of someone's sword. And then someone punched me. I believe you know them." I pointed at my left side.

"Bob or Tracey?"

"Both," Melina replied for me. I think we had both decided on not mentioning Tracey's new characteristics.

Dr. Finley bit her lip.

"Very well," she said. "Come in, I'll have a look at you. And you are?"

"Chris Borden," I said, extending my hand. She moved to take it and then noticed the sword at my waist. Her grasp was firm.

"Is that what I think it is, Chris Borden?"

"Yes, Ma'am."

We followed her inside to one of the examining rooms in the small private practice. It looked like half the building was devoted to an outpatient surgery ward, the other part offices, the waiting room and rooms like this one. I sat on the edge of the table, after dropping the sword in a chair.

"Take your shirt off." I complied. She walked over and began taking off the poor wrapping job I'd done this morning. The doctor paused when her eyes caught the marks on my neck.

"Yes, those are what you think they are too," I said. Melina plopped down into the other chair in the room and pulled her feet up in front of her. I winced as the doctor pushed slightly against my side.

"It's fractured." No, really. "But doesn't seem to be in danger of puncturing. I'll need to get an x-ray. Bob did this?"

"Yep. I think I may have broken his wrist. So I guess we're even."

"Follow me," said Dr. Finley, leaving the room briskly. I hopped down, collected the sword and my shirt and followed. Three doors down on the right past two examination rooms was a well equipped x-ray setup. Melina took my shirt and sword from me and I sat on the table. The doctor pushed my shoulders down, and then had me lift up my left arm slowly. She moved an arm over next my side and then adjusted the receptor on the other to match angles. Then she pulled up a lead vest in front of her chest, and snapped a switch.

"Turn on your right side," she said. She adjusted the machine and snapped another.

"Okay," she said. "Head back to the examination room, I'll get the slides."

We complied, and just after we entered the exam room again, Melina set down my stuff. I sat down in the same place as before. Melina then turned and walked towards me, looking at the dark bruise on my side. She touched the skin below it lightly. I realized she was slightly close. Dr. Finley walked in.

"All right, no snacking here," she said, almost warmly. Melina turned away and sat down. The doctor slapped two panes onto a glass and turned on the back light, clicking off the room lights in a practiced move. She stared at them for several seconds, while I looked over her shoulder.

"Well, Chris," she said. "It's not that bad. I don't see a danger of it making a puncture, either in or out. Not unless it is further injured. Which of course means I'm making the recommendation of not engaging in any more bouts with my family, or anyone else for that matter."

"I'm afraid that may be difficult. The anyone else part, at least."

"Figures. And from your other apparent use of your body as a shield for taking sword impacts, and other less violent losses, I'd say you're probably low on blood volume."

Melina looked away slightly.

"I'm not faulting you, Melina," she said. "I know how little it takes to keep you guys in your health. But I'm still suggesting concern with him."

That probably was a good idea at this point. The wine had gone more to my head than I'd normally expect after the large meal I'd had.

"Is there anything I should do?" I asked.

"Two options I'd recommend. One, is I can pump you up a bit with some saline. But I really don't feel like it, and it wont make that much of a difference. Not with the healing rate at least." She looked over at Melina.

"How's your potassium," she asked the vampire. "And when was your last test? I heard last that you were having some issues with your current host."

"I passed one last night.That's how I got the permit," she said, then pointed at me. "Since I only have his blood in me, it is as good as you can expect."

"Someday, someone's going to have to write a paper on the effects of second hand drugs on vampires. I'm sure the results would be quite interesting. It would probably allow us to figure out how to eliminate withdrawal effects and forestall the addiction. Ah, well. Since you only have Chris's blood in you, you must have bled yourself; how's your overall volume? Any headaches?"

I wondered where this was going, but decided to let it go on its own.

"Okay, I guess," Melina replied. Biting her lip. "It could have been worse, if, well. Someone stupidly fed me some blood with my wine less than an hour after."

"Stupid! You were passing out, Melina. What the heck was I supposed to do?"

Dr. Finley laughed. "I'll take it then that we can do it. If neither of you object?"

Melina shook her head. I raised my eyebrow. "Um, if I knew what I was being given the option of objecting to?"

Melina pointed to me, and then tapped two fingers against her neck. I turned to look at Dr. Finley, not making the connection.

"Direct injection is more effective, of course."

Huh?

"Oh, come on Chris; think. I'm a vampire, right? What happened when a vampire is injured. They heal quickly. You can cut off one of our arms, sew it back on, and give us some blood and we become whole again. Dr. Finley's asking you if want an injection of my blood. It'll heal you faster."

I closed my eyes and shuddered. The image that passed through my mind wasn't of an arm, but of a severed head. Melina's head. I shook the thought out and considered.

"Sorry, I am still new to this whole vampire thing. I didn't know that could be done. But it seems like there may be some side effects?" Yeah, like, some of the myths about people taking the blood of a vampire and turning?

"There are side effects to almost everything, Chris. If you get too drunk and Melina bites you, she will probably get sick. If you smoke cigarettes, they can experience vertigo. Sometimes seisures. The list goes on. In the other direction, you'll feel an odd burning sensation until the blood mixes fully. You'll also end up with a light headed feeling not unlike taking an antihistamine. Also, you will heal faster and be a little stronger for a small time. But it's a deceptive strength, which doesn't last. Like a shot of adrenaline."

"Anything else?" I asked. Melina laughed. I stuck my lounge out at her, making her laugh more.

"Okay, you two! What's the verdict? I have journals to read."

"Okay, I guess," I shrugged. "Turn about is often fair play. But I'll go with the direct injection. I don't think I could bring myself to bite her."

Now it was Dr. Finley's turn to laugh at Melina's turning red and looking away. The doctor nodded and washed and dried her hands at the sink. She put on a pair of nitrile gloves and extracted a 2 mL syringe and 17 gauge needle from a drawer. She kicked her stool over near Melina and dropped the wrappers in the trash bucket on her way. Melina offered her left arm and looked at the needle. The doctor grabbed her arm near the elbow, patted a small area with an alcohol swab, and with the same hand deftly inserted the needle. She drew out about 1 mL of blood, which looked a little lighter than usual for human blood.

Dr. Finley dropped the used needle off into a red container for such things and put another on the syringe. Using a second alcohol wipe, she gently pushed the air out of the syringe until a hint of blood formed on the tip. She wiped it off with the cloth and kicked over to me, tossing the wipe away in the same container and picking up another wipe. I raised my left arm.

"This will hurt a little," she said, wiping around the area of the impacts. I felt a stab and a slight burning sensation. It got worse, turning into an almost unbearable itch. I gritted my teeth and sucked in air. I felt another stab and more burning below the rib. Then she was done. The syringe, needle and wipe all went into the biohazard container. Dr. Finley turned back with a roll of something to wrap my chest with and some tape.

About five minutes later, I was wrapped up much better than I'd managed on my own. Breathing was a bit more difficult, but I could tell the wraps were succeeding in placing limits on the expansion of my chest, and thus on the movement of the damaged bone. I was also beginning to feel the burning spread slowly out from the area. It was also getting more bearable. I put my shirt back on and stood.

"Now, Melina," said Dr. Finley. "I'd suggest not taking too much of this guy's blood in the next few days. Only what you need. I know you're not the greedy type, but I also understand that blood of a wielder is probably a little harder to resist than the rest of us mear mortals."

Melina nodded. I strapped the sword back on my belt. We walked out the door to the lobby area. I recovered the borrowed coat from the rack next to the outer door. The rain had stopped.

"Thank you for your help, Dr. Finley," I said, extending my hand. She shook firmly.

"My pleasure Chris. Stay well. And don't let Bob push you around. He's really just an immature little kid at heart. Once you figure that out, you can get him to come around with greater ease."

"Thanks," I said. Dr. Finley turned to Melina, extending her hand. They shook as well.

"And you, you little vamp," she said. "Try to keep him out of trouble."

"I will," Melina smiled back. "Try at least."

"You think you'll go back? It's never too late."

Melina frowned slightly, but nodded. I wondered what they were talking about. Just that they weren't talking about me anymore.

Dr. Finley unlocked the door and motioned us out. "Now. Get!"

I laughed and followed Melina out the door and back to the car. Once we were inside and the car was moving, I glanced over at Melina.

"So that's why your bites heal so fast," I noted. "You're saliva helps heal the wounds, right?"

"Well," she replied. "That's part of it. I also use proper technique."

I laughed. "You're teasing me!"

"Nope," she said. "Notice I scratch first. That sets these things."

She rolled her index finger across her top teeth twice. The second time, she held her finger in place at the vry normal looking K-9 teeth and turned to me. I was stopped at the exit of the parking lot, so glanced over. It looked like two small hypodermic needles made of bone had extended from the pointy teeth.

"They make smaller holes, and allow for more control. And it's direct to our blood stream. Really sucks when you chip one though."

I pulled the rental into traffic.

"Neat."

"So, what kind of car you going to buy," Melina said, changing the subject. I didn't blame her. "There's a Chevy lot!"

I made a face. "I don't think so. I've got a thing for imports. Volvo, or Toyota. I don't want to spend too much of this money for transportation."

"Aren't those the boxy things?"

"You mean the boxy things with class? Yeah."

Melina didn't dignify that with a reply. I spotted a Volvo dealer on the other side of the highway and pulled into the lot. We got out of the rental and walked over near a row of sedans. A few other people were browsing the parking lot. A couple in an aging suv got out and started looking at the station wagons. I had a strange feeling we'd be overlooked. We were the only people in the lot not in business attire. I sighed and cut off one of the sales people who was vectoring to the newly arrived couple.

"Can I help you folks? I'm Tim." He was already sizing us up. He raised an eyebrow at the rental tag.

"Chris. S-60, R-Type," I immediately said while shaking his hand. "Any on the lot other than the one in the show room."

I didn't like the color. Something about beige and a sporty sedan just didn't go together in my mind. He thought for a moment.

"We have one that just came off a six month lease. I think it has about two thousand miles on it," he started walking us around the side of the building near a few sedans which had just came off a truck. The car on the end was just what I was looking for. Midnight blue, leather seats, and the all important 6-speed manual. I checked the odometer and nodded.

"Can we take her for a spin?" I asked. He didn't look like he was happy with the idea.

"You folks looking to buy soon," he asked. I nodded. Yeah, man. Cash. "Okay, can I grab your license to make a copy?"

I passed him my Florida drivers license and he went inside to get the keys. Melina put her hands on the roof and looked inside.

"It looks nice enough. A lot different than the Volvo's I remember," she said. "I thought most people didn't want stick shifts anymore?"

I shook my head. Only if they didn't like to row their own gears. I was about to comment when I noticed the sticker on the window. The decal on the back confirmed it. This was off lease, but off lease from another state. Which meaned no California ignition. I was happy. Tim passed me back my license and a key. I pocketed the license and unlocked the doors. Tim and Melina moved to get in the car, but I popped the hood. The sales man stopped halfway into the car, and then got back out. Melina laughed.

"He did this with the rental too," she explained while I checked the fluids. The oil was fresh. And the coolant was a touch low. I closed the hood. Then I glanced under the car briefly. It was fairly clean. Nodding to myself, I got in and started it up, after making sure the transmission was in neutral. Tim got the rest of the way in the passenger side and Melina hopped in the back seat behind him. I waited for them to buckle up and then put the car into gear. Seconds later I pulled out into the main road, spooling up through the gears smoothly. I loved it.

"So, you folks from Florida?" Tim asked. He was reaching for the AC control. Which I had shut off. I had my window down and it was messing with his hair. Poor guy.

"I am," I replied. "But I'm in the process of relocating for a new job."

"Just out of college?" he asked. I couldn't blame him. I didn't look that old. Melina didn't look over 19, and we were wearing jeans. Not the usual clientele for this lot at all.

"No," I replied simply. Let him think I hadn't gone. I've got a masters degree, thank you very much.

"You handle this thing pretty well," Tim said. "For a front wheel drive car, it is an extremely balanced vehicle."

"It's all wheel drive. The R-type's all wheel drive," I corrected.

"Oh, yeah," he said. "That's right. We don't get too many of them."

That's because they were special order only. I thought about asking him which turbo it had, but he'd probably get it wrong.

"The new sticker price is 37,500 base," I said. "What are you asking, since it's a lease."

"It was 46 new," Tim replied, at least he checked that. R-Types were up there a little. "39,900."

I was satisfied so I pulled a rather too quick U-turn, and headed back to the dealership. To make the point, I parked the sedan next to the rental. Tim gave me a look.

"Could you park it back over there," Tim asked.

"I'm going to buy it." I shut off the car and passed him the keys while unfastening my seat belt and opening my door.

Tim got out and looked at me over the top of the sedan with a bit of a smile.

"So, will you folks be financing?"

I didn't want to end the game yet. It was too much fun. "I'm not sure. Probably not."

The salesman seemed like he was pretty sure. I let him have his head.

"Lets go inside and look over the paperwork," he said. I nodded and pulled the envelope out of the rental car. Melina and I followed him into the showroom and over to a desk near the right side windows.

"So what's your credit like?" He asked after we sat down. I saw he was pulling up a credit report window on the computer. When I didn't answer him, he glanced over at me. I was about halfway through filling out a check.

"I think I'll just take care of it today," I said, after he stared at me for a few seconds. I paused with the check and passed him the certified bank letter. "You'll probably want to call the bank and double check that. And get me the total."

Tim calmly examined the letter and reached for his phone. After he dialed the number, he motioned for someone who had been walking past. The woman came over with a smile. Tim passed her the letter.

"I'm Claire Johnson, manager," she said, extending her hand in my direction, "it's nice to meet you Mr. Borden. I trust Tim has been seeing to your needs?"

"Quite, Mrs. Johnson," I replied, noticing the ring on her finger. I've dealt with enough clients to know it pays to notice details like that.

Tim spoke softly to someone on the phone. After a second or two, he thanked the other person and then hung up. He nodded at Mrs. Johnson.

"The total?" I asked of Tim. He began to speak.

"We'll take care of taxes and such for you Mr. Borden," the manager interjected. "The price mentioned should be quite sufficient."

I nodded and finished the check. I passed it to Tim and he got up and went to the back of the building to get some paperwork.

"Is there anything else we can do for you today, Mr. Borden?"

"Actually," I replied. "There is. Can you have someone return our rental? The agreement form is in the driver's door map pocket."

"I believe that can be arranged," she replied.

Tim returned and passed me several papers, which I looked through. He went and made a copy of my insurance card, even though it was out of state. After a few minutes, Mrs.

Johnson left to help a woman who was looking at the suv in the show room. I nodded to her as she left.

"Thank you for your business, Mr. Borden," said Tim, standing up and offering me his hand. I shook and then accepted the keys. He followed us out the door to the rental. After retrieving our stuff, I locked the car and passed him the key.

"Thanks Tim," I said, waving at him as Melina and I got in the sedan.

"That was quick," said Melina as I started the car and let out the clutch.

"Yeah, and a little bit fun too," I replied. The Volvo easily merged out into traffic. I pulled a u-turn and began looking for the next major road heading back towards the house in the hills. "How are we on time?"

Melina frowned. "Probably okay. It's still several hours till dark on the other side." It was starting to get dim here. It had taken longer than I thought at the doctors office. I turned the headlights on full.

"So where are you from?" I asked after an extended silence. Melina shrugged.

"I don't remember," she said. "I was taken as a baby."

I had been hopping to make light conversation. This didn't sound like too good a start along that path.

"Taken?" I asked.

"Some vampires have sick tastes," Melina said curtly. "I was either sold or kidnaped as a baby for blood."

I grabbed Melina's left hand and squeezed it. "I'm sorry, Melina. I didn't mean to bring it up." She squeezed back.

"It's okay," she said. "That was a while ago. I don't remember much of it anyway either. Willie and Charles got me out of it when I was five. After that, they pretty much raised me. Since they were both into swords and training techniques, they brought me up into it."

"I guess that explains the "Five Rings"."

"More or less. It probably wasn't the normal type of childhood for a girl. On the up side, I did end up taking the championship from Sir Finley when I was 13!"

Melina frowned and looked out the side window.

"Kind of young," I asked.

"Oh, well," she replied. "I lost it when I was turned. Which brings up the point of who has it now."

"That would be Neville, I guess?"

"No," she replied. "He's not very good with a normal blade. Tends to cut himself."

"You're pulling my chain, aren't you?"

"Yes, Chris," she said. "He's better than Finley now. You have no idea what you're getting yourself into, Chris."

"I'll face what I'll face," I replied. "Unless what I've seen from the stuff Trevor showed me is completely different than whatever the heck Neville does with his sword, I should be able to give him a challenge."

"He's much stronger than you."

"Faster than Finley?"

"Not really," she sniffed. "Shorter reach, and more power. Faster reactions, but not much quicker physically. So I guess that is a small advantage for you, Chris. You're guard is good, but a bit loopy."

"Loopy?" I asked, looking over at the vampire. "My guard is loopy? Gee thanks!"

"Well, you waver around way too much. And I think it shows your intentions. You're probably trying to stay focused on nothing. Good idea, but it's coming off badly. There's a difference on being focused on nothing, and being unfocused."

I considered this or a moment. That was the general idea I'd been taught.

"And you're tending towards the later. And he'll see it for what it is."

"My general inexperience," I replied. I wasn't too happy about the prospect. "Well, what do you expect. I've got to spend most of my time sitting down at a computer screen somewhere. I'm on the road at least one week in three. And I usually work 60 hour weeks. Kind of hard to work on a small hobby that I didn't even know would become this much of an issue."

"It may have just become your life, Chris."

"Yeah," I sighed. Perhaps.

"The ten year rule may be a bit of a problem for you," said Melina. Maybe she was getting a bit more comfortable in a car. This was about the most she'd said all day.

"So I may have to give up my job now? I've spent a lot of time on this career."

"If you've got to work with new tech, then you'll probably be asked to either stay main-side, or quit. It was what Dr. Finley had to decide. But you can't stay main-side and be our wielder."

Curtis will have a fit. I realized I'd forgotten to call him yet. Out of habit, I caught myself reaching for my cell phone. Which was other-side. In pieces. My hand went back to Melina's. I frowned.

"There's no chance of, say, getting a few months to wrap things up?"

"Possibly," Melina replied. "You can make your case to the Office of Technology. I'd talk with Lady Whitacre first. She can let you know how to best go about it." Melina paused. "You seem to be taking this well."

I shrugged. "Not much choice." Her hand pulled out of mine suddenly.

"You don't have a girlfriend or anything back in Florida, do you?"

"No, Melina," I replied quickly, almost laughing. "I had went on dates a few times with one of the engineers at work. But that stopped several months ago. I found out I don't necessarily get along with Chemical Engineers much. Something about my fear of Organic Chemistry."

Melina laughed. "Did you fail it or something? I didn't know organic was required for mechanical."

"It wasn't. I kind of made a stupid decision and found myself in the class. Made it through the intro stuff okay. And then we saw nomenclature. I half tanked. Then our first mechanisms. Not only did I have no clue what was going on, I was embarrassing myself in front of my reason for picking that major in the first place. And the reason was impressed with how someone else was handling the material. Needless to say, I failed the class. I switched to a more sensible major the next semester."

"And you didn't get the girl; poor Chris," she smiled at my expense. "Organic wasn't that bad. At least I didn't mind it much."

"Huh?"

"I told you I used to go to UCLA, Chris."

"Yeah, Biology."

"So you were paying attention," she teased. Brat.

I glanced over at her, and then struggled to extract my hand from hers to change gears as I slammed on the brakes. Melina squealed and grabbed for the door handle and pushed against the dash. Finally, I got the car into fourth and swung over two lanes to the left. The large black sedan which had been to the right of us was struggling to make the lane change. The far left lane opened up and we went past the sedan with a solid lane of slower traffic between us.

"Mind telling me what the hell that was about?" Melina asked through clinched teeth. I did some gritting of my own as the sedan bullied its way into the lane three cars behind us.

"There was a woman with a machine gun in the back seat of that car. She looked happy to see us."

"Oh."

Yeah, oh. As in not good. I spotted another sedan of similar vintage coming on the next ramp. The rear windows were down and a head popped out, looking in our direction.

"I guess it's a little late to say that warding would have been a good idea, Chris?"

"I was," I replied. Of course I wasn't warding the whole car. Just like with the creative parking job, making it disappear wouldn't have been a good idea. "I think that's how they found me. I may have been making us a bit too hard to focus on. Or something. I don't know how a lot of this stuff works. Yet."

After we got past a major turn off, the traffic began to thin. I pulled out ahead of the two sedans, but they quickly caught up. A third followed by a black van came out of a side ramp just ahead of me and moved to cut me off. The other two were right on our tail, both moving to box us in. I saw a shoulder come out of the car on the left. It was the same woman with the machine gun. She was aiming at the tires.

I decided I'd had enough. I pressed the accelerator and surged up until I made contact with the sedan in front of me. While still touching, I clutched, threw the car from fifth to third and began to push the car. Turning the wheel slightly to the right and giving it more gas, the strong Volvo overpowered the rear wheels of the larger sedan causing it to spin out to the left. I flew around the right side of the out of control car, tapping the sedan on that side in the process. In my mirror, I could see the sedan on the left crushing into the spinning car causing it to tip on its side. The van crashed into that one causing all three cars to enter into a slide at the gaurd rail.

Without waiting for the remaining sedan to recover, I quickly accelerated well past 100. After two slight turns in the highway, I lost sight of the sedan. Slowing down, I took an off ramp and relaxed slightly, taking several deep breaths. Melina extracted her right hand from the door handle. I glanced over at it and laughed uncontrollably. The handle had faired slightly better than those in the rental. It looked like I'd have to invest in some industrial strength vampire proof hand holds if I kept driving this chick around.

"You okay, Melina?"

She sniffed. I took a left at a road which I'd seen intersect the road into town.

"Mel?"

"They shouldn't know where the house is," she said. Her voice was very shaky.

"Melina, are you okay?" I slowed slightly and touched her arm.

"Just drive the car, Chris," she replied, a little stronger. I left my hand on her arm, but complied. Minutes later, and a u-turn, we pulled into the driveway. Melina surged out of the car and slammed the door. While she stood there with her eyes closed and taking deep breaths, I examined the damage to the nearly new Volvo. The right rear quarter panel just had some paint transfer. The front was a mess. Fortunately, it looked like the radiator was in one piece. The bumper was trashed and the hood and front grill were damaged. The right head light assembly was still functional, but half hanging out the side. I pushed it back in, cutting myself in the process.

The sun was just going down as I moved to stand behind Melina. I set my hands on her shoulders. She glanced over at me, and smiled slightly, backing into me. I let my arms drop around her. We stood long enough to watch the sunset. Just after the last rays faded beyond the horizon, Melina turned and kissed me, her arms around my neck.

After what seemed like an eternity, she broke the kiss and shoved me away. Her voice cracked. "Never put me through that again, Chris. Please."

Turning, Melina stormed off toward the house. I shook my head, grabbed my sword and hers from the car and followed. Yes, there were a lot of things I'd like to see this girl never have to go through again. A nasty car ride wasn't first on my list. But I'll definitely add it.

I paused on the steps of the house to look back over LA. My fingers absently ran over the marks on my neck from this morning. Yes, Melina, I'll try. I promise.

Chapter 19

Finally

Two glasses of water and 45 minutes of walking later I was regretting not having a third. On the upside, Melina seemed a lot happier. I was struggling to keep up with her fast pace. Every few minutes, I had to pull her back a bit. I made a mental note to add a good hiking backpack to my list of things to acquire. If I was going to be walking around this much, I should get in the habit of carrying water and food. Oh, and a first aid kit probably wouldn't hurt.

"We're early," she whispered as we arrived at what could be nothing other than another completely nondescript warehouse. I still didn't know exactly what was going on this evening, but it was obvious that Melina did. She pulled me into a doorway near the entrance of the warehouse and I found my arms full of vampire again. Her head was against my chest, arms wrapped around my waist. After several minutes, I think I was starting to dose off. Then the sound of cars approaching stirred me. Melina turned and grabbed my hand, pulling us towards the warehouse. We got to the main door just as two small pickups approached. Johny Danger jumped off the back of one of the trucks and opened the large door. Each truck had three people, two in the front and one in the bed. I saw Sara wave from the passenger side of the second truck. After the trucks passed, Johny motioned for us to follow them. The door shut behind us.

We walked around the end of a row of crates and then got to watch as the vampires loaded what looked like unmarked coolers from a hidden trap door in the floor of the warehouse. Melina moved to help, but Sara shook her head.

"We're almost done," she said, waving Melina off.

"Is that what I think it is?" I asked Melina after Sara had went back down the hole.

"What do you think it is?" Melina smirked back to me. I pinched her side and she squeaked, giving me a dirty look. Johny looked up at the noise and smiled at me. I smiled back.

"Blood?"

"Right-o," Melina replied.

"That's all guys," said Johny, sliding the trap door back in place. He skipped off to the main door. "Pile in."

"What, you mean we don't get to walk?" I asked with as much disappointment as I could manage. Sara climbed into the back of the second truck and motioned for us to take the front. Melina hopped in taking the middle, I pulled the door shut behind me. The vampire at the wheel extended his hand past Melina, I shook it. The whole side of her body was pressed against mine on the right side of the stick shift. I kind of liked it.

"Bill," he said.

"Chris," I replied immediately. Melina grabbed my hand when it returned from the shake. I let her.

The trucks pulled out of the warehouse and Johny hopped in to the back of ours with Sara. I think Bill would have spoken more, but he was having trouble with the gears. When he missed third the tranny screamed, its syncros spinning. Finally, he forced it into the sticky gear. I heard Johny say something rather nasty from the back of the truck. He could probably do better. I knew I could.

It seemed like we were making random turns, but overall heading northeast. Eventually, we came through a small alley way and then slowed right across from what was looking like our destination.

"That is most definitely a graveyard," I noted. "That would mean we're..."

"Waking up the kiddies," said Bill. Melina squeezed my hand. "Yeah. Nap time is over."

The two trucks made their way through the graveyard to one of several large buildings toward the back. Bill backed our truck next to the main door, so that the tail gate almost touched the top step. The other truck did the same. Everyone piled out. I reached back into the cab and clicked off the headlights. The woman who'd been driving the other truck nodded, set down the box she was carrying and did the same.

"Right," she said, walking back to the box. "No sense advertising."

"There never is," I replied.

Melina had gone inside. But I couldn't bring myself to do it. I think I was picking up on Johny's nervousness. While the vampires unloaded, I watched. After they were done, I heard several bangs from inside the building. A few minutes later, Sara came and stood next to me.

"Melina wants you to see the first one," she said softly. "Or at least, we're pretty sure she wants you to see it. She keeps stalling and Johny's about to have a cow."

I smiled. "It feels like we're being watched."

"We probably are," she replied, touching my arm. "Another reason to hurry. We have watchers here too."

I thought I could feel them too. It is interesting how much the dead still perceived. Or the sleeping. I nodded and let Sara guide me inside. The whole building was a crypt of sorts. The front and back walls were honeycombs for coffins. Several had been pulled out and were set on the the floor. A mental guess put the number at almost seventy. One was open. Melina was on the other side with her arms in the coffin. When I came around to the foot of the coffin, I could she Melina had her arms around a woman who looked to be asleep, perhaps in her early forties. I kneeled next to her and touched Melina's shoulder. She threw a quick smile in my direction, then glanced at a needle sitting on the floor. It had about 5 mL's of what was unmistakably blood in the barrel.

I picked up the needle, uncapped it and passed it to Melina. She took it, set the point against the woman's neck and then injected. The woman's eyes shot open and she gasped. Melina dropped the syringe to the ground. I winced as it bounced, but fortunately didn't break. Melina hugged the woman fiercely. I recovered the forgotten needle from near Melina's left knee.

The older woman pushed Melina away after a little while. Both of them had tears on their cheeks. Melina sniffed, wiped her eyes and then turned to me, still holding the woman's hands.

"Mom," she said. "There's someone I want you to meet."

The woman regarded me, noting both the borrowed coat and the sword.

"Chris Borden," said Melina nodding in my direction. "Meet my mom, Ginny."

I extended my hand. The woman took it, but her grip was extremely weak.

"Nice to meet you, Ma'am," I said. "You probably have a bit of a headache, no?"

With the question, I picked of the bag of blood from the cooler box and passed it to Melina. She clucked to herself and immediately hung the bag on a hook on the coffin lid.

"I'm glad that we have a wielder again," she said. "Well, that we finally have a wielder." She leaned back into the coffin while Melina unfurled the tube from the bag and set up an IV of sorts. Apparently the boxes were all vampire waking kits. The other vampires had begun on the other coffins in the building. From the box Johny was working on I heard cursing. The syringe was hurled from the box and it smashed against the opposite wall. The stream of curses continued. Johny slowly backed away.

"Did you have to wake her up?" asked Ginny, who had her eyes closed. I heard a bag being torn from the box. Then a sick gurgling sound. "She'll give herself gas doing it that way."

I laughed. Melina looked at me. Okay, maybe she would get gas guzzling that much blood. I still thought it was funny. A few seconds later, the empty plastic bag joined the shattered syringe on the floor with a splat. A woman surged out of the coffin and glared around the room. A few other vampires were sitting up and glancing at the sight from their coffins. Most of those administering revival packs didn't pay the woman any attention.

"Where the fuck is my sister?" she yelled. Johny gave her a toothy smile, then stymied it down to a blank expression as she turned back to him. "Why isn't my sister here?"

Ginny shot open her eyes and looked suspiciously at Melina. Melina shook her head and pointed at me with her thumb. The recovering vampire nodded and closed her eyes again.

I recognized the enraged vampire. It's kind of tough not to recognize the face of someone you kill. This had to be her twin. There was no question about it. Johny was a little off balance, so I stood and went to help. I remembered his comment about the vampire I killed and his past. This could get ugly.

"I believe your sister is dead," I said, standing a few paces away from Johny.

"What!?" The vampire had her hands at her sides, fingers locked into claws. I didn't know how fast she would get her strength back, but I didn't want to find out. I calmly set my left hand on my sword.

"I killed her," I said with regret. I did regret it. The vampire looked like she was going to charge me, but I held up my right hand. "Please don't do that. I didn't want to kill her and I don't want to kill you either."

It looked like she was considering this for a moment. Her eyes flicked between me, my hand and the sword and Johny. Then she lunged for my throat. She didn't make it. I'd taken the time to put a shield in front of me. When she came in contact with it, I closed the back of the shield, effectively locking her in place. She started to scream at me and bang on the shield. I tightened it to stop her from banging on it and then made the shield block outgoing audio.

I stepped right up to the shield and looked into her eyes.

"Vampire, hear me. You sister died while I was fighting against her for my life. She spent her last moments trying to strangle the life out of me even as my sword was through her heart. I assure you; I did not know the sword would kill her. And I assure you also that she did not know her sword would be useless against me. She died with honor, and because of my ignorance. I regret her death. If that means anything to you at all."

I saw a hint of understanding in the eyes. I decided to take a chance.

"Now. Will you control yourself if I let down the shield?"

She said something. I pointed to my ears, and then dropped the audio block.

"I'll behave," she repeated louder. I dropped the shield. With the vampire less than a foot away from me. I also didn't step back. We stared at each other for several seconds.

"Danger, when's the meeting?" she asked, bending over to pull a small bag from the coffin.

"Tomorrow night. Usual time."

"See you boys then," she said and stormed out the door. I turned to Johny.

"I think she needs a shower," I said. Then sniffed. He laughed so hard he had to put his hands over his stomach. Sara smiled as she helped a young male vampire out of a coffin. A few others were walking out on their own. I noticed Ginny had been almost the last one to stand, even though she was the first one whom we woke. I moved to steady her left arm.

Melina was on her right side.

"You okay, Lady?" I asked her. She snorted. Melina gave me a worried look.

"I've been out for a while," she replied. "Charles should be happy to see me."

The vampires were beginning to put the coffins back in the walls. It looked like we were about done with one side. There were still another hundred boxes of restorative left. I guess there was a round two. Ginny sat down on a bench near the door and Melina sunk down beside her, pulling her feet up onto the edge of the bench. They still held hands. I left them while Melina filled Ginny in on the past few days of events. I went outside.

My thoughts immediately went to the two vampires I'd killed. I still couldn't call it destroyed. To me they were individuals. As individuals, at my hands they had died. I felt a tear roll down my cheek. Some wielder I was.

My reverie was interrupted by motion approaching the building. My hand went to the sword. It was a cat.

The feline padded out between two gravestones and stared at me. The candle light from inside the building behind me shined in its eyes. It blinked, and then continued across the yard past the trucks. I laughed softly and shook my head. Here I am, standing in the middle of a graveyard at night, helping raise a bunch of sleeping vampires. A week ago, I didn't even believe in vampires. A week ago I was just an ordinary person with a job and a life. A job which I almost completely forgot about through the day. A job which may not be waiting for me if I don't get off my ass and call in. And a job which I may have to give up anyway. To keep doing things like waking vampires in the middle of a graveyard. At night. I'd have to remember to call first thing tomorrow.

Thinking of tomorrow. I believe that would be Tuesday other-side time. And Tuesday night just happened to be that meeting where I may end up facing down my most favorite character. I still hadn't gotten that chance to practice. I'd probably have to find an empty field somewhere. What I had in mind would not work too well inside. At least not if I screwed it up the first couple of times.

I was just about to turn and head back into the building to check on things when I suddenly felt someone next to me. Actually, I felt a little more than that. A very strong arm latched around my neck while the other stuck a needle into my arm. Between the arm crushing my wind pipe and the fire burning in my blood, I passed out.

Chapter 20

Wake up

I don't think I want to talk about the details. The short version was, I had a really bad dream about someone tearing my throat out with their teeth. This someone would have been a vampire. Then I was drowning in some liquid. That wasn't quite the consistency of water. Of course this would have meant I was a vampire. As I woke up and took stock, pretty much everything I thought about had something to do with me trying to tell myself it was just a dream.

I definitely had one hell of a headache. But then again, I'd been given a shot of something. My throat hurt a lot. Which may have been a good sign, since Vampires tend to heal. It also felt crushed, not lacerated. Also a good sign. Well, relatively good. My rib was also complaining a bit. Then again, the fact that I was laying on something hard may have done something to add to that. I tried rolling off the object and realized a few more things. My hands were tied behind my back. I couldn't feel my legs. No, no vampires had gone snacking, they were just asleep under me. From the straw and mulch under my face, I guessed I was in a stable of some sort. I didn't hear any horses though.

I'm not sure how I did it, but I managed to get into a relatively normal, pain minimizing, sitting position on the floor. While I sat there with my head spinning from the altitude change and blood rushing into my limbs, I heard a rustling sound. In the dim light I saw a shape move toward me. The movement quickened, then stopped with the sound of rattling bars. It looked like someone was in a cage a few feet from me. I heard a moan, and the figure dropped down to the floor.

Just as I was trying to get my voice to work, I heard voices approaching from outside.

"What the hell am I supposed to do with him?" asked a male voice. "No! For gods sakes! I can't touch that."

"I thought I was doing you a favor by bringing him here," replied a female voice. Which sounded extremely familiar. Actually, I'd been arguing with her not to long ago. I wondered whether she had gas yet.

"You are a crazy, sadistic vampire, Claria. It will be finished tomorrow night anyway," he said. Yeah, you can guess who it is.

"You could always feed him to Finley's daughter," Claria replied. A door opened and lights flicked on in the stables. I shut my eyes and tried to turn my head. "She is definitely hungry enough. You sure you know what you're doing, Sir Never?"

When I finally opened my eyes a crack, Claria was standing a few feet away with my sword wrapped up in the raincoat. Neville stood near the large cage. He had a dagger in his hand. Tracey Finley was in the locked cage, her whole attention focused on Neville and his dagger. The blade looked a lot like the one she had with her the other night.

With a practiced move, he touched the tip to his left forearm and then sheathed the blade. From his back pocket, he pulled a tissue and used it to dab the drop of blood from his arm. He extended the tissue over the cage and slowly lowered it. When Tracey reached for the tissue, he taunted her a few times, and then dropped it. With a sound of near joy, the woman grabbed the tissue from the air and brought it to her mouth. Yeah, she was a bit gone. Judging from the look on her face, actually, she was quite a lot gone.

"She was stupid enough to get turned. And then stupid enough to try and hide it. I wasn't just going to let such a worthwhile opportunity pass me by," he rolled down his left sleeve and turned towards me. "You know, my dear, that just might be a good idea. It's obvious now that I can't do anything to him. But accidents do happen with vampires. I was hopping that that slut would have had an accident of her own with him by now. But he seems to have her tamed."

No, I just happen to treat her like a human you gutless bastard.

"So, two options present themselves. I'm not sure which I like more. First, I could let her loose. She'd tear your throat out. Leave you to bleed to death. Oops! Dead wielder. Accidental gluttonous behavior on the part of the now uncovered unregistered vampire heiress to the Finley estate. Internal league matter. Case closed. We win.

"Or there's option two. Have her tear your throat out and keep at it until you die. Give a little blood back. Then, after a while, you wake up. Slightly stronger, faster, and hungry. Oops! Dead wielder. At least for all intents and purposes. Accidental turning in the throws of gluttonous behavior on the part of the same unregistered vampire-heiress to the Finley estate. Internal league matter. Case closed. We win."

"I think I like option two," said Claria.

"Can I get an option three?" I managed. Neville snorted. Claria moved to finger the latch of the cage. She started tapping it rhythmically. Tracey stirred in the cage, dropping the shreds of tissue and eyeing the door.

"No," said Neville, tossing the older vampire a key. Claria quickly popped the lock and tapped open the latch. "I think two it is."

Neville tossed his dagger to the floor near my hands. I quickly slid over it to try feeing myself. Not that it'd matter much.

"Tracey, turn him!" The cage door was swung open. Tracey got out of the cage and stood up. I struggled with the rope, managing to cut myself. Tracey sniffed, her steps towards me pausing. I was loose, and in the process of scrambling to my feet, blood coming from my left wrist where I'd sliced it with the dagger. I moved the blade to an attack position in my right hand, braced with my left at the hilt.

"You don't have to do this, Tracey. Really you don't." It didn't look like she heard me. Or she at least didn't seem to understand.

"I smell a lack of understanding," said Neville.

"And I smell blood. This wont take too long. Can I have a snack too?"

"No," barked Neville.

"A girl's gotta ask."

The hungry vampire was approaching me slowly, eyes focused on my face. I made a feint to the left, almost slipping in the process on the straw. The vampire actually went for the feint, and slowly recovered to track my move to the right. For a second I thought this may actually give me a chance. I slashed a warning, not really wanting to hurt Tracey. I hoped it would knock her out of this madness.

Instead of heading the warning, the girl stepped into the swing faster than I'd have expected. Her step turned into a lunge. I suddenly found myself with the dagger and my right hand trapped between us, the blade caught in her chest. I brought my left hand up to try and push her head away, only to have it yanked aside. Her left arm grabbed my chin and wrenched my head up and to the side. We crashed into the stable wall, my head cracking hard on an exposed stud.

"Stop!" yelled Sir Neville. "Stop it Tracey!"

She didn't stop. Her teeth stabbed into my neck. I felt her draw heavily, quickly. Then, just as suddenly, she tore away. I sunk to the floor, dazed, but relatively whole. I realized Neville was holding a handkerchief to my neck. He was also cursing under his breathe. I heard the cage door slam open and a struggle between the two vampires.

"It wont matter now," said Neville in anger. "Since she's fed."

"I thought you had her under control," snapped Claria back at him. I glanced up to see Claria release Tracey, who staggered against the side of the cage. The dagger was in Tracey's hand, but she was holding it at the hilt and blade junction. I then noticed my coat and sword were on a bench against the wall behind them.

"Shut up."

"Well, this still doesn't satisfy me," she continued, starting to babble. I took the hand-kerchief form Neville, dabbing to see if my neck was still bleeding. It was. "I mean he still must die. What difference does it make how or when. Why not now. I have the right to ask."

"Do you really?" Neville asked sharply. "You did leave my house after all. I'll offer you a cup for your services, but nothing more Claria. I still have to deal with this."

"I can deal with it for you," she prodded.

"I said no! Now go to the house and ask Alder for a cup like a good little vampire and get out of my sight. Sir Borden here will be taken care of in the circle tomorrow night as it should be. It's too late to change things."

"You're not letting him go? Are you?"

Yes, Neville, are you? Please let me go so I can beat your ass tomorrow night.

"Of course not. He'll arrive at the circle at the appropriate time. As for her," he pointed to Tracey, who was standing next to the cage with her eyes closed. "She may not be useful anymore. It depends on how strong his blood is."

"Strong," replied Claria. "Probably near yours. But without that oh-so-pleasant after taste of bile."

"Leave!"

"Yes, Sir Never, I leave," said Claria. She touched a finger to Tracey's jaw, flicking it to a side violently. Then she glared at me. I glared back from the floor. She turned and left, the door slamming behind her. Neville muttered something unkind. He crossed to Tracey and reached out his right hand. Tracey had her eyes half open, noted the hand, and set the dagger on it.

Neville immediately took the blade in a underhanded grip and slashed across her face. Tracey saw it coming and took the blow across her left cheek. The impact sliced through the flesh to bone, and sent her spinning down along the side of the cage.

"Hey," I said. "Come on! You ordered her to do it."

"Yes," he replied, turning and walking towards me. I started to try and get up, but didn't quite make it. "I did. I also told her to stop. She didn't. But this isn't about her."

He motioned the blade towards my neck. It had fluid dripping from the end. I got the idea, and bared my neck. Neville touched the blade to the wound, which stung a little as the fluid seeped into the damaged skin. The burning sensation spread and warmed the area slightly. I touched the handkerchief back to my neck and pressed. The warmth spread a bit more, and then subsided gradually. Neville offered me a hand, I swatted it away.

"Fine," he said. "But remember, I was not the one who took you, Borden. Word has it you have sworn to best me on the morrow. I swear to you that I will give you that chance."

"You've been reading too many books Neville."

He turned to Tracey and backed away. "Put him in the cage!"

Tracey moved over to me and offered me a hand. I just looked at it. She turned her palm to me. I got to my feet on my own, a knot on the back of my head surging with each pump of my heart. I managed not to sway. Tracey grabbed my arm and pushed me towards the cage. I thought of making a lunge for the sword near the wall, but Neville moved to block my path. The vampire also didn't seem to be willing to let go. I ducked down and into the cage opening, going to my knees. The top came to about mid chest.

"You too, Tracey. Keep him company." She complied, hitting her head on the way in.

Tracey crawled to the opposite side of the cage and sat down with her back to the wall. Neville closed and locked the gate. He then left the room, shutting off the light. I did not fail to notice he left the coat and sword.

I regarded my companion in the dim light seeping through from an exterior source. I could see the left half of her face, the other was shadowed. The cut from the dagger was obviously deep and painful, but it wasn't bleeding. A few rivulets of fluid had dribbled down her face from the lower end of the cut. Her eyes were focused on a point on the cage floor between us.

"I'm sorry," she said softly, after several minutes of silence. That did it. I couldn't take the condition of her face anymore. I tossed the handkerchief in her direction. She moved her left arm to catch it, but missed badly. Tracey picked it up from where it landed in her lap and stared at it. I motioned to her face. Languidly, she brought the handkerchief to her face, dabbing at the cut.

"I know it will heal," I said lamely. "But it looks painful." I'm sure it wasn't as painful as the stab wound I'd put in her side a few minutes ago. As if she read my mind, her right hand touched her chest. In the light, I could see it came away wet. But like the cut on her face, it wasn't actively bleeding. She shrugged.

"How's the headache."

"How'd you know?" she started. "Oh, Melina. Yeah. It's ebbing." She sighed.

"You need to work on your technique."

"Huh?"

"Tracey, you don't have to tear first to get a good bite. Just sort of scratch at the skin. It sets the needles."

"Oh," she said. "I haven't much practice."

I nodded and frowned. Neville, that bastard. I got to my knees and crossed to the cage door. Reaching through, I could finger the lock. There wasn't enough space between the bars to get a hold on it.

"Don't bother," said Tracey. "It's magicked. Can't be broken without the key."

"Oh, is that how it works?"

"Yeah. Once it's set, the whole cage is the same. Can't get in or out. I tried."

I remembered the condition of the walls in her room. I bet she tried. And she probably had a lot more to her tries than I could manage on a good day. This wasn't a good day. A part of me wondered whether Neville had used something similar in her apartment. It wouldn't do much good to ask.

I sat back down and faced the vampire.

"So why Neville?"

Tracey pulled the cloth away from her face to look at it, and then pressed it back in place.

I asked again.

"Showed up at my door with blood. I... I knew. But..."

"How soon after you were turned?" I figure I might as well find this stuff out now.

"Three days," she sniffed.

"And since then he's been stringing you along?"

She half nodded. Then shrugged.

"How'd you get turned? And I'm going to assume it wasn't consensual."

Finally, the vampire looked up at me and shook her head. "I was stupid," she said simply.

"Okay," I started. "Who turned you?"

Silence. I remembered that shirt with blood on it.

"And he wasn't always your source of blood? Was he? We've been to your apartment. And I don't think the t-shirt we found was Neville's."

Tracey stiffened and choked, while trying to swallow.

"But it wasn't your fault," I said firmly. "Tracey. You didn't choose to be turned."

"You wouldn't leave me to my horse before and you cant seem to allow me my gutter now. What is with you Chris?"

"As I remember, I think your saddle was falling apart. And you were in danger of dropping your reigns," I offered in reply. Tracey snorted.

"I thought I was showing admirable restraint in not tearing your throat out that night," Tracey said, finally meeting my eyes in the dim light.

"By drowning yourself in alcohol and covering up your scent with cigarettes?"

"Exactly," she replied. "Well, it works. Seems to have made it a bit tougher for my kin to see me for what I am."

"New and old," I muttered. She didn't hear me and raised an eyebrow. Then I remembered Lady Weiss's comment. And Samantha. "Hate to disappoint you. But some of them knew. Not your parents. But Lady Weiss knew and tried to warn me. She probably told a few of the other elders. They assumed you were being used to take someone out."

"I think that was the plan," Tracey admitted. "I'm not sure who though. He'd been saying something about getting me to transfer to a school called UNF, or something. I don't remember what state he said it was in."

"Florida," I replied instantly. I lived about ten minutes away from its campus. "Oh." That would mean I may have been the target. I let loose one of those curses I'd heard Melina use.

"Didn't you say you worked in..." she trailed off as I nodded.

"Same city and everything."

"What was that in your refrigerator?"

She gave me a look. Okay, fine. I really didn't want to know either. One of the outside lights clicked off, putting us pretty much in complete darkness. I sighed and laid my head back against the cage. I still wanted to know who turned her. But I didn't feel like ordering her to tell me. I wasn't sure how far or how fast that whole sensitivity thing established itself. I wasn't about to try it while locked in a cage without my sword either. Which reminded me that I kind of needed to get out of this cage sometime soon.

"Hmm," I looked at the lock. The sword was across the room, but I decided to try and look at the lock. Yes, that other way. I tried to shift.

At first it didn't seem to work. I tried a little harder, and slowly, I could feel things differently, then gradually see more. The spell for the lock was rather bright compared to anything else around. I tried to look harder at the workings of the spell. In exhaustion, I sunk back on my heels, then my butt. I almost blacked out. That was tough.

Sitting there, trying to clear my head, I thought about what I'd just done. Seconds into the process I slapped my forehead with my left palm. Stupid! You'd been using the sword before without being in physical contact with it you idiot! Sure, it was strapped to your waist, but it wasn't in direct contact. This was no different. Not in the ways that mattered.

With this in mind, I reached again and shifted. Much better. I looked at the spell for the lock. While laughing softly, I put my will to the lock and grounded it out for a fraction of a second. The U portion of the lock split out of the body and went sailing into the air. The body fell to the ground with a clank. And something screamed a warning from the remains of the lock. I stared at it, dazed for a second, and then smashed the rest of the spell down. But not before I felt the answering call from what was probably the key. Time to go.

I crawled out of the cage and unraveled the sword from my, still borrowed, raincoat. While belting on the sword, I turned to Tracey, who was still in the cage.

"Coming?" I asked. She looked at me pleadingly, as if in indecision. "Tracey, come on! Lets go."

That seemed to work. She crawled to the opening and got out. I swirled the coat around my shoulders and made for the door. In the large yard about 300 yards to the left was the main house. Lights were coming on in some of the rooms as I watched. And it looked like flashlights were starting to head this way from around the front of the house. To the right of the stable was a building that looked like a garage. I headed for it at a slow jog. My head was still throbbing.

With half a thought, the door fell inward off its hinges. I skidded to a halt. In front of me sat a nice little collection of antique cars. The second was nothing other than a perfect dark green Jaguar XJ120c. I bounded into the drivers seat, tapped the switches, and cranked the 6 right up. It roared to life. Tracey was standing in the headlights.

"Get in," I said loudly over the noise. She did. I motioned for the lap belt, fastening my own. With another thought, I severed the chain holding the counter weight and the door to this stall went sailing up. I double clutched, popped the car into first and launched it out of the garage onto the drive. Slamming it into second, and cranking on the throttle, I navigated the turn up the drive leading past the house to the main road. A trio of guards made a run at the car with swords out. Deciding not to see what happens when a vampire gets loose on such a nice car with a sword, I ran off into Neville's flower bed. The rear left wheel spun out a bit, kicking up plants and dirt. After passing the guards, I swung the Jag back onto the drive. I was up to almost sixty when I rounded the edge of the house.

Shifting into second and slamming on the brakes, I got the Jaguar down to a controllable speed to make the turn around the left side of the fountain and up the main drive. In the mirror I got the satisfaction of seeing Neville running down the front steps waving his sword and shouting. I almost didn't get the car slowed enough to make the turn onto the main road. The thing really wanted to go fast, and I had let it get a little ahead of me. Fortunately it stopped pretty well. I only left about 30 feet of skid marks as the car slid all the way through the right hander onto the road. It came about 6 inches from the left side curb at the apex.

Seconds later, I saw lights appear in my rear-view mirror. Probably the pair of sedans which were parked around the fountain. Piece of cake. I clutched into third, revving the engine and spooling up through the gears. The lights began to fade. After three bends in the road, and one near miss with someone riding a horse, I slowed slightly and turned to my passenger. Mostly to see if she was okay. She appeared so. As did the most obvious hand holds.

"Any idea how to get to your dad's from here," I shouted over the noise.

"Next left," she said. I didn't hear her. "Left!"

Crap, I braked, clutched and then let up. Slowing more gradually, and then pulling a three point turn in a drive. I didn't want to leave skid marks. Seconds later, I was on the side road, back up past sixty, pushing the old car through its paces.

"Right ahead," said Tracey, louder this time. I nodded, swung the car to the left lane while braking. Then I down-shifted, accelerated and swung into a delayed apex turn. After a few minutes, Tracey pointed to the left. I took this one with a little more caution. Another minute and I saw a familiar mark. We were a few blocks away from Finley's. I slowed to a stop at the Hausmann's. Lady Whitacre's was across the street. Tracey gave me a funny look. I thought for second more, and then swung the Jag into the Hausmann's drive. A thought opened the gate.

I parked the car behind the house, just in between a small tool shed and the back of a greenhouse. It would be hard to find, even by helicopter. I didn't even want to think about the cost of fuel for one of those.

"Out," I said. Tracey unfastened the belt and hopped out. I followed suite, then turned back to the car. I picked up a leaf from the ground and dropped it on the hood of the car. The car vanished, seeming to be replaced by a pile of leaves. Tracey gasped. I nodded in satisfaction and then took off at a brisk walk toward the gate. I almost lost my balance from the effort of the spell on top of the days activities.

"Try not to walk into anything. Or anyone," I said, turning right onto the sidewalk. Tracey followed with her head down. It was about ten minutes to the Finley's by foot. I warded us to oblivion.

Chapter 21

Awareness

We let ourselves in a side gate. And no I'm not guilty about the whole lock thing. I didn't care. I walked up the front steps and Johny Danger came out of the trees at a run. He skidded when he saw us and sprouted off a bark of laughter. Shaking his head from side to side, he bounded up the steps and opened the front door for us.

"Thanks Johny-o." I went into the foyer and took off the coat. Tracey walked past Johny, her head still hanging a bit. He glanced at her face and raised an eyebrow.

"No problem, boss," he replied. "You okay?"

After closing the door, he turned Tracey around and touched her cheek tenderly. And then looked at her side. He took her left hand in both of his. It looked like he was going to cry. "You should have told us girl. We could have helped you through this, really."

She gave him a weak smile and then turned away, taking her hand back. Johny shook his head again. I followed Tracey into the sitting room and poured myself a healthy glass of water. Then another for Tracey. I passed her the glass. We heard footsteps on the front steps, and then the front door slamming open. I drank half the glass and then set it down. I saw Sara talking to Johny in the hall. Melina came rushing into the room, and into my arms.

After several seconds of the embrace, my rib was starting to twinge a little. And I couldn't breath.

"Melina," I croaked. "Loosen up. You're being a bear."

She did, and looked up at me. In the light of the room, she easily spotted the fresh tears on my throat. Melina started to turn towards Tracey, anger alight in her eyes. I moved in front of her and kissed her instead. She broke it quickly, managing to push me half aside and keep moving towards the other vampire. I hugged her from behind and said softly in her ear.

"He ordered her Melina," I said. She paused for a second, her muscles still tense. I was bracing to get thrown across the room. I repeated the comment, hoping it would get through. "Neville ordered her to do it! You know what that means."

Melina relaxed, still glaring at Tracey. Who was still looking at the floor. Sir Finley took that moment to enter. He gave me a once over, noted Melina's glare, and then the marks on my neck. Then he crossed to his daughter. As Johny had, he inspected the damage. And then gently, took Tracey in his arms.

"Daddy," she said softly, as she tentatively wrapped her arms around him and started to cry on his shoulder.

I released Melina and pushed her towards the door gently. Grabbing my glass, I followed. Melina closed the door behind us and turned to me with fire in her eyes.

"Claria nabbed me," I said in explanation. No, I didn't run off on my own. She nodded, then kissed me. I almost dropped the water. A while later, someone cleared their throat behind us.

"Ahem," said Johny. "Get a room."

Melina giggled, and pushed me away slightly. I grabbed her right hand, putting my fingers through hers.

"Johny, if you see that old bat Claria, bash her head in for me. I'm going home. Tell Bob I'll see him in the morning. And tell him I don't think he should be going to work. There's some things we need to do, and I think I'll need his help."

"I'd love to let ya do that, Boss. But there's another errand we really need your help with. You, ah.. kind of checked out early."

"I'm really not in the mood," I said with a hint of steel.

"We woke them, but we still have to feed them," said Sara gently, passing me the cloak. I passed her back the glass of water and lead Melina out the door, cloak over my right arm.

"We can't make him do it Johny," Sara continued after I didn't reply. I had a pretty good idea what they were talking about. The two pickup trucks from before were parked just at the foot of the steps and to one side.

"It's in a kind of rough side of town," said Johny. "I guess we'll be alright. I just got off the line with Bill and the others said they'd already have most of the barrels out of the freezer by the time we get there. We didn't want to show up with the trucks before the stuff was ready to load. We were about to arrange to wait for tomorrow, but since you're back..."

"Fine," I resigned. "But I'm driving."

Johny threw half a smirk at Sara, who shook her head. Then he held his hand out. The female vampire pulled a bill out of her pocked and slapped it in his hand. I received a wink from him as he pocketed the money. I motioned for the trucks, Johny heading for the one on the right.

I stopped with my hand on the door and Melina biting her lip, giving me a look. It passed, and she turned and hopped in the side of Johny's truck. I laughed and got in the other.

"What was that about," asked Sara, getting the passenger seat. "I thought you two were getting along?"

I cranked over the little truck after putting it in neutral. Someone had left the parking brake off. No I didn't pop the hood. I didn't care at the moment.

"Melina doesn't really like my driving much." I clutched and forced the stick into first. Johny pulled out, with me tucking in behind him. I had to struggle to get the second gear to catch.

"I know," said Sara. "They're not in the best repair. Some day I'll find us some newer ones."

"So what exactly are we doing?" I asked, pulling the pickup out into the street.

"We'll pick up a load of barrels and move them to Lady Weiss's. She's got the storage space. And now the manpower to secure them."

I yawned.

"Perhaps we should have waited until tomorrow?" Sara asked.

Perhaps. "But I'd rather not make it difficult for your friends to get their strength back. No?"

"Yeah, there would probably be some grumbling," Sara replied. "I'm fortunate enough to have never gone through anything like that. I've always had a fall back position."

"You've been around for a while. Family?"

"Yes," she brightened a bit. "I've a daughter. From before I was turned. Her husband thinks I'm a weird cousin. I try to go and see them every once and a while. Of course the age thing is getting a bit weird. Considering I look younger than she does now."

"I guess that could make things a bit awkward. She have children of her own?"

"I'm a proud grandmother of two boys; 3 and 6," Sara said. Then the vampire sighed and looked down. "Just don't go mentioning it to a bunch of people. I'm fairly well respected as a good worker. But I do have a few enemies. Since my skills aren't that much beyond being dependable and stable, I'm not as disliked as a few other vamps. I'd like my "family" to not have to deal with anything they don't have to."

"I understand Sara," I said. "But thank you for telling me."

"Sorry. I guess I'm just sprouting out this nonsense because of the Hausmann's," Sara shuddered, clutching the door handle. "Seeing them brought back some memories."

I glanced over at her, raising one eyebrow. Before I could come up with anything worthwhile to say, I noticed a headlight in the mirror. Sara glanced back out the rear window.

"If that's mister split face on his motorcycle, I think I'm gonna run him through," I said.

"It is."

"Great," I sighed, and then grabbed Sara's arm as she moved to open her door just after we made a left turn. "You can drive a stick okay?"

"I could change this clutch in twenty minutes, Chris."

"I'll take that as a yes," I said hastely thinking. I grabbed a pen from the dash, thought hard on it, and then passed it to Sara. "Hang on to this. I'll meet you at the warehouse."

She accepted the pen as I clutched and brought the truck to a screatching halt. Leaving it in neutral with the parking brake on, I hopped out the door. Sara had the truck moving again within seconds.

I turned to face back to the corner, waiting for the bike to make it. The vampire spotted me, standing with my sword out in the middle of the road and came to a stop about ten feet in front of me. He kicked the stand out, which killed the engine, and then crossed his hands over the top of the handle bars.

"Heard you've been busy," he said.

"I'm in no mood to play," I said.

"Nor am I," he replied. "You almost got me dusted."

"Shall I rectify that?"

He leaned back in the seat. "Is that a threat?"

"Yes," I sighed. "Are you afraid of heights?"

He said something back that sounded oddly like a prayer. Then the vampire lunged off the bike, over the handle bars, while drawing his sword from a shoulder sheath. I probably wouldn't have been able to get out of the way. But I didn't have to, fortunately. Since he wanted to fly, I decided to give him a hand. With a fatiguing thought, I launched the vampire into the air. Hard. The circle of pavement I used to anchor the spell crumbled apart under the force.

I watched the vampire disappear, arching out of sight on his way back to the ground. Then I laughed. It kind of reminded me of a cartoon I'd seen once with a rabbit being thrown into the air by a mislayed snare trap. I gave the space cadet a silent salute with my sword before sheathing it and turning to the motorcycle. I hadn't ridden one in a while. Probably a pretty good way of getting around this place though.

Shaking my head, I hoped on the bike and pulled the helmet off the seat peg. The vampire hadn't been wearing it. I darn well was. I tapped up the kick stand and was about to crank the bike over then I realized there was someone standing in my headlights. Melina.

"I think I prefer your driving to that," she said, making a skyward motion. "Did you really have to?"

I shrugged, remembering her comment about taking a fall off a roof. I winced in apology.

"Hop on," I said.

Melina got on behind me, putting her arms around my waist. I pulled the clutch and cranked the small v-twin. It came alive easily.

"I mean, was that really necessary Chris?"

"Hang on," I said, ignoring her. "I haven't ridden two up in a while."

Thinking of the pen, I let out the clutch and gently throttled up. It wasn't so bad, other then having two vice grips around my waist. I tracked the pen to the warehouse about ten minutes later. At a motion from Johny, I parked the bike inside the warehouse and off to one side. Melina got off, which let me breath again, and I put the bike on its stand and killed the engine.

Melina said nothing, and went over to help get the last of the small barrels in the back of the trucks. Each was about 5 gallons in size. I sat down on a crate and closed my eyes. Tossing the vampire took a lot more out of me than I thought it would. Then again. I may not have had that much left in me after this evening's activities. At the sound of a tailgate being closed, I opened my eyes. Johny gave me a thumbs up. Melina dropped a barrel into the back of the other truck and Bill closed the tailgate.

"Is the bike clean?" asked Johny, coming over with Sara in tow.

"It runs well," I started. Then almost laughed at myself. I gave it a close look. "Yeah. It's clean. No danger. I seem to be into stealing vehicles tonight. What do we do with it?"

"If you fought the guy and made off with his ride; it's yours."

"The heck kind of law is that Johny?"

"Our kind," he replied. "Leave it here boss. You can come and get it later if you want. Or take it with you."

"I'll leave it. We set?"

"Yep." Bill and the others were looking anxious. Two had already walked out the door and disappeared into the street. Bill and the other three were standing near the door waiting to close up behind us. "Off to the Lady's house."

I nodded and got off my crate. Melina began to look apologetically in my direction, then shrugged her shoulders and followed me to the tail truck. Sara already had the other one moving. Johny hopped up onto the bed and sat down on the cab.

It took two cranks, but I got the other pickup moving.

"Sorry you saw that Melina," I said after a few seconds of silence. She laughed, and surprisingly, it didn't sound forced. The tranny whined as I tried to get the darn thing into third gear. Finally, I gave up, and went back to second for a moment, then to fourth. The engine groaned a bit, but made the change.

"It was actually kind of funny," Melina admitted. "I don't think Jules is a happy vampire right now. Between me splitting his head, you catching him at the Hausmann's and his test flight." She giggled. "I almost can't wait to find out where he landed."

"I was aiming for Neville's living room," I said, half jokingly. Melina responded by grabbing my hand.

"I'm sorry I didn't ride with you earlier, Chris," she apologized.

"It's fine. I had a nice chat with Sara."

"She's been a little strange since the other night," Melina replied.

"I think she saw a bit of herself in the situation," I said.

I had a little bit of trouble getting the truck stopped with the extra weight when Sara stopped the other vehicle at a stop sign.

"Sorry," I mumbled.

"Maybe you should have checked the brakes," Melina teased.

"It's just the extra weight. Probably a little too much for this little truck."

"I mean. The fluid may be low or something. And what about the oil. Or the power steering fluid."

"This doesn't have power steering," I said, emphasizing my point as I yanked the wheel around with both hands to make the right hand turn from a stop.

"And you didn't check the radiator either. What if it overheats?"

"Brat." She laughed. I gave in and grinned over at her.

A few minutes later, we turned into Lady Weiss's driveway. It looked like almost every window had a light on inside the house. Big change from the night before. I followed Sara around the side of her house and to a garage built onto the side of a hill. It looked like a three or four car building from outside, but most of that was show, as the building opened up into a cave section. Johny had gotten out of the lead truck and opened a door in one of the cave walls. A freezer door. A large freezer door. Sara backed the first truck into it, and I worked the other truck around to follow her. There was just enough room for both trucks front to back, and to open the doors on either side. I didn't want to know.

I got out and tossed the keys to Sara, quickly exiting the cold so Johny could get the door shut. Sara passed the keys to a little kid who'd followed us from the main gate.

"She'll be glad to see them, I suppose kido," said Johny, slapping the kid on the back. He didn't seem to like the attention. I was prepared to offer him a smile, but instead received an almost blank stare. The kid almost nodded when he saw my sword, and then frowned when he saw me grab Melina's hand.

"It's going to rain. And she's not home," he said. Before I could formulate anything in reply, he ran back to the house. I guess that meant we couldn't stay for dinner. And that we were going to get wet.

Johny shrugged and motioned us towards the cave exit and the garage. The wind had picked up a little. I stopped at the open doorway of the garage and shrugged the cloak a little higher and put up the hood.

"No chance of unloading and driving back to Sir Finley's in the trucks is there?"

"You can unload them." Sara said. "We'll watch."

"They are heavy man," Johny concluded. "And we just gave little Mike there our keys."

"They're what, five gallons each. Blood's a bit heavier than water, so, say fifty pounds per bucket."

"Actually," piped in Melina, while putting up her hood. "Just a touch over forty-four. It's only 1.07 grams per CC for blood." She stepped out and began walking toward the front gate.

It started raining slightly. I played with the idea of just lifting all the barrels out using my other methods. Deciding I didn't want to chance getting that much blood all over the place, I gave up and started walking after Melina. Johny and Sara pulled down the garage door and followed after us, catching up at the gate.

"More walking," I sighed, mostly to myself. Melina smiled over at Johny, who shook his head. "What?" I asked.

"Nothing," replied Johny.

"If there are any more errands tonight, I think I'm going to quit."

"Nah, boss. We're done."

"While we're out, we could handle that..." Sara trailed off. I spun around and gave her a look. "Or not."

I could tell from her expression that she was trying to get my goat. Giving up on the whole thing, I got to walking again, settling into a medium pace next to Melina. I could have sworn I heard her start humming to herself a few times. Johny and Sara were talking a little. Mostly softly, and mostly about the Hausmann's. And I think Sara's turning. From what I gathered, what she saw in the house that night was a mirror of her own experience.

Yeah, reminders can be tough. Like the one I gave Melina not too long ago.

"I really didn't know you were there, Melina."

"What?" She glanced over at me, "oh. That." Melina waved it aside. "I'm fine. I just. Well, he got the full package deal. I guess. Up and down. I just got to go down."

"I'd grab your hand or something," I said. "But it would get yours wet."

"That's sweet, Chris. But seriously. I'm fine," she tossed a strange look in my direction. "You can make up for it later."

Before I could figure out what to do with that statement, we heard the sound of sirens. The mage police, I guess. We stopped and Johny poked his head between our shoulders.

"I don't think they're on us, peeps," he said. "So lets just keep a goin."

"It's only a few more blocks," said Melina, smiling. "And maybe they're just responding to a call of a party crasher. Like the through-the-roof kind."

"I'm lost," said Sara. I shook my head and started walking again. I was pretty sure it was a left at the corner.

"Chris, um, *launched* I guess would be the best word to use. Well, he launched Jules like halfway across town. It was rather funny."

"I wanted to see if he'd turn into a bat," I added. "It didn't look like he was able to adapt in time."

"Lets make a good bet," began Johny, looking around expectantly at Sara. She shook her head emphatically. "What? What's wrong with it? Just a simple one; like what block did he land in or something."

We kept walking. I saw Sir Finley's main gate and quickened my pace slightly.

"No one wants to start a bet on it with me?"

"Not particularly," I said. "As I've none of your money anyway."

"He gets like this," said Sara. "At least it knockes his lingo a bit back to normal for a while."

Johny skipped ahead and opened the gate for us. I shooed him through and closed it, then almost tripped on a brick that was loose on the edge of the drive. Melina's hand was quicker than my thoughts and had me steady. I slide my fingers through hers in thanks.

"On second thought guys," I said aloud. Johny and Sara looked over their shoulders at us. "I'm gonna check out here. It's been a day."

"Will do boss."

"Night guys," I said. The two vamps looked at each other and then back at us. "Just tell Bob I'll see him first thing in the morning."

"Good night," Sara answered.

When we got to back out the gate and turned towards the Wielder's mansion, Melina pulled a little on my hand.

"What?" I asked, looking around in alarm. I was warding us, but not completely.

"I guess I should make sure I'm actually being invited."

I raised our twined hands up in front of her. "Consider it an invitation."

She didn't quite look satisfied, but we started walking again. The gate opened in front of us, I pushed it shut and we walked through the front drive. I released her hand and slid my arm around her slim waist instead. She did the same, setting her head against my shoulder. Some water dripped off her hair inside the front of my coat. I let go of Melina and opened the door. Tossing the coat to drip dry on a hook, and unstrapping the sword, I headed up the stairs. Melina followed after a few seconds. At the second bedroom, I tossed the sword inside the door onto a chair and continued on to the bathroom.

I wasn't about to go to sleep with dirt on my face and hands and blood on my neck. I cleaned up a bit in the sink and then drank some water straight from the tap. As I reached to shut off the tap, I noticed a set of towels to the right of the sink. Which I didn't remember seeing that morning. I must have missed them. I headed to the bedroom. Without turning on the light, I could tell Melina had taken the left side of the bed. I shut the door, and took off the polo shirt. I sat on the right side of the bed and untied my shoes, then stripped off the borrowed jeans with dirt stains on the knees from my crawling.

Sliding under the covers, I suddenly found myself with a vampire on top of me, nose to nose. It didn't seem like she had any pants on.

"Don't you ever do that again," she said in a strict, hard voice, her hand touching my neck gently where I'd been bitten. "Or I'll turn you myself, you idiot!"

"Yes Ma'am," I replied, setting my hands lightly on her bare legs. It didn't seem she was finished with the conversation. I was.

Just as she started to talk, I brought my arms up her sides slowly. She shivered and stopped talking as I reached up and kissed her.

"We're not finished with this," she said, breathing heavily after another kiss.

"Good," I replied, intentionally misinterpreting her. "I'm glad."

Her reply got silenced by another kiss. She wasn't trying very hard to stop me. Actually, she was helping out quite a lot.

A little while later Melina broke free from a kiss and pushed up a bit on her elbows, which were on either side of my head. Her hair was draped around us.

"Do you want to know what Samantha told me?" She asked softly, a playful edge to her voice.

"Not particularly," I managed, then tried to capture her lips again. She pulled back.

"You sure?" she asked. "I think you may want to hear it."

"Now?" I asked.

"Funny man," she replied. Okay fine. I laid my head back. She leaned forward and kissed me. This time I turned aside.

"Well?"

"She reminded me that vampires don't require birth control," she said rather clinically. I immediately got an image in my head of Samantha and Christopher that I didn't want.

"I'm not sure I wanted to know that. At least not about them."

Melina giggled, and then slid her arms around behind my head and said very softly in my ear, "are you sure you didn't want to know about that?"

"I guess I'll have to think about it," I replied playfully.

"Can I help," she whispered back. Her breath in my ear was driving me nuts.

"I don't see why not," I replied. She moved her head back to kiss me.

"Maybe this will help," she said. I was definitely losing that other mental image. I had a physical one of my own to think about. I later agreed with her entirely.

Chapter 22

Morning

I awoke with a headache, offset by a very comfortable weight laying on top of me. Melina felt me stirring, and pushed with her left arm to roll aside. I stopped her with my arms, and kissed the top of her head.

Then I heard what woke me. Footsteps on the stair. They just reached the landing for the floor. I rolled Melina off and started to get up in alarm. She grabbed my shoulders and kissed me. I pushed her away.

"Melina, the door. Footsteps," I managed to get out. She laughed and pushed me back down to the bed.

"Silly," she said. "They're your housekeepers. We woke them last night."

Oh. And how was I supposed to know that? There was a knock at the door. I looked down. Melina grabbed the sheet and pulled it up to her shoulders with one hand, the other tossed some of the fabric out over me. I pulled the side up a bit more.

"Come in," she said. I looked at her, but was slightly distracted by her hand on my chest. It slid down to my stomach as I sat up. The door opened and an old woman poked her head in, then the rest of her followed. She looked like she was in her 70's. Which I guess for a vampire could have put her at several hundred years old, depending on when she was turned.

"Sorry to disturb you, Sir," She said. "Walter and I were preparing to get some supplies and wanted to know if there was anything you had a preference for or against?"

"I'm sorry, Ma'am. And please call me Chris," I replied, giving Melina a quick look. "I didn't even know I had housekeepers until about two seconds ago. Probably anything is fine. I don't have any allergies either. What's your name by the way?"

"Ruth," she said. And then with a knowing smile. "Don't bother getting up. I'll do with a proper greeting later. I'm sure you still have other things on your minds."

Okay, the woman knew how to make someone blush. It definitely worked on me. Melina smiled shyly and turned away from the door.

"Well," she said. "We're off. Have a good day."

"Thanks Ruth," I managed. She closed the door. I pulled Melina down next to me and wrapped my arms around her.

"I'll get you back for that later," I said gently.

"Sure you will, Chris," she replied. "Good morning, by the way."

"That it is, I guess. Good morning to you too."

"How much did Tracey take?"

I sighed, and pulled Melina in a little tighter, turning to her as well.

"Chris?"

"A lot," I admitted. "At least it felt like it. I don't know if she would have stopped on her own, even though she'd been ordered to. Claria or Neville pulled her away."

"Wait, Chris. I thought you said Neville ordered her to bite you?"

"Actually, he ordered her to turn me. Just as she was reaching for my neck, he ordered her to stop. But she didn't."

Melina stiffened, "then she just bit you anyway?"

"Hey, Melina, remember what you were like the other morning? Well from what I could tell Tracey was way past that point. Way past it. She wasn't talking at all. Her reactions were slow as molasses. She seemed almost comatose. I don't blame her for it. You should have seen the way she was acting. It made me sick."

"You're too kind Chris," she replied, softening against me. "I guess I'm just worried. And a little jealous." She added the last softly. I kissed her forehead, she snuggled into my neck, and then kissed me there. I thought she'd bite, but she turned away. "Your blood is a little irresistible. So I guess I shouldn't blame her either. I mean, I almost couldn't keep myself from your neck the other night. And as bad as Tracey was..."

"So, I do think I can bear a small snack, Melina. By a lot, I mean she took more than you usually take. However, I don't think she knew what she was doing. As she put it later, Neville hadn't been letting her get much practice."

"You don't have to Chris," she replied quickly. "I'm more than capable of going a few days without."

"Melina," I said.

"Yes, Chris."

"Bite me," I said, rolling on top of her and nipping her neck.

Several minutes later she did bite me, taking very little. The effect was rather interesting. Afterwards, I found her arms and legs locked around me, almost unbearably tight. The gate alarm rang from downstairs. That would probably be Sir Finley. As we lay there, entwined together, I realized it was starting to get late. I tried to roll away, but Melina didn't let go.

"Just another minute, Chris," she asked. "Don't go yet."

"We have visitors," I said, hearing the bell to the gate ring again. I kissed her soundly and she reluctantly let go of me. I didn't want to get up either. I did anyway, glancing to the pants laying on the floor. Among other things. Of course, sitting on the back of a chair at a small antique desk was a shirt and fresh pair of pants. In the chair were a pair of underwear, socks and undershirt. It seems my house staff were rather efficient. Next to the door was the bag Melina had left at the Finley's with her clothes. Yes, they were efficient.

I found a dressing robe hanging on a hook next to the door. With a look back at Melina, I crossed the room and donned the robe, and the pair of slippers on the floor beneath the garment. I then went downstairs to let the guests in. With the palm of my hand, I tapped the button for the intercom system.

"Yeah?"

"It's us," said Sir Finley. "And it's getting late."

Yeah, it was. "Sorry, Bob. Come on in. I'll be about five minutes for a shower."

I tapped the control for the gate lock.

"We brought breakfast, too."

"You're a pal, Bob. Thanks."

I thumbed off the intercom and walked briskly back up the stairs. I opened the door to the bedroom, catching Melina in my arms. She slipped beneath the robe and kissed my neck.

"Hey, you," I said, my arms around her. "Enough."

"You're the one spoiling me," she said, her head against my chest.

"I think it's mutual," I replied. "I'm taking a quick shower. Bob's on his way up the drive."

She signed and stepped away from me. I reluctantly let her go. I gathered the clothes from the chair and headed to one of the two bathrooms on the floor. I'd discovered there were two only because the door to the second one had been opened sometime through the night by Ruth or Walter. There were fresh towels and such in that one as well. I went to the newly discovered one at the end of the hall past what looked like a fairly large study. Moments later, I was under the hot water, and instantly reminded of the knot on my head. There was actually a bit of dried blood in the area, and it was swollen. It stung a lot from the water. And the shampoo didn't help either.

In what I hoped was close to five minutes, I finished the shower, used the toilet, brushed my teeth with the fresh toothbrush, and exited the bathroom. It must have been the influx of vampire blood, but my arms were much better. I only rebandaged the left, which was still fairly bad, but not near what it looked like the previous morning. I was dressed in a decent pair of kaikis which fit snuggly, but were comfortable, and a garnet button down shirt. I yanked the socks on, put my feet back in the slippers and slipped out of the bathroom.

I pulled the other bathroom door shut on my way by. The shower was on. Melina wasn't in the bedroom when I got back to it to put my boots on and collect the sword. I ignored the dress shoes which had been set out near the rest of the clothes. Sword in hand, and struggling with the belt, I headed down the stairs, taking them two at a time.

I found the guests in the dining room, which I hadn't seen yet. Finley was setting out what looked like two omelets and two half omelets on plates already populated with fruits and toast.

"Coffee, boss?" Johny asked when I came in the room. He motioned to me with a thermos. The smell was beckoning strongly. I nodded. "Just black, thanks."

Johny nodded and poured me a cup, putting it in my hand. I accepted it, and sat down across from Bob. I realized they were both giving me funny looks. I also realized that I had a smile on my face when I walked through the door. I made myself stop, and buried my nose over the coffee cup, inhaling the aroma.

"Does Mr. Graves know you're breaking fast out of his hovering range?"

Bob choked on his orange juice. Johny cackled. "Oh, that's a good one Chris," said Johny.

"We had to have him restrained," said Bob, after swallowing. "He refused to give us the keys to the thermos drawer either. I had to have Johny pry it open with a spoon."

He was pulling my leg. I laughed with him anyway, imagining Mr. Graves getting shoved in a pantry. Melina walked in during the laughter, wearing a long skirt and a tank top. She nodded to the others and bent to kiss my cheek. I touched her face, briefly, and she sat next to me. Pulling the plate of fruits closer, she picked at a cantaloupe square. I looked back over to the others, realizing my attention had been completely stolen. They noticed it as well, and gave each other a look.

Bob pulled a bill out of his pocket and slapped it into Johny's hand. The vampire pocketed the money with a grin. Melina looked up at the transaction and took a sip of water.

"You sly dog, you," said Finley, looking at me with half a smirk on his face. I felt myself turning red. Melina found my hand under the table and squeezed it.

"Should I ask?"

"With these two, definitely not," said Melina. She was also slightly red, I was happy to note. "They're like little boys when it comes to certain things."

Bob was laughing softly into his napkin. Johny was trying not to grin. I shook my head.

"So, now that that's out of the way," I started, Johny lost it and cackled again. I ignored him. "I hope this wasn't too much of an imposition, Bob?"

"Not really," he said, setting down the napkin and sobering up. "I need to first thank you for bringing my daughter back to me, Chris. I mean it."

"I'm just glad to have gotten her away from Neville," I replied. And glad that I got away too. "Was she able to tell who turned her? We talked a little bit. But I was more worried about getting out of there, then getting answers."

Johny set a picture on the table. "Sara talked with her. Tracey met him at a club. Apparently this guy gave her some date-rape drug and got her back to her apartment. Neville watched while the guy turned her. Sick bastard even waited for her to come around, and shot her up with a bunch of his own blood. He's been stringing her out since."

"And the man's shirt in the room," Melina asked. I drew the picture towards me.

"Ex boyfriend from high-school. Dropped by to see her during a school break. She said she ended up biting him, but doesn't remember what happened. He turned up dead in police records. I don't think she killed him, not from what she said. Probably Neville offed him in retaliation."

I slowly set the picture down.

"We've got no clue who that guys is," said Johny pointing to the picture.

"I've got to go to work today after all," I said. I was now pretty pissed off. Melina raised an eyebrow.

"What does that have to do with this guy."

"His name's Gerald Russell. We hired him about a year ago. How hard is it to redirect the gate?"

"Should just be a simple bit. I can do mine myself usually, but only between predetermined locations. You should be able to add locations to yours," said Finley. "You just need a doorway that you've physically touched and a strong thought."

I nodded and got up. "Lets go. I think we need to ask this guy some serious questions." I stood up. Bob and Johny followed. Melina took a sip of water and got up as well. We went out into the main hall and toward the gate at the back. I looked at the gate, which was currently set to open on the front porch in LA. With a thought, I refocused it to my closet door in the office at my work in Jacksonville. I reached forward and opened the door, which now showed my messy office. Melina walked into the hall with her sword and dagger. I walked through the gate into the other side.

Chapter 23

Florida

"It looks like Neville has been trying to keep the seventh league without a wielder after all," I said softly after we all made it through the gate. It was a few minutes past four in the afternoon. I had just closed my office door, after checking to see who was still around. A few of the interns were working late in the bull pen, and there was a major job going on in the simulation room. Other than that, the boss was gone, and the secretaries had left early. The receptionist was probably still here. Not that the phones were ringing to anything but voice mail. As usual. Sean and Denise were in the simulation room. Gerald was nowhere to be seen.

"We thought that may have been the case," said Bob. "But we never had a connection. It's been a while since anyone was claimed by the blade. Of course, it'd be nice to know how he was finding out who the blade wanted."

"So, how should we handle this?" I asked, returning my attention to the matter at hand. Johny raised an eyebrow at me.

"I mean," I elaborated. "We need to apprehend him and bring him in to be charged, right?"

Melina gave me a blank look, then frowned and shook her head. "We could just take care of him when we see him. It was a forced turning. Family have the right."

Bob seemed to be in agreement.

"Um, guys," piped in Johny. "Shouldn't we be like, um finding him first. We can worry about what do with him after."

"He should be out there with Denise," I said. "Let me check the logs. See if he came in today."

I crossed behind my desk, set aside the stack of mail on the chair and logged in. After a few moments, I pulled up the access list for the day, and noted that Gerald logged out about a half an hour before.

"He just left."

"Figures," said Melina. "Probably heading on an airplane back to LA to coddle Sir Neville."

"I'll ask Denise. This may take a minute," I added, locking the screen, getting up and heading to the door.

I paused with my hand in front of the handle to check my wards. I just wanted the sword hidden. And I dampened the sound on the room, just in case. The door open, I stepped through and headed to the simulation room.

It looked like the pair was working on a waste water treatment plant design. The 3D plot was displayed on the large screen and several small blow-ups around it. It looked rather familiar. Actually, it looked like something I'd been working on a few weeks ago. As I walked in Sean looked up from the piping he was drawing and smiled at me. Denise went ballistic. I was the one who was supposed to be helping her with the piping design. It was our project. And it was due Thursday. They hadn't done much in the last two weeks.

"Where the hell have you been," Denise started. "You didn't call. You're cell phone is out of freaking order. You never check your emails. Oh, and we checked. You never checked out of you damn hotel room you moron. Might I remind you that this whole thing's due in 48 hours!"

"It's not due for another 53 hours," I snapped back. "And what the heck are you doing reworking the whole piping setup. I already did the piping before I left, Denise. You should have taken on the reactors."

She was a chemical engineer after all. It was her job.

"What do you mean, reworking the piping, Chris. You didn't do any of it!"

I pushed past Sean and tapped in a few commands, opening up the version I'd last worked on. With the complete piping structure all done in and tested. Sean sighed and leaned back in his chair.

"Fine," Denise said. Almost yelled, rather. "That would have saved us 10 hours yesterday while you were off in California doing lord knows what!"

"I had an emergency to attend to," I replied delicately. More or less accurate.

"Funny, they seem to be going around," said Sean. "Gerald left half an hour ago."

I know. More like 45 minutes, Sean. "And?" I leaded.

"And he had to catch a plane," Sean added.

"Family emergency of some sort. Went home to pack," said Denise. "So was yours a family emergency. Or was it just an I've-got-to-dump-stuff-on-poor-co-workers emergency?"

I wasn't listening anymore, and she knew it. She hit me in the arm. Or she would have, if I'd have let her hand get that far. Okay, Chris, think.

"Sean, give me your cell phone," I ordered. He looked up at me. "Now damn it!"

"Fine," he said coldly, passing it to me. I slipped it in a pocket.

"If Gerald comes back for any reason, ring me immediately," I said. "Then call the cops. And act normal."

"This is usually where you give a really good reason, and we all either have a good laugh, or call you crazy," Sean started. "You're not gonna? Are you?"

I left the room at a jog. That took far too long. As the door was swinging shut, I distinctly heard Denise, "he's completely barmy, he is. Out of his freakin mind. And you let him waltz off with your cell phone."

"It's the companies," Sean replied with a shrug. The door latched. I got to my office and motioned for my entourage to follow me out of the building. They didn't immediately move to follow.

"Well, that took a while."

Thanks Melina. Obvious.

"She your old girlfriend?" asked Johny. Melina gave me a look.

"A touching scene," insinuated Bob. "Two lovers. Their feelings obviously pined to the sticking place, for all to see."

"Can we go now?," I asked, letting a little of the annoyance I felt at my coworkers seep through. Bob nodded, but Johny looked like he wanted to continue berating me. Melina stopped him by giving him a shove towards the door while laughing.

It was a quick walk past the intern bull pen. On my way by the receptionists desk, I tore out the employee information card for Gerald Russlle. She was in the break room, as usual, watching a soap opera. We passed a few people from the downstairs graphics firm, and then were in the parking lot. I headed over to my car, parked in the corner of the lot from before the trip to L.A.

"Hop in," I said unlocking the door of the small wagon. When Melina walked by, I passed her the info card. We all piled in, Melina in shotgun, Sir Finley behind her and Johny behind me. Balanced vampires and humans. Funny. I started the car, buckled up and reached for Melina's hand with the address. After releasing her hand, I put the car in reverse, backed out and then pealed away from the lot into the pre-rush hour Jacksonville traffic.

"I know about where that is, but check to see how the heck I get to it off of Shamrock," I said to Melina. "There's a map in the glove box." Melina popped the latch, and found the map. She began looking. I slowed a little and pointed in the rough area to get her closer.

"I assume we're heading towards this guys house?" Asked Bob.

"Yep. But we're about a half an hour behind him," I said, making a right turn onto a major road at a red light. "The lady gets a rose: he's got a plane to catch."

"Can I trade the rose for his heart?" asked Melina. At first I thought she was joking. Her look over in my direction told otherwise. She definitely wanted to kill this guy. And I thought she didn't like Tracey.

"As far as I'm concerned Melina," said Bob. "You have my full blessing to destroy him on her behalf."

Melina nodded. I took a swallow and tried to concentrate on driving. A few moments later I pulled onto Shamrock.

"Well?" I asked.

"What road did we just come off of?" Melina asked calmly.

"61."

"Third left," she replied almost instantaneously. "Then it'll be a right about a quarter mile down."

I got into the far left lane and pulled into the turn lane at the appropriate road. Melina checked the road name, and motioned that it was the right one. The car barked a little bit into the turn as I cut it between two oncoming cars. One honked. The other didn't even notice me. They probably wouldn't have unless I actually ended up in their laps. A quarter mile down, I took a right onto the road and Melina looked down at the paper.

"3028," she said, "It'll be on the left side. You still have a ways to go."

"Thanks," I replied. I mean, I didn't even have to ask, and the chick let me know which side it was on. Nice.

"What happens if he's not home?" Asked Johny.

"Catch him at the airport." I didn't like the idea of trying to get swords through the security.

"And if we miss him there?" he countered.

"May be fun," said Melina. "Never fought in an airport before. Lots of space. And those luggage racks."

I glanced over at Melina, catching her with a wispy smile on her face. This was getting a bit odd.

"That look like it?" she half asked, pointing a few houses ahead.

"It's his truck," I said, noting the new silver pickup in the driveway.

"You two take the front. Since he knows you and Melina's agreed to take him, it'll work. Johny and I'll take the back."

I slowed, and stopped the car in the drive behind the pickup. We got out and split up. I waited until the other pair had slipped a ways around the side before we headed up the driveway to the door.

"What if he took a cab?" asked Melina.

"You're definitely on top of things today, Melina."

She smiled at me. "Got a little used to it, last night."

I grabbed her hand for a quick squeeze and then reached for the door bell. The tv was on inside. And the porch light was on as well. Strange, since it was still quite daylight. I rang again and knocked.

"Looks like you may be right again," I remarked, tuning to Melina. Who lunged past me, sword out, to bash the front door into kindling. Gerald stumbled back from the broken door and smashed into a cabinet, knocking several shelves out. He swung the remains of the cabinet away from the wall towards Melina, who deftly jumped around it and took a swing at the vampire. Gerald barely managed to get his sword up to bock her blade. In a fury of blows which raged over the living room, Melina showed a clear edge. Between her skill, the close confines of the room and her smaller size, Gerald was out matched. Johny and Bob had broken through the back door and were watching from the kitchen.

In almost no time, Gerald was obviously slowing down. His blocks were getting weak and he wasn't attacking much at all. Melina continued the barrage on the male vampire with one hand, and then pulled out her dagger with her left. Although he had been fading, the sight of the dagger gave Gerald a second wind. I took a close look at the small blade.

Then it dawned on me. Melina's dagger could kill other vampires. That was right, the Wielder's swords weren't the only ones. Just those and the ones she made.

Gerald slid backwards through some debris from what used to be the coffee table, and then he tripped and fell. By the time Melina closed, he was already halfway back to his feet. Melina's two blades caught Gerald's single sword with a clash. Then I noticed something. In terror, I ran at the pair as fast as I could, tearing my sword from its sheath. With a vicious down stroke I chopped the sword out of Gerald's hands and threw him backwards into the wall with a shield. I over did it a bit, as he went through the drywall and into the studs.

Melina was in front of me, swords out and bloody, hair flying and skirt slightly torn. And she was wondering what the hell I thought I was doing. I was wondering why she wasn't pissed at me.

"Boss?" Asked Johny already coming into the room with his sword out.

"Take a look at his sword," I said, still staring at Melina. She lowered her blades and took a step closer. I lowered mine as well. Johny bent and picked up the battered sword and brought it over to us. "You didn't know, Melina? Did you?"

She shook her head, bemused. I finally looked away from her and over to Johny. "Break it, Danger."

Johny looked over at Bob, who shrugged. He set the blade on the side of the fireplace and then jumped on the flat, snapping the sword into several pieces. Picking up some of the pieces he walked over to Melina and held them out. She looked down at them, recognizing immediately what they meant. More quickly than I thought was prudent with all the naked swords flailing about, Melina closed the distance between us and hugged me, bring my mouth down to hers.

After a few seconds, and probably because we were both becoming aware of the dangers of kissing with long sharp objects dangling from digits, we extracted ourselves. Johny had passed the pieces to Finley. He didn't look happy. Actually, he looked pretty ticked, and he was looking at Melina.

"I swear to you," she said, noticing the look. "It's not mine."

"And you didn't tell anyone," he asked, thought his anger was ebbing. "You're sure?

We ruled that you were to keep it secret. No one should know how to do that. Ever!"

"I did, Sir Finley!"

"It's different from hers," I said in her defense. "I think it does the same thing. But there's something a whole lot, well, darker about the whole thing. Hmm."

I sheathed my sword, motioning for Melina to come closer. She put her blades away and stepped next to me.

"They can't hear us," I said, after dropping a sound ward over our heads. She nodded and grabbed my hands. Her eyes had the hint of tears.

"I didn't tell anyone, Chirs," she said. "I really didn't."

"Shhh. I don't think you did. And I don't think Bob does either. I said Gerald's was different than yours. Which would probably mean it was made differently as well. There's something, unwilling, I guess in that thing. The hard part, I'm assuming would be the making the wood core? It sets the spell?"

Melina nodded her head. Then frowned.

"I'm not going to ask you to tell me. I think I already know." I dropped the ward. "Johny, how hard is it to scar a vampire's flesh."

"Hard. It usually doesn't scar at all."

"Unless we're not very healthy," added Melina. I figured.

"Has Tracey been having a lot of stomach aches recently, Sir Finley?"

The man paled and sunk to his knees, his head in his hands. So it was out; Sir Neville had been using Tracey to make blades fit to kill vampires. And this had been going on for quite a while. Which meant we were facing an unknown number of the deadly things. And as we just saw, there was a distinct danger due to the fact the people these blades would be wielded against probably wouldn't think much of them until it was too late.

"I believe it's time we left," I said. Johny checked his watch.

"Got that right," he said. "What do we do with him?"

"Take him with us," said Bob, his voice dripping with venom. He sniffed and then stood up. I decided not to argue.

"Throw him in the back of the Subaru," I said. Johny began extracting the guy from the wall while Melina tossed the broken pieces of the blade into a plastic container she found in the kitchenette. Bob couldn't keep his eyes off of Gerald.

In minutes, we were all piled into the car, vamps in the back. I popped it into gear and tore our of the drive. Two quick turns through a side neighborhood got us out of the area. Apparently someone had called in the noise of us bashing down the door. I heard sirens approaching.

The ride back to work was a quiet one. And a fast one. It ended fast too. A police car had just turned into the office parking lot in front of us. They moved fast. I spun into the lot next door and parked between two of their large moving trucks. We piled out, quietly.

"I've got a back window," I said. "I'd rather not actually have a run-in with law enforcement. If I can help it."

The others nodded agreement. With Gerald over Johny's shoulders, we went through the small stand of trees between the businesses.

"I don't think Melina likes your driving much, boss," said Johny.

"Hush," Bob directed back at him. Melina smiled weakly over her shoulders. I stepped ahead of them and hopped the small fence. Johny passed Gerald to me and Bob, but Melina pushed between us to help ease his still unconscious body down to the ground.

I thought the lock open and then threw the window to my office open. We all heard the front door of the office close. Melina hopped in and gave a hand dragging Gerald over the window sill.

Bob went through the gate first, then the vamps. I put the mail back on the chair, locked the terminal and hopped through after them. Just as someone knocked rather loudly on the door.

Chapter 24

Rush

"Where's Tracey?" asked Bob immediately upon our entrance to his house. Sara frowned and finished buckling on her sword. Johny dumped Gerald unceremoniously at her feet, causing her to jump back.

"On the back porch, second floor," she said. "She just woke up. Mister Graves gave her some wine a moment ago."

"Bob, she may have been ordered not to tell about the blades," I started. He nodded after a quick thought.

"That may be. But we need to know how many!"

"And she may not know that either," I countered.

"Can I talk to her?" asked Melina softly. I nodded, but looked to Bob. It was his house and his little girl.

He sighed and waved her out to the back. After her skirt swished through the door down the hall, he turned his eyes to Gerald, who was finally starting to stir. I threw a shield over him as he tried to sit up.

"Man," Gerald winced as his head bounced off my shield and then off the hard wood floor. He coughed a few times and took a deep breath. "The hell."

"We could ask him too," said Johny.

Bob considered this for a moment. "No, I think we'll bleed him though. Then bring him to the meeting," he sighed. "Go ahead and let him up: you need to save your strength, Wielder."

I frowned. Thanks Bob. I needed that. I let the vampire go, who tried to stagger to his feet. Johny and Sara each grabbed an arm and began hauling him out the door. Bob followed. I really didn't feel like watching a vampire have his blood let, so I went looking for the kitchen instead. It was past lunch time. Well past lunch time.

The door located, mostly by the smells of supper preparation, I pushed it open. Only to face the master of the domain; Mister Graves.

"Any chance of me making myself a sandwich," I asked before he had the chance to finish inhaling. I feigned as much nonchallanace as I could manage. Which was a fair amount.

"Preposterous!" he managed, cutting his breath short. "Out! Out! Out!"

"Look, dude," I began. "I don't want to get in your way. I just want to grab a snack."

"Not in MY kitchen-" I cut him off by holding up hand. "I–"

"Shh."

"Don't 'shush' me, Sir!"

I clamped my hand over his mouth, watched his eyes go buggo and he started to stagger back. I didn't let him finish, making a snatch past him, then turning on my heel and lunging out the door. In my spoils: a huge fresh muffin the size of my hand.

"And stay out," came the shout from behind me. I smirked a bit, and then picked up the pace, lunging up the stairs three at a time. I made it out to the second floor balcony to see Tracey and Melina talking softly. The latter looked up and smiled at me. Tracey wouldn't, letting her eyes drift out over the rear lawn. A nearly empty wine glass was in her left hand. Her right absently rubbed her cheek where there was still a mark from her own blade.

"Thirty," said Melina, patting the patio chair next to her, which would put me across from Tracey and keep my back to the house. I sat and raised an eyebrow. "Possibly more."

"More what?" I asked. I wasn't thirty yet. I hoped I wasn't looking it.

"Blades," elaborated Tracey. Her voice was barely audible. "I'm not sure! I keep..."

"Dreams," said Melina flatly. She winced, shaking her head. "They tend to stick."

I didn't know if her word choice was the best, so I took a bite out of the muffin.

"For there to be no weakness, there is to be no sense of strength," Melina paraphrased. "The only strength is in understanding the power you now have, Tracey."

The two vampires locked eyes for a moment. Then Tracey noticed by muffin.

"You get that from the kitchen?" asked Tracey.

I nodded.

"How?"

"Snatched it.." I mumbled.

Melina gave me an odd look. "And he saw you?"

"Actually," I swallowed. "He was standing about a foot away when I effected the grab. Don't worry, I know the type. I can deal with his."

I stopped because Tracey was choking on her wine. She almost dropped the glass. I was about to ask if she was okay when it became apparent that she was laughing. Her eyes flashed up, with a bit of a glow. And then the moment passed, her gaze dropped back into the wine, and she swallowed the last of the laughter.

A moment later, Martin skidded to a stop in the doorway of the porch. Tracey took a deep breath. He crossed to sit down at the fourth chair next to his sister. Melina gave me a quick look, and I nodded, getting up and heading for the door. Her hand slipped into mine after we entered the house and I started to head to the stairs.

We got down into the main hall, and I tossed away the wrapper from the muffin in a trash bin. I felt a bit out of sorts.

"I can't go out the front, because I really don't want to see a vampire being bled. And shouldn't go out the back because of the little family time thing. So now what?"

"Third floor practice rooms?"

"I guess that'll work," I replied, already being dragged in the general direction of the stairs. The same ones we just walked down. "Wind scroll. Right?"

"'It is impossible to prevail without reason'."

I snorted. "Yeah, reason. That I have."

"Do you?" She asked. "Do you really? Or are you just playing at it; like in one of your books."

I almost dropped her hand. Then thought the better of it.

"Honestly?" I asked. Mostly of myself.

"Honestly, Chris."

"Maybe," I replied. She opened a door into a large, high ceilinged hall on the third floor. It looked like it was almost as big as that entire side of the house. Probably 15 meters by 40. I drew my sword and sat down in the center of the room, looking down at the blade. Melina sat cross legged in front of me in a swish of skirts.

"Maybe I've not dealt with this all yet. Some isn't still real to me. At least not as real as it should be."

"That blade is real."

I flipped it over and studied the edge. Yes it was. A magnificent sword, which I still felt I had no right to. I could wield it, it seemed. But was it truly mine? Was being able to flash it around and call forth some magic enough to call it mine? I wasn't sure.

"This house, this place is real."

I looked around the room and took a deep breath. Yes, this place was real too. Different, but real. The time passed in odd cycles. Yet the air was indeed air. The soil substantial and the feeling of life pervasive. But did I belong here? Here among the mages. Here among vampires. And who knows what else. Again, I wasn't sure.

"I'm real."

A simple statement. I looked up at her as she leaned forward on her knees and placed her hands over mine on the hilt of the sword. Our eyes met.

Yes, Melina was real. Vampires were real. I'd seen, and felt, enough to realize that in its entirety. Real as the day is long. More true here than else, due to the longer days. But what was she to me? I'd grown used to having her around these past few days. Used to her presence, her persistence and character. What did that mean? Was it all due to the circumstances which I precipitated by walking into Charles's shop what seemed like ages ago and seeing that box?

Since then, it had been nearly constant motion. And I needed to slow things down. Center. Find some peace, if only temporary. Else, I'd not know the difference between strong and weak. I would not have reason. And thus, I would find victory impossible.

Melina sat back on her haunches slowly, still studying my face. My mind went down to the blade, held in my hands. I almost cautiously dropped my awareness into its hilt, looking at what made it what it was. I'd have to face a similar blade soon. And would have to unravel it's mysteries, at least a little, in order to manage what I'd intended.

The settings were phenomenally more complex than anything I'd looked at before. At first I was lost in the winding of the core of the blade. I found an end, an anchor point in the stone on the hilt, and followed it through, tracing the line as I would a circuit. I knew networks, I'd built them and troubleshooted them for years. I could do this. So I examined and learned.

Occasionally, I'd touch on a path, and it would change, or shift. But after a while, I'd learned what to look for in the patterns. There was a decisive difference between the "feelers" and the backbone.

More importantly, I knew how to shatter that spell. There were seven nodes. I couldn't tell what they did, exactly, but they were the substructure for the entire network. Short them, and the whole package would fall apart. And the sword would shatter. How violently I knew not. I just knew I didn't want to experiment with this particular blade. I'll wait for Sir Neville's.

I opened my eyes to find Melina still staring at me.

"Better?" she asked.

I took a deep breath, letting it out slowly. "Mostly. If I can find the nodes of Neville's blade, I can break it," I said. "Are they made the same?"

"Probably. As they were all made by the same people at the same time," she said. "But Chris, you'll not have a half an hour or so of contemplation. Perhaps not but a few moments."

I considered this, frowning slightly.

"Then I'll have to be quick."

She returned my frown, not my smile.

"Then you'll be dead," she didn't seam to like that idea. I didn't really either.

"I could stall a fair amount," I mused.

"You don't know anything but one way of using the blade Chris. You'll see a lot more from Neville. Things that you haven't had the chance to examine."

"'And defense is an unreliable entanglement, which is the product of a distracted mind'." I almost smiled at her.

"Now whose doing the paraphrasing of the Wind Scroll," she shook her head. "Poorly I might add."

I sighed, but it was a contented one. I was coming to embrace what I'd have to do.

"Tell me of the typical challenge; what Neville will be used to. What are the customary progressions?"

"The challenge begins with the two in circle, warded by the seven highest mages at the meeting. Once in, as you'd expect, neither can leave until the agreed upon terms of the challenge have been met. Sometimes this is just to first blood. Others, to disarming. Others to death."

"I think I know which terms will be adopted for this challenge," I said flatly.

"Anything in the circle, except sound, stays. The two face one and other. When called for, the challenge begins. Usually, blades only at the outset. A match of skill till first blood. At that point, anything goes till the challenge is finished."

"Air?" I asked.

"What about it?"

"Is air allowed in and out of the circle? Or just sounds. In other words, do we have a fixed amount of air in the circle?"

"That's a good question. I'd say no, since we never smell fire until after the circle falls. But I don't know for sure. You could ask I guess."

"I think I'll assume it's sealed," I mused. Or possibly something with shields and oxygen.

"Or at least slightly diffusive. Maybe permeable to nitrogen and oxygen, but not large molecules," continued Melina. Oh, yeah. She did say she was starting a biology degree. I'd just nod and agree until she started talking about partition coefficients. That's where my handle on diffusion ended.

"And his sword style?"

"The rudiments are like Sir Finley's," she started. "Guard problem is I think there on the left side. Probably from the same source as Finley's; as they had the same instructor early on. I don't expect you'll find anything lacking with Neville's foot work. And I don't think he dips his right."

"And of course, he's faster than Bob, and thinks quicker. Right."

The vampire nodded.

"But he is slow on the take," I stated. "Slow changing gears when he sees the unexpected."

"That was how I nearly tore him apart."

"What if I just jump right in and try bashing him apart with some shield tricks?"

"I'd say you have a better chance of getting a lucky shot in on him with the blade. Unless your trick with the nodes will work."

"Hmm."

"Oh, and there's one more thing," Melina sighed. "He may be taking infusions of vampire blood to up his strength."

Great. I winced. Then shrugged.

"I made a promise. I have a reason. And I have a way. It is left but to make them all march in rhythm," I intoned. Melina didn't seem to think this was convincing enough.

"You're taking this seriously, Chris. But I don't think seriously enough."

"There is no time left for anything else. I face him and hold my own until we go the the more extraordinary measures allowed by the swords. I shield like hell, which should catch him off guard as I've got some filters in mind that'll throw him for a loop. I've also got something in mind for taking the oxygen out of his space.

"And all I need is a little bit of time. To find the nodes. After that, I can keep my promise."

I moved to my feet, noting on the way that the clock on the wall said nearly 6:00. The meeting was at 7:30.

"Am I still allowed to worry?"

I looked down at Melina, who didn't seem too happy about the situation. I really wasn't either. She stood up and hugged me. I was pleased to note my ribs didn't hurt anymore. And thanks to her.

"The spell can be broken, and the blade unbound. I know this."

"But do you understand why?"

"It's just currents and voltages and resistances. Energy, but not electrical. Not really."

"Misunderstanding is a delusion," she added sternly, looking up to my eyes.

"And not true emptiness," I concluded. The Scroll of Emptiness. "It is Neville who does not understand the sword. I know how it works, though not all it can do. One does not need to know how to drive a car in order to make it fail."

She laughed slightly. "I just got a mental image of you slashing his tires with a pocket knife."

"I was thinking more along the lines of igniting his gas tank." It'll work. It had to. I'd promised.

We left Bob's house a few minutes later after a quick bite to eat. Tracey seamed slightly more animated, and Martin wouldn't leave her side. Good kid. Johny and Bill from the other night let us out the front gate.

The walk back to the Wielder's house was slow and deliberate. I had to change. Melina carried a bag with her that had materialized itself as we were heading towards the front door from one of the maids. Mister Graves popped out just enough to make sure the bag was delivered and give me an icy glare. I'd have to find out his first name. It was required.

"Aren't you going to ask what's in the bag," Melina asked after we passed the edge of the Finley estate along the sidewalk.

"No." I figured it was clothes. It was in the same bag as the delivery I received the other morning from Samantha.

"Fine."

"Fine what?"

"Considering I've nothing else with me to wear, I guess I'll have to show it to you anyway."

"If you're trying to tease me, it wont work. Not now anyway," I said with half a smile."And if your trying to distract me. Consider me already distracted. But I'm afraid I'll be quite distant until this is done."

She sighed. We got to the gate and I opened it, letting Melina through and closing it behind us.

"A part of me doesn't want this to be over," said Melina softly. "That's rather stupid and petty of me. Isn't it."

"Consider it mutual," I replied. "I'm not looking forward to dealing with the consequences of this week's adventures." I caught a glance from Melina. "As far as work is concerned," I added quickly. Considering her friendship was one of the consequences of said adventures. "I've a lot of projects, all requiring tech much newer than 10 years old. And I hate going back on commitments."

I pushed it aside, shaking my head.

"I agree," the girl stepped away to skip up two stairs ahead of me and opened the door. There was a note inside on the table next to the coat rack from Ruth. It seems they were out getting some items and would be back that evening later on. Melina headed upstairs, I presumed to put on what was in the bag. I followed a few moments later.

My thoughts were already detaching themselves from concerns. I was getting ready. Tests were either a hell or a panacea. I held that each should be passed or failed in advance. I'd done my studying. Asked my questions. Found my answers. There was nothing else left to do. Sort of.

I'd probably have to tell myself this about another fifty times before I faced Neville down.

I found Melina in a nice red dress down in the back hall in front of the gate. She was biting her lip, but stopped and smiled when she saw me.

I had on the jerkin from the other morning and similar garb, freshly delivered, I assumed. And yes, I was wearing my boots. Oh, of course, the coat was, well, you know. My attention was slightly caught up by the vampire, but I let it slide aside and I almost walked right past her.

"Later," I said softly. "And remind me to compliment you on the dress then as well." I refused to let myself look down at her. She looked like she was about to cry. Which didn't help my resolve in the least.

"Melina.." I started.

"Please just hug me, Chris," she almost pleaded. I complied. I really didn't have any choice. "Please try and come out of this alive."

I held her for a few moments longer, then tipped up her chin to capture her mouth quickly. There went the last of my resolve.

We broke the kiss, and I glanced up at the clock. Still 15 minutes to go. I wanted to be early. I released Melina, reluctantly, and set the gate with a thought to the meeting hall. It knew where it was. Grabbing Melina's hand, we walked through.

I almost wish I'd stayed where I was. Of course that would have meant all sorts of terrible things may have happened. Then again. All sorts of terrible things happened anyway. I'll let you be the judge. However. I'll say this; I'll never be satisfied with allowing myself a fifteen minute window again. Now it's never less than a half an hour. Damn him.

Chapter 25

Entrance

Kind of funny walking into a mess. And this was it. Some bastard had decided to try starting the meeting a half an hour earlier. The doors finally sealed less than three seconds after Melina and I made our entrance. A woman was trying to call the meeting to order, yelling for people to sit down. I immediately caught Neville's eyes, just about ten meters away from me. He had turned to look back at the sound of our gate.

I squeezed Melina's hand and then let it go.

"I assume this means we're definatly going to be challenged?" I asked calmly to no one in particular. Looking around showed we were in a huge cathedral. The circle on the floor was about twenty meters in diameter. And the ceiling at least forty tall. It reminded me of a theater from ancient Rome. At least in the seating features. About a quarter full of people, some arguing, others entranced on the action.

Lady Weiss was fuming next to Lady Whitacre and Dallas. I saw Cleary and Naber. None of the others. The vampire Claria was in deep argument with Whitacre and Dallas, who I now noticed was a vampire himself. I hoped to find Samantha here, and instead looked to the Lady Weiss. I walked over in their direction.

"Not quite yet," intoned an older woman standing in the center of the circle. I assumed she was replying to my question. "Please take your seats. This meeting has gotten off to a strange start. And I'd like to move things along."

"And there's a particular reason it's started yet at all?"

The woman stared at me and motioned toward Lady Weiss. "Talk to your elder, blade."

I gave Neville a glare, and walked over to the Lady. I was certain Neville was behind this mess. The others had all dispersed to take seats. Across the circle from the terminus area were seven mages standing in front of chairs. At even intervals around the circumference were wooden booths, taken up by each league's seniors. There were three seats in each booth. The rest of the audience sat in graduated rows around raised above the booths. Neville took his seat around the right side with two elders from his league. One looked decisively uncomfortable. The other was talking rapidly, yet softly to a woman leaning over the back of the booth. She kept nodding every few words. It looked like there was one blank space across from the mages allowing them an unobstructed view of the gates. Still, three booths on one side and four on the other. Strangely unsymetrical. If there had been an eighth booth in the original plans, it had never been constructed.

The seven mages stood in an arc along the circle edge. There were chairs behind them. One looked to be the man who'd been in charge of the police group that collected the goons from the Hausmann's. The others I didn't recognize. I looked around the lower row of booths at the league elders and wielders. A few nodded at me. A few scowled.

I sat next to Lady Weiss and the Lady Whitacre took up the seat on her other side. Neither looked at me, though Weiss had a half smile on her face. I only counted five wielders in the room. Not good, since it meant we were missing one. Well, two if you count Seamus.

"Sorry I'm only fifteen minutes early," I said softly. "I assume they decided to make a go at things a bit ahead of schedule?"

"Bloody hell wielder," she said in the same tone. "Glad you're punctual. He challenged your right to the sword directly as a precursor to calling quorum. It was fortunately denied by the arbiter. So then they called quorum for some stupid reason. They will probably challenge our league's right to add to the consolidated vote. Morons. If they loose, it doesn't matter how we vote, they can't challenge our decision. But our side's down a wielder."

"The Fourth League will present it's position," the arbiter nodded to Neville's box from the center of the circle. The guy in the center of the fouth league's box, still looking uncomfortable, stood and cleared his throat.

"Thank you," he coughed into his hand and then looked around the hall. "We joined with leagues one and three to this position. We have issue to declare. Petition is issued to promote the education, well-being and success of this enclave. It is asked that the technology limit and associated bans be dropped. Efforts should be made to revitalize our standing in the world. And in order to do this, we must not keep ourselves from participating in the advancements of the main-side. "

"Is that the full of your position?"

"Yes arbiter."

"And do leaders of leagues one and three give their vote to this position in consolidation?"

Both leaders nodded.

"Is this where things get complicated?" I whispered to Lady Weiss. She kicked me in the shin.

"The congress accepts your vote," the Arbiter glanced around the circle. "Are there any other consolidations?"

"Yes, Congress," said one of the other leaders. He was a short dark man with silver hair from the second league.

"Proceed."

"Leagues two, five, six and seven will vote a mind."

"I do not see a wielder next to you, Robinson. Are you certain?"

"She would have been here if the quorum wasn't called early," the man snapped.

"We've been through that already; the vote passed. Do the leaders of leagues five, six and seven concur?"

All three nodded.

"Well with two voting positions, I assume there is to be a challenge?"

"There is," said Neville. "We challenge the right of league seven to enter a vote."

Lady Weiss inhaled and let out a small laugh. "Well, then it's perfect. If you win," she added the last with a smirk in my direction. "Else; what does it matter anyway."

"Does the seventh league accept the challenge? Lack of acceptance automatically withdraws the league's vote."

"That's up to you Mr. Borden," Weiss said, jabbing me in my side with her finger.

Neville had stood and crossed to stand next to the Arbiter. I stood next to the booth and took a deep breath.

"Well, have you accepted it?" asked Neville with feigned impatience. He didn't look too happy. He also didn't look like his animosity was entirely directed at me. I remembered his promise to me the other night about us facing off. Had he been stalling?

I was confused slightly. Neville shouted something again, but I was pointedly ignoring him. At least it appeared as if I was ignoring him. Actually he had my full attention. "Interesting. So I walk in and beat him and then the meeting continues with our vote incontestable. Our position wins, 4 to 3. Seems like a plan."

"If you win," the lady added. I nodded, turned and walked the few paces to the edge of the circle. Melina's eyes caught mine as I glanced over my shoulder. I saw in them a whirlwind of emotions, toped by fear. I didn't want to disappoint this lady either, offering her a weak smile. She struggled to return it, then I continued into the circle, scanning the faces in the audience on my way.

I finished my inspection facing Neville. The arbiter nodded at me and then stepped out of the circle. I purposefully walked to the center, with hand on hilt but not drawing.

Something felt different, and a glance over at the mages revealed that they'd all nearly collapsed back into their chairs. I guessed the wards were up. The circle was closed. Sir Neville glanced at me, noting my look at the mages. I ignored him and started stretching out cautiously.

"What the hell are you doing?" he snapped.

"The meeting starts at 7:30," I said calmly. I didn't feel calm, but I was not going to let myself get flustered. I nodded up at the clock, and then switched to stretching out my left leg. Which still hurt a little bit. "We still have three minutes."

He almost laughed.

"How'd you get out of the cage?"

"I had my trusty lock pick set."

"You didn't have a set of pick-locks that could pick that!"

"I used my teeth," he looked like he was getting a little angry. Not that I minded that possibility.

"It was not my choice to start this early," he said. "I was not allowed an option."

"By who; those black clothed guys over there? The same ones who tried to off us main-side after you picked up Tracey?"

"I am glad you popped through in time, Borden. And think about it this way," he smiled slightly. "If you win, I've even done you a favor. The other two leagues didn't have wielders here. I could have challenged both of them."

"I hear a but there, Neville?"

"You wont win."

"You don't know how I got out of a cage that would hold you, yet you are assured of winning against me?" I stood up. Noted the clock touched off at 7:30. "Looks like we get to find out after all."

"I much prefer this, Borden," said Neville, drawing his sword. "You've been an honorable foe, and I'll make sure you die with dignity."

I backed away a step while drawing my own blade. He stepped closer, and I circled to the left, making him follow me. I'd not been idle while stretching, and already found three of the nodes. His blade was complex, and perhaps slightly twisted. The wielder himself was feeding back into the blade in an odd way. And it seemed to stem from the extra strangeness I felt about him. Like Melina suggested, he'd been taking some infusions. I wondered if he realized what it was doing with his interactions with the blade. I didn't have any more time to consider this as a hail of blows began.

The first came after a two step lunge at my right side. I turned away slightly and swatted the blade, mimed a counter attack, but was forced to abandon. His blade had already made it back into position for a stab at my shoulder. I turned it aside. Another strike at my left arm. A hapless block. Then a slash across my stomach. I let it by, stepping back. He paused for a second, which allowed me enough of a breather to consider his footwork. Just like Finley. He was leading slightly. But he wasn't patterning. At least not that I could tell.

The respite over, I had to lunge back again after two brutally strong strikes at my head. Both left my arms tingling. He went for a third, but I anticipated it with an attack of my own at his left side. He had to drop back and give up the stroke to make the block. Then he laughed.

"Weak," he said. He tried another power swing at me. It rung against my sword.

"Slow," I remarked back at him, performing the same preemptive attack. I followed it with another three, at almost random points along his inner and middle circles. I was surprised he let me in that far with the blade. Something told me he was baiting me, so I backed off a little ways.

Just in time, as he suddenly got a lot quicker with those power swings. I took three more on the blade but ducked the fourth and lunged under his guard to kick him in the stomach. On the way up, I slashed at his left side, which he had wide open. The blade cut deeply into his arm. My right leg swept out and took his feet out from under him.

The larger man rolled right through it, skittering back and to his feet a ways away. He quickly backed off and regathered himself. I used the time to find the fourth node. And began working on the fifth. He approached again.

"That wasn't bad," he concluded. Then he attacked again, even stronger than before. And I wasn't ready, having to scramble back for five or six strokes. But at least I was avoiding the brunt of most of them. One I'd turned aside only to have it reopen my left arm. I'd been used to it hurting, so was ignoring it easily. Seeing my break again, I let one swing past and then went on the offensive, but made myself stay in his middle circle. Just as I felt he was going to try something, I pulled back from my down stroke, stepped aside, and then hacked across his exposed left side.

I succeeded in opening a gash in the side of his shirt. I couldn't tell if I'd struck flesh or not. Neville simply ignored the slash and drove his sword down at my head. I rose to block it, but managed to only deflect the blade. It sunk into my left shoulder. I was already swinging my right leg to take out his left knee. After making the kick, I staggered back, knocking aside two stabs at my stomach with the sword in my right hand. Fortunately, he didn't manage to break my collar bone. He didn't follow. And yes, his weight was almost all on his right leg.

"Have you had enough yet?" He asked. I think he said something else, but I was concentrating on finding the fifth node. He staggered back one more step as I felt the node and locked down it's position. The air around me started tingling.

I switched gears and tried to get a shield up in time, but it was smashed aside by the veritable lightening storm that suddenly swarmed around me. I went down, under a few shocks. Before the third one, I somehow had turned my useless shield into something that could deal with electricity. Yes. I wasn't prepared to deal with electricity. Kind of ironic.

The attack changed to fire. Which I dealt with by adding another layer of shield, linked to the first. I setup a bank of capacitors to the side and fed a filtered line from the shields into them. No sense bleeding all the energy coming at me to ground. I could use it to keep shields running on their own later. I thought for a second about pulling the energy back into me from the virtual capacitors, but I didn't want to try.

I got a little warm, but not singed. So Neville switched to ice. I added a layer. He tried ice and lightening. I winced, and added a filter, using the two shields to feed almost directly off each other. It took a few seconds for me to get a nasty oscillation out of one of the lines, but it worked. Suddenly, the whole building shook. Neville raised his arms above his head and brought them down a second time. The shields flared, but the physical blow was blocked by the lowest layer. I simply added a few more capacitors. Another hit. I assumed he was using something like shields to batter against me.

Since my network was anchored to one of the foundation pillars of the building, things would get interesting if he managed to crack that. Another hit. I threw some tunable parameters into the shields so I could adjust them more quickly, felt that there was enough of a filtering system on the capacitors that I could leave them alone. So I looked into finding the sixth node.

Neville began to throw everything he had at the shields. I paid a small amount of attention to them, occasionally tweaking a capacitor or adding some resistance between a diode and ground. I found the sixth quickly. And then the seventh.

The other wielder stood a few meters away from my shield, sweating bullets while huffing and puffing. His side and arm were bleeding profusely. As was my shoulder. He'd roared something at me.

"You didn't leave anything left for an attack," he barked a second time. "Did you?"

I was feeling a little drained. But most of it was from the foot battle. I shrugged. My mind wrapped around the nodes of his sword, preparing to short them and break the spell. Perhaps I should make him drop the blade? I wasn't sure how violent this thing would be when it fell apart. Something told me he wouldn't listen. I almost set the ground, beginning to isolate myself first by severing my link to the potential. One of the nodes changed at my isolation.

I frowned, reset my connection, and the node went back to the way it was. I repeated the test. Realization struck; the node was a connection from his sword to mine. Call it a pointer. Something that referenced my sword. A quick look at the other nodes in this way identified most as pointers to other swords in the room. And some that weren't in the room. Well, two Wielders weren't here. Thanks to the early call time and the trial.

So if I shorted out this guys sword, would the others fail? Yes, I realized. They would. Fail but not shatter. They would just stop working until the connections could be reset to bypass the missing node. It was as minor a change as fixing the wards at Trevor's shop. I made the changes to my blade, forcing the pathways to reroute from the node for Neville's sword in mine back into the anchor point in the hilt. No need to be fancy.

Again, I almost shorted his sword. I paused. Seven nodes. Seven Leagues. Seven mages managing the circle. Seven Wielders and seven swords. Each sword is a node in another. But there's seven nodes referencing other swords. Not six. I laughed. Neville looked like he was about to explode. This made me laugh more, as he may have been about to do just that.

"I don't want to kill you," I told the other wielder, after getting myself back under control. "But I tell you in all seriousness, that if you do not drop your sword and step away, you may die!"

"What?"

"Drop your sword or you may die, Sir Neville. I mean it!"

"You've got to be joking!"

I wasn't. I stared at him, getting to my feet. I stared some more and slowly shook my head from side to side. For a moment, I saw fear cross his eyes. He brushed it away.

"Then I'll try to make this as quiet as possible," I took a deep breath. I couldn't make him drop the sword. So I'd just have to be careful. And I readied to throw a shield over this guy after I popped his breakers.

"Tell me, Neville," I began. "Have you ever shorted out a car battery?"

"What does that have to do with..."

"Everything."

I set the connections, though his sword fought me. They fell into place all at once. And everything went to hell rather quickly. The spell from the sword flew apart violently, first launching Sir Neville across the circle to hit the shield wall about two meters above the ground. I threw my readied shield over him to hopefully keep the guy alive. Then I had my own problems to worry about.

There was a lot of power in that blade. And the spells took a long time to completely unravel. The first blast was only a taste. Perhaps only the surface of the sword. The spells holding the blade's edge, or it's warding spells. After that, it was a scramble to keep the shields around me.

It finished a few minutes later, with me a mess on the ground. I felt burned and drained from all the energy that I'd handled. With a sigh, I let down the shields, discharging what little was left in my capacitors to ground. I looked over at Neville, who was lying in a crumpled heap across the circle, his clothes smoking. Then I glanced up to the mages. Who, I might add, were not looking happy.

I staggered to my feet, using the sword to help me up. I almost slipped on a slightly large spot of blood on the ground. Carrying it low before me, as I lacked the energy to sheath it, I crossed to look at the mages. So now what.

"Are we finished yet?" I asked. Well, croaked, more like.

The one in the center shook his head, then pointed to Neville. I looked over.

"I'm not going to kill him," I said. "There's no point."

He didn't seem to accept this. Well, I wasn't going to kill an unarmed and unconscious man. Even one I didn't like all that much.

"Let us out," I said sternly. A few of the mages inhaled or raised their eyebrows. "The challenge is over."

Mister leader shook his head again. I turned around. "Fine," I said softly. I raised the sword slightly, and closed my eyes. Felt for the anchor points of the huge shield above us. And very gently grounded them out. I was inside and didn't really want to vaporize either myself or the building. The spell ceased, causing a few curses from the group behind me. I ignored them, crossing the circle to where my league was sitting. Well, a few were sitting. Most everyone seemed to be standing. And I didn't quite expect the sound of applause.

Chapter 26

Aftermath

I said the evening would get a bit worse. And the fact that a large number of people weren't clapping should have cued me into that rather quickly. A flash of light and the hiss of steel to my right brought me around. One of Neville's friends was about a meter away and looked pissed. There were two more behind him, similarly angered.

I was tired. I turned, and lowered my sword, dropping a net shield on their heads. The first one went down and the tail to his left. The third waved it off. And, from the looks of her, she was preparing something a bit nasty in a reply. I fortunately didn't get to find out as Melina promptly hit her in the side of the head with her sword. The woman fell, snarling. Melina grabbed my left arm, which caused me to almost pass out. I tried to complain, but didn't get anything out as I found myself getting literally dragged out of the circle. Dallas and Claria were swinging blades with one another just outside the circle. He looked like he wasn't doing too well. Weiss was standing next to my terminus, her side bloody. And I realized one of our friendly Wielders was tailing Melina and I.

We paused, for the vampire to set me back on my feet. My comrade wielder had a really grave expressions on his face. Another wielder walked over. One that had been in Neville's camp. She had a half grin on her face and a pack of swords with her. The fellow wielder behind us turned to face the oncoming group. The woman shook her head.

"Things have changed, Garett. My league offers my sword," the woman wielder said. The man, Garrett, stiffened slightly but shrugged.

Of the thirty or so black garbed interlopers, most were fighting a rear guard to aid in getting out the main doors at the other side of the cathedral. One interesting battle was occurring between the woman who I could have sworn Melina downed and one of the mages that set the circle. The mage fell under an wall of fire.

"Werewolf," murmured Melina in my ear. "We've got to get you out of here. But the mages still haven't opened the hall. Damn them."

They appeared to be a bit distracted at the moment. I then saw another one of the wielders from Neville's combined group try and use his sword to block one of the black clothed men. What ever he tried didn't work. The man fell, his sword sliding along the floor. I shuddered as the body disintegrated before touching the ground.

"Melina," I said through clinched teeth, and quietly. "Their blades don't work. And they don't all know it."

"This could get bad then," she said. And it wasn't already? "Can you open the hall? I think they'll leave if they could."

Can I do what? Oh. I focused, and found the locking spell. A moment and it was down. The huge double doors opened with a bang at the other end. Rain and wind poured in the opening. A crack of lightening sounded. Fitting. Of course the storm may have formed due to my little experiment with Neville's former blade.

The main-siders disengaged in pairs and trios, beginning to slide out the doors. I saw a group of them heading for Neville's downed form. Quickly, I broke away from Melina and almost ran over to Dallas, who wasn't looking like himself anymore. I slapped Claria's blade aside, struck twice more to knock her back and yelled at her to get Neville. She swung at me once, but I stopped her with a shield and used it to shove her in the general direction, my eyes daggers. The vampire got the point and turned away, cursing.

Dallas nodded his thanks. The hall was emptying through the various openings. I caught a salute from the woman wielder who put in with us as she stepped through her terminus. I let Melina help me through my own and back to the wielder's mansion. Well, I didn't have much choice.

We went through the gate, and Melina let me fall into a chair off to the side of the back hall. My head was swimming. Lady Whitacre was frowning down at me, pressing something onto my shoulder. It hurt like hell. Bob and company came sliding into the room from the front. Someone must have let them in.

"Stupid wielder," admonished Lady Weiss. I laughed, and then wished I hadn't.

"At least he's alive," said Bob. Thanks man. "Casey. She'll hate us for it, but she'll be able to take care of him."

"Can he set the gate, or will we have to take him through your house?" the elder vampire asked.

"He's been there," said Melina. I nodded and got to my feet with the help of Melina and Johny who'd appeared at my other side.

"Just you four," said Lady Weiss. "The rest of us will head home. And try and put the pieces together from the night's events. I'll have Samantha meet you there soonest."

I reset the gate to the doctor's front door. Bob went through first, followed by the rest of us. I think I passed out a few moments after tripping and falling on my face in the middle of the Doctor's busy waiting room. But not before I got to hear her string of curses and Bob's attempts at an explanation. It was a little funny.

I came to on a table, with my shoulder thankfully numb. And the unmistakable sound of suture thread through flesh greeting my ears. I shuddered.

"Hold still," said the Doctor Finley. I thought she was being rather loud, since her mouth was only about ten centimeters from my head. She went back to berating Bob about his party's entrance. Melina and Johny didn't seem to be in the room. I sighed and let my head back down on the table.

"No choice, my ass! You could have taken him to that hospital over there. It's not the best, but Jesus Bob! They could have managed this well enough."

"There wasn't much time," he defended himself. "As you said. And he didn't know the hospital, so he couldn't set the gate."

"Maybe he just wanted to see you," I offered.

"Don't start wielder," she said. "I'm," she tugged, "not", again, this one hurt through the numbness, "not," ouch, "getting," I winced and hissed. I heard the string break. "Crap."

"Involved?" Bob offered. I couldn't help it. I laughed. It hurt. The doctor glared down at me.

"Three more and you're done," she said, threading another suture into the hook needle. I think the local was starting to wear off a bit, I hissed again as the needle went through the skin.

"Hurts?" she asked. I nodded. She almost said good. Bob shrugged his shoulders apologetically. I raised my eyebrows at him, mouthing Tracey's name.

"Not yet," he replied. I frowned and nodded.

I let Dr. Finley finish in silence. She tossed away the remains of the suture kit, slaved some antibiotic over the stitches and covered them with a bandage. My left arm received a similar treatment of cream and bandage. I slowly got to a sitting position. With a double snap, the pair of gloves Dr. Finley used flew into the trash can. She washed her hands, while I stood up slowly. My head hurt.

"You should tell her Bob," I said. He nodded.

"Tell me what?" his wife asked, suspiciously.

"Thanks Doctor," I said, grabbed my shirt and left the room, closing the door behind me. I heard something a bit loud about her having patients to get to. I kept walking. A look at the shirt was all it took to trash it. I really didn't want to put something on that was half covered in my dried blood. Especially not while hanging around vampires. I'd guess it would be considered rather rude. I ignored the evil look from one of the nurses and grabbed a surgical scrub shirt from a closet next to the nurses desk.

A few more steps, and I walked out into the waiting room. It was rather packed, but Melina and Johny had chairs across from one an other. There wasn't another chair available in the place and it looked like the two patients in line with the receptionist would be needing chairs soon. I motioned for the door. We went outside, and Melina gently hugged me, worry on her face.

I hugged her back, but pushed her away in favor of the water fountain next to her. She gave me a dirty look, which made Johny laugh. I looked back up at her with a grin. Then I remembered the message being told between the Finley's.

"This may take a little while," I said, grabbing Melina's hand and sitting down on the low wall of the entry room with my back to the glass. It was uncomfortable, but kept us out of the way, and gave us some privacy. Melina sat down next to me, but Johny kept standing. Her grip on my hand was rather firm.

"Tracey?" asked Melina. Johny nodded for me.

"You okay boss?" he asked.

"Pretty much. Drained. Mine's not in there, is it." I guessed that Melina's and Johny's sword were wrapped up in my borrowed coat, which Johny held in his arms. I reached out for my sword and felt it back in the wielder house, leaning against the chair.

Melina started to apologize, but I smiled.

"It looks like we'll be taking a slightly longer way back, boss."

"I know where it is, Johny," I said. "And that's all I need to know."

The two vampires looked at me like I was nuts. Well, I was. A late 80's BMW pulled into the parking lot, screeching tires as it squeezed into a parking space. I smiled slightly when Samantha and Jennifer got out of the car. The later still had her apron on from the restaurant. Samantha looked like she had been through hell, but came out victorious. The door flew open.

"What the hell are you doing out here?" she said, taking in the scene.

"Trying to be inconspicuous," I replied. "Bob's telling the Doc about Tracey. Why didn't you tell them?"

"Another time wielder," Samantha replied. "Well, I guess a 'good job' is in order, though I still don't know what all happened. I gather something rather unorthodox and nasty?"

When we didn't offer anything, she continued.

"It seems that if we ever get," she sniffed. "Oh, bloody hell. Are you warding?"

"Yes, ma'am," I said.

"Well, when or if we ever manage to get the congress together again, it seems we will be well off. I already have messages from two of the other leagues that they intend to vote with us. Which leaves Neville's league, which is without a sword, but still somehow has a wielder from what I hear. Of that I won't ask.

"And there's the matter of the Mage's being enraged at your meddling. The quick message from them was that they were going to investigate your use for possible illicit sources or something. Again, I won't ask now. Hopefully whatever you did to them will pan out."

I almost smiled. They wouldn't let me out. I wanted out. It wasn't like I didn't ask nicely.

"Which brings me to the most disturbing messages, from two of our consolidated fellow Wielders; they can't use their blades. That I have to ask on. Do any of the swords work?"

"Mine does," I said simply.

"Show me," she said sharply. Melina and Johny exchanged looks. I made a little shield activate the water fountain next to Melina, fill up another little shield with water, and marched that over to me. I took a sip from the air cup.

Jennifer laughed. Samantha seemed satisfied and the other two vampires seemed perplexed.

"So, is the damage to their swords permanent? If so, I think you'll not be very popular, Chris."

I thought for a moment. Perfect. "Have them go see Trevor. He can straighten them out."

"Trevor?"

"Yeah," I said. "You know, the guy you sent Melina and I to to have her dagger recharged and give me some lessons. He'll be able to get them working again. It's just a quick little adjustment."

The league leader didn't entirely swallow this, but at least she let it drop.

"Bob's inside?" she asked.

I nodded.

"Hm... Okay. You guys go ahead and get back to the estate. I think Lady Weiss said she'd have to stay there tonight. Someone broke into her house when she was getting ready to leave for the meeting. Johny, you go with them and then stay with Weiss when she leaves. I'll go speak with Bob and my sister."

I nodded, and the two women went inside. I saw the receptionist shake her head in annoyance when they walked right past her.

"That's pretty low," I said. "Not telling your own sister that your niece is a vampire."

"Maybe she didn't actually know until we told her," offered Melina.

"Ah, well. Either way, I think she only suspected it, even if she told us she knew. Let's go guys," I said and waved to the front door. I stood and opened it for Johny.

"Right-o, man," he said, stepping across the threshold and back into the wielder's house. Melina was still sitting on the wall. I smiled at her.

Finally, she got up and crossed to stand next to me. Rather closer than necessary. I looked down at her, trying to figure out the expression on her face.

"You're changing our world Chris," she said softly, touching my left arm gently, then my cheek. "Changing my world."

"Perhaps it needed to be changed."

"Perhaps," she agreed. "It's changed you too."

Yes, that it has. In many ways. Should I tell her there was an eighth sword? Tell her I think it pointed to her as the wielder? Maybe after I found it. And I would find it. For her.

Seven nodes plus one. Eight swords in all.

"That it has, Melina."

I leaned down and kissed her, my right hand on her shoulders. Then pushed her backwards through the door into the other side.

Epilogue

I set my sword down on the bench next to me and drank half a glass of water. My shoulder still hurt a fair amount. Of course, sparing with Melina wasn't helping. Well, that wasn't entirely true. It made it hurt more, but it was better that I was getting the shoulder working again. I smiled up at her, catching her eye after she knocked Bob back, almost out of the ring. He was working up his wrist, and getting used to a new blade. While watching the two go at it, my thoughts went back over the past few weeks of craziness. There's still some loose ends. So here goes.

I believe I'll start with Charles, since he was the first person I met in this weirdness that became my life. I still have his damn coat and haven't seen him. Him and Ginny went off on some vacation or something before I could get it back to him. I guess I could drop it off at the store, but for some reason always have second thoughts. It's not that I don't go to the store; I do. More on that later.

Neville would be next, and believe me, he wasn't very well liked after the fiasco in the circle. I don't believe he comes to the other side at all. Pretty much sticks to teaching history. I will mention that we noticed he was the associate dean of admissions for the College of Arts and Sciences at UCLA. Again, something to remember for a bit later.

Trevor called me up a few days after the ill-fated meeting wondering what the hell he was supposed to do about the blades of the other wielders, and why I sent them to him in the first place. I think his language (and that of his wife in the background) was a little more vulgar than that. I didn't show him. And he figured it out for himself. Afterwards we both agreed to keep the existence of the other blade quiet for now. His practice grew a great deal as a result. I'm glad I pushed it on him.

The other day, I actually heard him say 'no' to Lucy. She almost blew up at him, threatening to leave him. His response was something approximating a shrug of the shoulders. She didn't leave and I think they get along a lot better now. Oh, and she closed her shop to work with him full time. Kind of funny.

Bob and Casey have mostly reconciled. Because of the practice, the doctor still has to stay main-side much of the time, but they're at least doing better. Tracey went back to classes after a few days and seems to have bounced back a fair amount. Their whole family and house is helping out with that. Martin's alledgidly got himself a girlfriend at Georgia Tech. So I've got to remember to bug him about it next time I have supper at their house. And I found out Mister Graves's first name from Lady Weiss. Hehe... I can't wait for the ideal opportunity to use it.

The Lady herself recovered well from getting attacked in her home by a bunch of wood core blade wielding vampires. She took two out herself in the process. We put up a bounty for the wooden blades destruction. A few were turned in. I'm sure we'll be seeing more of them. And not in the way I'd prefer. Which brings us to someone else, and how often I'd be seeing her.

Melina decided to make a go at finishing her degree in biology. I had a pretty sure fire way of getting her re-admitted. I can't wait to see the look on Neville's face when I show up in his office and present the suggestion. Anyway, she was back in her apartment. At least until the lease runs out. In the days, she was tending the store for Charles. I saw her almost every day that I could. Which wasn't too often. We'd try and find her a good apartment near UCLA once the semester changed.

I had made my peace with the guys at the engineering firm and gave three months notice. Well, that was how much time the Office of Technology gave me to get my affairs in order and move into the wielder house full time. Of course that meant that the firm had me by the toenails for a full three months and persisted in efforts to extract as much work out of me as possible.

I also applied for a teaching position at the university. I didn't like Los Angeles that much, but the league was based there, essentially. I figured, simpler was a bit better. No, or at least I tell my self no, Melina's desire to stay with UCLA didn't have anything to do with it. Sure it didn't. And I'm not fooling myself. Not in the least. Right.

I laughed out loud and the two fighters turned to give me funny looks. I shook my head. It was too hard to explain. Bob lunged around and tried to cut below Melina's left guard. She effortlessly turned his blade and popped the sword out of his hand. He cursed, and Melina blew me a kiss. Then curled a finger and motioned me up off my duff.

I sighed, and grabbed my sword. I was starting to love this girl. But she was definitely a handful. I stood and stepped into the circle. Great. Her eyes were twinkling. Lovely. But I wouldn't have it any other way.